Amanda Quick is a pseudonym for Jayne Ann Krentz, the author, under various pen names, of more than fifty *New York Times* bestsellers; there are more than 35 million copies of her books in print. She lives in Seattle.

Visit her website at www.amandaquick.com

The Paid Companion

Amanda Quick

PIATKUS

PIATKUS

First published in the United States in 2004 by G.P. Putnam's Sons,
a member of Penguin Group (USA) Inc., New York
First published in Great Britain in 2005 by Piatkus Books
Reprinted 2005 (twice), 2010, 2011, 2013

A CIP catalogue record for this book
is available from the British Library.

ISBN 978-0-7499-3554-2

Typeset by Phoenix Photosetting, Chatham, Kent

Piatkus
An imprint of
Little, Brown Book Group
Carmelite House
50 Victoria Embankment
London EC4Y 0DZ

An Hachette UK Company
www.hachette.co.uk

www.littlebrown.co.uk

Acknowledgements

My thanks to Catherine Johns, former curator, Romano-British Collections, at the British Museum, and Donald M. Bailey – again – this time for the fascinating bits on the lost rivers of London. Any errors are, of course, mine and mine alone, but given that they are lost rivers, maybe no one will ever discover my mistakes.

Prologue
Arthur

Arthur Lancaster, Earl of St. Merryn, was sitting in front of a crackling fire in his club, drinking a glass of excellent port and reading a newspaper, when he received word that his fiancée had eloped with another man.

"I'm told young Burnley used a ladder to climb up to her window and assist Miss Juliana down to the carriage." Bennett Fleming lowered his short, sturdy frame into the chair across from Arthur and reached for the bottle of port. "They are headed north, by all accounts. No doubt making for Gretna Green. Juliana's father has just set out after them, but his coach is old and slow."

A great hush fell upon the room. All talk stopped. No papers rustled; no glasses moved. It was almost midnight and the club was full. Every man in the vicinity appeared to be frozen in his chair as he strained mightily to eavesdrop on the conversation taking place in front of the fire.

With a sigh, Arthur folded his newspaper, set it

aside and took a swallow of his port. He looked toward the window where wind-driven rain beat furiously against the glass panes.

"They'll be fortunate to get ten miles in this storm," he said.

As was the case with every other word he spoke that night, the remark became part of the St. Merryn legend. . . . *So cold-blooded that when he was told that his fiancée had run off with another man, he merely commented upon the damp weather.*

Bennett hastily downed some of his port and then followed Arthur's gaze to the window. "Young Burnley and Miss Juliana have an excellent, well-sprung carriage and a strong, fresh team." He cleared his throat. "It is doubtful that the lady's father will catch them, but a single man mounted on a good horse might be able to overtake the pair."

Expectation seethed in the crystalline silence. St. Merryn was indisputably a single man, and it was no secret that his stable housed some extremely prime horseflesh. Everyone waited to see if the earl would elect to pursue the fleeing couple.

Arthur got to his feet in a leisurely manner and picked up the half-empty bottle of port. "Do you know, Bennett, I seem to find myself suffering from the most extreme case of boredom this evening. I believe I will go see if there is anything of interest happening in the card room."

Bennett's brows shot up toward his receding hairline. "You never gamble. I can't even begin to count the number of times that I have heard you claim that it is illogical to wager money on a roll of the dice or a hand of cards."

"I am feeling unusually lucky tonight." Arthur started toward the card room.

2

"Devil take it," Bennett muttered. Homely features creased in alarm, he climbed to his feet, seized his half-finished glass of port and scrambled to catch up with the earl.

"Do you know," Arthur said midway across the unnaturally silent room, "it occurs to me that I miscalculated rather badly when I asked Graham for his daughter's hand in marriage."

"Indeed?" Bennett slanted Arthur an uneasy glance, as though examining his companion for indications of a fever.

"Yes. I believe that the next time I set out to find myself a wife, I will approach the project in a more logical manner, just as I would one of my investments."

Bennett grimaced, aware that their audience was still paying rapt attention to everything Arthur said. "How in blazes do you intend to apply logic to the business of finding a wife?"

"It occurs to me that the qualities that one requires in a wife are not unlike those one would expect in a paid companion."

Bennett sputtered and coughed on a mouthful of port. "A *companion*?"

"Only consider the matter closely." There was a clink as Arthur tilted the port bottle over his glass. "The ideal companion is a well-bred and well-educated lady possessed of a sterling reputation, steady nerves, and a meek and modest manner in both her actions and her dress. Are those not the exact specifications one would set down if one were to describe the perfect wife?"

"A paid companion is, by definition, impoverished and alone in the world."

"Of course she is poor and without resources."

Arthur shrugged. "Why else would she apply for such a humble post?"

"Most gentlemen would prefer a wife who can bring them a fortune or some property," Bennett pointed out.

"Ah, but that is where I have a great advantage, is it not?" Arthur paused at the door of the card room and surveyed the busy tables. "Not to put too fine a point on it, I am filthy rich and getting richer by the day. I do not require a wealthy wife."

Bennett halted beside him and reluctantly conceded the point. "True."

"One of the great things about paid companions is their condition of dire poverty," Arthur continued. "It makes them suitably grateful for whatever employment is offered, you see."

"Huh. Hadn't thought of that." Bennett swallowed more port and slowly lowered the glass. "I think I am beginning to follow your reasoning."

"Unlike sheltered, romantic young ladies whose views of love have been sadly warped by Byron and the novels of the Minerva Press, paid companions must, of necessity, be a far more practical lot. They have learned the hard way just how harsh the world can be."

"No doubt."

"It follows, then, that your typical companion would not be inclined toward behavior that would cost her to lose her post. A man could expect, for example, that such a lady would not run off with another man shortly before the wedding."

"Perhaps it is the port, but I believe you are making excellent sense." Bennett frowned. "But just how would one go about finding a wife with all the qualities of a paid companion?"

"Fleming, you disappoint me. The answer to that question is glaringly obvious. If one wished to choose such a paragon of a wife, one would naturally go to an agency that supplies companions. One would interview an assortment of applicants and then make one's selection."

Bennett blinked. "An agency?"

"How could a man go wrong?" Arthur nodded to himself. "I should have thought of the idea a few months ago. Just think of all the trouble I would have avoided."

"Uh, well—"

"If you will excuse me, I believe there is an opening for a player at that table in the corner."

"The play will be deep," Bennett warned. "Are you quite certain—"

But Arthur was no longer paying attention. He crossed the room and sat down at the card table.

When he got to his feet a few hours later, he was several thousand pounds richer. The fact that the earl had broken his own ironclad rule against placing wagers and proceeded to win a sizeable sum that night added yet another facet to the St. Merryn legend.

The first light of a gray, drizzly dawn was just beginning to show above the rooftops when Arthur left his club. He got into the waiting carriage and allowed himself to be driven back to the big, gloom-filled house in Rain Street. He went straight to bed.

At nine-thirty the next morning he was awakened by his elderly butler, who informed him that his fiancée's father had found his daughter at an inn where she was sharing a room with her handsome young rescuer.

5

There was, of course, only one thing to be done in order to preserve the lady's reputation. The outraged papa had decreed that the couple would be wed immediately by special license.

Arthur thanked the servant politely for the news, turned over and went immediately back to sleep.

Prologue
Elenora

The news of her stepfather's death was delivered to Elenora Lodge by the two men to whom he had lost everything in a poor business investment. They arrived on her doorstep at three o'clock in the afternoon.

"Samuel Jones dropped dead of a fit of apoplexy when he found out that the mining scheme had failed," one of the men from London informed her with no sign of sympathy.

"This house, its contents and the land that adjoins it from here to the stream all belong to us now," the second creditor announced, waving a sheaf of papers that carried Samuel Jones's signature on every page.

The first man squinted at the small gold ring Elenora wore on her little finger. "The deceased included your jewelry and all personal possessions, with the exception of your clothing, on the list of goods he put up as collateral for the loan."

The second creditor jerked a thumb to indicate the very large individual who stood slightly behind and to the side. "This is Mr. Hitchins. We hired him from Bow Street. He's here to make sure you don't take anything of value out of the house."

The hulking, gray-haired man who had accompanied Samuel Jones's creditors had hard, watchful eyes. He carried the Bow Street Runner's badge of office: a baton.

Elenora faced the three aggressive-looking men, aware of her housekeeper and maid hovering anxiously in the front hall behind her. Her thoughts flew to the stable lads and the men who tended the gardens and the home farm. She knew full well that there was very little she could do to protect them. Her only hope was to make it sound as though it would be foolish to dismiss the staff.

"I assume you realize that this property produces a very comfortable income," she said.

"Aye, Miss Lodge." The first creditor rocked on his heels, well pleased. "Samuel Jones made that clear, right enough."

The second man surveyed the neatly kept grounds with an air of anticipation. "A very handsome farm it is."

"Then you will also be aware that the only reason the property is valuable is because the people who work the land and maintain the household are highly skilled individuals. It would be impossible to replace them. If you let any of them go, I can promise you that the crops will fail and the house will decline in value within months."

The two creditors frowned at each other. Obviously neither of them had considered the problem of the servants and laborers.

The Runner's grizzled brows climbed at that announcement and an odd expression lit his eyes.

But he said nothing. Why would he? she thought. The business end of this matter had nothing to do with him.

The two creditors reached a silent accord. The first one cleared his throat.

"Your staff will stay on," he said. "We've already arranged for the sale of the property, and the new owner made it clear that he wants everything to stay just as it is."

"With the exception of yourself, of course, Miss Lodge." The second creditor bobbed his head with a wise air. "The new owner won't be needing you."

Some of Elenora's tension eased. The people who worked for her were safe. She could turn her attention to her own future.

"I assume you will allow me time to pack my clothes," she said coldly.

Neither of the two creditors appeared to hear the acute disdain that laced her tones. One of them hauled a watch out of his pocket.

"You have thirty minutes, Miss Lodge." He nodded at the big man from Bow Street. "Mr. Hitchins will remain with you at all times while you pack, to make sure that you don't steal any of the silver. When you're ready to leave, one of the farmers will take you into the village and leave you at the inn. What you do after that is up to you."

Elenora turned with as much dignity as she could muster and found herself confronted with her sobbing housekeeper and the distraught maid.

Her own head was whirling in the face of the disaster, but she knew that she had to maintain her composure in front of these two. She gave them both what she hoped was a reassuring smile.

"Calm yourselves," she said briskly. "As you just

heard, you are to remain in your posts, and the men will keep their positions as well."

The housekeeper and the maid stopped crying and lowered their handkerchiefs. Both went limp with relief.

"Thank you, Miss Elenora," the housekeeper whispered.

Elenora patted her shoulder and hastened toward the stairs. She tried to ignore the mean-looking Runner who stalked behind her every step of the way.

Hitchins stood just inside the opening of her bedchamber, hands clasped behind his back, feet braced, and watched as she hauled a large trunk out from under the bed.

She wondered what he would say if she were to inform him that he was the only man who had ever set foot in her bedchamber.

"This was my grandmother's traveling trunk," she told him instead, throwing open the lid to reveal the empty interior. "She was an actress. Her stage name was Agatha Knight. When she married my grandfather, there was a terrible uproar in the family. Such a scandal. My great-grandparents threatened to disown my grandfather. But in the end they were forced to accept the situation. You know how it is with families."

Hitchins grunted. Either he did not have any experience with a family or else he found her personal history extremely dull. She suspected the latter.

In spite of Hitchins's lack of conversation, she continued to chatter nonstop while she dragged her clothes out of the wardrobe. Her goal was to distract him. She did not want him to become curious about the old trunk.

"My poor mother was mortified by the fact that her

10

mother had gone on stage. She spent her entire life trying to live down Grandmother's notorious career."

Hitchins checked his watch. "Ye've got ten minutes left."

"Thank you, Mr. Hitchins." She gave him a steely smile. "You're being very helpful."

The Runner proved to be inured to sarcasm. He no doubt experienced a lot of it in his profession.

Elenora yanked open a drawer and took out a pile of neatly folded linen. "You might want to avert your eyes, sir."

Hitchins had the grace not to stare at her chemise and nightgown. But when she reached for the small clock on the bedside table, his thin mouth tightened.

"Ye're not to take anything except your personal clothing, Miss Lodge," he said, shaking his head.

"Yes, of course." So much for sneaking in the clock. Pity. It might have been worth a few pounds to a pawn dealer. "How could I have forgotten?"

She slammed the lid down and locked it quickly, a chill of relief shooting down her spine. The Runner had not shown the least bit of interest in her grandmother's old theater trunk.

"I am told that I look just like her when she was my age," she said in conversational tones.

"Who would that be, Miss Lodge?"

"My grandmother, the actress."

"Is that a fact." Hitchins shrugged. "Ready, are ye?"

"Yes. I trust you will convey this downstairs for me?"

"Aye, ma'am."

Hitchins hoisted the trunk and carried it down to the front hall. Outside, he loaded it into the waiting farmer's cart.

One of the creditors stepped into Elenora's path as she made to follow Hitchins.

11

"That little gold ring on your hand, if you please, Miss Lodge," he said sharply.

"Indeed."

With a bit of precise timing, she managed to remove the ring and drop it just as the creditor reached out to take it from her. The circlet of gold bounced on the floor.

"Damnation." The annoying little man leaned down to retrieve the ring.

While he was bent over in a parody of an awkward bow, Elenora swept past him and went down the steps. Agatha Knight had always emphasized the importance of a well-staged exit.

Hitchins, showing an unexpected turn of manners, handed her up onto the hard, wooden bench of the farm cart.

"Thank you, sir," she murmured. She settled herself on the seat with all of the grace and aplomb she would have employed getting into a fine carriage.

A gleam of admiration appeared in the Runner's eyes.

"Good luck to ye, Miss Lodge." He glanced into the rear of the cart where the trunk loomed large. "Did I mention that my uncle traveled with a company of actors in his younger days?"

She froze. "No, you did not."

"Had a trunk very similar to yours. He said it was quite useful. He told me that he always made certain he had a few essentials packed inside in the event that he was obliged to leave town in a hurry."

She swallowed. "My grandmother gave me the same bit of advice."

"I trust ye heeded it, Miss Lodge?"

"Yes, Mr. Hitchins, I did."

"Ye'll do all right, Miss Lodge. Ye've got spirit." He

winked, tipped his hat and walked back toward his employers.

Elenora took a deep breath. Then, with a snap, she unfurled her parasol and held it aloft as though it were a bright battle banner. The cart lumbered into motion.

She did not look back at the house where she had been born and had lived all of her life.

Her stepfather's death had not come as a great surprise, and she felt no grief. She had been sixteen years old when Samuel Jones had married her mother. He had spent very little time here in the country, preferring London and his never-ending investment schemes. After her mother had died three years before, he had rarely showed up at all.

That state of affairs had suited Elenora quite well. She did not care for Jones and was quite content not to have him underfoot. But of course that was before she had discovered that his lawyer had managed to shift her inheritance from her grandmother, which had included the house and surrounding property, into Jones's control.

And now it was all gone.

Well, not quite all, she thought with grim satisfaction. Samuel Jones's creditors had not known about her grandmother's pearl and gold brooch and the matching earrings hidden in the false bottom of the old costume trunk.

Agatha Knight had given her the jewelry right after her mother had married Samuel Jones. Agatha had kept the gift a secret and had instructed Elenora to hide the brooch and the earrings in the trunk and not tell anyone about them, not even her mother.

It was obvious that Agatha's intuition about Jones had been quite sound.

Neither were the two creditors aware of the twenty

pounds in bank notes that were also inside the trunk. She had kept the money aside after the sale of the crops, and had tucked the notes in with the jewelry when she had realized that Jones was going to take every penny from the harvest to invest in his mining scheme.

What was done was done, she thought. She must turn her attention to the future. Her fortunes had definitely taken a downward turn, but at least she was not entirely alone in the world. She was engaged to be married to a fine gentleman. When Jeremy Clyde received word of her dire predicament, she knew that he would race to her side. He would no doubt insist that they move the date of the wedding forward.

Yes indeed, she thought, in a month or so this terrible incident would be behind her. She would be a married woman with a new household to organize and manage. The prospect cheered her greatly.

If there was one skill at which she excelled, it was that of organizing and supervising the myriad tasks required to maintain an orderly household and a prosperous farm. She could handle everything from arranging for the profitable sale of crops to keeping the accounts, seeing to the repairs of the cottages, hiring servants and laborers, and concocting medicines in the stillroom.

She would make Jeremy an excellent wife, if she did say so herself.

Jeremy Clyde galloped into the inn yard later that evening, just as Elenora was instructing the innkeeper's wife on the importance of making certain that the sheets on her bed were freshly laundered.

When she glanced out the window and saw who had

arrived, Elenora broke off the lecture and rushed downstairs.

She went straight into Jeremy's open arms.

"Dearest." Jeremy hugged her quickly and then put her gently away from him. His handsome face was set in lines of grave concern. "I came as soon as I heard the news. How dreadful for you. Your stepfather's creditors took *everything?* The house? All of the property?"

She sighed. "I'm afraid so."

"This is a terrible blow for you, my dear. I do not know what to say."

But it transpired that Jeremy did, indeed, have something very important to say. It took him some time to get around to it, and he prefaced it with the assurance that it broke his heart to have to tell her, but he really had no choice.

It all boiled down to a very simple matter: Due to the fact that she had been stripped of her inheritance, he was forced to terminate their engagement immediately.

He rode away a short while later, leaving just as quickly as he had come.

Elenora climbed the stairs to her tiny room and sent for a bottle of the innkeeper's least-expensive wine. When it was delivered, she locked her door, lit a candle and poured herself a brimming glass of the tonic.

She sat there for a long time, looking out into the night, drinking the bad wine and contemplating her future.

She truly was all alone in the world now. It was a strange and disturbing thought. Her orderly, well-planned life had been turned upside down.

Only a few hours before, her future had seemed so clear and bright. Jeremy had been planning to move into her house after the marriage. She'd had a com-

15

fortable vision of herself as his wife and lifetime partner; a vision in which she managed the household, raised their children and continued to supervise the farm's business affairs. Now that shimmering bubble of a dream had burst.

But very late that night, after most of the wine in the bottle was gone, it came to her that she was now free in a way she had never been before in her entire life. For the first time ever, she had no obligations to anyone. No tenants or servants depended upon her. No one needed her. She had no roots, no ties, no home.

There was no one to care if she made herself notorious or dragged the Lodge name through the muck of a great scandal, just as her grandmother had done.

She had a chance to plot a new course for herself.

In the pale light of the new dawn she glimpsed a dazzling vision of the very different future she would craft.

It would be a future in which she would be free of the narrow, rigid strictures that bound one so tightly when one lived in a small village; a future in which she controlled her own property and her own finances.

In this grand, new future she would be able to do things that she could never have done in her old life. She might even allow herself to sample those uniquely *stimulating pleasures* that her grandmother had assured her were to be found in the arms of the right man.

But she would not have to pay the price that most women of her station in life paid to know those pleasures, she promised herself. She would not have to marry. After all, there was no one left to care if she ruined her good name.

Yes, this new future would be glorious indeed.

All she had to do was find a way to pay for it.

Chapter One

The ghastly, corpse-pale face appeared suddenly, materializing out of the depths of the fathomless darkness like some demonic guardian set to protect forbidden secrets. The lantern light spilled a hellish glare across the stark, staring face.

The man in the small boat screamed at the sight of the monster, but there was no one to hear him.

His shriek of horror echoed endlessly off the ancient stone walls that enclosed him in a corridor of endless night. His shocked start of surprise affected his balance. He staggered, causing the small boat in which he traveled to bob dangerously on the current of the black waters.

His heart pounded. He was abruptly drenched in a chilling sweat. He stopped breathing.

Reflexively he gripped the long pole he had been using to propel the little craft up the sluggish stream, and fought to steady himself.

Mercifully the end of the pole dug solidly into the

riverbed, holding the boat steady as the last reverberations of his dreadful cry died away.

The eerie silence descended once more. He managed to breathe again. He stared at the slightly-larger-than-human-sized head, his hands still shaking.

It was merely another one of the ancient classical statues that lay like so many dismembered bodies here and there along the banks of the underground river. The helmet on this one identified it as a figure of Minerva.

Although it was not the first such statue he had come across in the course of this strange journey, it was certainly the most unnerving. The thing resembled nothing so much as a severed head that had been tossed heedlessly into the mud beside the river.

He shivered again, tightened his grip on the pole and shoved hard. He was annoyed at his reaction to the figure. What was the matter with him? He could not allow his nerves to be so easily unsettled. He had a destiny to fulfill.

The little boat shot forward, slipping past the marble head.

The craft rounded another bend in the river. The lantern light picked out one of the low, arched foot-bridges that spanned the stream at various points along the way. They were passages to nowhere, ending as they did at the walls of the tunnel that enclosed them. The man ducked slightly to avoid banging his head.

As the last of his terror left him, the surging thrill of excitement returned. It was all just as his predecessor had described in his journal. The lost river truly did exist, twisting beneath the city, a secret waterway that had been covered over and forgotten centuries before.

The author of the journal had concluded that the Romans, never the sort to pass up a potential engineering project, had been the first to enclose the river so that they could contain it and build upon it. One could see the evidence of their masonry work here and there in the lantern light. In other places, the underground tunnel through which the river passed was vaulted in the Medieval style.

The enclosed waters no doubt functioned as an unknown sewer for the great city above it, carrying storm waters and the runoff from drains to the Thames. The smell was foul. It was so silent here in this place of eternal night that he could hear the skittering of rats and other vermin on the narrow banks.

Not much farther now, he thought. If the directions in the journal were correct, he would soon come upon the stone crypt that marked the entrance to his predecessor's secret underground laboratory. He hoped with all his might that he would find the strange machine there, where it had been left all those years before.

The one who had come before him had been forced to abandon the glorious project because he had not been able to unravel the last great riddle in the ancient lapidary. But the man in the boat knew that he had succeeded where his predecessor had failed. He had managed to decode the old alchemist's instructions. He was certain that he could complete the task.

If he was fortunate enough to find the device, there were still many things to be done before it could be made to work. He had yet to locate the missing stones and get rid of the two old men who knew the secrets of the past. But he foresaw no great difficulties in that endeavor.

Information was the key to success, and he knew how to obtain that commodity. He moved in Society, so he had some useful connections in that world. But he also made it a point to spend a great deal of time in

19

the disreputable hells and brothels where the gentlemen of the ton went to seek more unwholesome pleasures. He had found such places to be veritable oceans of rumor and gossip.

There was only one person who knew enough to be able to realize what he intended, but she would not be a problem. Her great weakness was her love for him. He had always been able to use her affection and trust to manipulate her.

No, if he found the device tonight, nothing could stop him from fulfilling his destiny.

They had labeled the one who had come before him a madman and refused to acknowledge his genius. But this time matters would unfold in a very different fashion.

When he had finished constructing the deadly device and demonstrated its enormous destructive energy, all of England, indeed all of Europe would be forced to hail the second Newton in its midst.

Chapter Two

She won't do. Too timid. Too meek." Arthur watched the door close behind the woman he had just finished interviewing. "I thought I made it clear, I need a lady with spirit and a certain presence. I am not looking for the typical sort of paid companion. Bring in another one."

Mrs. Goodhew exchanged a glance with her business partner, Mrs. Willis. Arthur sensed that they were both nearing the end of their patience. In the course of the past hour and a half he had spoken with seven applicants. None of the subdued, painfully dowdy women on the Goodhew & Willis Agency roster had come close to being a potential candidate for the post he was offering.

He did not blame Mrs. Goodhew and Mrs. Willis for their growing exasperation. But he was beyond being exasperated. He was desperate.

Mrs. Goodhew cleared her throat, folded her large, competent hands on top of her desk and regarded

Arthur with a stern air. "My lord, I regret to say that we have exhausted our list of suitable applicants."

"Impossible. There must be someone else." There had to be another candidate. His entire plan hinged on finding the right woman.

Mrs. Goodhew and Mrs. Willis glowered at him from behind their matching desks. They were both formidable females. Mrs. Goodhew was tall and grandly proportioned with a face that could have been stamped on an ancient coin. Her associate was as thin and sharp as a pair of shears.

Both were soberly but expensively attired. There was a judicious amount of gray in their hair and a considerable measure of experience in their eyes.

The sign on the front door outside declared that the Goodhew & Willis Agency had supplied paid companions and governesses to persons of quality for over fifteen years. The fact that these two had established this agency and operated it at an obvious profit for that period of time was a testimony to their intelligence and sound business sense.

Arthur studied their determined expressions and considered his options. Before coming here, he had gone to two other agencies that boasted a selection of ladies seeking work as paid companions. Each had produced a handful of insipid prospects. He had felt a distinct pang of pity for all of them. He understood that only the most dire conditions of genteel poverty could induce any female to seek such a post. But he was not in the market for a woman who aroused the emotion of pity in others.

He clasped his hands behind his back, widened his stance and confronted Mrs. Goodhew and Mrs. Willis from the far side of the room.

"If you have run through all of the suitable

candidates," he said, "then the answer is clear. Find me an *unsuitable* female."

The two stared at him as though he had taken leave of his senses.

Mrs. Willis recovered first. "This is a respectable agency, sir. We do not have any *unsuitable* females in our files," she said in her razor-edged voice. "Our ladies are all guaranteed to possess reputations that are entirely above reproach. Their references are impeccable."

"Perhaps you would do well to try another agency," Mrs. Goodhew suggested in quelling tones.

"I don't have time to go to another agency." He could not believe that his carefully calculated scheme was about to fall apart simply because he could not find the right female. He had assumed that this would be the simplest, most straightforward part of the plan. Instead, it was proving to be astonishingly complicated. "I told you, I must fill this post immediately—"

The door slammed open behind him with resounding force, effectively putting an end to his sentence.

Together with Mrs. Goodhew and Mrs. Willis, he turned to look at the woman who blew into the office with the force of a small storm off the sea.

He saw at once that she had, possibly by accident although he suspected more likely by design, tried to distract attention from her striking features. A pair of gold-framed spectacles partially veiled her vivid amber-gold eyes. Her glossy, midnight-dark hair was pulled back in a remarkably severe style that would have looked more appropriate on a housekeeper or maid.

She wore a serviceable gown of some heavy, dull material in a peculiarly unattractive shade of gray. The garment looked as though it had been deliberately

23

fashioned to make its wearer appear shorter and heavier than she actually was.

The connoisseurs of the ton and the obnoxious dandies who loitered about on Bond Street ogling the ladies would no doubt have dismissed this woman out of hand. But they were fools who did not know how to look beneath the surface, Arthur thought.

He watched the purposeful yet graceful way in which she moved. There was nothing timid or hesitant about her. Lively intelligence glittered in her exotic eyes. Spirit and determination radiated from her.

In an attempt to maintain his objectivity, he concluded that the lady lacked the sort of smooth, superficial perfection that would have caused the men of the ton to hail her as a diamond of the first water. Nevertheless, there was about her something that drew the eye, an energy and vitality that created an invisible aura. In the right clothes she would not go unnoticed in a ballroom.

"Miss Lodge, please, you cannot go in there." The harried-looking woman who occupied the desk in the outer office hovered uncertainly in the opening. "I told you, Mrs. Goodhew and Mrs. Willis are discussing a very important matter with a client."

"I do not care if they are discussing their wills or their funeral arrangements, Mrs. McNab. I intend to speak with them immediately. I have had quite enough of this nonsense."

Miss Lodge came to a halt in front of the twin desks. Arthur knew that she had not noticed him standing behind her in the shadows. The thick fog outside the windows was, in part, responsible. The mist allowed only a vague, gray light into the office. What little illumination there was did not penetrate far.

Mrs. Willis heaved a long-suffering sigh and

assumed an expression that implied she was resigned to some inevitable fate.

Mrs. Goodhew, obviously made of sterner stuff, surged to her feet. "What in heaven's name do you think you are doing interrupting us in this outrageous manner, Miss Lodge?"

"I am correcting what appears to be the mistaken impression that I am seeking a post in the household of a drunkard, or a lecherous rakehell." Miss Lodge narrowed her gaze. "Let us be clear about this. I am in need of an immediate position. I cannot afford to waste any more time interviewing employers who are obviously unacceptable."

"We will discuss this later, Miss Lodge," Mrs. Goodhew snapped.

"We will discuss it now. I have just come from the appointment you arranged for me this afternoon, and I can assure you that I would not take that post if it were the very last position you had to offer."

Mrs. Goodhew smiled with what could only be described as cold triumph. "As it happens, Miss Lodge, it is, indeed, the very last post that this agency intends to make available to you."

Miss Lodge frowned. "Don't be absurd. As annoying as this process is for all concerned and most especially for me, I fear we must press on."

Mrs. Goodhew and Mrs. Willis exchanged glances. Mrs. Goodhew turned back to Miss Lodge.

"On the contrary," she said icily. "I see no point in sending you out on even one more interview."

"Haven't you been paying attention, Mrs. Goodhew?" Miss Lodge snapped. "I told you, I am in need of a new position immediately. My current employer will be leaving town the day after tomorrow to join her friend in the country. She has graciously consented to allow me to stay with her until she departs, but after that I will be obliged to find new lodgings. Lodgings which, due to the extremely poor wages I have been paid for the past few months, I cannot afford at the moment."

Mrs. Willis shook her head with what appeared to be sincere regret. "We have done our best to secure another post for you, Miss Lodge. You have had five interviews with five different clients in the past three days, but you have failed at each attempt."

"I am not the one who failed those interviews. The prospective employers failed them." Miss Lodge raised one gloved hand and began to tick off her fingers as she continued. "Mrs. Tibbett was well into her cups when I arrived, and she continued to nip at her bottle of gin until she toppled over and fell sound asleep on the sofa. Why she seeks a paid companion is beyond me. She was unable to carry on a coherent conversation."

"That is quite enough, Miss Lodge," Mrs. Goodhew said through set teeth.

"Mrs. Oxby said nothing during the entire interview. Instead she allowed her son to conduct the proceedings." Miss Lodge shuddered. "It was obvious that he is one of those dreadful men who inflicts himself upon the weak and helpless females in his own household. The situation was impossible. I have no intention of living under the same roof with such a despicable man."

"Miss Lodge, if you please." Mrs. Goodhew seized a paperweight and thumped the top of her desk.

Miss Lodge ignored her. "And then there was Mrs. Stanbridge, who was so ill that she was forced to conduct the interview from her bed. It was clear to me that she will not survive the fortnight. Her relatives are dealing with her affairs. They cannot wait for her to cock up her toes so that they can get their hands on her money. I could see immediately that it would have been highly unlikely that I would have been able to collect my fees from them."

Mrs. Goodhew drew herself up to her full height and bristled. "It is not the prospective employers who are to blame for your predicament, Miss Lodge. You are the one who is responsible for your failure to secure new employment."

"Nonsense. I had no difficulty whatsoever in obtaining a suitable position six months ago when I first applied to this firm."

"Mrs. Willis and I have concluded that that bit of luck came about solely because of the fact that your first employer happened to be a noted eccentric who, for some incomprehensible reason, found you amusing," Mrs. Goodhew declared.

"Unfortunately for you, Miss Lodge," Mrs. Willis added with ghoulish good cheer, "our list of clients is quite short of eccentrics at the moment. Generally speaking, we do not cater to that type of client."

It occurred to Arthur that the tension in the room had escalated to the point where the three women had forgotten that he was there.

Miss Lodge flushed an angry shade of pink. "Mrs. Egan is not an eccentric. She is an intelligent, well-traveled woman who holds enlightened views on a vast number of subjects."

"Twenty years ago she had a string of lovers that was said to include half the ton, both male and female," Mrs. Goodhew shot back. "She is rumored to be a devoted follower of Wollstonecraft's odd notions regarding female behavior, she refuses to eat meat, she is a student of metaphysics and everyone knows that she once traveled all the way to Egypt and back with only two servants for company."

"Furthermore, it is a well-known fact that she will only wear garments made of purple cloth," Mrs. Willis announced. "Rest assured, Miss Lodge, eccentric is the most polite label we can apply to your current employer."

"That is grossly unfair." Miss Lodge's eyes sparkled with outrage. "Mrs. Egan is an estimable employer. I will not allow you to slander her."

Arthur found himself both amused and strangely entranced by her loyalty to her soon-to-be-former employer.

Mrs. Goodhew snorted. "We are not here to discuss Mrs. Egan's personal qualities, however estimable you may deem them to be. The fact is, there really is nothing more that we can do for you, Miss Lodge."

"I don't believe that for a moment," Miss Lodge said.

Mrs. Willis beetled her brows. "How do you expect us to find a place for you, Miss Lodge, when you have steadfastly refused to adopt the appropriate demeanor required of a successful paid companion? We have explained time and again that meekness, humility and quiet, restrained speech are imperative."

"Bah, I have been meek and humble to a fault." Miss Lodge appeared sincerely affronted by the criticism. "And as for quiet speech, I challenge either of you to prove that my conversation has been anything but quiet and restrained."

Mrs. Willis raised her eyes to the ceiling, evidently seeking help from a higher power.

Mrs. Goodhew snorted. "Your notion of appropriate behavior differs markedly from that of this agency. We are unable to do anything more for you, Miss Lodge."

Arthur noticed that Miss Lodge was starting to look worried now. Her firm, elegant jaw tightened visibly. He could see that she was about to change tactics.

"Let us not be too hasty here," she said smoothly. "I am certain there must be other potential employers in your files." She gave both women a sudden, brilliant smile that could have lit up an entire ballroom. "If you will allow me to look through them, I can no doubt save all of us a good deal of time."

"Let you examine our client files?" Mrs. Willis flinched as though she had touched an electricity machine. "Out of the question. Those files are confidential."

"Calm yourself," Miss Lodge said. "I have no intention of gossiping about your clients. I merely wish to peruse the files so that I may make an informed decision concerning my future employment."

Mrs. Willis squinted at her down the long length of her sharp nose. "You do not seem to grasp the salient point here, Miss Lodge. It is the *client* who makes the decision when it comes to filling the post, not the applicant."

"On the contrary." Miss Lodge took a step closer to Mrs. Willis's desk, leaned over slightly and flattened her gloved hands on the polished surface. "It is you who fail to comprehend. I cannot afford to fritter away any more time on this project. Allowing me to examine the files seems an entirely sensible approach to the problem we face."

"*We* do not face a problem, Miss Lodge." Mrs. Goodhew raised her brows. "You face one. I fear that from now on, you must face it somewhere else."

"That is quite impossible," Miss Lodge looked at her. "I have already explained that there is not enough time left for me to apply to another agency. I must have a position before Mrs. Egan departs for the country."

Arthur made his decision. "Perhaps you would care to consider one more offer of employment from this agency, Miss Lodge."

Chapter Three

The sound of his voice, dark, chilled, controlled and seemingly emanating from the gloom behind her, unnerved Elenora to such a degree that she very nearly dropped her reticule.

She whirled around with a tiny, stifled gasp. For a few disturbing seconds she could not make him out clearly, but she knew instantly that whoever he was, he could well prove dangerous. An oddly exhilarating thrill of anticipation swept through her.

Hastily, she tried to shake off the sensation. She had never reacted like this to any man. It was no doubt a trick of the poor light. The fog had closed in very snugly around the windows, and the two small lamps on the desks of Mrs. Goodhew and Mrs. Willis created more shadows than they dispelled.

Then she realized that she was still wearing the spectacles she had borrowed from Mrs. Egan to enhance her appearance as a proper companion for today's interviews. She reached up very quickly, plucked the eyeglasses from her nose and blinked a couple of times to refocus her vision.

She could see the man in the shadows quite clearly now, but that did not do much to alter her initial impression. If anything it only heightened her feelings of wariness and excitement.

"Dear me," Mrs. Willis said quickly. "I had quite forgotten you were standing there, sir. I beg your pardon. Allow me to introduce Miss Elenora Lodge. Miss Lodge, the Earl of St. Merryn."

St. Merryn inclined his head ever so slightly. "A pleasure, Miss Lodge."

No one would ever label him handsome, Elenora thought. The power, control and harsh intelligence that stamped his features left no room for elegance, refinement or traditional masculine beauty.

His hair was a deep shade of brown. Unfathomable smoky green eyes watched her from some concealed lair deep inside. He had the bold nose, high cheekbones and distinctive jaw that one associated with creatures that survived on their hunting skills.

She realized with a start that she was allowing her imagination to get the better of her. It had been a very long day.

She pulled herself together and made her curtsy. "My lord."

"It would seem that we might be of service to each other, Miss Lodge," he said. His gaze never wavered from her face. "You are in need of a position. I have a distant relative, the widow of a cousin on my father's side, who is staying with me for the Season. I require a companion for her. I am prepared to pay you triple your usual fees."

Triple her usual fees. She was suddenly a little breathless. Steady now, she thought. Whatever else she did, she must maintain an air of dignified calm. She had a feeling that if St. Merryn detected any indication that she suffered from delicate or easily excitable nerves, he would withdraw his offer.

Raising her chin, she gave him what she hoped was a coolly polite smile. "I am prepared to discuss the position, sir."

She heard Mrs. Goodhew and Mrs. Willis murmur between themselves, but she paid no attention. She was too busy watching the satisfaction that glittered briefly in the earl's enigmatic eyes.

"There is a bit more to the post than the duties that are generally expected of a paid companion," St. Merryn said very deliberately.

She recalled the old adage about things sounding too good to be true and steeled herself.

"For some reason, I am not surprised to hear that," she said dryly. "Perhaps you would be so good as to explain?"

"Of course." St. Merryn switched his attention to Mrs. Goodhew and Mrs. Willis. "I would prefer to have this conversation in private with Miss Lodge, if you two ladies do not mind." He paused a beat and smiled faintly. "The situation involves a family matter. I'm sure you comprehend."

"Certainly," Mrs. Goodhew said. She seemed relieved to have the excuse to exit the room. "Mrs. Willis?"

Mrs. Willis was already on her feet. "After you, Mrs. Goodhew."

The two women stepped smartly around their desks and crossed the room. They closed the door very firmly behind them.

A heavy silence descended. Elenora did not like the feel of impending dread that accompanied it.

Some of her initial excitement faded. It was

replaced with wariness. Her palms tingled with a strange chill. She sensed the weight of the heavy fog pressing at the windows. It was so thick that she could not see the buildings across the narrow street. Was it just her imagination that made the room seem suddenly very small and intensely intimate?

St. Merryn walked deliberately across the office and came to a halt in front of one of the windows. He meditated for a while on the featureless mist that shrouded the narrow street. She knew that he was debating just how much to tell her.

"I may as well come straight out with it, Miss Lodge," he said after a moment. "What I told Mrs. Goodhew and Mrs. Willis was not the full truth. I am not in need of a companion for my relative, although she is, indeed, staying in my house."

"I see. What do you require, sir?"

"A fiancée."

Elenora closed her eyes in despair. Just when she had begun to believe that the nature of the potential employers in the files of Goodhew & Willis could not get any worse, she was confronted with a madman.

"Miss Lodge?" St. Merryn's voice cracked like a whip across the room. "Are you all right?"

Jolted, she opened her eyes and summoned what she hoped was a soothing smile. "Of course, my lord. I am perfectly all right. Now then, perhaps there is someone who should be summoned?"

"I beg your pardon?"

"A family member or a personal servant, perhaps?" She hesitated delicately. "Or an attendant?"

The poor sent their insane relatives to the horrors of the hospital known as Bedlam. But among the wealthy, it was customary to secure an afflicted family member in a private asylum. She wondered when St. Merryn had escaped and whether anyone had noticed yet that he was missing from his locked cell.

"An attendant?" St. Merryn's expression hardened. "What the devil are you talking about?"

"It is rather bleak and gloomy outside, is it not?" she said gently. "One can easily become lost in a fog like this." *Especially if one's mind is also filled with strange vapors and visions,* she added silently. "But I'm certain that there is someone who will come and guide you home. If you could just let Mrs. Goodhew and Mrs. Willis know where to send a message . . ."

Understanding and then icy amusement lit St. Merryn's eyes. "You think I'm mad, don't you?"

"No such thing, my lord. I was merely trying to be helpful." She took a cautious step back toward the door. "But if there should happen to be a tiny problem here, I am confident that Mrs. Goodhew and Mrs. Willis will be able to deal with it."

Concluding that it would not be wise to turn her back on a lunatic, she groped awkwardly behind herself, searching for the doorknob.

"No doubt." His smile was wry and fleeting. "I'll wager those two are capable of dealing with just about anything, including a deranged client. But, as it happens, Miss Lodge, I am not mad." He shrugged. "At least, I do not believe that I am. If you will take your hand off that doorknob, I will attempt to explain."

She did not move.

He raised his brows slightly. "I promise you, I will make it worth your while."

"In the *financial* sense?"

His mouth tilted a little at one corner. "Is there any other sense?"

Not as far as she was concerned, she thought. In her current predicament, she could not afford to overlook any reasonable offer of employment. The shimmering dream of a new future for herself that she had created out of thin air that long, lonely night six months before, had proved far more difficult to achieve in real life than she had ever imagined. Money was the sticking point. She needed this post.

St. Merryn might be mad, but he did not appear to be a depraved rakehell or a drunkard as had been the case with two of her potential employers that afternoon.

In point of fact, she thought, he was starting to sound more and more like a man who understood how to conduct a business negotiation. She admired that quality in a gentleman.

And he was most certainly not on his deathbed, either, as the third potential client that day had been. Quite the contrary, there was a disconcerting, intensely intriguing air of masculine vitality about him that stirred her in a way she could not describe. He was not handsome, at least not in the manner in which Jeremy Clyde had been. But the whispers of awareness lifting the little hairs on the nape of her neck were oddly stimulating.

Reluctantly, she released the doorknob. She stayed where she was, however, within inches of escape. A successful paid companion learned to be prepared for the unexpected.

"Very well, sir. I am listening."

St. Merryn moved to the front of Mrs. Goodhew's desk, leaned back against it and stretched his arms out to the sides. The position pulled his excellently cut coat snugly across his strong shoulders. It also allowed her to notice that he had a broad chest, flat stomach and lean hips. There was nothing thin or soft or weak about him.

"I have come to London for a few weeks this Season

for the sole purpose of conducting some rather complicated business affairs. I will not bore you with the details, but the long and short of it is that I intend to form a consortium of investors. The project requires secrecy and privacy. If you know anything about Society, you will be aware that both conditions are extremely difficult to achieve. The Polite World lives on a steady diet of gossip and rumor."

She allowed herself to relax slightly. Perhaps he was not mad after all.

"Pray continue, sir."

"Unfortunately, given my current situation and a certain incident that occurred a year ago, I believe it will be somewhat difficult for me to go about my business without a great deal of annoying interference unless I am seen to be quite clearly off the marriage mart."

She cleared her throat. "Your situation?" she asked as delicately as possible.

He raised one brow. "I have a title, several rather nice estates and a substantial fortune. And I am not married."

"How nice for you," she murmured.

He looked briefly amused. "Sarcasm is not generally considered a desirable quality in a paid companion, but given the fact that I am just as desperate as you are, I am prepared to overlook it on this occasion."

She blushed. "My apologies, sir. It has been a somewhat trying day."

"I assure you, mine was equally unpleasant."

It was time to get back to the subject at hand, she decided. "Yes, well I do see that your *situation* makes you an extremely interesting commodity in certain social circles."

"And no doubt quite boring in other circles."

She had to work to hold back a smile. His wry, self-deprecating humor caught her by surprise.

St. Merryn did not appear to notice her startled amusement. He drummed his fingertips in a single staccato pattern on the desk. "But that is neither here nor there. As I was saying, my situation is further complicated by the fact that last Season, I was engaged for a time to a young lady who eventually eloped with another man."

That information took her aback more than somewhat. "Never say so."

He gave her an impatient look. "There are any number of people who would be happy to tell you that the young lady in question had a narrow escape."

"Hmm."

"What the devil does that mean?"

"Nothing really. It just struck me that perhaps you are the one who had the narrow escape, sir. I had a similar escape myself, six months ago."

Cold curiosity gleamed in his eyes. "Indeed? And would that explain why you find yourself applying for a post as a paid companion today?"

"In part." She swept out a hand. "But given what I now know about my former fiancé, I can tell you in all truth that I would rather be looking for a new post this afternoon than married to a liar and a deceiver."

"I see."

"But enough of my personal life, sir. The thing is, I do, indeed, understand your dilemma. When word reaches Polite Circles that you are in town, it will be assumed that you have come back to try your luck again on the marriage mart. You will be viewed as so much fresh, raw meat by the matchmaking lionesses of the ton."

"I could not have put it more succinctly myself. And that, Miss Lodge, is why I need a lady who can pose convincingly as my fiancée. It is really very simple."

"It is?" she asked warily.

"Certainly. As I said, although I am here to conduct some extremely private business, Society will assume I have come back to shop for another bride. I do not want to find myself tripping over every young chit who has been brought to town to find a husband this Season. If I am perceived to be securely engaged to be married, the huntresses of Society will be forced to focus their attentions on other game."

She sincerely doubted that St. Merryn's scheme would prove to be the least bit simple. But who was she to argue with him?

"It sounds a very cunning plan, my lord," she said politely. "I wish you the very best of luck with it."

"I can see that you do not think for a moment that it will be successful."

She sighed. "Far be it from me to remind you that many a man in your situation has underestimated the cleverness and determination of a mother who is intent on securing a good catch for her daughter."

"I assure you, madam, that I have the greatest respect for the female of the species. Hence my plan to parade a fraudulent fiancée in front of Society for the next few weeks. Now then, will you accept the post that I am offering?"

"Sir, do not mistake me, I am not at all opposed to accepting the position. Indeed, I believe that I would quite enjoy it."

That comment clearly intrigued him. "Why do you say that?"

"My grandmother was a very fine actress who gave up the stage to marry my grandfather," she explained. "I have been told that I resemble her to a striking degree. I have often wondered if I got a measure of her talent, as well as her looks. Acting the role of your fiancée would no doubt prove interesting, even challenging."

"I see. Well, then—"

She held up a hand. "But we must be realistic, sir. The truth is, as much as I would like to tread the boards, as it were, and as desperately as I want those excellent wages you offered, the fact is that it would be extremely difficult for me to masquerade as your intended bride."

His jaw tightened with impatience. "Why is that?"

Where to begin? she wondered.

She moved a hand down her skirts to indicate her dull, gray gown. "For starters, I lack a proper wardrobe."

He gave her a long, considering look that took her in from head to toe. She felt like a prize mare up for auction at Tattersall's.

"Do not concern yourself with the problem of your wardrobe," St. Merryn said. "I never expected that a woman who was applying for a position as a paid companion would possess the sort of gowns needed for this charade."

"Yes, well, in addition to the clothes, there is the matter of my age." This was proving to be an extremely embarrassing interview, she thought. Most of the other potential employers had considered her a bit young for the positions they were offering. However, in this instance, she was definitely too old.

"What is wrong with your age?" He frowned. "I had assumed that you are somewhere in your late twenties. I trust you are not about to tell me that you are considerably younger than you appear? I am most definitely not in the market for a green chit fresh out of the schoolroom."

She set her back teeth and reminded herself that this

morning when she had dressed for her interviews, she had deliberately made herself up in what she hoped was the very image of a typical paid companion. Nevertheless, she was somewhat irritated to learn that he had erred on the high side when he had calculated her age.

"I am six and twenty," she said, striving to keep her words entirely neutral.

He nodded once, evidently satisfied. "Excellent. Old enough to have acquired some common sense and knowledge of the world. You'll do."

"Thank you," she retorted caustically. "But we both know that gentlemen of your rank and fortune are expected to marry very young, extremely sheltered ladies straight out of the schoolroom."

"Hell's teeth, madam, we are discussing a paid post, not a genuine betrothal." He scowled. "You know perfectly well that it would be impossible for me to employ a seventeen-year-old girl for this position. Not only would she be highly unlikely to possess the skills and self-confidence required to carry it off, she would no doubt expect me to go through with the damn wedding at the end."

For some reason that remark sent a chill through her. She did not understand why, however. Logic told her that of course the Earl of St. Merryn would not even consider marriage to the woman who played the role of his fiancée for a few weeks. Why, such a woman would be no better than an actress. Wealthy, powerful gentlemen of the ton had affairs with actresses; they certainly did not marry them.

"Speaking of which," Elenora made herself say briskly, "just how do you intend to end this fictitious engagement when you have concluded your business here in town?"

"There will be no problem with terminating it," he

said. He shrugged. "You will simply disappear from Society. It will be put about that you cried off and returned to your family's estates somewhere in the far North."

You will simply disappear.

Alarm slithered across her nerves. That sounded decidedly ominous. On the other hand, he was right. Vanishing from exclusive circles would not be so very difficult. The rich and the powerful lived in a very small, self-contained world, after all. They rarely strayed outside the borders of that glittering sphere, nor did they notice those who existed beyond it.

"Yes, I suppose that will work," she said, thinking it through carefully. "Few, if any, of my future employers are likely to move in the same exalted circles of Society that you and your acquaintances inhabit. Even if they do go into the Polite World and even if I were to come into contact with some of their elevated friends, I doubt that anyone would take any notice. Once I revert to my role as a paid companion, no one will pay any attention to me."

"People see what they expect to see," he agreed.

A thought struck her. "Perhaps I should use another name while I play this role, to help ensure that no one recognizes me while I am in the part."

He chuckled. "I can see that the notion of taking a stage name appeals to you, but I do not think it necessary, and it will only complicate matters in the event that someone from your own past does happen to recognize you."

"Oh, yes, I see what you mean." She was somewhat disappointed, but she had to admit that he was correct. "It is unlikely, but if I should meet up with an acquaintance here in London, it would be difficult to explain my new name."

"Truthfully, I am not at all disturbed by the notion of you encountering someone you know while you play your part. There is no reason why such an event would affect our script. As long as I claim you as my fiancée, you will be accepted as such. I am considered something of an eccentric, so no one will be unduly shocked that I wish to marry a lady with no social connections."

"I see."

His smile was cold. "Who will dare to contradict me?"

"Yes, of course," she said, a little awed by his unshakable arrogance. But his point was well taken. Who, indeed, would dare to question his claim? And as for the future, well, she would worry about that when it was necessary to do so. She could hardly afford to pass up this extremely profitable arrangement because of some vague fear of being recognized as the earl's cast-off fiancée six months from now.

"Indeed." She nodded once, satisfied. "Very well, I think it is safe to assume that no one looking at a companion will see the Earl of St. Merryn's former fiancée, so I should have no difficulty obtaining future employment." She hesitated. "But where will I live while I am in your employ? I do not have any lodgings of my own. It is quite expensive here in town, you know."

"You will stay in my house, of course. We will tell people that you are visiting from the country to shop and enjoy the pleasures of the Season."

"You expect me to live under your roof, sir?" She raised her brows. "That would invite the sort of gossip that I'm sure you would not want."

"There is no need to be alarmed on account of your reputation, Miss Lodge. I promise you that you will be properly chaperoned. The tale that I gave Mrs. Goodhew and Mrs. Willis concerning my widowed female relative staying with me for a few weeks was quite true."

"I see. Well, then, my lord, your scheme just might work."

"Miss Lodge, for your information, my schemes *always* work. That is because I am very good at making plans and executing them."

He said that without any trace of arrogance, she realized. It was a simple statement of fact as far as he was concerned.

"Nevertheless, this particular scheme seems somewhat complicated," she murmured.

"Trust me, Miss Lodge. It will work. And at the end of it, I will pay you not only triple your fees, but a bonus."

She went very still, hardly daring to breathe. "Do you mean that, sir?"

"I need you, Miss Lodge. Something tells me you are perfect for the part I want you to play, and I am quite willing to pay you handsomely for your talents."

She cleared her throat. "As it happens, I have been saving every penny I can afford to put aside in order to invest in a certain business venture."

"Indeed? What sort of venture would that be?"

She pondered briefly and then decided that there was no reason not to tell him the truth. "I hope you will not be too terribly shocked, sir, but my goal is to go into trade."

"You are going to become a shopkeeper?" he asked in an astonishingly neutral manner.

Braced for strong disapproval, she felt almost lightheaded with relief when he did not condemn her scheme out of hand. In the view of well-bred people, going into trade was a dreadful move to be avoided at all costs. In the eyes of Society it was preferable by far to scrape by in genteel poverty rather than become the proprietor of a business.

"I realize that my plans must strike you as beyond the pale," she said. "But as soon as I have obtained enough money, I intend to open a bookshop and a circulating library."

"You do not shock me, Miss Lodge. As it happens, I have made my fortune through various investments. I have some skill when it comes to business."

"Indeed, sir." She gave him another polite smile.

He was being very gracious, she thought. But they both knew that the gulf between a gentleman's business investments and the notion of going into trade was vast and deep in the eyes of Society. It was all very well for a person of quality to purchase shares in a shipping venture or a housing construction project. It was another matter altogether for a well-bred individual to become the proprietor of a shop.

Nevertheless, the important thing was that St. Merryn did not seem the least bit put off by her plans. Then again, she thought, he had made it clear that he was not in a position to be choosy.

He inclined his head in somber acknowledgment of her intentions. "Very well, then, do we have a bargain, Miss Lodge?"

The generosity of his terms completely dazzled her, as he had no doubt intended. She had one remaining qualm about the post she was accepting, but she crushed it down quite ruthlessly. This was the first turn of good fortune that had come her way since that dreadful day when her stepfather's creditors had arrived on her doorstep. She would not risk losing a golden opportunity simply because of a petty uncertainty.

Scarcely able to contain her delight, she smiled again.

"We do indeed, my lord."

St. Merryn stared at her mouth for several seconds, as though riveted. Then he gave his head a slight shake and frowned slightly. She got the impression that for some reason he was annoyed, not with her but with himself.

"If we are to achieve our objective of projecting an air of intimacy about our association," he said dryly, "I think you must learn to call me Arthur."

That would not be easy, she thought. There was a forbidding quality about him that would make such easy familiarity difficult.

It was not until she was outside in the street, hurrying back to Mrs. Egan's townhouse to give her the good news, that the qualm she had squelched earlier rose up once more to plague her.

It was not the earl's formidable temperament or his bizarre plan to parade her in front of Society as his fiancée that worried her, she thought. She could deal with those things.

What made her uneasy about this too-good-to-be-true post was the fact that she was almost positive that St. Merryn had not told her the whole truth.

He was keeping secrets, she thought. Her intuition warned her that St. Merryn's scheme involved something far more dangerous than a plan to put together an investment consortium.

But his private affairs were none of her concern, she concluded with rising excitement. The only thing that mattered to her was that if she successfully carried off the role St. Merryn had assigned to her, she would be well on her way to realizing her dream by the time he brought his little drama to a close.

Chapter Four

It is just barely possible that my streak of extremely bad luck is about to come to an end." Elenora sank gratefully into the depths of the wingback chair and smiled at the two women perched on the sofa across from her.

She had first met Lucinda Colyer and Charlotte Atwater six months before, in the offices of Goodhew & Willis. The three of them had arrived on the same day, seeking employment as companions. After a particularly trying afternoon of interviews, Elenora had suggested that they all go to the tea shop just around the corner and commiserate.

As it happened the three of them were quite different in temperament, but that fact paled in comparison to the things that they did have in common: They were all in their mid-twenties, well past the age when a good marriage was still a viable option. They were all from respectable backgrounds; well-bred and well-educated. And due to a variety of unfortunate circumstances, all three found themselves alone in the world and without resources.

In short, they shared the common bonds that drove women such as themselves into the paid companion profession.

That first afternoon tea together had become a regular Wednesday affair. After they had obtained posts, Wednesday was the one day of the week that each of them had free.

For the past few months they had been meeting here in the parlor of Lucinda's elderly employer, Mrs. Blancheflower. It was not an environment calculated to lift one's spirits, in Elenora's opinion, and she knew the others did not find it particularly cheerful either.

The atmosphere was one of intense gloom due to the fact that Mrs. Blancheflower was dying somewhere upstairs. Fortunately for Lucinda, who had been hired to keep the lady company in her remaining days, her employer was taking her time about making her transition to a higher plane.

As Mrs. Blancheflower slept most of the time, Lucinda had found her post to be quite undemanding. The chief drawback was that her employer's relatives, who seldom came to call, had decreed that the housekeeper maintain a suitably funereal décor. That meant that there was a great deal of black cloth hung everywhere. In addition, the drapes were always kept pulled tightly closed to ensure that no hint of cheerful spring sunlight could squeeze into the somber rooms.

While the gloom weighed on one, Elenora and her friends endured it every Wednesday because there was one very significant advantage to holding their visits here: The tea and cakes were free, thanks to Mrs. Blancheflower's unknowing largesse. That meant that the three women could all save a few pennies.

Elenora had asked St. Merryn to allow her to tell her friends the truth about her new post and had assured him that neither of them went about in Society. Lucinda's employer was on her deathbed and Charlotte's was an elderly widow who was confined to her house by a failing heart. *"Not that either of them would breathe a word about my role even if they were to encounter someone who was acquainted with you, sir,"* she had added with great certainty.

St. Merryn had seemed quite satisfied, even unconcerned with her friends' ability to keep silent about her role as his phony fiancée. He truly was not the least bit worried about them spreading gossip, for the simple reason that he knew full well that no one in Society would pay any attention to such a wild rumor put about by a couple of impoverished paid companions. Who would take Lucinda's and Charlotte's word over that of a wealthy, powerful earl?

Lucinda and Charlotte had at first been astonished by the news that she was to play the role of St. Merryn's fiancée and live in his house. But after learning that she would be properly chaperoned by one of his lordship's female relatives, they had concluded that the post was a very exciting one.

"Just think, you will be able to go to all the most exclusive balls and soirées," Charlotte said, looking dazzled. "And you will wear elegant gowns."

Lucinda, ever the pessimist, affected an air of dark foreboding. "If I were you, I would be very cautious around St. Merryn, Elenora."

Elenora and Charlotte both looked at her.

"Why do you say that?" Elenora demanded.

"A few months before I met you, I was employed as a companion to a widow who had connections in Society. She was unable to leave her bed, but in the months that I was with her, I learned that her chief pleasure was to keep up with the affairs of the ton. I recall some gossip about St. Merryn."

"Go on," Charlotte pressed eagerly.

"At the time he was engaged to marry a young lady named Juliana Graham," Lucinda continued. "But the *on dit* was that she was terrified of him."

Elenora frowned. "Terrified? That is a rather strong term."

"Nevertheless, she evidently regarded him with great fear. Her father accepted St. Merryn's offer, of course, without bothering to consult with Juliana. After all, his lordship is extremely rich."

"And then there's the title," Charlotte murmured. "Any papa would want such an alliance in the family."

"Precisely." Lucinda poured herself another cup of tea. "Well, as it happened, the young lady was so frightened of the prospect of marrying St. Merryn that one night she climbed down a ladder from her bed-chamber and fled into the teeth of a terrible storm with a man named Roland Burnley. At dawn, Juliana's father found the pair in the same bedchamber at an inn. Naturally the two were wed immediately."

Charlotte tilted her head slightly. "You say that it was the young lady's father who pursued the couple? Not St. Merryn?"

Lucinda nodded, her face somber. "The story is that when he received the news that his bride-to-be had eloped, St. Merryn was in his club. He calmly announced that the next time he chose a fiancée, he would go to an agency that supplies paid companions and select one. Then he went into the card room and played until dawn."

"Good heavens," Charlotte breathed. "He must be as cold as ice."

"He is, by all accounts," Lucinda confirmed.

Elenora stared at Lucinda, dumbstruck. And then the humor of the situation overtook her. She started to laugh so hard that she was forced to put her teacup down before the contents spilled onto the carpet.

Lucinda and Charlotte stared at her.

"What is so amusing?" Charlotte asked sharply.

Elenora clutched her sides. "You must admit, St. Merryn has certainly made good on his vow to obtain his next fiancée from an agency," she managed between giggles. "Who would have thought the man had such an ironic wit? What a great joke he is going to play upon Society."

"No offense, Elenora," Lucinda muttered, "but your new employer sounds even more eccentric than Mrs. Egan. I would not be at all surprised if he proved to be the type who will attempt to perpetrate outrages upon your person."

Charlotte shivered, but her eyes were very bright.

Elenora grinned. "Nonsense. I have interviewed a sufficient number of truly lecherous employers to know one when I see one. St. Merryn is not the sort who would force himself on a lady. He possesses far too much self-control."

"He certainly does not appear to be a very passionate or romantic gentleman, either," Charlotte said, clearly disappointed.

"Why do you say that?" Elenora asked, startled by the observation. She thought about what she had glimpsed in the earl's smoky green eyes. Something told her that the reason St. Merryn wielded so much self-control was precisely because he did possess a passionate nature.

"Any other gentleman endowed with even a modicum of romantic sensibilities who had been told that his fiancée had run off with another man would have given chase," Charlotte declared. "He would have snatched his lady from the arms of the man who had carried her off, and then challenged the other gentleman to a duel."

Lucinda shuddered. "They say St. Merryn's blood runs cold, not hot."

Chapter Five

Perhaps it was the steady drizzle that made the mansion in Rain Street appear to loom on some other dark,
metaphysical plane. Whatever the reason, there was an
air not only of gloom but of neglect about the place,
Elenora thought. It reminded her of the house where
Lucinda kept watch over her dying employer, but on a
far grander scale. It was as if something had expired
inside the St. Merryn mansion a long time ago and the
big house had begun to decay.

Elenora checked the card St. Merryn had given her
to make certain that the hackney had brought her to the
right address. Number Twelve Rain Street. There was
no mistake.

The door of the hack opened. The driver handed her
down and then unloaded the trunk that contained her
personal possessions.

On the point of leaving her there in the street, he
eyed the front door of the mansion with a dubious
expression.

"Yer certain ye've come to the right place, ma'am?" he asked.

"Yes, thank you." She smiled, grateful for his obvious concern. "Someone will be out to collect my trunk in a moment. There is no need for you to hang about."

He shrugged. "If ye say so."

He clambered back up onto the box and let out the reins. Elenora squelched her own serious misgivings as she watched the vehicle disappear down the street.

When the hackney was gone, she was conscious of being very alone in the mist-shrouded street.

Just as well, she told herself as she went briskly up the steps. Better that no one had witnessed St. Merryn's new fiancée arriving in a hack. This way her sudden appearance in Society would be all the more intriguing and curious in the eyes of the Polite World. At the end of this business she would simply disappear in the same mysterious fashion.

A small thrill swept through her. She was about to become a woman of mystery, *an actress.* She had the oddest feeling that she had spent her whole life waiting in the wings, preparing to take the stage, and now the moment had arrived.

She had donned her favorite gown for this occasion, a deep, claret-red walking dress that Mrs. Egan had ordered for her from her own personal dressmaker. Pinned to the bodice was the elegant little watch that her former employer had given her as a parting gift.

"You'll do just fine, my dear," Mrs. Egan had declared with maternal satisfaction when she had given Elenora the watch. *"You've got spirit and nerve and a kind heart. Nothing can keep you down for long."*

She reached the top step and banged the heavy brass knocker. The sound seemed to echo endlessly deep inside the big house.

For a moment she heard nothing. Then, just as she was starting to wonder if she had, indeed, made a mistake in the address, she caught the faint patter of footsteps on a tile floor.

The front door opened. A young, very harried-looking maid looked out at her.

"Yes, ma'am?"

Elenora considered how to proceed. St. Merryn had told her that he intended to maintain their charade in front of his servants. But she was well aware that the staff of any household generally paid considerably more attention to the doings of their employers than said employers realized. She had a hunch that even if the maid and the other servants had not already realized that there was no genuine fiancée, they had, at the very least, deduced that there was something distinctly amiss about the situation.

Nevertheless, there was no use going about this in a halfhearted manner, she decided. She was being paid to act, and she must do so as convincingly as possible. The maid, like those in the Polite World to whom she would soon be introduced, was part of her audience.

"You may inform your employer that Miss Elenora Lodge has arrived," she instructed in a polite but authoritative tone. "I am expected. Oh, and please have one of the footmen fetch my trunk from the street before it is stolen."

The maid managed a hasty little curtsy. "Yes, ma'am." She stepped back to allow Elenora into the hall.

Elenora waited until the young woman had vanished through a doorway before allowing herself to breathe a small sigh of relief.

She turned slowly on her heel, taking stock of the front hall. It was just as bleak and forbidding as the outside of the house. Very little light penetrated through the high windows above the door. The heavily carved wooden panels darkened the interior still further. A number of classical statues and Etruscan-style vases occupied the shadowy niches around the room. The place had the musty, dusty air of a museum.

Curious, she stepped to the nearest marble pedestal and drew her gloved fingertip lightly across the surface. She frowned at the distinct line that appeared and brushed her hands together to get rid of the dirt that had accumulated on the tip of her glove. No one had cleaned thoroughly in here in quite some time.

Footsteps sounded in the hall, heavier than those of the maid. Elenora turned around.

She found herself gazing at the most astonishingly handsome man she had ever seen in her entire life. From his high, noble brow to his finely chiseled features, smoldering eyes and artlessly curled hair, he was a vision of masculine perfection.

If not for the fact that he wore a butler's formal coat and trousers, he could have modeled for an artist seeking to paint a vision of a romantic poet in the style of Byron.

"I am Ibbitts, madam," he said in a deep voice. "I apologize for any inconvenience you may have suffered. His lordship is waiting for you in the library. If you will follow me, I will announce you."

A tiny warning bell clanged somewhere in her mind. There was nothing objectionable about his words, she thought, but she was convinced that there was a thinly veiled disdain buried in them. Perhaps it was her imagination.

"Thank you, Ibbitts."

She handed him her bonnet. He immediately turned to set it on a dusty marble-topped table.

"Never mind," she said quickly, snatching the hat out of his hand before he could put it on the grimy table. "I'll keep it with me. About my trunk. I do not want it left out there in the street."

"I very much doubt that anyone would steal your trunk, madam." Ibbitts could not have made it plainer if he had tried that he was certain her trunk contained nothing of value.

She had had enough of his polite sarcasm. "Send a footman for it now, Ibbitts."

Ibbitts blinked owlishly, as though confused by the unsubtle reprimand. "Any thief with a bit of common sense knows better than to steal from this household."

"That is only somewhat reassuring, Ibbitts. I fear that there are a great number of thieves who lack common sense."

Ibbitts's expression tightened. Without a word, he reached out and yanked hard on a velvet bell pull.

A tall, thin, gangly-looking young man of about eighteen or nineteen years appeared. He had red hair and blue eyes. His pale skin was sprinkled with freckles. He had a nervous, rabbity air.

"Ned, fetch Miss Lodge's trunk and take it upstairs to the bedchamber Sally prepared this morning."

"Aye, Mr. Ibbitts." Ned scurried out the front door.

Ibbitts turned back to Elenora. He did not actually say, *there, are you satisfied now?* But she was certain he was thinking the words.

"If you will come with me," Ibbitts said instead. "His lordship does not like to be kept waiting."

Without waiting for a response, Ibbitts led the way along a dimly lit hall toward the back of the big house.

At the far end of the corridor he ushered her into a long room paneled in heavy, dark wood. She was relieved to see that the windows in the library were not covered by heavy curtains as they were at the front of the house. Instead, the thick, brown velvet drapes had been tied back to frame the view of a wild, chaotically overgrown, rain-drenched garden.

The library was furnished with a murky carpet badly in need of cleaning and several items of substantial furniture in a style that had been out of fashion for several years. The high, shadowy ceiling had been painted with a dreary scene of a twilight sky at some point in the distant past. Bookshelves lined most of the walls. The leather-bound volumes were old and dusty.

A narrow, circular staircase studded with wrought iron balusters twisted upward to a balcony that was lined with more bookshelves.

"Miss Lodge, my lord." Ibbitts made his announcement as though he was reading Elenora's name from an obituary notice.

"Thank you, Ibbitts." At the far end of the room, near the window facing the unkempt garden, Arthur rose from behind a heavily carved desk.

Silhouetted against the poor light his hard face was unreadable. He came around the front of the desk and walked toward her down the length of the room.

"Welcome to your future home, my dear," he said.

It dawned on her that he was playing his part in front of the butler. She must do the same.

"Thank you. It is so good to see you again, sir." She made her best curtsy.

Ibbitts backed out of the room and closed the door.

The instant the butler disappeared, Arthur halted midway down the room and glanced at the clock. "What the devil took you so long? I thought you would be here an hour ago."

So much for his role of gallant fiancé, Elenora

thought. Evidently her new employer did not intend to maintain the charade when they were private.

"I apologize for the delay," she said calmly. "The rain made the traffic quite difficult."

Before he could respond, a woman spoke from the balcony overhead.

"Arthur, please introduce me," she called down in a warm, soft-spoken voice.

Elenora looked up and saw a tiny bird of a woman who appeared to be in her mid thirties. She had delicate features and bright hazel eyes. Her hair, dressed in a simple chignon, was the color of dark honey. Her gown appeared to be relatively new and made of expensive fabric, but it was not in the latest style.

"Allow me to present Margaret Lancaster," Arthur said. "She is the relative I mentioned, the one who will be staying here while I conduct my business affairs. She will go about with you and lend her services as a chaperone so that your reputation will not suffer while you are in this household."

"Mrs. Lancaster." Elenora dropped another curtsy.

"You must call me Margaret. After all, as far as the world is concerned, you will soon be a member of the family." Margaret started down the circular staircase "My, this is going to be so exciting. I am quite looking forward to the adventure."

Arthur went back to his desk and sat down. He looked at Elenora and Margaret in turn.

"As I have explained, I want the pair of you to do whatever is necessary to distract the attentions of Society so that I can conduct my business affairs with the greatest degree of privacy possible."

"Yes, of course," Elenora murmured.

"You will make arrangements immediately to attend the most important and most fashionable balls and soirées so that everyone in Society will see that I really do have a fiancée."

"I understand," Elenora said.

He looked at Margaret. "As Elenora's chaperone and female guide, you will deal with the details involved in making certain that she creates an immediate and convincing impression on the Polite World."

"Yes, Arthur." Margaret's expression seemed somewhat strained.

"She will need suitable gowns, hats, gloves and all the fripperies that go with them," Arthur continued. "Everything must be in the most current mode, of course, and purchased from the right shops. You know how critical fashion is in Society."

There was a short pause during which Margaret seemed to collect herself.

"Yes, Arthur," she said again. This time her smile was decidedly shaky.

Elenora glanced at her in surprise, wondering what was amiss.

Arthur, however, did not seem to be aware that anything was wrong.

"Very, well, I think that is all for now," he said, reaching for a leather-bound journal and a pen. "You may both go. I'm sure you have a number of things to do to prepare yourselves. Let me know if you have any questions."

Elenora wondered if he realized that he was dismissing them as if they were members of his staff. Of course, she reminded herself, in her case that was the simple truth.

Margaret's relationship to him was a different matter entirely, but to Elenora's astonishment, the other woman did not appear to be offended. In fact she seemed suddenly desperate to escape the library.

Elenora thought about her reaction of a moment before, when Arthur had casually informed her that she would be responsible for all matters of fashion and style.

She was fairly certain that what she had glimpsed in Margaret's eyes was an expression of glazed horror.

Arthur waited until the door closed behind the two women. Then he put aside the journal and got to his feet. He went to stand at the window facing out into the garden.

He knew that Elenora suspected that he had not told her everything. She was right. But he considered it best that she did not know the full truth. There was no need to tell Margaret, either. Both women would find it easier to act their parts if they did not know what had really prompted him to write the play in which they were performing.

He remained there in front of the window for a long time, staring out into the misty garden and thinking about how much he disliked this house.

His grandfather had brought him here to live shortly after his parents had died in an inn fire. He had been six years of age at the time. He had not known his grandfather until then because he had never met him. The old earl had been furious with his son for making a runaway marriage. Arthur's mother had been a young lady possessed of neither fortune nor social connections. The old man had refused to receive her or his grandson.

His grandfather had certainly known how to hold a grudge, Arthur thought.

But the shock of losing his son in the fire had forced the old man to realize that Arthur was the only heir that he was going to get. He had brought his grandson back to the big, gloomy house in Rain Street, and then he had dedicated himself to the task of ensuring that Arthur did not follow in what he saw as his son's romantic, irresponsible footsteps.

He had learned his lessons well, Arthur thought. His grandfather had drilled his obligations and responsibilities into him from that very first day. Ten years later, when he had lain on his deathbed, the old man had still been at his self-appointed task. His last words to Arthur had been, "Remember, you are the head of the family. It is your duty to take care of the rest of them."

The only bright spots during the decade he had spent with his grandfather had occurred during frequent extended visits to the home of Arthur's eccentric great-uncle, George Lancaster.

It was Uncle George who had provided the positive, supportive influence that had enabled him to weather the old earl's bleak and rigid temperament, Arthur thought. Unlike the others in his vast and far-flung family, George Lancaster had not expected anything more of him than that he be what he was, a growing boy with a boy's hopes and dreams and curiosity.

It had been George, not his grandfather, whom Arthur had come to love in the way that he had once loved his father.

Now George Lancaster was gone, murdered less than two months before.

"I will avenge you," Arthur vowed quietly. "On my oath, the murderer will pay."

Chapter Six

The maid, Sally, had just finished unpacking Elenora's trunk when there was a soft knock on the door of the bedchamber.

Sally opened the door to reveal an anxious-looking Margaret standing in the hall.

"I wonder if I might speak to you, Elenora?" Margaret glanced to either side, evidently assuring herself that the corridor was empty. "It is somewhat urgent."

"Yes, of course. Come in." Elenora smiled at Sally. "That will be all for now. Thank you."

"Yes, ma'am." Sally hurried out of the room, closing the door behind her.

Elenora looked at Margaret. "What is the problem? I could see that something made you quite anxious downstairs in the library."

"Anxious is a mild word." Margaret flung herself into a chair. "Stricken with panic would be a more accurate way to put it."

"And why is that?"

Margaret rolled her eyes. "Because I am here under false pretenses, of course."

Elenora was amused. "So am I, when you consider the matter."

"Yes, well, in your case that is not a problem. Arthur hired you from that agency." Margaret waved a hand. "He interviewed you. He knows precisely what he has got in you, and he has written your part with that in mind. But my situation is quite different, and when he discovers that I am not at all what he believes me to be, he will be furious."

Curious now, Elenora sank down slowly on the side of the bed and studied Margaret. "Would you care to explain?"

"I suppose I should begin at the beginning. A fortnight ago Arthur came to see me. He explained his plan to present a false fiancée to Society and asked if I would agree to act as a chaperone. I told him that I would be happy to assist him in his scheme."

"That was very kind of you."

"Kind? Bah. I leaped at the chance. This is the first opportunity that I have had to come to London since my Season fourteen years ago."

"I see."

Margaret grimaced. "My husband was a middle-aged man when I married him. He suffered from gout and he detested travel of any sort. During our time together I was unable to do anything more than make occasional visits to my mother and my aunt. Do you have any idea of what it is like to be trapped in a tiny village for fourteen years?"

"Well, yes, as a matter of fact I do."

"Oh." Margaret winced. "Sorry. I did not mean to carry on that way. The thing is, I am a writer."

"Really? How exciting." Elenora was entranced. "Have you been published?"

Margaret smiled. "Yes, as a matter of fact. I write for the Minerva Press. I use the name Margaret Mallory because I am quite certain that my prickly Lancaster relatives would not approve of having a writer of novels in the family."

"This is wonderful. I have read two of your books, *The Secret Wedding* and *The Proposal*. I adored both of them."

"Thank you." Margaret blushed. "Very kind of you to say so."

"It is the truth. I am a great fan of your work, Miss Mallory. I mean, Mrs. Lancaster."

"Please, you must call me Margaret."

Elenora hesitated. "You say your identity is a secret from everyone in the family? Including his lordship?"

"Arthur is the very *last* person I would wish to have discover the truth." Margaret made a face. "He is a man of many exceptional qualities when it comes to investments and such, but I fear that he takes his role as head of the family far too seriously. His grandfather's influence, no doubt."

Elenora thought about the fierce self-control she had perceived in the earl's enigmatic eyes. "Yes, I can see that there is a certain sternness in his nature."

"Not to put too fine a point on it, Arthur can be inflexible, autocratic and downright dictatorial. Furthermore, he does not approve of the current fashion for novel reading, and I shudder to think of how he would respond if he discovered that I actually wrote such books. At the very least, he would never have asked me to come to London to chaperone you. Promise me that you will not reveal my secret."

"I promise."

"Thank you. Now then, as I was about to explain, I have been having trouble with several parts of my latest manuscript. They all involve scenes at fashionable parties and meetings with high-flyers in Society. But I cannot write those bits with any conviction because I know almost nothing about life in Polite Circles."

"I thought you said you had a Season?"

"It lasted less than a fortnight because Harold made his offer almost immediately after he met me. In any event, that was fourteen years ago, so I am very much out of touch."

"I think I begin to understand your dilemma."

Margaret sat forward. "When Arthur asked me to help him with his scheme I thought it would be the perfect opportunity to come to London to observe and record details of the Social World. So naturally I told him that I would be delighted." She threw up her hands in despair. "But that was before I realized that he also expected me to deal with the gowns and all of the rest of what it takes to go into Society."

"Ah."

"I am very sorry, Elenora, but I do not have any notion of how to go about locating the most fashionable dressmaker or milliner or glove maker. I feel I should confess to Arthur, but if I do he will surely send me home and find someone else to act as your chaperone."

"Hmm."

Margaret gave her an expectant look. "What are you thinking?"

Elenora smiled. "I am thinking that there is no reason to bother Arthur with these pesky problems. I'm sure we can handle them without too much trouble." She thought about the pile of cards she'd spotted heaped on the tarnished salver on the hall table.

"Arthur's title and position will ensure that we have any number of invitations. All we really need is the name of a skilled dressmaker. She will be able to guide us to all the most fashionable shops."

"How do you propose to find the right dressmaker?"

Elenora chuckled. "My former employer was somewhat unusual when it came to her taste in clothing. She preferred to wear only garments made of purple fabric."

"How odd."

"Perhaps. But Mrs. Egan is nothing if not a lady of fashion. I can assure you that every single one of her purple gowns was created by a most exclusive dressmaker, one with whom I am well acquainted because I accompanied my employer on several trips to her shop."

"But she will surely recognize you."

"I do not think that need concern us," Elenora said. "During my time with Mrs. Egan I learned that good dressmakers rise to the heights of their profession not just through skill but also because they have a talent for discretion when it comes to the affairs of their most important clients."

Margaret's eyes sparkled. "And as the future bride of the Earl of St. Merryn, you certainly qualify as a very important client."

Chapter Seven

Ibbitts stood in the darkness of the linen closet and
considered closely the conversation he had overheard
earlier.

It was quite by accident that he had discovered the
small hole in the hidden wall panel that made it possible for someone inside the closet to eavesdrop on conversations in the library. He suspected that the secret
opening had been cut many years before, by a clever
servant who'd had the good sense to keep track of his
employers' business.

One thing was certain, Ibbitts thought. He had been
right about Miss Lodge. He had known from that very
first moment when he had caught her examining the
dusty table in the hall that there was something strange
about her. True, she had smiled at him, the way women
always did, but he had not detected the telltale flash of
lust in her eyes. Not even a glimmer of sensual interest.

She had admired him the way one might admire an

attractive painting or work of art; with appreciation but nothing more.

It was most unusual and somewhat disturbing. His face was his fortune, as his mother had predicted, and people, especially women, always responded to his fine looks.

He had been aware straight from the cradle that his handsome features were a great asset. Even as a young boy, he'd understood that people regarded him in a way that was markedly different than the manner in which they viewed his brothers and sisters and the other children in his village.

His face had made it easy for him to obtain that first, fateful post in the household of the fat, aging baron who had lived just outside of the village. The old man had recently married a lady several decades younger than himself. It transpired that his lordship's new bride was very pretty and very bored. She had been delighted with Ibbitts; dressing him in handsome livery and insisting that he wait upon her at every meal.

The first night that she had invited him into her bed he had quickly understood that he possessed another great asset in addition to his face. In that moment when he had knelt behind her plump, soft buttocks, burrowing deep into her snug heat, he had glimpsed a vision of the bright, successful future that awaited him.

It had dawned on him that fateful evening that the world was likely well-populated with rich, attractive young wives who, for reasons of money and social connections, had been married off to fat, old men. He had concluded that London would afford him the best career opportunities.

He had been correct. When the aged baron had died in his sleep a few months later, his widow had wasted no time moving her entire household to town. She had taken Ibbitts with her, promoting him to the rank of butler. He had remained in her employ for more than a year before growing weary of her unceasing demands.

He had eventually left her service and sought another post. It had not taken him long to find an even more lucrative position in another wealthy household. Once again he had found himself called upon to satisfy a young wife whose bald, middle-aged husband spent most of his nights with his mistress.

Like his first employer, the lady had been very generous, not just with her favors and his quarterly wages, but also, more important, with expensive gifts.

For a few years he had pursued his career with great diligence. In addition to a number of posts in which he was obliged to meet the demands of several astonishingly lusty ladies, he had obtained one or two positions in the service of wealthy gentlemen. The men had been just as appreciative of his two great assets as the women.

But a year ago, disaster had struck. True, he had long since grown weary of the tiresome demands of his employers. Work that nature had intended to be pleasurable had become, well, *work*. Nevertheless, he had told himself that the pay and the gifts were worth the labor.

Then one night, to his great horror, a problem arose. Rather, to be more precise, his second great asset had failed to arise.

His face might have been his fortune, but it was not much good on its own. His excellent career depended just as much, if not more, upon his reliability and endurance in bed.

To his dismay, he had been ignominiously let go from his post. But once again luck had been with him. Seven months ago he had found his present position here in the mansion in Rain Street. The elderly man-of-business who had hired him had given him a few simple instructions. Ibbitts was to supervise a small staff suitable for maintaining the large house and ensure that the earl's London residence would be ready for its owner on the rare occasions that St. Merryn elected to come to town for one of his brief stays.

Ibbitts had found his new post to be ideal in every respect. Not only was there no employer to be kept satisfied in the bedchamber, but St. Merryn had not even bothered to put in an appearance.

Until now Ibbitts had been free to do as he liked in the big house. He had used the opportunity to set about making arrangements for an early and comfortable retirement.

Things had been going well until St. Merryn had arrived a few days before, unannounced, expecting the household to be prepared for him. Ibbitts had been terrified for the first twenty-four hours after the earl had taken up residence. Emboldened by the long absence of his employer, he had made several modifications in the staff. The result was that the mansion was not in the best order.

He had made the changes for an excellent reason: economy. There had been no point retaining the cook or the housekeeper or the second chambermaid or the gardeners when the mansion's owner was not around to make use of their services.

He could only hope that St. Merryn would not stay long, Ibbitts thought. In the meantime, he would learn as much as possible about the earl's private affairs.

Over the course of his career, he had discovered that there was often a very good market for information about his employers' secrets.

Chapter Eight

Bennett lowered himself into the chair across from Arthur and glanced back once more toward the lean, angry young man who was just leaving the club. "I see Burnley is here this afternoon."

"Yes." Arthur did not look up from his newspaper.

"I saw him watching you a few minutes ago. I swear, if looks could kill, you would have cocked up your toes by now."

Arthur turned the page. "Fortunately, looks do not have that effect upon me. At least, Burnley's do not."

"I believe that he has conceived a deep hatred of you," Bennett warned quietly.

"I cannot comprehend why. He is the one who got the lady, not me."

Bennett sighed and sank deeper into his chair. It worried him that Arthur refused to show any signs of concern about Roland Burnley's clear and unwavering dislike of him. But, then, at the moment his friend was focusing all of his attentions on his scheme to catch his great-uncle's murderer. And when Arthur concentrated on a venture, it consumed him until it was completed.

Such intense single-mindedness could be a decidedly irksome trait at times, Bennett thought. But he was forced to admit that it was likely the reason why Arthur had, in the matter of only a few years, managed to rebuild the once-depleted St. Merryn fortunes to their current very high level.

Although he knew that Arthur was not interested in hearing any warnings about Roland Burnley, Bennett felt obliged to deliver another one.

"Rumor has it that Burnley's financial situation has deteriorated to a very low point," he said, trying to ease into the subject from another angle. "He is trying to recoup his gaming losses in the hells."

"If he has resorted to gambling to provide an income, his financial status will only decline further."

"No doubt." Bennett leaned back in his chair and steepled his fingers. "I do not like what I see in his face when the two of you are in the same room."

"Then do not look at his expression."

Bennett sighed. "Very well, but I advise you to guard your back."

"Thank you for the advice."

Bennett shook his head. "I do not know why I bother."

"I apologize if I do not seem to be suitably grateful. The thing is, I have other matters on my mind at the moment. I am about to proceed to the next step of my plan."

Once Arthur set one of his convoluted schemes in motion, there was no known force that could halt it, Bennett reminded himself. Usually his friend's elaborate machinations concerned financial investments.

But occasionally he applied his talents toward other types of strategies, invariably with the same degree of success. A smart man did not get between Arthur and his goal, whatever it happened to be.

"The word has gone out that your mysterious new fiancée is in town to enjoy the pleasures of the Season for a few weeks," Bennett said. "There is a good deal of speculation about her, of course. As you instructed, I let it be known in certain quarters that she is from a wealthy, landholding family in the North."

"There are no rumors going around to the effect that I obtained her from an agency?"

"Of course not," Bennett snorted. "Everyone remembers the vow you made last year, naturally, but they all assumed at the time that it was a great joke. No one believed then and no one believes now that a man in your position would actually go through with such a nonsensical notion."

"Excellent. Then all is going according to my plan in that direction."

"I still cannot believe that you intend to use a paid companion to aid you in this bizarre scheme." Bennett frowned. "What is she like?"

"You will meet Miss Lodge soon enough." Arthur lowered the paper, smiling a little with satisfaction. "She is quite intelligent, and she has been out in the world long enough to have acquired some useful experience."

"I see," Bennett murmured. In other words, Miss Lodge was no blushing virgin.

"She is rather striking in her looks," Arthur continued, warming to his topic. "Extremely self-possessed. She has a certain air of authority that will cause people to think twice before they ask impertinent questions. In addition, her grandmother was an actress. I am hoping that the talent runs in the blood. All in all, she is quite perfect."

Hell's teeth, Bennett thought, stunned by the long list of Miss Lodge's accomplishments, which had rolled so freely off Arthur's tongue. What was going on here? He had not heard his friend speak this enthusiastically about any woman in years. No, that was not right. He was quite certain that in the entire time he had known him, he had *never* heard Arthur speak of any lady with such glowing approval.

Of course, Bennett thought, Arthur, with his unusual perspective on such things, was the only man he knew who would view such qualities as *worldly experience* and a *talent for acting* as desirable attributes in a well-bred lady. Any other man would consider them more suited to a courtesan or a lover.

"Just the woman you were looking for," Bennett muttered.

"Indeed."

Bennett tapped his fingers together twice. "I still say that you should tell her what this is all about."

"Absolutely not. The less she knows, the less chance that she might inadvertently allow the truth to slip out at the wrong moment."

"I understand your concerns, but I do not think that it is fair to keep her in the dark." Bennett paused a beat before firing his last, most convincing argument. "Furthermore, have you considered that if you were to tell her the entire tale she might be able to assist you in your inquiries?"

Arthur's eyes narrowed. "That is the very last thing I want. It is none of her affair."

"I can see it is no use arguing the point with you." Bennett exhaled deeply. "Did your chaperone arrive?"

"Yes." Arthur stretched out his legs and rested his

arms on the sides of the chair. "To tell you the truth I had a moment or two of doubt about Margaret this afternoon."

"Thought you said she was the only one of your female relatives you could tolerate having under your roof for an extended period of time."

"She is. But when I told her that I expected her to handle all of the arcane matters associated with introducing my fiancée into Society, I could see that she knew nothing about the business. Indeed, I am quite certain that I saw outright panic in her eyes."

"That is hardly surprising. You did tell me that other than a brief Season several years ago, Mrs. Lancaster has never lived in town."

"True." Arthur grimaced. "I suppose I just assumed a lady who had been married for fourteen years would know how to handle that sort of thing. But today I realized immediately that it is Margaret who is the innocent from the country, not Miss Lodge."

Bennett frowned, thinking of the elaborate preparations his long-dead wife had made before every ball and soirée. "You will need someone who can deal with all the details," he warned. "A fashionable lady must have the right gowns, gloves, dancing slippers and such. She must have a hairdresser or a maid who can manage her headdress. She must shop at the most stylish shops."

"I am aware of that."

"See here, Arthur, if Mrs. Lancaster is not capable of organizing the venture, you must find another relative who can handle it. Otherwise you will be facing a social disaster. Trust me on this matter. I have some experience, if you will recall."

"There is no need to bring anyone else into this affair." Arthur looked quietly pleased. "Margaret will remain because I must have another woman in the household for propriety's sake. I know who is who in the ton, thanks to my business dealings, so I will select the invitations that I want Miss Lodge to accept. You will escort the pair to the first couple of affairs and introduce my fiancée to a few of the right people. I do not want her to become a complete wallflower."

"Yes, well, I will be happy to do my best with the introductions, but what of the *clothes,* man? I promise you that is a very crucial aspect of this thing."

Arthur shrugged. "I'm sure Miss Lodge can handle the clothes."

Such unshakable confidence in another person, let alone in a lady, was most unlike Arthur, Bennett thought, intrigued. When it came to carrying out his labyrinthine schemes, he rarely reposed such complete confidence in anyone, male or female.

Bennett counted himself one of those few whom Arthur did trust, and now, it seemed, Miss Lodge had been added to that very short list. How interesting.

"Well, what of the social aspect?" Bennett persisted. "You know how treacherous the waters are in a fashionable ballroom. If Miss Lodge is seen talking to the wrong person, it will destroy the impression that you are trying to make. It will be worse yet if she dances with the wrong man or goes out into the gardens with him. Very young ladies are protected by their mamas or a skilled chaperone, but from what you've told me, Miss Lodge will have no one to hover over her."

"That is not quite correct, Bennett." Arthur smiled slightly. "I intend that she will have you to hover over her."

Bennett uttered a heartfelt groan and closed his eyes. "I was afraid that you were going to say something like that."

Chapter Nine

The following morning Elenora surveyed her bed-chamber, her hands on her hips, one toe tapping.

The dark, somber furnishings included an ornately carved wardrobe, a massive, heavily draped bed and a dark, dingy carpet. The wallpaper was from an earlier era when lush, exotic patterns had been the height of fashion. Unfortunately the colors had faded to the point where it was impossible to make out the twining vines and flowers.

The degree of cleanliness in this room was of a piece with what she had seen throughout the mansion. Only a minimum of dusting, sweeping and polishing had been done. There was a thick layer of grime on the frame of the octagonal mirror and on the headboard. The cloudy view through the window was evidence that no one had washed the panes in recent memory.

If she was going to be living here for the next few weeks she would have to do something about the deplorable condition of the household, she decided.

Opening the door, she let herself out into the gloomy hall. She was not looking forward to breakfast. The evening meal the night before had consisted of tasteless stewed chicken, dumplings that could have served as ballast for a ship, vegetables cooked to an unwholesome shade of gray and a boiled suet pudding.

She and Margaret had dined alone together in the somber dining room. Arthur had had the good sense to take himself off to his club. She did not blame him. She would have preferred to dine elsewhere, also.

She descended the stairs, noting the dust that had collected between the balusters, and went in search of the breakfast room. She wandered into two closed, curtained chambers filled with draped furniture before she chanced upon Ned.

"Good morning," she said. "Will you kindly direct me to the breakfast room?"

Ned looked baffled. "I think it's somewhere at the end of the hall, ma'am."

She raised her brows. "You don't know where the breakfast room is located?"

Ned reddened and started to stammer. "Beggin' yer pardon, ma'am, but it hasn't been used in all the time that I've been working here."

"I see." She possessed herself in patience. "In that case, where will I find breakfast this morning?"

"In the dining room, ma'am."

"Very well. Thank you, Ned."

She went down another passage and walked into the dining room. She was somewhat surprised to see Arthur seated at the end of the very long table.

He glanced up from the newspaper that was open in front of him, frowning slightly as though he did not quite know what to make of her there at that hour.

"Elenora." He rose to his feet. "Good day to you."

"Good day to you, sir."

The door that led to the pantry swung open. Sally appeared looking even more frazzled and anxious than she had the day before. Her forehead glistened with perspiration. Long tendrils of hair had escaped her yellowed cap. She stared at Elenora and wiped her hands on a badly stained apron.

"Ma'am," she said, making an awkward curtsy. "Didn't know you would be coming down for breakfast."

"I noticed," Elenora said. She nodded meaningfully toward the long table.

The maid rushed to the sideboard and yanked open a drawer.

While the girl set a second place, Elenora crossed the room to examine the dishes that had been provided.

The situation in the kitchen had not improved since the night before. The eggs had congealed. The sausages were an unappetizing color and the potatoes reeked of old grease.

In desperation she selected a couple of slices of limp toast and poured herself a cup of lukewarm coffee.

When she turned back to the table, she saw that Sally had set the second place at the opposite end of the table from where Arthur sat.

She waited until the girl had left the room before picking up the napkin and silver. She moved the place setting up the table to a position on Arthur's right, where she sat down with her limp toast and coffee.

There was a moment of awkward silence.

"I trust you slept well last night," Arthur said eventually.

"Very well, indeed, my lord." She sampled the coffee. It was not only very cold, it was dreadful. She set

81

the cup down. "Do you mind if I ask if your household staff has been with you for a long time?"

He looked mildly surprised by the question. "Never saw any of them before in my life until I arrived a few days ago."

"You don't know any of them?"

He turned the page of his newspaper. "I spend as little time as possible here. In fact, I haven't used the place at all in the past year. On the rare occasions when I come to London, I prefer to stay at my club."

"I see." His lack of interest in the mansion certainly explained a few things, she thought. "Who oversees the servants?"

"My grandfather's elderly man-of-business takes care of all matters concerning this household. I inherited him together with the mansion, and managing the place is his only remaining task. I do not use him for any other business." He picked up his cup. "Why do you ask?"

"There are a few housekeeping details that require attention."

He tasted his coffee and winced. "Yes, I noticed. But I do not have time to deal with them."

"Of course not," she said. "I, however, do have some time. Do you have any objection to my making one or two changes in the management of your home?"

"I do not consider it my home." He shrugged and lowered his cup. "In fact, I am thinking of selling it. But please feel free to make any changes you like while you are here."

She nibbled at the drooping toast. "I can certainly understand why you would wish to sell. This is a large and expensive residence to maintain."

"The cost has nothing to do with it." His eyes

hardened. "I simply dislike the place. When I marry, I will require a house in town for occasional use, but I will purchase another residence for that purpose."

For some reason his comment caused her to lose what little interest she'd had in the toast. Naturally he was contemplating a real marriage, she thought. Why had mention of it depressed her spirits? He had a duty to the title and his family. Furthermore, when he did get around to selecting his countess, he would do what other men in his situation did: He would look for a sheltered young lady just out of the schoolroom, the sort of female he had deemed too delicate and too innocent to be employed as a make-believe fiancée.

St. Merryn's bride—his real bride—would be a lady with a pristine reputation; one whose family was unsullied by scandal or a connection to trade. She would bring him lands and a fortune, even though he had no need of either, because that was how things were done in his world.

It was time to change the subject, she decided. "Is there any news of interest in the papers?"

"Just the customary gossip and scandal broth." Disdain ran deep in his voice. "Nothing of importance. What do you have on your schedule for today?"

"Margaret and I plan to go shopping."

He nodded. "Excellent. I want you to make your appearance in Society as quickly as possible."

"We should be ready to attend our first party tomorrow evening," she assured him.

Ibbitts entered the dining room carrying the badly tarnished salver from the front hall. The tray was heaped with a pile of cards and notes.

Arthur looked up. "What have you got there?"

"Another batch of calling cards and an assortment

of invitations, m'lord," Ibbitts said. "What do you wish me to do with them?"

"I will deal with them in the library."

"Yes, m'lord."

Arthur crumpled his napkin and got to his feet.

"You will excuse me, my dear," he said. "I must be off. Later today I will let you have the list of social affairs that you are to attend this week."

"Yes, Arthur," she murmured in her most dutiful tones. She would not take his *my dear* seriously, she told herself. The endearment was solely for Ibbitts's benefit.

To her astonishment, he leaned down and kissed her; not on her cheek but directly on her mouth. It was a very brief, very possessive kiss; the sort of kiss a man bestowed upon a real fiancée.

Who would have guessed that Arthur was such an excellent actor? she mused, a bit dazed.

She was so rattled by the unexpected display of fraudulent affection that she could not speak for a moment. By the time she recovered, Arthur had left the dining room. She heard the muffled ring of the heels of his elegantly polished Hessians out in the hall.

"Will there be anything else, madam?" Ibbitts asked in a tone that suggested strongly that there could not possibly be anything of the sort.

"As a matter of fact, there is something else." Elenora dropped her napkin on the table. "Please bring me the household accounts for the past two quarters."

Ibbitts stared, uncomprehending, for several seconds. Then his cheeks turned a dull red. His mouth worked a few times before he managed to speak.

"I beg your pardon, madam?"

"I think that I made myself quite clear, Ibbitts."

"The old earl's man-of-affairs keeps the household

accounts, ma'am. I do not have them. I merely keep a tally of the expenses and give the information to Mr. Ormesby."

"I see. In that case, perhaps you can answer some questions for me."

"What questions, ma'am?" Ibbitts asked warily.

"Where is the cook?"

"She quit her post a few months ago, ma'am. Haven't been able to replace her. But Sally seems to be working out well in the kitchen."

"Sally is, indeed, working very hard, but she is not cut out to be a cook."

"I hope to hire a new cook from an agency soon," Ibbitts muttered.

"Do you, indeed?" Elenora got to her feet and started toward the kitchen door.

"Where are you going, ma'am?" Ibbitts demanded.

"To consult with Sally about kitchen matters. Meanwhile, I suggest that you direct your efforts toward securing a new cook and another maid. Oh, yes, and we will require a couple of gardeners as well."

Ibbitts's eyes darkened with anger but he said nothing. Elenora felt a cold chill between her shoulder blades when she turned her back on him to enter the kitchen.

Chapter Ten

The killer made another adjustment to the heavy iron-and-brass machine and stood back to examine his handiwork.

He was so close. He had solved the last great mystery in the ancient lapidary, the one his predecessor had failed to unravel. One or two final adjustments and the device would be complete. Soon the mighty power of Jove's Thunderbolt would be his to command.

A feverish elation flashed through him, as hot and cleansing as an alchemist's fire. His whole being thrilled to the prospect of success.

He glanced at his watch. It was nearly dawn. He walked through the laboratory, turning down the lamps. Then he picked up the lantern and entered the crypt.

He had learned that there were two secret entrances to the laboratory. The iron cage that descended from the ancient abbey overhead was useful, but he did not like to employ it frequently because he was concerned, as his predecessor had been, that oft-repeated use would invite the curiosity of those who lived nearby.

True, most people in the vicinity feared the abbey, believing it to be haunted. But some bold person might be tempted to overcome his dread if he happened to notice a fashionably dressed gentleman coming and going from the chapel every night. Therefore the killer reserved the iron cage for those occasions when he was in a hurry.

The lost river was the safer if more tedious route for his regular nightly trips to the laboratory.

At the rear of the crypt, water lapped at the secret underground dock. He got into one of the small, shallow-bottomed boats he kept there. Balancing carefully, he set the lantern on the bow and picked up the pole.

A firm shove sent the little boat into the current of the long-lost river. The vessel floated gently in the dark, foul-smelling water. The killer was obliged to crouch now and again to avoid the ancient stone footbridges that arched overhead.

It was an eerie, unsettling journey. Although he had made the trip many times now, he did not think that he would ever become accustomed to the oppressive darkness and the foul odor. But he took a thrilling comfort in the knowledge that his predecessor had come and gone to the secret laboratory countless times along this strange route. It was all a part of his great destiny, he thought.

One of the ancient relics that littered the riverbanks came into view. The lantern light danced across a marble relief partially submerged in the mud. It depicted the scene of a strange god wearing an odd cap. The figure was shown in the act of slaying a great bull. *Mithras,* according to the remarks in his predecessor's journal, the mysterious lord of a Roman cult that had once flourished in these parts.

The killer averted his gaze the way he had learned to do whenever he came upon one of the old statues. The accusing stares in those sightless eyes always made him uneasy. It was as if the old gods could see that place inside him where the strange energy that fueled his genius seethed and simmered; as if they understood that it was not entirely under his control.

Chapter Eleven

The following day, shortly after ten o'clock in the evening, Elenora stood with Margaret and Bennett Fleming in the shelter of a cluster of potted palms.

"The first dance is critical," Bennett explained, assessing the crowd with the wise air. "We must make sure that it is with the right gentleman."

Elenora peered through the palm fronds. The chamber was ablaze with lights from the pendulous chandeliers. Mirrors lined one entire wall, reflecting the glow of the dazzling scene.

Brilliantly gowned ladies and gentlemen dressed in the height of fashion laughed and gossiped. Elegant couples floated across the dance floor. Music poured down from the balcony where the musicians were ensconced. A small army of servants in blue livery made their way through the throng carrying trays of champagne and lemonade.

"I do not see why I cannot dance with you first," Elenora said to Bennett.

She had decided immediately upon meeting Bennett Fleming that she liked him very much. One look at his sturdy frame and earnest eyes and she had understood why Arthur trusted him. Bennett Fleming gave the impression of being one of those rare, good-hearted, steadfast people that one knew one could rely upon in a crisis.

"No, no, no, that will never do," Bennett assured her. "Whoever goes first will set a certain standard, you see. Whoever he is, he has the power to make you instantly fashionable."

Margaret regarded him with open admiration. "How do you know such things, sir?"

Bennett turned a dull red. "My late wife was a lady who enjoyed the pleasures of the Polite World. One learns things when one is married to an expert."

"Yes, of course," Margaret murmured. She reached into her reticule and took out a small pad of paper and a tiny pencil.

Bennett frowned. "What are you doing?"

"Making notes," Margaret said airily.

"Whatever for?"

"My journal."

Elenora swallowed a laugh. She wondered what Bennett would say if he knew that Margaret was doing research for her new novel.

"I see." Bennett's brows came together in a narrow-eyed expression. He took a swallow of champagne and assumed the air of a man preparing to go into battle. "As I was saying, the question of which gentleman should be allowed the privilege of being the first is extremely important."

"Hmm," Elenora mumured. "The process of selection sounds very similar to that of choosing one's first lover."

Bennett coughed on his champagne.

"Like the process of choosing a lover," Margaret repeated to herself, scribbling furiously on her notepad. "Yes, I like that turn of phrase. Makes it all sound quite intriguing, does it not?"

Bennett stared at her. "I cannot believe you wrote that down for your journal."

"It will make for interesting reading later, don't you think?" Margaret gave him a bright smile and dropped the notepad into her reticule.

Bennett evidently decided not to respond to that question. Instead he turned his attention back to the dance floor. Quite suddenly he brightened with obvious relief.

"There he is," he announced in low tones.

"Who?" Elenora asked.

"The man who will be the first to lead you out onto the floor." Bennett angled his chin.

Elenora followed his gaze and saw a tall, distinguished-looking gentleman in a blue coat standing near the French doors that opened onto the gardens. He appeared to be in his late fifties. He was engaged in conversation with another man. Something about his stance and expression made it clear that he was unutterably bored by the colorful scene going on around him.

"Who is he?" Margaret asked. "And why do you say that he is the right choice for Elenora's first dance partner?"

"That is Lord Hathersage," Bennett explained. "He is a wealthy man with tentacles throughout Society. His wife died two years ago without giving him an heir, and it is understood that he is in the market for a new bride."

"In that case, why would he want to dance with

93

me?" Elenora asked curiously. "I'm supposed to be engaged."

"Hathersage is known to be extremely particular when it comes to the ladies," Bennet said patiently. "Indeed, he considers himself a connoisseur. A turn on the dance floor with him will draw a good deal of attention. Every other man in the room will be eager to discover what he sees in you. In short, Hathersage can bring you into fashion."

"What if it transpires that he does not want to dance with me?"

For the first time Bennett's friendly eyes lit with secret amusement. "I do not foresee any problem in that direction."

Margaret gave him a quick, searching glance. "Why do you think he will be happy to dance with Elenora? Even from this distance, I can see that he is likely one of those gentlemen who suffer from a surfeit of ennui."

"Hathersage and Arthur have done business together often over the years," Bennett said. "In addition, Hathersage owes Arthur a great favor."

Curious, Elenora slowly unfurled her fan. "I hesitate to ask, but I cannot resist. What sort of favor?"

"Arthur is a genius when it comes to investments. Six months ago there was a flurry of interest in a mining venture in Yorkshire. Arthur knew the project was likely a swindle that would end in disaster. He heard that Hathersage was about to purchase a share in the project and sent him a note warning him that it was probably not a sound investment. The entire scheme fell apart a short time later, and everyone involved lost their money. But because of Arthur's advice, Hathersage avoided the disaster."

No doubt the mining venture of which Bennett spoke was the same one that had destroyed her stepfather and stolen her inheritance, Elenora thought. What a great pity that Samuel Jones had not been a friend of Arthur's. Then again, Jones had never been one to listen to good advice.

Bennett looked at her. "I can arrange this first dance, but what happens after that will be entirely up to you. Once you are out on the floor with Hathersage, you must try to come up with something witty in the way of conversation. If you can amuse him, even for a moment or two, he will be pleased."

Elenora wrinkled her nose. "You make me feel like a paid courtesan instead of a paid companion, Mr. Fleming."

Bennett winced. "My apologies."

"Paid courtesan instead of a paid companion," Margaret repeated softly. "Excellent." She opened her notebook.

"Never mind." Elenora chuckled. "I will do my best to think of something entertaining to say to Lord Hathersage."

Bennett summoned a footman and sent him to Hathersage with a short message.

Five minutes later, Elenora found herself on the dance floor. She smiled up at her tall, gray-haired companion. Hathersage was all that was polite, but it was clear that as far as he was concerned he was merely repaying a favor. This close, the ennui in his expression was unmistakable. She wondered that he had not expired long ago of his severe case of boredom.

"It is very kind of you to allow Mr. Fleming to press you into service in this manner, sir," she said.

"Nonsense. I am delighted to be of assistance," Hathersage said, giving no indication that he meant the words. "It is certainly no great hardship to dance with an attractive woman."

"Thank you," she replied. How on earth was she supposed to carry on a conversation with a man who obviously wished to be somewhere else?

"I must tell you, I envy St. Merryn," Hathersage continued dryly. "He has managed to find himself a fiancée without having to subject himself to the rigors of the Season. I, on the other hand, am in the position of having to endure an endless string of silly young misses fresh out of the schoolroom."

His attitude started to irritate her. "I suspect that the process of making a good match is just as arduous for the young ladies as it is for gentlemen such as yourself, sir."

"Impossible." He looked deeply pained. "You cannot imagine how difficult it is for a man of my years and experience of the world to make conversation with a young chit of seventeen. All the little creatures want to talk about is Byron's latest nonsense or the newest fashions from Paris."

"You must look at the situation from the young ladies' perspective, sir. I assure you, it can be mind-numbingly difficult to make conversation with a man who is old enough to be your father when you would much rather dance with a handsome young poet."

Hathersage looked briefly disconcerted. Then he frowned. "I beg your pardon?"

"A man, furthermore, who is only interested in your looks, your reputation and your inheritance." She made a tut-tutting sound. "When that exceedingly dull gentleman displays no knowledge whatsoever of the subjects that are of interest to a young lady, it is a wonder she is able to make any sort of conversation at all, is it not? One certainly cannot imagine her rushing home to write any romantic reminiscences in her journal about such a dance partner, can one?"

There was a startled pause while Hathersage digested that observation.

A reluctant spark of genuine interest gleamed in his eyes. "Where the devil did St. Merryn find you, Miss Lodge?"

She flashed him her most polished smile. "As you are acquainted with my fiancé, you are no doubt aware that he possesses an extremely logical mind. He naturally applied his talents for analysis and sound reasoning to the task of finding a suitable bride."

"Logic and reason, eh?" Hathersage was fascinated now. "And where did those skills direct him to go in search of such a paragon?"

"Why, to an agency that specializes in supplying paid companions to the most exclusive sort, of course."

Hathersage chuckled, evidently having decided to go along with the jest. "Ah, yes, he did indeed vow to do just that."

"It is a sensible approach. When one comes right down to the nub of the matter, husbands and wives are, in essence, companions, are they not?"

"Hadn't considered the institution of marriage in that light before this moment, but I will concede that you have a point."

"Only consider the brilliance of St. Merryn's tactics, sir. At the agency he was provided with an extensive selection of well-educated ladies who all possessed the most excellent references and reputations above reproach. Rather than being obliged to dance with all of them and endure a series of potentially dull conversations, he was, instead, able to conduct detailed interviews."

"Interviews." Hathersage grinned. "How very clever."

"The beauty of the process is that it works both ways. The candidates for the position he offered were, in turn, able to question him as well. They were thus saved the necessity of having to amuse and entertain any number of elderly gentlemen who know nothing of Byron's latest works and who are only looking for an attractive heiress who will provide them with an heir."

Hathersage brought her to a halt in the middle of the dance floor. For a terrible moment Elenora thought she had miscalculated badly and had initiated a complete disaster.

Then Hathersage threw back his head and laughed uproariously.

Every head in the room turned. Every eye was riveted.

By the time Hathersage returned Elenora to Bennett and Margaret, the line of gentlemen waiting to request a dance extended from the potted palms all the way to the entrance to the card room.

"Consider the favor repaid in full," Bennett told Hathersage.

"On the contrary," Hathersage said, still chuckling. "This has been the most entertaining evening I have had in a long time."

Chapter Twelve

Arthur braced both hands on the balcony railing and searched the crowded ballroom for Elenora. It was after midnight, and he was not in a good mood. He had just concluded another night of inquiries that had yielded few results. Granted, he had discovered more information concerning one of the mysterious snuff-boxes that he sought, but so many other questions remained unanswered. He had the inexplicable sensation that time was running out quickly.

It took him a few minutes to spot Elenora. When he did catch a glimpse of her gleaming dark hair on the far side of the ballroom, he finally realized why it had been so difficult to find her: She was surrounded by a sea of males, all of whom appeared to be vying eagerly for her attention.

She was chatting in an extremely familiar manner with a circle of gentlemen she could not possibly have met before tonight. Not only that but her high-waisted, emerald-colored gown was cut far too low, revealing too much of her soft bosom and gently molded shoulders. She glowed like some exotic jewel, one he was certain that every man in the vicinity coveted.

Where were Bennett and Margaret? he wondered. They were supposed to be keeping an eye on the situation.

As he watched, one of the gentlemen near Elenora bowed over her gloved fingers and escorted her out onto the dance floor. Whatever she was saying to her companion must have been vastly amusing, Arthur decided grimly. The man was grinning like a fool.

His evening had been deteriorating for the past few hours, he thought. The sight of his phony fiancée enjoying herself on the dance floor with a complete stranger was the last straw. Matters were clearly out of control down there in the ballroom.

He shoved himself away from the railing and started toward the stairs.

"Allow me to congratulate you on your charming fiancée, St. Merryn," a familiar voice drawled behind him.

He paused and looked back at the tall man coming toward him along the balcony. "Hathersage."

"I had the great pleasure of dancing with Miss Lodge earlier this evening. A most unusual lady." Hathersage stopped and glanced down at the dancers. He chuckled. "Indeed, I am giving serious consideration to employing your strategy in my own search for a wife."

"What do you mean?"

"Why, I am referring to your brilliant notion of interviewing candidates for the position at an agency that specializes in supplying paid companions, of course."

Arthur's blood ran cold. Had Elenora told Hathersage the whole truth about the deception? Surely not.

"She mentioned the agency?" he asked warily.

"I vow it was the most amusing tale I have heard in weeks." Hathersage replied. "It will be on everyone's lips tomorrow. Such lively wit is a valuable asset in a wife, just as it is in any other type of *companion*."

Elenora had given Hathersage the truth, but because it was so outrageous, he had not believed it, Arthur realized, relaxing somewhat.

The rest of the Polite World would follow Hathersage's lead, he thought. All was well.

"She is quite unique," Arthur said.

"Indeed." Hathersage's eyes narrowed slightly. "You will want to keep an eye on her, St. Merryn. I wouldn't be surprised to discover that some of those men hanging around her down there right now are already plotting to lure her away from you."

Damnation. Was it possible that Hathersage himself might be contemplating such a move? He was said to be in the market for a new wife, and he was certainly wealthy enough to be able to look past a lady's finances.

Anger splashed through Arthur. He fought it with the force of his will and a dose of logic. Hathersage was merely amusing himself.

"If you will excuse me, I believe I will take your advice and go downstairs to see about protecting my interests," he said calmly.

"Be prepared to stand in line."

Arthur waited until Elenora's partner led her back off the dance floor before he descended into the ballroom. He had no intention of standing in line. But he was irritated to discover that he had to use some force and a certain degree of raw intimidation to make his way into Elenora's inner circle.

When he finally arrived, Elenora did not appear to be overjoyed to see him. After her small start of surprise, she gave him a polite, somewhat quizzical smile.

"What are you doing here, sir?" she asked in a low voice meant for his ears alone. "I thought you had other plans for the evening."

She was acting as though he was the last person she had wanted to see tonight, he mused. Conscious of the disgruntled gentlemen loitering about in the vicinity, he smiled the way a man smiled at a lady who belonged to him.

"What plans could possibly be more important than dancing with my lovely fiancée?" he asked, bending over her hand. He took her arm and steered her firmly toward the dance floor. "Where are Bennett and Margaret?" he growled.

"They disappeared into the card room an hour or so ago." She studied him with mild concern. "What is the matter, sir? You appear to be somewhat perturbed."

"I'm not perturbed, I'm annoyed."

"I see. Well, you really cannot blame me for not being able to distinguish between the two states of being. In your case they appear remarkably alike."

He refused to be teased out of his bad temper. "Bennett and Margaret were supposed to keep an eye on you."

"Ah, so that is the problem. You were concerned about me. Well, there is absolutely no need, sir. I assure you, I am perfectly capable of taking care of myself."

He thought about the cluster of gentlemen that had surrounded her earlier. "I do not like the idea of you being left alone in the middle of a ballroom with a crowd of strangers."

"I was hardly alone, sir, and I am making friends at a great rate."

"That is not the point. You are a very competent woman, Elenora, but there is no getting around the fact that you have not had a great deal of experience swimming in Society." Bennett's admonition came back to him. "These waters can be extremely treacherous."

"I assure you, there is no need to worry about me. That is one of the reasons you went to an agency to hire a paid companion, if you will recall. Among other requirements, you wished to employ a female who had been out in the world; one who possessed a degree of common sense."

"And that is another thing." He tightened his grip on her. "What were you thinking when you told Hathersage that I had found you at an agency?"

"Bennett warned me that I would have to say something to Hathersage that would cause him to sit up and take notice, as it were. I had heard about your infamous vow a year ago, the one about seeking your next bride at an agency. I decided that if I referred to your little jest, Hathersage would be amused. That is precisely what happened."

"Huh." He did not like it, but he had to admit she was right. Hathersage had found Elenora very entertaining. "Who told you about those remarks I made a year ago?"

"Evidently everyone has heard about them. Indeed, they appear to have become a part of your personal legend."

He winced. "At the time I intended them as a bit of wit, one of those things one says to deflect sympathy or unwanted inquiries."

"I understand. But later, when you realized you needed a lady who could pose as your fiancée, it occurred to you that the idea was actually a very good one, is that it?"

"It was either that or employ a professional actress," he agreed. "I was reluctant to do that for fear that she might be recognized by, uh," he hesitated, searching for a diplomatic turn of phrase. "Someone who had seen her perform onstage."

She caught his slight pause and raised her brows. "Or by some gentlemen who had enjoyed her favors offstage?"

"No offense to your grandmother," he said dryly.

"None taken. She would have been the first to acknowledge that actresses and opera dancers have always enjoyed a certain reputation among the gentlemen of the ton."

He was relieved that she did not appear to be the least bit touchy or outraged by the subject. What a relief it was to be able to talk openly to a woman, he thought, his mood lifting for the first time that evening. With Elenora he did not have to concern himself with the possibility that he might accidentally ruffle her female sensibilities. She was, indeed, a woman of the world.

"Nevertheless," he continued, recalling the point he was attempting to make, "it would have been best if you had not made any reference to my comments about selecting a paid companion for a wife. It will only serve to make people all the more curious about you."

"I beg your pardon, sir, but was that not the whole point of the deception? Your goal is to use me to deflect Society's attention while you conduct your private business, correct?"

He grimaced. "Yes."

"It seems obvious that the more people are consumed with curiosity about me, the less notice they will take of what you are doing."

"Enough," he growled. "You are right and I admit defeat. Indeed, I do not know why I bothered to start this discussion. I must have had a momentary lapse of memory."

But that was a lie, he acknowledged silently. He had started the small quarrel because he had been badly jolted by the possibility that Hathersage might have his eye on Elenora. The sight of other males paying so much attention to her disturbed him for reasons that he did not want to analyze too closely.

She laughed. "For heaven's sake, sir, no one in his right mind would actually *believe* that you went to an agency to find a wife."

"No, probably not."

She gave him a reproving look. "Really, sir, you must calm yourself and stay focused on your business affairs. I will deal with the tasks that you are paying me to manage. I trust your plans are going well?"

It occurred to him that she was the only part of his elaborate scheme that was actually working. He would very much like to discuss the other aspects of the affair with her, he thought suddenly. He wanted to talk to someone. Elenora was an intelligent, worldly woman who was not easily shocked. Furthermore, he was convinced now that she could keep his secrets.

He was also quite desperate for some fresh ideas. His failure to make any progress in the past few days was worrisome.

Bennett had advised him to tell Elenora the truth. Perhaps that was not such a bad notion after all.

He came to a halt at the edge of the dance floor.

Ignoring the polite inquiry in her eyes, he guided her toward the glass-paned doors that opened onto the terrace.

"I am in need of some air," he said. "Come, there is something I want to discuss with you."

She did not argue.

The night was pleasantly cool after the heat of the crowded ballroom. He took Elenora's arm and led her across the terrace, away from the lights. They went down the stone steps into the lantern-lit gardens.

They walked for a distance before he stopped at the edge of a large fountain. He considered his words carefully before he started into his tale.

"I did not come to town to form another consortium of investors," he said slowly. "That is merely the tale I have put about to cover my real purposes."

She nodded, showing no indication of surprise. "I had a feeling there was more to this business. A man of your intelligence and resolute nature would not employ a lady to pose as his fiancée merely to avoid the inconveniences of having every eligible young lady of the ton tossed into his path."

He grinned reluctantly. "That comment only goes to show how little you know about such inconveniences. Nevertheless, you are right. I employed you to provide cover for me so that I could go about my real business."

She tipped her chin with an expectant air. "And that would be?"

He hesitated another second or two, gazing steadily into her clear eyes, and then he consigned his remaining qualms to the nether regions. Every instinct he possessed told him that he could trust her.

"I am attempting to find the man who murdered my great-uncle, George Lancaster," he said.

At that news, she went very still, watching him intently. But she remained remarkably composed, considering his words.

"I see," she said neutrally.

He remembered how she had once briefly mistaken him for an escaped madman. "I suppose you really do think me crazed now."

"No." She looked thoughtful. "No, in truth, such a bizarre objective does indeed explain your rather strange decision to employ me. I was quite sure that you were not conducting business in the usual manner."

"Whatever else this is," he said wearily, "it is most certainly not business in the usual manner."

"Tell me about your great-uncle's death."

He put one booted foot on the fountain and rested his forearm on his thigh. For a moment he studied the dark waters in the pool, gathering his thoughts.

"It is a long and involved story. It begins, I suppose, many years ago, when my great-uncle was a young man of eighteen. He made the Grand Tour that year, and as it happened he was even then obsessed with science. The result was that he spent most of his time immersed in various ancient libraries in the countries that he visited."

"Go on."

"While in Rome he came across the books and journals of a mysterious alchemist who lived some two hundred years ago. My great-uncle was fascinated with what he discovered."

"They say that the line between alchemy and science has often been blurred and difficult to distinguish," Elenora said quietly.

"It is true. In any event, my great-uncle came upon an ancient lapidary called the *Book of Stones* in the alchemist's collection."

She raised her brows. "Old lapidaries are treatises on the magical and occult properties of various gemstones, are they not?"

"Correct. This particular lapidary had been written by the alchemist himself. The book was bound in heavily worked leather. The front cover was set with three strange dark red gems. Inside there was a formula and instructions for the construction of a device called Jove's Thunderbolt. It was all written down in some obscure alchemical code."

"How strange. What was the purpose of the machine?"

"Supposedly it was capable of creating a powerful beam of light that could be used as a weapon similar to a thunderbolt." He shook his head. "Occult nonsense, of course, but that is what lies at the heart of alchemy."

"Indeed."

"As I said, my great-uncle was young and lacking in experience at the time. He told me that he became quite excited by what he discovered in the lapidary. According to the alchemist's notes, the three red stones sewn into the cover of the *Book of Stones* were the key to producing the furious energy emitted by the device."

"What did he do with the lapidary?"

"He brought it back to England and showed it to the two men who were his closest friends at the time. All three were fascinated by the possibility of constructing the machine."

"I assume that they were not successful."

"My great-uncle said that although they succeeded in constructing a device that looked similar to the drawing in the lapidary, they could not figure out how to draw out the strange energy supposedly concealed in the red stones."

She smiled a little. "That is hardly surprising. I'm sure the alchemist's instructions were nothing more than crazed fantasies."

He looked down at her shadowed face. Her eyes were dark, compelling pools, more mysterious by far than any alchemist's formula. The skirts of her jewel-toned gown gleamed in the moonlight. He had to fight a sudden urge to touch the soft, delicate skin at the nape of her neck.

He forced himself to concentrate on his tale. "My great-uncle told me that eventually he and his two companions came to precisely that conclusion. Jove's Thunderbolt was a fantasy. They put their experiments with the device aside, having learned their lesson about the futility of alchemical research, and moved on to more serious studies in natural philosophy and chemistry."

"What did they do with the stones and the device that they had constructed?"

"One of the three men kept the machine, supposedly as a memento of their flirtation with alchemy. As for the stones, they all decided to have them set in three snuffboxes as an emblem of their friendship and commitment to the true path of modern science."

"One snuffbox for each of them?"

"Yes. The boxes were enameled with scenes of an alchemist at his work. Uncle George said that he and his companions formed a small club and called it the Society of the Stones. They were the only members. Each man took a coded name drawn from astrology and had it engraved on his snuffbox."

"That makes sense," she said. "Alchemy has always had a strong link to astrology. What were the names they chose?"

"My great-uncle called himself Mars. The second

man was named Saturn. The third was known as Mercury. But he never told me the real names of his old acquaintances. There was no reason for him to mention them. I was just a boy when he told me the story."

"This is a fascinating tale," Elenora whispered. "What happened to the Society of the Stones?"

"The three remained close for a time, sharing notes on their researches and experiments. But after a while they drifted apart. Uncle George mentioned that one member of the Society died while still in his twenties. He was killed in an explosion in his laboratory. The second man is alive, as far as I know."

"But your great-uncle is dead," she said.

"Yes. Murdered in his laboratory only a few weeks ago."

Her brows came together in a gentle frown. "You're certain that he was killed? It was not an accident?"

Arthur looked at her. "He was shot twice in the chest."

"Dear heaven." Elenora drew a breath. "I see."

He watched the waters splash in the fountain. "I was very fond of my great-uncle."

"My condolences, sir."

The sympathy in her voice was genuine. He was oddly touched by it.

He roused himself from the moody reverie and returned to his story.

"The Runner I employed to investigate the crime was useless. He concluded that my uncle had been murdered either by a burglar whom he surprised in his laboratory, or, more likely, by the young man who assisted him in his experiments."

"Have you talked to the assistant?"

He set his jaw. "Unfortunately, John Watt fled the night of the murder. I have not been able to find him."

110

"Forgive me, but you must admit that his disappearance adds credence to the Runner's theory."

"I am well acquainted with Watt, and I am convinced that he would never have committed murder."

"What of the other theory?" she asked. "The one concerning a burglar?"

"There was a burglar, right enough, but he was no random footpad. I searched my great-uncle's house quite carefully after his death. The *Book of Stones* was nowhere to be found." He tightened his hand into a fist on his thigh. "And his snuffbox, the one set with the red stone, was also gone. Nothing else of value was missing."

She contemplated that. "Are you certain?"

"Absolutely certain. I believe that my great-uncle was murdered by someone who was after the lapidary and the snuffbox. Indeed, I am convinced that those three snuffboxes are important clues. If I can find the two that belonged to my great-uncle's old friends, I may learn something useful. It is in that direction that I have been focusing most of my efforts lately."

"Have you had any luck?"

"Some," he said. "Tonight, I finally managed to discover the address of an elderly gentleman who may be able to tell me about one of the snuffboxes. I have not yet been able to speak with him, but I plan to do so soon."

There was a short silence. He was aware of the music and the laughter from the ballroom, but both seemed to come from far away. Here beside the fountain there was a sensation of privacy that bordered on the intimate. The flowery scent of Elenora's perfume tugged at his senses and tightened the muscles in his belly. He realized that he was becoming aroused.

Control yourself, man. The last thing you need now is that sort of complication.

"You say you have disregarded the Runner's conclusions," Elenora continued after a moment. "Have you formulated some conjecture of your own regarding the identity of your great-uncle's killer?"

"Not precisely." He hesitated. "At least, not one that makes any sense."

"You are a man of logic and reason, sir. If you are considering a theory, however bizarre, I suspect there is some serious foundation for it."

"Not in this case. But I will admit that I find myself reflecting again and again upon a remark my great-uncle made when he told me about his three friends and the Society that they had formed."

"What was it?" she asked.

"He mentioned that one of the three members of the Society, the one who called himself Mercury, never truly overcame his fascination with alchemy, although he pretended to do so. My uncle said that Mercury was the most brilliant of the trio. Indeed, there was a time when they all believed that he would someday be hailed as England's second Newton."

"What became of him?"

He looked at her. "Mercury was the member of the Society who was killed by the explosion in his laboratory."

"I see. Well, that makes it rather difficult to conclude that he might be the killer, does it not?"

"It makes it damned impossible." He sighed. "Yet I find myself returning again and again to that possibility."

"Even if he were still alive, why would he wait all these years to murder your great-uncle and steal the lapidary and the stone?"

"I do not know," Arthur said simply. "Perhaps it took him this long to unravel the secret of drawing the energy from the red stones."

"But there is no secret." She spread her hands. "Your great-uncle told you that the alchemist's tale was no more than a fantasy."

"Yes, but Uncle George also told me something else," Arthur said slowly. "Something that has been weighing on my mind. He claimed that, as undeniably brilliant as Mercury was, he was also showing signs of mental instability, perhaps even of outright madness, toward the end of his life."

"Ah." Thoughtfully, she tapped her fan against her palm. "So this Mercury might have begun to believe in the power of the red stones."

"Yes. But even if that were the case, it all happened a long time ago. Mercury, whoever he was, has been in his grave for a very long time."

"Perhaps someone has stumbled upon his notes or journals and decided to pursue his research."

Arthur experienced a flash of new respect. "That, Miss Lodge, is a very interesting theory."

A woman's light, teasing laughter stopped him in mid-sentence. The sound came from the other side of the tall hedge. A man's voice murmured a response.

"Yes, I saw her with Hathersage," the lady said. "Miss Lodge is certainly an Original, is she not? But if you ask me, there is something extremely odd about her." She sniffed daintily. "About the entire situation, come to that."

"What makes you say that, Constance?" the man asked. He sounded both amused and curious. "It appears to me that St. Merryn has found himself a most intriguing fiancée."

Arthur recognized the voice. It belonged to a man named Dunmere, a member of one of his clubs.

"Bah." Constance did more than sniff this time. She gave a small snort of disgust. "St. Merryn cannot be serious about marrying her. That much is obvious. When a man of his rank and position takes a wife, he selects a young heiress from a good family. Everyone knows that. This Miss Lodge has obviously been on the shelf for several years. No one knows anything about her family background. Furthermore, judging by her manner and what I have heard of her conversation, I would venture to say that she is no naïve innocent."

Arthur glanced down and saw that Elenora was listening intently to the conversation on the other side of the hedge. When she met his eyes, he put a finger to his lips, signaling for silence. She nodded in understanding, but he noticed that she was frowning.

With luck, he thought, the gossiping pair would wander off in another direction.

"I disagree," Dunmere said. "St. Merryn is considered to be something of an eccentric. It would be quite in keeping for him to choose a wife who is not out of the usual mold."

"Mark my words," Constance retorted, "there is something very strange about his betrothal to Miss Lodge."

Arthur could hear footfalls on the gravel and the soft rustle of skirts now. So much for avoiding Constance and Dunmere. They were making their way toward the fountain.

"Perhaps it is a love match," Dunmere suggested. "St. Merryn is rich enough to be able to afford such an indulgence."

"A love match?" This time Constance's laughter was thin and brittle. "Are you mad? This is St. Merryn we are discussing. He is as cold-blooded as they come.

Everyone knows that the only things that arouse his passions are his investments."

"I will admit that he does not appear to possess any strong romantic sensibilities," Dunmere conceded. "I was in the club that night when he was told that his fiancée had eloped. I will never forget his astonishingly casual reaction."

"Precisely. Any man possessed of even a modicum of romantic sensibility would have given chase."

"No offense my dear, but a fiancée who has betrayed her future husband with another man is not worth risking one's neck for in a dawn appointment."

"What of St. Merryn's honor?" Constance demanded.

"It was not his honor that was at stake," Dunmere said dryly. "Rather, it was the young lady's. Rest assured that there is no man in the ton who would dream of questioning St. Merryn's honor."

"But from all accounts, St. Merryn behaved as though the entire affair was nothing more than a singularly dull bit of theatrics that was more suited to Drury Lane."

"Perhaps that is how he considered it," Dunmere said in a thoughtful tone.

"Rubbish. I tell you, St. Merryn is as cold as the sea. That is why he did not give chase that night. And that is why I am certain that whatever else it is, this new betrothal is no love match."

Arthur looked down and saw that Elenora was still listening closely to the couple's conversation. He could not, however, discern from her expression just what she was thinking. For some reason, that worried him.

"My dear Constance," Dunmere said slyly, "it sounds as though you learned the lesson concerning St. Merryn's cold nature the hard way. What happened?

Did you attempt to make him the target of one of your charming seductions only to have him decline the offer of your very inviting bed?"

"Don't be absurd," Constance snapped quickly. "I have no personal interest in St. Merryn. I am merely relating what everyone knows to be the truth. Any man who would play cards at his club while his bride-to-be was carried off by her lover lacks feeling. He would, therefore, be incapable of falling in love."

Constance and Dunmere had almost reached the end of the hedge. In another moment or two they would round the corner. Arthur wondered if there was time to get Elenora out of sight behind the far end of the hedge.

Before he could signal his intentions, she leaped to her feet. His first thought was that she was about to flee from the impending encounter with the gossiping pair.

He was stunned when she threw her arms around his neck and pressed herself against him instead.

She put one hand behind his head, urging him closer.

"Kiss me," she commanded in a breathless whisper.

Of course, he thought. How clever of her to realize that the best way to defuse the gossip was to be seen engaged in a passionate embrace. The lady was very quick-thinking.

He pulled her closer and covered her mouth with his own.

In the next instant he forgot all about the little play they were supposed to be staging. Heat, searing and dazzling in its intensity, swept through him.

He was vaguely aware of Constance's startled gasp and Dunmere's amused chuckle, but he ignored both in favor of deepening the kiss.

Elenora's fingers tightened abruptly around his shoulders. He knew his sudden, fierce reaction had startled her. He slid one hand down her back to the place where the curve of her hips began. Very deliberately he pressed her into the intimate space created between his legs, one of which was still propped on the edge of the fountain.

The position allowed him to feel the softness of her stomach against his erection. A sweet, hot ache filled his lower body.

"Well, well, well," Dunmere murmured. "It would seem that St. Merryn is not quite as cold as you believed, my dear Constance. Nor does Miss Lodge appear to be unduly terrified at the prospect of suffering a fate worse than death at his hands."

Chapter Thirteen

Margaret settled into the cushioned seat of the carriage and smiled at Arthur with a hopeful air. "I think that went very well, don't you, sir?"

Arthur lounged on the other side of the cab. The yellow glow of the interior lamps etched his face in shadow and mystery.

"Yes," he said in his low, dark tones. But he was looking at Elenora, not at Margaret. "I think we all gave excellent performances tonight."

A small shiver of apprehension or perhaps uncertainty went through Elenora. She concentrated very hard on the sight of the crowded streets and managed to avoid Arthur's considering gaze.

She had intended that kiss in the garden to be nothing more than a convincing bit of fiction designed to quell the gossips. But she had lost control of the situation almost immediately.

She was still unable to comprehend what had happened. One moment she had been urging Arthur to embrace her for the sake of their small audience; the next she had been shocked and stirred all the way to her toes.

The kiss had left her flushed and strangely disoriented. Indeed, she was certain that if Arthur had not been holding her so tightly when Constance and Dunmere rounded the end of the hedge, she would have lost her balance. The back of her neck still tingled with an unnerving sense of awareness.

"You have got the distraction you wanted," Margaret went on, cheerfully oblivious to the dangerous undercurrents shifting through the shadows of the carriage. "Everyone at the ball tonight was overcome with curiosity. I vow, the tongues wagged even faster after you two came back from taking the fresh air out on the terrace."

"Really?" Elenora made herself say very vaguely.

"Yes, indeed," Margaret assured. "I don't know how you did it, but Mr. Fleming and I agreed that both of you managed to affect the appearance of two people who had just concluded a very ardent bit of lovemaking out there in the gardens. It was an astonishing piece of acting, I must say."

Elenora dared not take her eyes off the night-shrouded streets "Mmm."

"I was rather pleased with the results of that scene in the gardens, myself," Arthur said, sounding for all the world like a hard-to-please theater critic.

Desperate to change the subject, Elenora summoned up a bright little smile for Margaret. "Did you enjoy the evening?"

"Oh, yes, very much," Margaret replied dreamily. "Mr. Fleming and I spent a good deal of the time discussing the latest novels. It happens that he is a great fan of Mrs. Mallory's works."

Elenora managed, just barely, to conceal her amusement behind her handkerchief. "Mr. Fleming is obviously a man possessed of excellent taste."

"That was certainly my opinion," Margaret concurred.

Arthur frowned. "I have warned Bennett time and again that his habit of reading novels is likely the reason he takes such an unrealistic, ridiculously romantic view of the world."

The carriage rumbled to a halt at the front steps of the St. Merryn mansion some twenty minutes later. The door was opened by a sleepy-looking Ned.

Margaret used the back of her gloved hand to pat a dainty yawn. "Gracious, I am exhausted after such a long evening. If you two will forgive me, I believe I shall take a candle and go straight to bed."

She swept up the staircase with what Elenora could only describe as a spring in her step. Margaret did not appear the least bit tired, she thought. In fact, there was not only a lightness in her movements that seemed new this evening, there was also a certain brightness in her eyes.

Elenora was still pondering Margaret's subtle new glow when she realized that Arthur was holding the candle aloft, surveying the room with a considering frown.

"Does this hall look different to you?" he asked.

She glanced at the furnishings. "No, I don't think so."

"It does to me. The colors appear brighter. The mirror is not so dark and the statues and vases seem newer."

Startled, she took a closer look at the nearest marble figure. Then she chuckled. "Calm yourself, sir, there is nothing strange about the fresh look. Earlier today I gave instructions that this hall was to be properly cleaned while we were out. Judging from the layer of dust on the furnishings, it evidently had been some time since that was done."

He looked at her with a speculative expression. "I see."

His gaze made her uneasy for some obscure reason. "Well, then, it is quite late, is it not?" she said, striving for a polished, professional sort of demeanor. "I had best be off to bed myself. I am no more accustomed to these hours than Margaret."

"I would like to speak with you before you go upstairs," Arthur said.

It was an order, not a request. A sense of foreboding hovered over her. Was he going to let her go because of what had happened in the gardens?

"Very well, sir."

Arthur glanced at Ned. "Off to bed with you. Thank you for staying awake until we got home, but it was unnecessary. We are perfectly capable of letting ourselves in when we return at such a late hour. In the future, do not bother to stay up. You require your rest."

Ned looked quite startled by his employer's gesture of appreciation. "Aye, sir. Thank you, sir." He left quickly.

A moment later Elenora heard the door to the lower part of the house close with a muffled thud. Ned had vanished into the servants' quarters downstairs.

The front hall suddenly seemed very close and—there was no other word for it—intimate.

"Come, Miss Lodge. We'll go into the library to have our conversation."

Arthur picked up a candle and led the way down the hall.

She followed cautiously. Was he annoyed by the overly enthusiastic manner she had exhibited during that kiss? Perhaps she could explain that she had been equally surprised by her heretofore unexpected acting talents.

Arthur ushered her into the library and closed the door with an unmistakable air of finality.

Elenora felt a sense of doom descend upon her.

Without a word, Arthur set the candle down and crossed the carpet to the hearth. He went down on one knee and coaxed the embers into a blaze. When he was satisfied, he rose, untied his neckcloth and tossed it over a nearby chair. Then he unfastened his white linen shirt far enough to reveal a few curling dark hairs on his chest.

Elenora forced herself to look away from his bare throat. She must concentrate, she thought. Her post was at stake. She could not let him dismiss her out of hand simply because she had kissed him with a little too much exuberance. All right, make that a great deal of exuberance, she amended silently. Either way, it was not her fault.

She cleared her throat. "Sir, if you disapprove of my suggestion that we embrace earlier this evening, I apologize. However, I must point out that you did hire me in large part for my acting skills."

He picked up the brandy decanter. "Miss Lodge—"

"I would also like to remind you that my grand-mother was a professional actress."

He poured two measures of brandy and nodded solemnly. "Yes, you have mentioned your grand-mother on several occasions."

"The thing is, it may be that I got more of her thespian abilities than I had realized, if you see what I mean." She gestured widely with her fan. "That would account for the degree of drama in my, uh, performance. I assure you it took me every bit as much by surprise as it did you."

"Is that so?" He handed her a glass of brandy and then propped himself on the corner of his desk. He swirled the contents of his glass and regarded her with a brooding expression.

"Yes." She gave him what she hoped was a reassuring smile. "In future, I shall try to moderate my talents in that area."

"We will return to the subject of your acting talents in a moment. First I want to finish the discussion we were engaged in when we were interrupted by that pair of rumormongers in the gardens."

"Oh." She looked down at the glass he had given her and concluded that she needed something to fortify herself.

She took a healthy swallow of the fiery spirits and nearly stopped breathing altogether when the stuff hit the back of her throat. It was as if she had swallowed the sun.

Arthur evidently noticed something was amiss because he raised his brows.

"Perhaps you should sit down, Miss Lodge."

She dropped like a stone onto the sofa and breathed deeply.

"This is very strong brandy," she wheezed.

"Yes, it is," he agreed, raising his own glass to his mouth. "It is also very expensive. I find that it is best sipped rather than gulped."

"I shall remember that in future."

He nodded. "Now then, I told you that I had uncovered the name of a gentleman who may know something concerning the snuffboxes. I plan to talk to him.

I would appreciate any notions you might have on the question of locating my great-uncle's assistant, John Watt, however."

"The man who disappeared the night of the murder?"

"Yes. I have spent the past three days going about his old haunts, the coffee houses and taverns he favored, the neighborhood where he grew up, that sort of thing. But thus far I have discovered no trace of him. It is as if he simply vanished."

Elenora thought about that. "Have you talked to the members of his family?"

"Watt was an orphan. He had no family."

"And you're quite certain he is not the killer?"

Arthur started to shake his head, but he paused and then opened one powerful hand, palm up. "When it comes to human nature, anything is possible, but I do not believe that Watt is the villain of this piece. I have known him for years. He is honest and hardworking. Furthermore, he was devoted to my great-uncle, who trusted him and paid him well. I cannot envision Watt turning on him."

"He stole nothing that night? None of the silver was missing?"

"No."

"Then perhaps you looked in the wrong places when you went to the coffeehouses and taverns where Watt was accustomed to meeting his friends," Elenora said slowly.

"Where would you look?" he queried.

"It is none of my business," Elenora said carefully. "And heaven knows I have had no experience whatsoever in solving crimes. But it seems to me that an honest, hardworking man who fled in fear of his life but who also neglected to take any valuables to help

125

pay for his food and lodging would have only one thing on his mind."

"And that would be?"

"Finding employment as quickly as possible."

Arthur did not move. Comprehension gleamed in his eyes. "Of course," he said very softly. "I have overlooked the obvious. But that still leaves a great deal of territory to be covered. How does one go about finding a single man in this city?"

"Are you certain that he was single?"

"What do you mean?"

"You said he was a young man with no family. Is there, perhaps, a sweetheart in the picture?"

Arthur raised his half-finished brandy in a deliberate toast. "An excellent notion, Miss Lodge. Now that you mention it, I recall a certain young maid in my great-uncle's household who seemed quite fond of Watt. I will interview her first thing tomorrow."

She relaxed slightly. He seemed pleased now. Perhaps he would not let her go after all.

Arthur came away from the desk and went to stand in front of the fire. The flickering light of the flames made the brandy in his faceted glass glow like a liquid jewel.

"I had a hunch that talking to you might help me clarify my own thoughts," he said after a moment. "Thank you for your observations and comments."

His praise warmed her more than the fire. She felt herself blush slightly. "I hope you will find them useful. I wish you good luck, sir."

"Thank you. I will no doubt need it." He continued to study the flames as though seeking answers or, perhaps, insight. "Now we come to the second subject that I wish to discuss tonight."

She braced herself. "Yes, my lord?"

"That kiss in the gardens this evening."

She gripped the brandy glass. "The lady's comments about our relationship made me think that she did not believe that we are, indeed, engaged, sir. It occurred to me that if word got around that ours is a love match, the Polite World might be more inclined to accept our little fiction."

"It was a very clever move on your part," he said. "I congratulate you on your quick thinking."

Enormously relieved, she took a quick, tiny sip of the brandy.

"Thank you, sir," she said, trying to sound professional and competent. "I did my best to make my performance realistic."

He turned around to look at her with eyes that reflected the heat of the fire. Something deep within her tightened once more, just as it had earlier in the gardens when he had returned her kiss.

A dangerous, seductive excitement crackled invisibly in the air between them. She sensed that he was as affected by the strong passions echoing around them as she was herself. The brandy glass in her hand trembled.

"You certainly achieved your objective." He set his own glass on the mantel and started toward her with a slow, deliberate stride. His eyes never left hers. "In fact, I was so caught up in the moment that I wondered if, perhaps, you were not merely acting."

She tried, but she could not think of a single intelligent thing to say in response to that observation. She sat there, frozen in place on the edge of the sofa, and watched him close the space between them.

He stopped directly in front of her and gently removed the brandy glass from her fingers. He put it down on the table without taking his gaze off her face.

His hands closed over her shoulders. He brought her to her feet.

"Was it all pretense?" He drew his thumb across her parted lips. "Are you that good an actress, Miss Lodge?"

The velvety rasp of his fingertip on her mouth stole her breath. The small caress was exquisitely intimate. She ached with the need for more of his touch.

Words failed her. A good actress could lie through her teeth when called upon to do so, she reminded herself. But for some peculiar reason she could not summon the denial she knew she should issue.

Instead, she touched the tip of her tongue to the edge of his thumb. The texture of his skin sent a delicious little shiver through her.

Arthur smiled slowly. Elenora flushed. She could not believe that she had done that with her tongue. Where had the urge to taste him come from? she wondered, a little panicked.

"I think that answers my question." Arthur wrapped his fingers around the nape of her neck and lowered his mouth until his lips hovered just above hers. "I must confess that I was not acting either, this evening out there in the gardens."

"Arthur."

He kissed her as though savoring some forbidden elixir. But she was the one who was sampling the unknown tonight, she thought. Feverish thrills raced through her, leaving her hot and cold and strangely euphoric. She clamped her fingers around his shoulders and clung for dear life.

He took her clutching fingers as an invitation and deepened the kiss. When she felt his tongue slide along her lower lip she was startled, but she did not pull back.

This was that stimulating pleasure that her grandmother had told her could be found in the arms of the right man. What she had felt when Jeremy Clyde had kissed her had been only a shallow brook compared to this raging waterfall of sensation.

She wanted to throw herself over the edge and sink all the way to the bottom of the mysterious pool.

Arthur took the pins from her hair, his movements so exquisitely intimate that she trembled. No man had ever taken down her hair.

And then his mouth was on her throat. She felt the edge of his teeth.

Lucinda's remark concerning Arthur's runaway fiancée drifted through her dazed mind. *She was terrified of him.*

Arthur cradled her breast in his palm. She could feel the heat of his hand burning through the fine green silk of her bodice.

She moaned softly and moved her arms up around his neck.

But instead of responding by tightening his hold on her, he muttered something soft and rueful, something that might have been a muffled curse. Reluctantly he raised his head and set her a short distance away.

He cupped her face in his hands and smiled wryly.

"This is neither the time nor the place," he said. His voice was rough with passion and regret. "You hold a unique post in this household, but that does not alter the fact that you are a member of my staff. I have never taken advantage of any woman in my employ, and I certainly do not intend to make an exception with you."

For a second she could not believe she had heard him aright. He still thought of her as just another member of his household staff? After that passionate embrace? After he had taken her into his confidence and asked her advice on how to conduct his investigation?

Reality slammed back, ripping apart the delicate web of sensual pleasure and desire that she had spun around herself. She did not know whether to be furious or mortified. Indeed, the mix of anger, frustration and embarrassment that swirled through her left her almost speechless.

Almost, but not quite.

"Forgive me, sir," she said, layering each word with a thick coating of ice. "I had no notion that you viewed me as just another member of your staff—"

"Elenora."

She stepped back, forcing him to drop his hands from her face. "And I would not dream of allowing you to violate your strict rules regarding your conduct toward females in your employ."

"Hell's teeth, Elenora—"

She gave him her most brilliant smile. "Rest assured, I will endeavor not to forget my place again. I certainly would not want to be responsible for putting such a high-minded employer in such an untenable position again, sir."

His jaw hardened. "You are misinterpreting my words."

"They seem quite clear to me." She made a show of glancing at the tall clock. "Gracious, the hour grows late, does it not?" She sank into her most elegant curtsy. "If you have no further need of my *services* this evening, I will bid you good night, sir."

He narrowed his eyes in warning. "Damnation, Elenora."

She spun on her heel, giving him her back, and walked quickly toward the door.

His stride was longer than hers. He got to the door ahead of her. For a frantic moment she tried to decide what she would do if he barred her path.

But he did not try to stop her from making her grand exit. Instead, he opened the door for her with a graceful flourish and inclined his head in a mocking bow.

When she swept through the opening, head high, she glimpsed his wicked smile out of the corner of her eye.

"When this affair is over, Miss Lodge, I shall, of course, be forced to terminate your employment in this household," he said coolly. "When that day comes, I assure you, we will return to this conversation and consider carefully what course our association will take in future."

"Do not depend upon having any such a considered discussion, my lord. I see no reason to offer again what has already been rejected once."

She did not dare look back to see how he had reacted to that comment. Instead she forced herself to walk, not run, toward the stairs.

An hour passed before she heard the steady, muffled thud of his footsteps in the hall outside her bedchamber. The sound seemed to reverberate with the beat of her heart.

He paused at her door. The tension was unbearable. Would he knock softly?

Of course he would not knock, softly or otherwise. He had just made it very clear that he would not do any such thing.

But she sensed him there, on the other side of her door, and she suddenly knew, as clearly as though she could read his mind, that he was thinking about knocking; thinking quite hard.

After a while she heard him go on down the hall to his own bedchamber.

Chapter Fourteen

Elenora opened her eyes very cautiously. She was vastly relieved to see the crack of light in the drapes that meant morning had finally arrived. The clock on the table read nine-fifteen. She was surprised to realize that she had finally managed to get some sleep.

It seemed to her that most of the night had been spent alternating between strange dreams and long, restless bouts of wakefulness during which she relived the kiss in the library a hundred times.

She shoved aside the covers and put on her slippers and wrapper. She washed quickly at the washstand, wincing at the bracing sting of the cold water. When she was through, she twisted her hair up into a neat knot and pinned a pristine white cap over it. Then she went to the wardrobe to survey the array of gowns hanging inside.

The pretty new clothes that she had ordered from Mrs. Egan's longtime dressmaker were a positive feature of this new post, she thought. Not that they would do her any good when she left for her next position. It was highly unlikely that any of her future employers would want to hire a professional companion who dressed in such a fashionable manner.

As she had anticipated, the dressmaker had been only too happy to observe discretion on the subject of her knowledge of her new client's recent post in Mrs. Egan's household. But, then, any ambitious dressmaker worth her needles would have had sense enough not to gossip in such a situation, Elenora thought.

As for her own situation, she refused to worry about future wardrobe problems. With luck there would not be a great number of new employers or new posts to concern her, she thought, reaching for a cheerful yellow-orange morning gown trimmed with pale green ribbons. Thanks to the triple wages and the bonus that St. Merryn was paying her, she would have almost enough money to secure a lease on a small bookshop when she left this household. If she was fortunate in her next post, another six months of employment would ensure that she had sufficient funds to stock her shop with the latest novels.

And then she would be free and independent at last.

While she dressed, she forced herself to concentrate on her shiny new future instead of Arthur's heated kisses.

She found the hallway empty when she opened the door of her bedchamber a few minutes later. She wondered if Arthur had already gone downstairs to breakfast. In spite of what had happened the night before, she discovered that she was quite looking forward to seeing him again this morning. She went quietly toward the staircase, careful not to make any noise that might awaken Margaret.

At the foot of the stairs she turned and went along the corridor that took her to the back of the house.

Taking a deep breath, she raised her chin, assumed a grand air and swept into the dining room as though absolutely nothing had happened the night before.

Her performance was for naught. The room was empty.

So much for showing Arthur that his kisses were completely unmemorable. Sighing, she went through the doorway that opened into the pantry and descended the narrow steps to the lower floor where the kitchens were located. Her slippered feet made no sound on the treads.

A cup of tea and a slice of warm toast would be enough for her this morning, she decided.

She heard the muffled voices just as she arrived at the bottom of the steps. They were coming from behind a closed door. She recognized them immediately. Ibbitts and the maid, Sally.

"Stop your damned sniveling, you stupid creature," Ibbitts snarled softly. "You'll do as I say or you'll find yourself on the streets again."

"Please don't make me do this, Mr. Ibbitts." Sally was sobbing. "It was one thing to go through Miss Lodge's personal things when I unpacked her trunk. I didn't like it but at least I wasn't doing her any harm. This is different. If you make me steal her pretty little watch, I could be arrested and hung."

"Bah. Even if he caught you in the act, St. Merryn wouldn't turn you over to the Runners. I've served in enough households to know the type of employer who would do that, and he's not one of 'em. Too softhearted by far."

Ibbitts did not sound particularly approving of Arthur's kind temperament, Elenora noted.

"At the very least, he'll turn me off without a reference." Sally cried harder. "You know how badly I need this post. Don't make me risk it."

"You'll lose your precious post for certain if you don't do as you're told, girl. I'll see to that. Remember what happened to young Paul when he refused to give me my fee. Straight out onto the street he went, and without a reference. Wouldn't be surprised if he's making a living as a footpad by now. Probably hanged by Christmas."

Elenora heard Sally's great, gulping gasps very clearly through the panels of the door.

"I just can't, sir. I'm a good girl. I've never done anything this bad. I just can't."

"A good girl, are you?" Ibbitts laughed harshly. "Not according to your last employer. She tossed you out for seducing her son, didn't she? Found you on your back in the still room, your feet kicking in the air, her precious boy between your legs, didn't she?"

"That's not how it was," Sally croaked. "He attacked me, he did."

"Because you tempted him. I'll wager you thought he'd give you some money for your efforts."

"That's not true."

"It makes no matter," Ibbitts shot back. "The thing to remember is that you didn't get a reference, and we both know that you'd be servicing gentlemen in alleys by now if I hadn't taken you in. You're lucky to have any post at all."

"Please, sir. I've done everything you asked so far, and I give you your fee out of my quarterly wages. I can't do this thing you want. I just can't. It's not right."

Elenora had had enough. She tried the doorknob. It twisted easily in her hand. She shoved the door open with such force that it slammed against the wall and bounced a couple of times.

Startled, Ibbitts and Sally stared at her, open-mouthed.

Ibbitts's statue-perfect features transformed themselves into a mask of rage.

Rising panic bloomed in Sally's gaze. She put her hand to her throat and made a small, frantic, squeaking sound not unlike a little bird that has fallen from its nest.

Elenora rounded on Ibbitts. "Your vile behavior is unacceptable. You will collect your things at once and leave this house immediately."

Ibbitts recovered quickly, his fine mouth twisting into a sneer. "Who the bloody hell do you think you are to interfere in my private business like this?"

Now would probably be an excellent time to fall back on the authority that came with her fictitious role as Arthur's fiancée, Elenora decided.

"I am the future mistress of this household," she announced coldly. "And I will not tolerate your despicable actions."

"Future mistress, eh?" An unholy glee leaped in Ibbitts's eyes. But instead of launching a verbal assault, he jerked his thumb at the hapless Sally. "Get out of here, girl. Go to your bedchamber. I'll finish with you later."

Sally blanched. "Aye, Mr. Ibbitts, sir."

She scurried toward the door, where Elenora stood blocking the exit.

"Beggin' yer pardon, Miss Lodge," she pleaded through quivering lips. "Please let me leave."

Elenora handed her a handkerchief and stepped aside. "Go on, Sally. Dry your tears. All will be well."

Sally gave no sign that she believed that for an

instant. She seized the square of embroidered linen and used it to cover her face as she rushed out of the room.

Elenora was alone with Ibbitts.

He looked her up and down, dismissing her with a degree of disdain that would have done justice to an arrogant gentleman of the ton. "Well, now, Miss Lodge, I reckon it's time we got something settled here. We both know that you will never be the future mistress of this household, don't we?"

Her stomach turned over, but she kept her face impassive. "I have no idea what you're talking about, Ibbitts."

"Just because his lordship managed to pass you off as a fine lady in front of the quality, don't think you've got me fooled. You're no more than a paid companion. You're in this house on a temporary basis. When St. Merryn no longer needs you, you'll be let go just like any other member of the staff whose services are no longer required."

Elenora's palms tingled. She had been right when she'd warned Arthur that it would be difficult to deceive the servants. Her only hope was to bluff her way through this confrontation.

"You have obviously been eavesdropping on your employer, Ibbitts," she said evenly. "A very bad habit, indeed. And as is often the case when one listens to conversations not meant to be overheard by others, you have got the facts wrong."

"Bah. I've got the facts right enough, and well you know it. St. Merryn hired you from that agency, Goodhew and Willis, didn't he? I heard him tell Mrs. Lancaster about his scheme. He's paying you a fee to play the role of his fiancée. Do you know what that makes you, Miss Lodge? An actress."

"Enough, Ibbitts," she snapped.

"We all know about actresses, don't we?" He gave a

snort of disgust. "Like as not, you'll be warming his lordship's bed before you're finished with this post."

Ibbitts had known the truth all along, she thought. That explained the thinly veiled contempt she had noticed in his attitude toward her from the moment she arrived. But judging by the way he had sent Sally out of the room just now, it was clear that he had kept the secret to himself, no doubt intending to wait until he could turn it to his advantage.

Disaster loomed, Elenora realized. Arthur would be furious once he realized that his butler was aware of his plan. He would likely conclude that his strategy to have her pose as his fiancée had to be abandoned. If he had no further use for her, she might very well find herself back at the offices of Goodhew & Willis before the day was out.

Well, there was nothing she could do but go forward. Ibbitts was a dreadful man. One way or another, he had to be banished from this house.

"You have half an hour to pack your things, Ibbitts," she said very steadily.

"I'm not going anywhere," Ibbitts rasped. "And you're not going to be giving any more orders around here if you know what's good for you. From now on you'll dance to my tune, Miss Lodge."

She stared at him. "Are you mad?"

"Not mad, Miss Lodge, just a good deal more clever than you realize. If you try to turn me out of this house, I'll see to it that his lordship knows that I'm aware of his scheme." Ibbitts snickered. "What's more, I'll tell him that I learned about it from you because you like to chatter in bed."

"That would be a very dangerous thing to do, Ibbitts," she said softly. "St. Merryn would not believe you, in any event."

139

Ibbitts's smile would have looked more appropriate on a viper. "When I tell him about the fancy blue ribbons on that pretty white linen nightgown of yours, I'm certain that he'll believe every word I say."

"You know what my nightgown looks like because you forced Sally to describe it to you."

"Aye, but his lordship will assume that the reason I can describe it so accurately is because I've seen you in it, won't he? And even if he doesn't fall for that tale, the damage will have been done as far as you're concerned. If he finds out his plans are no longer secret, he'll abandon them. And that means he won't have any use for you, Miss Lodge. You'll find yourself out on the street about ten minutes after me."

"You are a very foolish man, Ibbitts."

"You're the fool, Miss Lodge, if you think you can get rid of me so easily." Ibbitts gave a coarse laugh. "But you're in luck because I'm going to make a bargain with you. Keep your mouth shut about what you heard in this room a few minutes ago, and I won't let on to his lordship that I know about your nightgown or his secrets."

"Do you really believe that I will allow you to blackmail me, Ibbitts?"

"Aye, Miss Lodge, you'll do as you're told, just like Sally and Ned, and you'll be grateful." He chuckled derisively. "So grateful, in fact, that you'll pay me my usual commission, same as the others do."

She folded her arms. "Just what is your usual commission?"

"Sally and Ned give me half their quarterly wages."

"And what do they get for that fee?"

"Why, they get to keep their posts, that's what they get for it. You'll agree to my bargain, too, because we both know that you've got a lot more to lose than I do."

"Do I?"

"Aye, you silly bitch." His mouth twisted. "With this face, I can always find another post. But after you get tossed out of this house, you'll likely never get another respectable place. Expect you'll end up lifting your skirts for drunken gentlemen in doorways around Covent Garden before the year is out."

She did not bother to respond to that. Turning, she went out into the tiny hall.

Ibbitts's low, cruel laughter followed her.

She found Ned hovering anxiously at the top of the kitchen steps.

"What happened, Miss Lodge? Sally says we're going to be let go."

"You and Sally will not lose your posts, Ned. It is Ibbitts who will soon be on his way."

"Not him." Ned shook his head sadly, resigned. "His kind always wins out in the end. He'll see to it we're both sent away without references for causing him trouble like this."

"Calm yourself. His lordship is a fair-minded man. When I explain the situation to him, he will understand. You and Sally will be fine."

I am the one who will soon be looking for another position, she thought. Regardless of how the problem with Ibbitts was resolved, there was no getting around the fact that once St. Merryn knew his secret was in the hands of a despicable, untrustworthy creature like Ibbitts, he would be forced to end the charade.

Well, she had known that the post was too good to be true right from the start, had she not?

Arthur stood in the stable doorway and watched John Watt use a pitchfork to shift hay into a stall. The young man looked a lot different than he had the last time Arthur had seen him.

When he had worked in George Lancaster's household, Watt had always kept himself clean and neat. The shirt and pants he was wearing today were most likely the garments he had had on the night he'd run away. They had not stood up well to the demands of Watt's new career. Six weeks' worth of use in a livery stable had converted what had once been good clothing into little more than torn, badly stained rags.

Watt's hair was tied back with a strip of cloth. Sweat streamed off his brow. But true to his nature, he was working hard, even though it was highly unlikely that his new employer was paying him anything close to the wages he had received from George Lancaster.

"Hello, Watt," Arthur said quietly.

Watt jerked violently and spun around, pitchfork raised, face working in alarm. When he saw Arthur, he groaned.

"So it's you, sir." He swallowed heavily and slowly lowered the fork, as though defeated. "I knew ye'd find me sooner or later."

Arthur walked toward him. "Why did you run off, Watt?"

"You must know the answer to that, sir." Watt propped the pitchfork against the side of the stall, wiped his forehead with a gritty hand and heaved a massive sigh. "I was afraid you'd think I was the man who murdered Mr. Lancaster."

"Why would I believe that?"

Watt scowled, confused. "On account of I was the only one in the house with Mr. Lancaster that night."

"My great-uncle trusted you. So do I. And so does your Bess."

Watt started. "You've talked to Bess?"

"She's the one who told me that you had changed your name and taken a job here at the livery stable."

Watt squeezed his eyes shut in pain. "I shouldn't have told her where I was. But she was so anxious about me that I had to let her know that I was safe. I begged her not to tell anyone. She's an honest girl, though. I suppose it was too much to ask her to lie for me, especially to you, sir."

"You must not blame Bess. I had a very long talk with her a short time ago. She loves you with all her heart, and she would have kept your secret if she thought I meant you harm. She certainly didn't tell anyone else, not even the Runner who questioned her."

"A Runner questioned her?" Watt was horrified. "Oh, my poor Bess. She must have been scared to death."

"I'm sure she was. But she did not tell him that she knew where you were. She only confided in me because I convinced her that I believe you are innocent."

Watt gnawed nervously on his lower lip. "Bess told me that the Runner thinks I'm the one who murdered poor Mr. Lancaster."

"I let the Runner go after he came to that conclusion. I knew that he was wrong."

Watt's eyes crinkled in astonishment. "Why are you so sure it wasn't me who killed Mr. Lancaster?"

"You forget that I've known you for years, Watt. I am well aware that you aren't the type to turn violent. You are a patient man, slow to anger and steady in your ways."

Watt blinked a couple of times. "I don't know how to thank ye, sir."

"You can thank me," Arthur said deliberately, "by telling me everything you can about what went on in the days leading up to my great-uncle's murder, and by recalling for me every single fact concerning the events that occurred on the night of his death."

An hour later, satisfied that he had learned all he could from Watt, he sent the young man back to his sweetheart and promised him that he and Bess would both be given new posts on one of the Lancaster estates.

His next stop before returning to the mansion in Rain Street was at the home of the elderly man-of-affairs he had inherited from his grandfather.

He found the house hushed and dark. The servants went about with somber faces.

"The doctor says Mr. Ormesby won't live out the week," the housekeeper told him, wringing her hands in her apron as she led the way to the bedchamber where her employer lay on his deathbed. "It was kind of ye to come by to say farewell."

"It was the least I could do," Arthur said. He took a closer look at the woman and realized that she was getting on in years. This was likely the last post she would be able to obtain. "Did Ormesby arrange for a pension for you?"

Her eyes widened in surprise at the question. "It's kind of you to ask, sir, but I'm sure he was good enough to remember me in his will. I've worked for Mr. Ormesby for going on twenty-seven years."

Arthur made a mental note to make certain that Ormesby had left his housekeeper enough to allow her to survive her retirement.

Ormesby and the old earl had had a lot in common. Neither of them had been known for their generosity.

Elenora was putting the last of her personal possessions into the trunk when Margaret bustled anxiously into the bedchamber.

"What in heaven's name is going on here?" Margaret came to a halt in the middle of the room and glared at the trunk as though it were the enemy. "Sally just interrupted me in the middle of a scene that I have been working on for two days to tell me that you are preparing to leave."

"I'm sorry to say that St. Merryn's grand scheme has come apart at the seams."

"I don't understand."

"Ibbitts knows why I am here, and he made it clear that he will not hesitate to use the information for his own purposes. When his lordship learns that his plans are in ruins, he will no longer need my services. I thought I might as well pack and make ready to leave."

"This is absurd."

"Hardly." Elenora sighed. "I confess that I've had a feeling all along that St. Merryn's elaborate charade was doomed to fail."

She straightened and surveyed the bedchamber, aware of an odd sense of loss that had nothing to do with financial matters. She did not want to leave, she realized, and not just because it meant that she would be obliged to go through the dreary process of finding another post.

It wasn't the house she would miss, it was the little thrill of delight that went through her every time she walked into one of the rooms and saw Arthur.

Stop this maudlin behavior at once. You do not have time to indulge yourself in brooding thoughts. You must concentrate on the future.

"My dear Elenora, this is terrible," Margaret declared. "I'm quite sure there is some mistake. You can't leave. Please, do not make any hasty decisions until after you have spoken with Arthur. I'm certain he can straighten this out."

Elenora shook her head. "But I do not see how he can continue to use me in his scheme as he intended. The entire project has been compromised by Ibbitts."

"Arthur is very resourceful. I'm sure he will find a way to proceed with his plan."

The sound of carriage wheels in the street drew Elenora to the window. She looked down and watched Arthur get out of the coach. He carried a large package under one arm, and he looked quite serious.

"The earl has returned," she said to Margaret. "I had best go down and conclude this affair."

"I will come with you." Margaret hurried to follow. "I'm sure this will all come right."

"I do not see how," Elenora said, trying not to show any trace of the sad emotions she could feel churning deep inside. "His lordship has no further need of my services."

"Allow me to tell you, my dear," Margaret continued as they went down the stairs, "that when it comes to Arthur, it is best not to try to predict his actions. The only thing one can say about him with any great certainty is that once he sets a course, it is almost impossible to make him change it. Just ask anyone in the family."

Sally and Ned stood anxiously in the hall, talking quietly. When they saw Elenora and Margaret, they broke off their conversation. They both looked stricken.

"What is it?" Elenora asked. "Has something else happened?"

"It's Ibbitts, ma'am," Ned said. "He's in the library

with his lordship this very minute. There's no telling what lies he's feeding to the master."

Margaret glowered. "What makes him think that St. Merryn will take his word over Elenora's?"

"I don't know, ma'am," Sally whispered. "But Ibbitts was smiling when he went into the library." She shivered. "I've seen that smile before."

Chapter Fifteen

Arthur leaned back in his chair and watched Ibbitts closely while the butler told his tale.

"I assure you, there's no great harm done, sir," Ibbitts concluded with grave sincerity. "I won't breathe a word about your secret plans."

"Indeed?"

"Of course not, sir." Ibbitts raised his noble chin and set his broad shoulders. "I am nothing if not loyal to you."

"You say Miss Lodge let the secret slip when she tried to lure you into her bedchamber?"

"Naturally, I did not accept the invitation, sir, even though she was dressed in nothing but a white linen nightgown trimmed with little blue ribbons. I take my responsibilities to my post very seriously."

"I see."

Ibbitts sighed. "In fairness, you should not place too much blame on Miss Lodge's frail shoulders."

"Why do you say that?"

Ibbitts made a tut-tutting sound. "A lady of her age and station in life has little hope of contracting any sort of respectable marriage, does she? Her sort has no choice but to look elsewhere when the urge takes 'em, if you know what I mean."

The door opened abruptly. Elenora stormed into the library. Margaret was directly behind her.

"Do not listen to a word Ibbitts says." Elenora strode briskly across the room. She was flushed with anger. "He is a liar and a blackmailer who takes advantage of the other servants. I have informed him that he must quit this house immediately."

Arthur rose politely to his feet. "Good morning, Miss Lodge. He inclined his head to Margaret. "Please be seated, both of you."

Margaret sat down immediately, her face bright with anticipation. "Well, now, this should prove interesting," she said to no one in particular.

Elenora appeared not to have heard his suggestion that she take one of the chairs. Instead, she halted in front of his desk, her eyes snapping with anger.

"Ibbitts forces the other servants to give him half of their wages," she announced. "That's what he charges them to allow them to keep their posts. It is despicable. Sally and Ned told me it is also the reason why the housekeeper, the cook and the gardener left a few months ago, leaving this household woefully under-staffed."

Ibbitts gave her a pitying expression and shook his head. "I fear that Miss Lodge is suffering from an affliction of the nerves, sir. Female hysteria, no doubt. I've seen this sort of thing before in unmarried ladies of a certain age. A vinaigrette is sometimes helpful."

Elenora gave him a look of utter contempt. "Do you deny it?"

"Of course." Ibbitts drew himself up proudly. "If his lordship wishes to verify my innocence in this matter, he has only to question the servants. I'm quite certain that both Sally and Ned will tell him that I make no such demands of them."

"Sally and Ned are both terrified of you, Ibbitts," she said. "They will say anything you order them to say."

It was interesting to watch Elenora when she was blazing with righteous anger, Arthur thought. Unfortunately, he did not have time to indulge himself in this scene today.

"Will you please sit down, Elenora?" he said quietly.

"In addition to his despicable treatment of Sally and Ned, Ibbitts eavesdropped on you," she said.

"That is a lie." Ibbitts whirled back to confront Arthur. "I would not dream of listening to my employer's private conversations. It was young Sally who overheard you, sir, and came straight to me with the news that Miss Lodge was merely a paid employee. Naturally I ordered her and Ned to keep silent about your private affairs. They will do as they are told. I stand ready to assist you in your plans in any way I can."

"Rubbish," Elenora said through her teeth. "He is attempting to blame Sally—"

"Sit down, Elenora," Arthur repeated. This time he put an edge on the words, making them into a command.

Reluctantly, she obeyed.

Ibbitts gave her a scathing look. "Begging your pardon, my lord, but did you examine Miss Lodge's references before you selected her for this post?"

"It was your references I failed to examine," Arthur

151

said. "And evidently neither did Ormesby, due to his poor health."

"I assure you, my references are excellent," Ibbitts said quickly.

"Because you wrote them yourself, I'll wager," Elenora muttered.

"That is a lie," Ibbitts hissed. He turned back to Arthur. "I will be happy to supply letters from previous employers, sir. I think you will find them all quite satisfactory."

"That won't be necessary." Arthur reached for one of the volumes that he had brought back with him after paying his respects to the dying Ormesby. "I glanced through these on my way back here this morning. The entries for the past year tell me everything I need to know about you, Ibbitts."

Ibbitts stared, uncomprehending, at the journals. "What are those, sir?"

"The household accounts." Arthur opened the most recent journal and drew a finger down the page to the entry he had marked earlier. "It seems that as recently as last month, you regularly submitted requests for the payment of wages for a staff that included a number of people who are no longer employed here." He looked at Ibbitts. "Among them are the housekeeper, the cook and the gardeners, all of whom evidently departed last fall."

Ibbitts took a step back, clearly caught off balance. "There must be some mistake, sir."

Arthur closed the leather-bound volume. "The mistake was not letting you go several months ago, Ibbitts. However, I intend to rectify that error now. You will pack your bags and leave this house immediately."

"Sir, you said yourself that your man-of-business is

ill." Ibbitts was both furious and frantic. "He must have written down the wrong amounts."

"He has been too ill to leave his house in order to see what was happening for himself, but he is entirely lucid, I assure you. These amounts were paid to you so that you could, in turn, pay the servants. You obviously did not inform Ormesby when members of the staff gave notice. Instead, you continued to collect their wages. I suspect you have pocketed that money. I want you out of here within the hour."

Elenora leaped to her feet. "I knew you would do the right thing, sir."

Arthur sighed. "Please sit down, Elenora."

Her mouth tightened, but she sat.

Ibbitts was stunned. "You're letting me go?"

"Of course I'm letting you go." Arthur reached behind his chair and tugged on a velvet bell pull. "You're a liar and a blackmailer. Consider yourself fortunate that I'm not having you placed under arrest."

The library door opened. Ned stood there, looking scared but determined.

"Yes, m'lord?" he said.

"Ibbitts is no longer employed in this household. You will accompany him to his room while he packs his possessions. Make certain that he does not help himself to any of the silver on the way out the door. Is that clear?"

Ned glanced from Arthur to the scowling Ibbitts and back again. The anxiety evaporated from his eyes.

"Aye, sir," he said in a firmer tone. "I'll see him out the back door for ye."

Ibbitts's face twisted with fury and scorn. "I suggest that you ask Sally and Ned for references concerning their characters, m'lord. You'll soon find out that they cannot supply any. Sally lost her post because she lifted her skirts for her employer's heir. Ned here lost his because he took her side when she tried to deny what she'd done."

Ned's hands tightened into fists.

Elenora came up out of her chair. "I do not doubt Sally and Ned's version of the story for a moment. It is Ibbitts who has proved himself untrustworthy."

Arthur rubbed the bridge of his nose. "I would appreciate it if you would stay seated, Miss Lodge. All this popping up and down is rather tiresome."

"Sorry."

She sank back down into her chair with obvious reluctance. Arthur could see the toe of one of her slippers tapping impatiently on the carpet. It occurred to him that her short career as a paid companion had done little to alter what was obviously her natural inclination to take command.

In spite of all the problems facing him at the moment, he was amused. Elenora no doubt found this business of deferring to him extremely vexing.

He fixed his attention on Ned. "You and Sally will both remain in your present posts. Furthermore, I will see to it that the wages Ibbitts forced you to pay to him are refunded immediately."

"Thank you, sir," Ned stuttered, clearly astonished.

Arthur gestured toward the door. "On your way, Ibbitts. I have wasted enough time on this matter."

Ibbitts's jaw clenched with rage. He gave Elenora a vengeful glare as he stalked past her.

Arthur waited until Ibbitts had reached the door before he spoke again.

"One more thing, Ibbitts," he said, steepling his fingers. "There seems to be some confusion regarding Miss Lodge's status in this household."

"I know her status right enough," Ibbitts muttered. "She's nothing more than a paid companion."

"You are mistaken in that assumption." Arthur kept his tone very even. "I intend to marry Miss Lodge. She will most certainly be the future mistress of this household. If you make the mistake of spreading tales to the contrary, you will have cause to regret it. Do I make myself clear?"

With a quick sideways glance, he saw Elenora's eyes widen.

Ibbitts bared his teeth. "Whatever you want to call her is your affair, m'lord."

"Yes," Arthur agreed. "It is. You may go now."

Ibbitts stomped through the doorway. Ned closed the door and followed him, leaving Arthur alone with Margaret and Elenora.

"Well," Margaret said. "That was certainly exciting." She smiled at Elenora with great satisfaction. "I told you that Arthur would settle matters. Now you can instruct Sally to unpack your trunk."

Arthur went cold inside. He looked at Elenora, trying not to let his reaction show on his face.

"You packed?" he asked.

"Yes, of course." She cleared her throat. "I did not think that you would be needing my services after you discovered that Ibbitts was aware that I am merely an employee and not your real fiancée."

Margaret looked at him. "When Elenora confronted him, Ibbitts revealed that he knew all about your scheme. He actually tried to blackmail her, if you can believe it."

Arthur sat back in his chair, thinking about what had just happened. "Ibbitts tried to extort money from you in exchange for keeping silent about your position here?"

"Yes." She brushed that aside. "But that was nothing compared to the vile manner in which he treated Sally and Ned. I can take care of myself. Those two are far more vulnerable."

Arthur wondered if she knew how rare her sense of responsibility was among those who moved in Polite Circles. In that world chambermaids were routinely let go when a male member of the household got them pregnant, and an aging housekeeper might be dismissed without a pension when she was no longer able to carry out her duties.

Elenora shook her head. "I did warn you, sir, that it would be extremely difficult, if not impossible, to keep secrets from your staff."

"I would take it as a kindness if you would refrain from pointing out the error of my ways," he said mildly.

She flushed. "My apologies, sir."

He sighed. "Never mind, you were right."

Her brows drew together in a troubled expression. "I really do not see how I can remain in my present position now that someone as untrustworthy as Ibbitts is aware of the truth."

"I see no reason to alter course," he said. "The scheme appears to be working as I intended. Society is riveted on you, leaving me free—" He paused, reminding himself that Margaret was still in the room. "Free to conduct my business."

"But if Ibbitts succeeds in starting gossip concerning my true position in this household, your scheme will no longer be viable."

Her insistence on trying to remove herself from the role he had employed her to act struck an unexpected spark against the flint of his self-control.

"What I see," he said, pronouncing each word with

deliberate emphasis, "is that you are the only hope I've got of carrying out this plan. Furthermore, given the rather handsome wages I am paying you, I think I have every right to expect a most convincing performance. Wouldn't you agree?"

Margaret blinked in astonishment at his sharp words.

Elenora merely inclined her head with excruciating formality, letting him know that she was annoyed but not intimidated.

"Of course, my lord," she said dryly. "I will endeavor to give satisfaction."

"Thank you." What the devil had made him snap at her like that? He never allowed himself to lose his temper.

Margaret hastened to smooth over the unpleasantness. "Really, Elenora, you must not be concerned about what Ibbitts might say. Who in Society would take the word of a butler dismissed without references over that of the Earl of St. Merryn?"

"I know, but he is aware that the story we have put about as a jest is, indeed, the truth."

"Even if Ibbitts were to gossip about you, he can do no harm. He will only be seen to be repeating the tale," Margaret assured her.

"She is correct," Arthur said. "Calm youself, Elenora. Ibbitts need not cause us any concern."

"I suppose you are right," Elenora said. But she did not look satisfied.

Margaret sighed. "Well, that's settled, then. You're staying, Elenora."

Elenora frowned. "That reminds me, we seem to find ourselves somewhat short of staff."

Yet another problem to be resolved before he could proceed with his investigation, Arthur thought wearily.

157

He picked up a pen and reached for a sheet of paper. "I will send a message around to an agency."

"There is no need to waste your time dealing with a series of candidates sent out by an agency," Elenora said crisply. "Sally has two sisters in need of employment. One of them is evidently an excellent cook. The other will be happy to take on the duties of a chambermaid. I think Sally will do well as our new housekeeper. Also, Ned has an uncle and a cousin who are skilled gardeners. As it happens, their last employer just sold his townhouse and let his entire staff go, so they are looking for positions. I suggest we hire the lot."

Margaret clapped her hands. "Good heavens, Elenora, you are amazing. It sounds as though you have the problem of staffing completely in hand."

Arthur was so greatly relieved to be rid of the burden of finding new servants that he could have swept Elenora up into his arms and kissed her.

"I leave the matter in your hands," he said very formally instead.

She acknowledged that with a casual nod, but he thought she seemed rather pleased.

That was one pressing issue out of the way, he thought, spirits rising.

"If you will both excuse me, I must go upstairs to change my gown." Margaret rose to her feet and went toward the door. "Mr. Fleming will be here soon. We are going to visit some bookshops this afternoon."

Arthur got to his feet and crossed the room to open the door for her. She hurried out into the hall and disappeared. When he glanced back and saw that Elenora was about to follow, he held up a hand.

"If you don't mind," he said quietly. "I would like to discuss with you what I learned from John Watt."

She stopped midway across the carpet, her face brightening with excitement. "You found him?"

"Yes, thanks to your suggestion that I talk to his sweetheart." He glanced at the clock. "It is after four. I will send for the carriage and we will take a turn around the park. The sight of you and me together will serve to reinforce the notion that we are, indeed, engaged, and we will have privacy for our conversation."

Chapter Sixteen

It was just going on five o'clock when Arthur drove the sleek carriage through the gates of the large park. Perched next to him, dressed in her new blue carriage gown with its matching hat, Elenora reminded herself for the thousandth time that she was merely a paid companion who had been employed to perform a part. But deep down she could not resist the temptation to pretend for just a little while that the play had become reality and that Arthur had invited her to drive with him because he wanted to be with her.

The scene spread out before her was lively and colorful. The spring afternoon was sunny and warm and, as was the custom in town, many in the Polite World had come to the park to see and be seen.

The tops of many of the vehicles had been lowered to better display the elegantly dressed passengers. Several gentlemen rode exquisitely turned-out mounts on a neighboring path. They paused frequently to greet those in the carriages, exchange gossip and flirt with the ladies. Couples who took a turn around the park together were, in fact, announcing to Society that marriage plans had either been arranged or were being seriously considered.

Elenora was not surprised to discover that Arthur handled the reins the way he did everything else, with a smooth, efficient skill and quiet authority. The beautifully matched, well-schooled grays responded instantly to his touch.

"I located Watt in a livery stable," Arthur said.

"Was he able to tell you any details concerning your great-uncle's death?"

"Watt said that on the day of the murder, he and Uncle George spent the better part of the afternoon working on some experiments in the laboratory. After the evening meal, George retired to his bedchamber upstairs. Watt went to bed, too. His bedchamber is located downstairs, near the laboratory."

"Did he hear anything that night?"

Arthur nodded grimly. "Watt said he was sound asleep but was jolted into wakefulness by some odd noises and what he thought was a muffled cry from inside the laboratory."

"He went to investigate?"

"Yes. It was not uncommon for Uncle George to go back into his laboratory late at night to check on the results of an experiment or make notes in his journal. Watt feared that he had had some mishap. But the door of the laboratory was locked. Watt had to retrieve a key from his bedside table. While he was doing so, he heard two pistol shots."

"Dear heaven. Did he see the killer?"

"No. By the time he got into the laboratory, the villain had fled through a window."

"What of your great-uncle?"

"Watt found him on the floor, dying in a pool of blood."

Elenora shuddered at the thought of that scene. "How dreadful."

"Uncle George was still partially conscious. He mumbled some words before he died. Watt said that they made no sense to him. He assumed that George was experiencing some strange hallucination brought on by the mortal injury."

"Did Watt recall what he said?"

"Yes," Arthur said evenly. "According to him, my great-uncle's dying words were meant for me. George said, *Tell Arthur that Mercury is still alive.*"

Elenora caught her breath. "Then you are right, sir, this does concern your great-uncle's old companions and those strange red stones."

"Yes. But I have been proceeding on the assumption that Mercury was dead." His mouth twisted. "I ought to have known better than to arrive at any conclusions without proof."

She studied the tight brackets at the corners of his mouth. Her earlier irritation evaporated. "Tell me, my lord, are you always so quick to shoulder all of the responsibility when things go wrong?"

He gave her a quick, frowning glance. "What sort of question is that? I assume the responsibility that is mine."

"And then some, I think." She noticed that two expensively garbed ladies in a passing carriage were watching her and Arthur with the avid expressions of a pair of cats eyeing potential prey. Quite deliberately she angled her dainty parasol to block their view. "It has become clear to me in the short time that I have known you that you are far too accustomed to the dictates of duty. You accept whatever obligations are thrust upon your shoulders as though they were your lot in life."

163

"Perhaps that is because responsibility *is* my lot in life," he said dryly. "I control a considerable fortune, and I am the head of a very large family. In addition to any number of relatives, a great many tenants, farmers, servants and laborers depend upon me in one way or another. Given that situation, I do not see how I can escape the demands of duty."

"I did not mean to imply that you should attempt to evade your obligations," she said quickly.

He was amused. "I am pleased to know that you did not intend any criticism, because my intuition tells me that you and I have a great deal in common when it comes to the manner in which we feel the weight of our responsibilities."

"Oh, I hardly think—"

"Take, for example, the way in which you rushed to Sally's rescue today. There was no need to get involved."

"Rubbish. You know very well that one cannot listen to such vile threats and remain silent."

"Some people could have done so without a qualm, telling themselves that they had no *responsibility* in the matter." He drew in the reins slightly. "I think we are also alike in other ways as well, Miss Lodge."

"What do you mean?" she asked, wary now.

He shrugged. "Having interrupted that scene between Ibbitts and Sally, you could have surrendered to Ibbitts's blackmail in order to protect your position in the household."

"Nonsense."

"There was, after all, a fair amount of money at stake. Triple your wages plus a bonus. Even split in half with an extortionist, that is far more than you can expect to make in a year's employment as a companion elsewhere."

"One cannot give in to extortion." She adjusted the parasol. "You know very well that had you been in my shoes, you certainly would not have done so."

He merely smiled, as though she had proved his point for him.

She frowned. "Oh. I see what you mean. Perhaps we do share some character traits. But that was not quite what I meant."

"What did you mean, Miss Lodge?"

"I believe that what I am trying to describe may have more to do with your excessive sense of self-mastery. Your notions of what is right and proper for you to do. I believe you may demand more of yourself than is strictly necessary, if you see what I mean."

"No. I don't see what you mean, Miss Lodge."

Exasperated, she moved the parasol in a somewhat random manner. "Let me put it this way, my lord. What do you do to make yourself happy?"

There was a short, stark silence.

Elenora held her breath, wondering if he thought that she had overstepped her bounds as an employee yet again. She braced herself for an icy set-down.

Then she noticed the twitch at the corner of his mouth.

"Is this a polite way of informing me that I am not particularly charming, witty, clever or amusing?" he asked. "If so, you could have saved your breath. Others have already made that observation."

"I once loved a man who was charming, witty, clever and amusing," she said. "He claimed to love me in return. In the end he proved to be a faithless liar and a coldhearted fortune hunter. As a result, I am not very keen on the charming, witty, clever and amusing sort."

He slanted her an enigmatic sidelong glance. "Is that a fact?"

"It is," she assured him.

"He was a fortune hunter, you say?"

"Oh, yes. Not that I had a great fortune to be hunted compared to yours, my lord." She could not repress a little wistful sigh. "Still, it was a rather nice house and some excellent land that, when properly managed, produced a tidy profit."

"Who managed it? Your father?"

"No. My father died when I was an infant. I never knew him. My mother and my grandmother managed the land and the household. I learned the skills from them. The property was to be my inheritance. My mother eventually remarried, but my stepfather was only interested in the income that came from the farm."

"What did he do with the money?"

"He fancied himself a skilled investor. But he generally lost more than he made. His last financial venture involved a certain mine in Yorkshire."

Arthur's jaw tightened. "I recall that project. If it is the one I am thinking of, it was a swindle from the outset."

"Yes. Well, unfortunately, my stepfather lost everything in it and the shock brought on a fatal fit of apoplexy. I was left to deal with his creditors. They took everything." She paused. "Or, almost everything."

He made a minute adjustment to the reins. "And your fortune hunter? What became of him? Did he simply disappear?"

"Oh, no. He showed up almost immediately, having received word that I was no longer due to inherit. He promptly ended our engagement. Two months later I learned that he had run off with a young lady from Bath whose father had settled a great deal of money and some very nice jewels on her."

"I see."

There was a short silence during which she became acutely aware of the muffled thud of the horses' hooves,

166

the clatter of carriage wheels and the sounds of voices drifting across the park.

She suddenly realized that she had said far more than she had intended about her personal affairs. They had started out discussing a murder. What in heaven's name had led her to this subject?

"My apologies, sir," she muttered. "I certainly did not mean to bore you with my personal history. It is an exceedingly dreary topic."

"You said that your stepfather's creditors got almost everything?" Arthur asked, sounding curious.

"On the day I was confronted with the creditors, things were a bit hectic, as you can imagine. I was obliged to pack my personal things under the eye of the Runner who had been brought along to oversee the eviction. I used my grandmother's trunk, the one she had acquired in her acting days. It had a false bottom."

"Ah." A small smile flickered at the corner of his mouth. "I begin to see where this is going. What did you manage to smuggle out of the house, Miss Lodge?"

"Just the items that I had hidden in the trunk: my grandmother's gold and pearl brooch, a pair of earrings and twenty pounds."

"Very clever of you."

She wrinkled her nose. "Not nearly as clever as I had hoped to be. Do you have any idea how little the pawn dealers will give one for a perfectly lovely brooch and a pair of earrings? Only a few pounds. I managed to get myself to London and find a post through Goodhew and Willis, but I assure you, there was very little left over."

"I understand."

She squared her shoulders and adjusted the parasol again. "Enough of that depressing topic. Let us return to the matter of your investigation. How do you intend to proceed?"

167

He did not respond immediately. She got the impression that he wanted to continue discussing her deplorable financial situation.

But he flexed his gloved hands on the reins, sending a subtle signal to the grays, and returned to the subject of his great-uncle's murder.

"I've been thinking about that problem," he said. "I believe my next step will be to try to locate the third member of the Society of the Stones, the one who called himself Saturn. In addition, I think it might be a good idea to keep a close watch on Ibbitts."

"Ibbitts?" She was startled. "Why is that? You assured me that he could do us no harm."

"I am not concerned with any gossip about your position that he might attempt to spread," Arthur explained. "But I would be very interested to know if anyone attempts to contact him now that he is no longer employed in my household."

"Why would anyone do that?"

Arthur looked at her. "If I were a killer who was trying to remain hidden, I would be extremely curious to know if someone from my victim's family was making inquiries and, if so, whether or not I was a suspect. Who better to interview than a disgruntled servant?"

She was impressed. "That is a brilliant notion, my lord."

He grimaced. "I'm not sure that it qualifies as brilliant, but I do feel that it should be considered. It is possible that Ibbitts overheard more than a conversation concerning your status as a paid employee."

She suddenly understood. "We talked about John Watt and your investigation last night in the library. Yes, of course. Ibbitts may well know that you are hunting a killer."

He nodded. "If someone were to contact Ibbitts, I

could assume that he is the murderer and that he may be anxious or curious to know what is happening in Rain Street."

"Presumably no one else would bother to talk to a dismissed butler," she agreed. "But how will you arrange for Ibbitts to be watched night and day?"

"I have been considering that question. I could use street lads, although they are not always dependable. The alternative is a Runner. But many of them are no more reliable than the street boys. In addition, it is common knowledge that they can be easily bribed."

She hesitated, recalling her one and only experience with a Runner. "If you elect to go to Bow Street, there is one man there you might find trustworthy. His name is Hitchins."

Before Arthur could question her about Hitchins, a man mounted on a handsome, prancing bay came alongside the carriage. Elenora glanced at him, absently noting the excellence of the horse and the polish on the rider's gleaming boots.

She started to look away, and then the shock of recognition slammed through her.

Impossible, she thought. It couldn't be him. With a gathering sense of dread, she raised her gaze to the gentleman's handsome features.

She found him staring at her, equally stunned.

"Elenora," Jeremy Clyde said. His eyes lit up with the smoldering warmth that had once made her pulse race. "It *is* you. I thought I must have been mistaken when I noticed a familiar-looking lady in this carriage. What a pleasure to see you again, my dear."

"Good day, Mr. Clyde. I understand that you were wed several months ago." She gave her most wintry smile. "Please accept my congratulations. Is your wife here in town with you?"

Jeremy seemed slightly disconcerted by the direction of her conversation. She got the impression that he had forgotten that he had a wife. She thanked the fates that she had not married this man. If she had, she would no doubt have found herself in the position of being the inconvenient spouse whom Jeremy had trouble recalling to mind.

"Yes, of course, she is here," Jeremy said, evidently recovering his memory. "We have taken a house for the Season. Elenora, I had no notion that you were in town. How long will you be staying?"

Arthur glanced briefly at him and then looked at Elenora. "An acquaintance of yours, my dear?"

"I beg your pardon." Flustered at having forgotten her manners, she pulled herself together and quickly made the introductions.

Jeremy inclined his head politely in acknowledgment, but Elenora noticed the flash of astonishment in his eyes when he realized whom he was meeting. He had not recognized Arthur by sight, which was hardly surprising, Elenora thought, since the two men had never moved in the same circles. But Jeremy certainly recognized the name and the title.

Amusement bubbled through her, suppressing her initial dismay. The sight of his discarded fiancée sitting intimately close to one of the most mysterious and most powerful men of the ton had clearly flummoxed Jeremy.

But even as she watched his face, she could see his confusion and surprise transforming into cunning speculation. Jeremy was already trying to think of a way in which he could turn her connection to Arthur to some advantage.

Why had she not noticed this side of him while he had been wooing her? Now that the scales had fallen from her eyes, she could only wonder what it was that had once attracted her to him.

"How do you come to be acquainted with my fiancée, Clyde?" Arthur asked in the dangerously casual manner that Elenora was learning to recognize.

Jeremy's face went as blank as a sheet of foolscap.

"Fiancée?" he repeated. He sounded as though the word had caused him to choke. "You are *engaged* to Elenora, sir? But that's impossible. I don't understand. It cannot be—"

"You did not answer my question," Arthur cut in, wheeling the grays around another vehicle. "How do you come to be acquainted with my fiancée?"

"We are, uh, old friends." Jeremy was obliged to urge his mount to a swifter pace in order to keep up with the carriage.

"I see." Arthur nodded, as if that explained everything. "You must be the fortune hunter, the one who ended his engagement to Elenora when he discovered that she had lost her inheritance. Ran off with a young heiress instead, I understand. Now that was a piece of very shrewd business on your part."

Jeremy stiffened. His anger must have transmitted itself directly through the reins, because his high-strung mount reacted with a nervous toss of the head and began to dance anxiously about on the path.

"Obviously Elenora has given you a very distorted version of events," Jeremy said, yanking fiercely on the reins. "I assure you our relationship did not end because of the disastrous state of her finances." He paused meaningfully. "Unfortunately, there were other reasons involving Miss Lodge's private *affairs* that obliged me to end our connection."

The dark hints that she had compromised herself with another man left Elenora so furious she could hardly breathe.

"What other reasons?" Arthur asked, for all the world

171

as though he had entirely missed the subtle implications of Jeremy's words.

"I suggest you ask Miss Lodge." Jeremy struggled with the reins of his sidestepping, head-tossing mount. "After all, a gentleman does not discuss a lady's *intimate* affairs, does he?"

"Not if he wishes to avoid a dawn appointment," Arthur agreed.

At the sound of those unambiguous words, several heads swiveled instantly toward the carriage. Elenora realized that she and Arthur and Jeremy were suddenly the focus of every member of Society who happened to be in the vicinity. It was rather like being caught in the fierce heat of a burning lens.

Jeremy's jaw dropped. Elenora did not blame him. She was almost certain that her own mouth had fallen open as well.

She could scarcely believe what she had just heard. Arthur had threatened Jeremy with a duel.

"Now, see here, sir, I don't know what—" Jeremy broke off to jerk violently on the reins of his agitated horse.

The additional insult was too much for the beast. It reared wildly, hooves flailing.

Jeremy lost his balance and began an inevitable slide to one side. He fought frantically to regain his seat, but when the horse took off at full gallop, he had no chance. He fell hard on the path, landing on his rear.

Feminine giggles and raucous masculine laughter emanated from passing carriages and riders nearby who had witnessed the debacle.

Arthur ignored the entire scene. He tweaked the reins and the grays moved out in a snapping trot.

Elenora looked back over her shoulder and watched Jeremy pick himself up, dust off his rump and stalk away across the grass. The one glimpse she got of his flushed face was sufficient to send a shudder through her. Jeremy was furious.

She turned around quickly and sat, gazing straight ahead, clinging tensely to her parasol. "I apologize for that unfortunate scene," she said tightly. "I was caught by surprise. I certainly never expected to find myself face-to-face with Jeremy here in London."

Arthur guided the horses toward the gates. "I believe we shall go home now. Thanks to Clyde, we have achieved our purpose. Our presence here in the park this afternoon was most certainly noted and will no doubt be remarked upon at length this evening in every ballroom in town."

"No doubt." She swallowed and glanced at him quickly, uncertain of his mood. "It is generous of you to take such a positive view of the situation."

"My good nature has some limitations," he said. "I will expect you to keep your distance from Clyde."

"Of course," she said, appalled that he would think that she might want to have anything to do with Jeremy. "I assure you, I have no wish to speak to him again."

"I believe you. But he may well try to presume on your previous association."

She frowned. "I do not see how."

"As you yourself noted, Clyde is nothing if not an opportunist. He may convince himself that he can find a way to turn his acquaintance with you to his advantage."

She was hurt that he thought for even a moment that she needed to be warned. "I promise you, I will be careful."

"I would appreciate that. This situations has already become complicated enough as it is."

Her heart sank. He was certainly not pleased, she

thought. And why should he be, come to that? The incident with Jeremy was the second complication in which she had been involved that day.

If she found herself connected to any more irksome problems, Arthur might well conclude that she was more trouble than she was worth.

Judging from his pensive, brooding expression, she suspected that he was thinking similar thoughts.

Concluding that it would be a very good idea to change the subject, she seized upon the first one that came to mind.

"I must compliment you on your excellent acting talents, my lord," she said with an approving air. "Your implied threat to issue a challenge to Jeremy should he spread unpleasant gossip about me was extremely convincing."

"Do you think so?"

"Yes, indeed. It was only a single line, but you delivered it in a most gripping manner, my lord. Just the right degree of cool understatement, if I may say so. Why, your words even sent a shudder through me."

"It remains to be seen if Clyde was similarly affected," Arthur said thoughtfully.

"I'm certain that he was." She chuckled. "For a moment, you actually had me persuaded. I vow, had I not known that you were merely acting a part in this play we are staging, I would have sworn that you meant every word you said."

He gave her a curious look. "What makes you think that I didn't mean exactly what I said?"

"Really, sir, you are teasing me," she said.

They both knew that he had not meant that threat, she thought. After all, if Arthur had not bothered to pursue his real betrothed when she had run off with another man, he was hardly likely to engage in a duel over the honor of an imitation fiancée.

It was only much later, when she was going upstairs to her bedchamber, that she remembered that Arthur had never answered her question: He had not told her what he did to make himself happy.

Chapter Seventeen

The buxom serving wench made one more attempt to snag his attention when she saw that he was making for the door of the smoky tavern. Ibbitts gave her a brief, contemptuous survey, letting her know that the sight of her full breasts spilling out of the stained bodice of her dress filled him with disgust, not lust. Her cheeks went red. Anger and humiliation flashed across her face. With a swish of her skirts, she whirled and hurried off toward a table of raucous patrons.

Ibbitts muttered a curse and opened the door. He had been in a foul temper since St. Merryn had let him go two days earlier. Several hours of drinking bad ale and throwing bad dice tonight had done nothing to improve his mood.

He slouched down the steps into the street, turned and started toward his new lodgings. It was just going on midnight, and there was a full moon; an ideal setting for footpads. A number of carriages rattled up and down the street. He knew they were filled with drunken gentlemen who, bored with their clubs and ballrooms, came to this neighborhood in search of more earthy pleasures.

He shoved one hand deep into the pocket of his coat and wrapped his fingers around the hilt of the knife that he had brought along for protection.

The silly serving wench was a fool to think that he would even consider lifting her skirts. Why would he want to share the filthy sheets of a tavern girl who likely bathed only once a week, if that? In the past few years he had become accustomed to tumbling the clean, perfumed ladies of the Quality; ladies who dressed in silks and satins; ladies who were ever so grateful for the attentions of a strong, well-made man who could satisfy them in bed.

A figure moved in the shadows of the alley up ahead. He tensed, nervously tightening his hand around the hilt of the knife. He heard the slap of shoes on pavement and glanced back at the tavern door, wondering if he should make a run for it.

At that moment a drunken whore stumbled out of the darkness, singing an off-key ballad to herself. She spotted him and stumbled to a halt.

"Well, now, yer a fine-looking one, ye are," she called out. "What d'ya say to a bit o' sport? I'll give ye a good price. Half the gennelmen's rate. How does that sound?"

"Get out of my way, you stupid woman."

"No call to be rude." She hunched her shoulders and headed toward the lights of the tavern. "That's always the way with the handsome ones. Think they're too good for the likes of a hard-working girl."

Ibbitts relaxed a little but quickened his pace. He was anxious to get back to the safety of his new lodgings. It was time to contemplate his future. He had plans to make.

He still had his looks, he reminded himself. With luck he would keep them for a few more years. He would soon find another post. But the sad truth was that it was unlikely he'd ever again turn up a situation as comfortable and as profitable as the one he'd just lost.

The bleak prospect stoked his rage. What he wanted was revenge, he thought. He'd give a great deal to make St. Merryn and Miss Lodge pay for ruining his pleasant arrangement at the mansion in Rain Street.

But the only way to do that was to find a means of using the information he had obtained by eavesdropping. Thus far, he had not been able to come up with a promising scheme.

The big hurdle was that he did not know who in Society to approach. What member of the ton would be willing to pay for the news that St. Merryn was trying to find his great-uncle's killer or that the amusing jest concerning Miss Lodge's origins in an agency was actually the truth?

And there was another obstacle. Who would take the word of an unemployed butler over that of the powerful earl who had dismissed him?

No, he was probably doomed to return to his former career, he decided as he arrived at his new address. And it was all the fault of St. Merryn and Miss Lodge.

He let himself into the dingy hall and went up the stairs. The only good news on the horizon was that he was not going to have to start looking for a new post immediately. Over the course of the past few months, he had surreptitiously removed some lovely silver items and a couple of excellent rugs from the Rain Street house and taken them to the receivers in Shoe

Lane who dealt in stolen goods. As a result he had some money put aside that would enable him to take his time selecting his next situation.

He stopped in front of his room, dug out his key and fitted it into the lock. When he opened the door he saw the weak glow of a candle flame.

His first befuddled thought was that he had somehow unlocked the wrong door. Surely he had not been so foolish as to go off and leave a candle burning.

Then the voice came out of the darkness, chilling him to the bone.

"Come in, Ibbitts." The intruder moved slightly in the corner. The folds of a long black cloak shifted around him. His features were hidden beneath a heavy cowl. "I believe that you and I have some business to transact."

Visions of the legions of husbands he'd cuckolded over the years blazed in his brain. Had one of them learned the truth and taken the trouble to hunt him down?

"I . . . I . . ." He swallowed and tried again. "I don't understand. Who are you?"

"You do not need to know my name before you sell me the information you possess." The man laughed softly. "In fact, it will be infinitely safer for you if you do not learn my identity."

A glimmer of hope leaped within him. "Information?"

"I understand that you have recently left the employ of the Earl of St. Merryn," the man said. "I will pay you well if you can tell me anything of interest concerning that household."

The cultured, well-educated voice marked the intruder as a gentleman. The last of Ibbitts's anxiety evaporated. Euphoria took its place. He had learned the hard way over the years that the men who moved in the elevated circles of Society were no more to be trusted than those who lived in the stews, but there was one significant difference between the two groups: The men of the ton had money to spend and were willing to pay for what they wanted.

His fortunes had turned yet again, Ibbitts thought. He sauntered into the room, smiling the smile that had always turned heads. He made certain that he stood within the circle of light provided by the candle so that the man in the cloak could see his handsome features.

"You're in luck, sir," he said. "I do, indeed, have some interesting information to sell. Shall we discuss the terms of our bargain?"

"If the information is of use to me, you may name your price."

The words were music to Ibbitts's ears.

"In my experience, gentlemen only say that sort of thing when they are pursuing women or vengeance." He chuckled. "In this case, I expect it's the latter, eh? No sane man would go to such lengths to get his hands on an irritating female like Miss Elenora Lodge. Well, sir, if it's revenge against St. Merryn you're after, I'm more than happy to help you."

The intruder said nothing in response, but his very stillness renewed a measure of Ibbitts's nervousness.

It did not surprise him to learn that St. Merryn had such a determined and relentless enemy. Men as wealthy and powerful as the earl always managed to annoy a few people. But whatever the intruder's reasons might be, Ibbitts had no intention of inquiring into them. He had survived in the households of Society all these years because he had learned the fine art of discretion. Take, for example, the way he had been very careful not to let St. Merryn know that he was aware of the inquiries the earl was making into his uncle's murder.

"A thousand pounds," he said, holding his breath. It was a very daring price. He would have settled for a hundred or even fifty. But he knew that the Quality never respected anything unless it came at considerable cost.

"Done," the intruder said at once.

Ibbitts allowed himself to breathe again.

He told the man in the cloak everything he had overheard in the linen closet.

There was a short pause after he finished.

"So, it is as I anticipated," the intruder said, speaking softly as though to himself. "I do, indeed, have an opponent in this affair, just as my predecessor did. My destiny grows more clear by the day."

The man sounded odd. Ibbitts grew uneasy again. He wondered if he had given away too much information before getting his hands on the money. The Quality did not always feel an obligation to keep their bargains with his sort. Oh, they were quick enough to pay their gaming debts because those were considered matters of honor. But gentlemen were content to let shopkeepers and merchants wait forever when it came to their bills.

With a deep sigh, Ibbitts prepared to accept a much lower fee, if it proved necessary. He was not in a position to be particular, he reminded himself.

"Thank you," the man said. "You have been most helpful." He stirred again in the shadows, reaching one hand inside the flowing folds of the cloak.

Too late Ibbitts understood that the stranger was not reaching for money. When his hand reappeared, moonlight danced evilly on the pistol he held.

"No." Ibbitts stumbled backward, clawing for the knife in his pocket.

The pistol roared, filling the small room with smoke and lightning. The shot struck Ibbitts in the chest and flung him hard against the wall. A searing cold immediately began to close around his vitals. He knew that he was dying, but he managed to cling to the knife.

The damned Quality always won, he thought as he started to slide down the wall. The ice spread inside him. The world began to go dark.

The intruder came closer. He took a second pistol out of his pocket. Through the gathering haze that clouded his vision, Ibbitts could just make out the wings of the cloak that swirled around the man's polished boots. Just like one of those winged demons out of hell, Ibbitts thought.

Rage gave him one last burst of energy. He shoved himself away from the wall, the knife clutched in his fingers, and flung himself toward his killer.

Startled, the villain swerved to the side. His booted foot caught on the leg of a chair. He staggered, trying to find his balance, the cloak flaring wildly. The chair crashed to the floor.

Ibbitts struck blindly; felt the blade pierce and rip fabric. For a second he prayed that he would bury the knife in the demon's flesh. But it snagged harmlessly in the thick folds of the cloak and was jerked from his hand.

Spent, Ibbitts collapsed. Dimly he heard the knife clatter on the floor beside him.

"There is a third reason why a man might tell you to name your price," the intruder whispered in the darkness. "And that is because he has no intention of paying it."

Ibbitts never heard the second shot that exploded through his brain, destroying a large portion of the face that had always been his fortune.

The killer rushed from the room, pausing only to put out the candle and yank the door closed. He stumbled down the stairs, his breath coming and going in great gasps. At the bottom of the steps he suddenly remembered the mask. Yanking it out of the pocket of the cloak, he fitted it over his head.

Things had not gone entirely according to plan tonight.

He hadn't been expecting that last desperate assault from his victim. The two old men had died so easily. He had assumed that the damned butler would be equally obliging.

When Ibbitts had flung himself at him, knife in hand, blood soaking the front of his shirt, it was as if a dead man had been shocked by an electricity machine into a semblance of life.

The sense of raw terror he had experienced was still upon him, rattling his nerves and clouding his usually well-focused brain.

Out in the darkened street the unlit hackney waited. The coachman huddled into his greatcoat, nursing his bottle of gin. The killer wondered if the man on the box had heard the pistol shots.

No, he thought. Highly unlikely. Ibbitts's lodgings were at the back of the old, stone building, and the walls were thick. In addition there were several carriages in the street, rattling and clattering loudly.

If the coachman's ears had picked up any sounds at all, they would have been greatly muffled.

For a second or two he hesitated, and then he

decided that there was nothing to be concerned about in that quarter. The coachman was quite drunk and had little interest in his passenger's activities. All he cared about was his fare.

Even if the driver were to grow curious or decide to talk to his friends in the tavern, there would be no risk, the killer thought as he bounded up into the cab of the vehicle. The hackney driver had never seen his face. The mask concealed his features quite adequately.

He dropped onto the worn cushions. The coach rumbled into motion.

The killer's breathing gradually steadied. He reviewed the events of the past few moments, going over each twist and turn with his brilliantly honed, logical mind. Methodically he searched his memory for errors or clues that he might have inadvertently left behind.

Eventually he was satisfied that the matter was under complete control.

He was still breathing a little too fast; still a bit light-headed. But he was pleased to note that his nerves had calmed. He raised his hands in front of his face. There was no light inside the cab, so he could not see his fingers clearly, but he was fairly certain that they no longer trembled.

In place of the frantic sensation he had experienced after the unanticipated attack, waves of giddy excitement were now sweeping through him.

He wanted—no, he *needed*—to exult in his great success. This time he would not go to the exclusive brothel he had used after he had killed George Lancaster and the other old man. He required a far more personal celebration, one that befitted his unfolding destiny.

He smiled in the darkness. He had anticipated the need to savor this thrilling achievement and had planned for it, just as he had planned all of the other aspects of the business.

He knew exactly how he would mark this bold triumph over his opponent.

Chapter Eighteen

The old man gazed into the crackling fire, one gouty foot propped on a stool, a glass of port in his gnarled fingers. Arthur waited, his arms resting on the gilded sides of his chair. The conversation with his companion had not gone smoothly. It was obvious that for Lord Dalling time had become a deep pool in which the currents of the past and the present were intermingled, rather than a river that ran in only one direction.

"How did ye happen to learn of my interest in old snuffboxes, sir?" Dalling asked, frowning in a befuddled manner. "Collect 'em yourself, do ye?"

"No, sir," Arthur said. "I visited several shops that specialize in selling fine snuffboxes and asked for the names of those clients the proprietors considered their most knowledgeable customers. Your name came up in several of the best establishments."

There was no need to add that it had been considerably more complicated obtaining the old man's current address. Dalling had not made any additions to his snuffbox collection in years, and the shopkeepers had lost track of his whereabouts.

In addition, the elderly gentleman had moved two years previously. Most of his contemporaries were either dead or suffering great gaps in their memories and could not remember the location of their old friend's new lodgings. But fortunately one aging baron who still played cards every night at Arthur's club had recalled Dalling's new street and number.

They sat together in Dalling's library. The furnishings and the books on the shelves dated from another era, as did their owner. It was as if the past thirty years had never happened, as if Byron had never written a word, as if Napoleon had not been defeated, as if men of science had not made astonishing strides investigating the mysteries of electricity and chemistry. Even his host's tight breeches dated from another time and place.

The tall clock ticked heavily in the silence. Arthur wondered if his last question had sent his companion back into the murky depths of the pool of time, never to resurface.

But Dalling stirred at last. "A snuffbox set with a large red stone, you say?"

"Yes. With the name Saturn worked into the design."

"Aye, I recall a box such as you describe. An acquaintance carried it for years. Quite a lovely little box. I recall once asking him where he had purchased it."

Arthur did not move for fear of distracting the old man. "Did he tell you?"

"I believe he said that he and some companions had commissioned a jeweler to create three similar boxes, one for each of them."

"Who was this gentleman? Do you remember his name?"

"Of course I remember it." Dalling's face tightened fiercely. "I'm not senile, sir."

"My apologies. I never meant to imply that."

Dalling appeared somewhat mollified. "Glentworth. That was the name of the man who owned the Saturn snuffbox."

"Glentworth." Arthur got to his feet. "Thank you, sir. I am very grateful for your assistance."

"Heard he died recently. Not long ago. Within the past week, I believe."

Hell's teeth. Glentworth was dead? After all the effort it had taken to track him down?

"I didn't attend the funeral," Dalling continued. "Used to go to all of them, but there got to be too many, so I gave up the habit."

Arthur tried to think of how to proceed. Everywhere he turned in this maze, he met with a blank wall.

The fire crumbled. Dalling took a jeweled snuffbox out of his pocket, flipped the lid open and helped himself to a pinch. He inhaled the pulverized tobacco with a quick, efficient little snort. Closing the box, he settled deeper into his chair with a heavy sigh of satisfaction. His heavy lids closed.

Arthur started toward the door. "Thank you for your time, sir."

"Not at all." Dalling did not open his eyes. He fingered his exquisite little snuffbox, turning it over and over in his hand.

Arthur had the door open and was about to step out into the hall when his host spoke again.

"Perhaps you should talk to the widow," the old man said.

Chapter Nineteen

The costume ball was a crush. Lady Fambridge had displayed what Elenora had learned was her well-known flair for the dramatic in the décor she had chosen for the evening. The large, elegant room was lit with red and gold lanterns rather than blazing chandeliers. The dim illumination steeped the space in long, mysterious shadows.

A number of potted palms had been brought in from the conservatory. They had been strategically placed in clusters along the walls to provide secluded niches for couples.

Costume balls, Elenora had quickly discovered, were all about dalliance and flirtation. They provided opportunities for the jaded members of Society to play their favorite games of seduction and intrigue even more openly than was usual.

Arthur had admitted that morning at breakfast that when he had elected to accept the invitation, he had not realized the event would require a domino and a mask.

That was what came of leaving social decisions to a man, Elenora thought. They did not always pay attention to the details.

Margaret and Bennett both appeared to be enjoying themselves thoroughly, however. They had disappeared half an hour before. Elenora had a hunch that they were making good use of one of the palm-shrouded bowers scattered strategically around the room.

She, on the other hand, was making her way through the crowd toward the nearest door. She needed a rest.

For the last hour she had dutifully danced with any number of masked gentlemen, rarely bothering to hide her own features behind the little feathered mask she carried in one hand. The point was for her to be recognized, after all, as Margaret had reminded her.

She had carried out her responsibilities to the best of her ability, but now she was not only bored, her feet were also beginning to hurt inside her soft leather dancing slippers. A steady diet of balls and soirées took its toll, she thought.

She had almost reached the door when she noticed the man in the black domino making his way determinedly toward her. The cowl of the enveloping cloak-like garment had been drawn up over his head, casting his face into deep shadow. As he drew closer she saw that he wore a black silk mask.

He moved like a wolf gliding through a flock of sheep in search of the weakest lamb. For an instant her spirits rose and she forgot all about her sore feet. When he had left the house earlier that evening, Arthur had taken a black domino and a black mask with him. He had said he would meet her at the Fambridge ball and accompany her home.

She had not expected him to arrive so early, however. Perhaps he had met with success in his inquiries and wanted to discuss the new information with her. She took some comfort in the knowledge that, although he seemed intent on ignoring the attraction between them—at least for now—he had more or less made her a consultant in this affair.

The stranger in the domino arrived in front of her. Elenora's excitement evaporated instantly. This was not Arthur. She was not certain how she knew that with such certainty before he even touched her, but she did know it.

It was not the man's voice that gave him away—he did not speak. There was nothing odd about that. He was not the first gentleman that night to use gestures to invite her to dance. Voices were easy to identify, and several guests preferred to play their games anonymously. Nevertheless, she had recognized most of her partners, especially those with whom she had danced the waltz on previous occasions.

The waltz was a surprisingly intimate sort of exercise. No two men conducted it in quite the same manner. Some went about the business with military-style precision. A few steered her around the floor with such energetic enthusiasm that she felt as though she was engaging in a horse race. Still others took advantage of the close contact to try to rest their hands in places where propriety dictated they did not belong.

She hesitated when the man in the black domino offered his arm in a graceful flourish. He was not Arthur, and her feet really did hurt. But whoever he was, he had made a considerable effort to get to her in the crowd. The least she could do was dance with him, she thought. After all, she was being paid to perform a role.

The man in the mask took her arm. In the next breath, she regretted her decision. The touch of his long, elegant fingers sent an inexplicable chill through her.

She caught her breath and told herself that it must be her imagination. But her senses rejected that logic. There was an aura about the stranger that stirred her nerves in a most unpleasant manner.

When he guided her into the steps of the waltz, it was all she could do not to wrinkle her nose in reaction to the unwholesome odor that emanated from him. She could tell that he had recently perspired very heavily, but the smell of his sweat was not that which was produced by normal exertion. It was tainted with some essence that she could not identify; a vapor that filled her with disgust.

She studied the small portion of his face that was not covered by the mask. In the lantern light his eyes fairly glittered through the slits cut in the black silk.

Her first thought was that he was intoxicated, but she discarded that theory when she realized that he was not the least unsteady or lacking in coordination. Perhaps he had just won or lost a fortune in a game of whist or hazard. That might account for his air of unnatural excitement.

Tension tightened the muscles in her body. She wished with all her heart that she had not accepted the cowled man's offer of a dance. But it was too late. Unless she wanted to cause a scene, she was trapped until the music ended.

She was positive that she had never danced the waltz with this man before tonight, but she wondered if she had met him at some other affair.

"Are you enjoying the evening, sir?" she asked, hoping that she could tempt him into speaking.

But he merely inclined his head in a silent, affirmative response.

The long fingers gripped her own so tightly that she could feel the outline of the ring he wore.

She felt his gloved hand tighten at her waist and almost stumbled in response. If he attempted to move his palm lower, she would end the dance immediately, she told herself. She could not abide him touching her any more intimately.

She shifted her fingertips from his shoulder to his arm in an effort to put a little more distance between them. The movement caused her palm to glide across a long, jagged tear in the voluminous folds of the heavy black cloth of the domino. Perhaps the garment had got caught on the door of his carriage. Should she mention the rip in his cloak to him?

No, the less said between them the better. She did not want to make polite conversation, even if he proved willing to talk.

And then, without a word, the man in the mask brought her to a halt at the edge of the dance floor, bowed deeply, turned and strode swiftly toward the nearest door.

She watched him leave, slightly stunned by the strange episode and exceedingly relieved that it was over.

The folds of her own cloaklike domino suddenly felt much too warm. She needed that breath of fresh air now far more than she had a few minutes before.

Raising her mask to conceal her face, she managed to escape the shadowy ballroom without attracting any more attention. She went down a quiet hall and sought refuge in the Fambridges' moonlit conservatory.

The large greenhouse radiated the wholesome, soothing scents of rich soil and thriving foliage. She paused at the entrance to give her eyes time to adjust to the shadows.

After a moment she discovered that the pale glow of the full moon flooding through the panes of glass provided sufficient illumination to make out the shapes of the workbenches and the masses of greenery.

She wandered down an aisle of broad-leaved plants, enjoying her moment of solitude and silence. She had danced with any number of mysterious masked strangers that evening, but Arthur had not been among them. Even if he had come to her in a mask and a domino and said not one word, she would have known his touch, she mused. Something in her reacted to his nearness as though they shared some sort of metaphysical connection. Surely he experienced some of the same awareness when he was near her. Or was she fooling herself?

She reached the end of the corridor of potted plants and was about to turn back when something, a brush of a shoe against the tile or perhaps the soft swish of a domino, told her that she was no longer alone in the conservatory.

Her pulse quickened. Instinctively she moved deeper into a patch of shadow created by a towering palm. What if her dance partner had followed her?

The conservatory had seemed a safe enough retreat, but it occurred to her that she could be trapped here at the far end of the glass house. The only way back into the ballroom would take her past whoever had followed her here.

"Miss Lodge?" The woman's voice was low and tremulous.

Relief cascaded through Elenora. She did not recognize the newcomer, but knowing that she was dealing with a female eased her tension. She stepped out of the shadow of the tall palm.

"Yes, I'm here," she said.

"I thought I saw you come this way." The lady came toward her along the plant-lined aisle. Her domino was fashioned of a light-colored fabric that reflected the moonlight: pale blue or green, perhaps. She had the cowl pulled up over her head to shield her face.

"How did you recognize me?" Elenora asked, curious and somewhat surprised to discover that she was still a bit wary. The waltz with the masked stranger had unsettled her usually unflappable nerves more than she would have believed possible.

"I saw you arrive in St. Merryn's carriage earlier." The woman was small and rather ethereal-looking in her pale costume. She seemed to drift toward Elenora as though her feet did not quite touch the ground. "Your mask and domino are quite distinctive."

"Have we been introduced?" Elenora asked.

"No, forgive me." The lady reached up with one dainty, gloved hand and lowered her cowl to reveal an elegant coiffure. Her hair was most likely a golden blonde shade, but in the eerie light it had the appearance of magically spun silver. "My name is Juliana Burnley."

Arthur's former fiancée. Elenora managed, barely, not to groan aloud. The evening was progressing from bad to awkward. Where was Margaret when she was needed?

"Mrs. Burnley," she murmured.

"Please, call me, Juliana." She removed her mask.

Elenora had heard enough in the way of gossip to guess that Juliana was very pretty. The reality was somewhat daunting. Even here in the weak light of the moon, it was easy to see that Juliana was nothing short of beautiful. Her features were finely etched and delicately made.

Everything about her was so dainty and lovely as to be a little unreal. Here, amidst the moonlit foliage, Juliana looked like a fairy queen holding court in a moonlit garden.

"As you wish." Elenora lowered her own mask. "You obviously know who I am."

"St. Merryn's new fiancée." Juliana floated to a halt a short distance away. "I suppose I should offer my congratulations." She ended the sentence on a rising note, as though asking a question.

"Thank you," Elenora said coolly. "Was there something you wanted?"

Juliana flinched. "I'm sorry, I'm not handling this very well. The truth is, I'm not sure how to go about it."

Nothing was so irritating as a person who hemmed and hawed and refused to get to the point, Elenora thought.

"What, precisely, are you attempting to accomplish?" she asked.

"This is so difficult. Perhaps it would be easier if you would allow me to start at the beginning."

"If you feel that will help."

Juliana turned slightly away and examined a nearby plant as though she had never seen anything like it in her entire life. "I'm sure you've heard the gossip."

"I know that you were engaged to St. Merryn and that you eloped with Roland Burnley, if that is what you mean." She did not bother to conceal her impatience.

Juliana clenched one gloved hand. "I had no choice. My parents were determined to marry me off to St. Merryn. They would never have allowed me to end the engagement. I am certain that if I had confided to Papa that I couldn't bring myself to go through with the wedding, he would have locked me in my room and fed me bread and water until I agreed to obey him."

"I see," Elenora said neutrally.

"You don't believe me? I assure you, Papa is very strict. He will not tolerate any disagreement. Everything must be done according to his dictates. And Mama would not go against him. I would have done almost anything to escape the marriage they intended for me. My dear Roland came to my rescue."

"I see."

Juliana smiled wistfully. "He is handsome and noble and very, very brave. There is no other man I know who would have stood up to both my father and his own, not to mention St. Merryn, in order to save me from a horrid marriage."

"You're certain that marriage to St. Merryn would have been horrid?"

"It would have been intolerable." Juliana shuddered. "During the weeks that I was engaged to him I used to lie in bed at night and cry until dawn. I pleaded with Papa to find another husband for me, but he refused."

"What, precisely, made you so sure that you could not bear to be married to St. Merryn?"

Juliana's neat brows came together in a delicate frown of confusion. "Why, because he is exactly like Papa, of course. How could I possibly wish to marry a man who would treat me the way Papa always treated me? A man who never paid the least attention to my opinions? A man who never allowed me to make my own decisions? A man who insisted upon playing the tyrant in his own home? Why, I would rather have entered a convent."

The light of understanding began to dawn. It was abruptly quite clear why Juliana had run off with her Roland.

"Well, that does explain a few things, I suppose," Elenora replied.

Juliana searched her face. "You're not the least bit afraid of St. Merryn, are you?"

The unexpected question caught Elenora by surprise. She thought about it briefly. She had a good measure of respect for Arthur, and she certainly had no wish to arouse his temper unnecessarily. Nor would she care to cross him. But fear him?

"No," she said.

Juliana hesitated and then nodded. "I can see that it is different for you. I must admit that I am envious. How do you do it?"

"How do I do what?"

"How do you make St. Merryn pay attention to what you have to say? How do you stop him from taking command of your life? How do you prevent him from having his own way in everything?"

"That is a rather personal question, Juliana," she said. "I wonder if we might get to the reason why you sought me out here in the conservatory?"

"I am sorry. I did not mean to pry. It is just that I cannot help but be curious about the woman who, uh—"

"Took your place?" Elenora suggested.

"Yes, I suppose you could put it like that. I merely wondered how you deal with him."

"Let's just say that my relationship with St. Merryn is considerably different than the one you had with him."

"I see." Juliana nodded again, this time with a sage air. "Perhaps you do not fear him because you are so

200

much older than me and have so much more experience of the world and of men."

Elenora discovered that she was gritting her teeth. "No doubt. Now, if you don't mind, what was it you wished to say to me?"

"Oh, yes, of course." Juliana straightened her shoulders and raised her chin. "This is very difficult, Miss Lodge, but I come to you as a supplicant."

"I beg your pardon?"

Juliana held out one hand in a graceful, beseeching gesture. "I must beg you for a great favor. You are my only hope. I do not know where else to turn."

Elenora wondered for a moment if Juliana was playing some sort of bizarre game. But the other woman's desperation was plain. It was clear that whatever else was going on here, she was entirely serious.

"I'm sorry," Elenora said, softening her tone in spite of her irritation. Juliana really did seem quite anxious. "I fail to see how I could possibly be in a position to be of service to you."

"You are engaged to St. Merryn."

"What has that got to do with it?" Elenora asked warily.

Juliana cleared her throat. "The gossip is that, although you are not yet wed, the two of you appear to be on very *intimate* terms."

Elenora went cold. Intimate terms was a polite euphemism and everyone knew it. She told herself that it was only to be expected that Society would speculate that she and Arthur were involved in an affair. Indeed, she ought to have anticipated such rumors. Unlike Juliana, she was not an obviously innocent eighteen-year-old living under the stern protection of her parents.

As far as the Polite World was concerned, Elenora

reminded herself, she was not only a mature woman, she was a lady of mystery who was residing under the same roof as her even more mysterious fiancé. Margaret's presence in that household gave the situation a socially acceptable façade, but that did not keep tongues from wagging.

It should have come as no surprise to learn that the scandalmongers were convinced that she was *intimate* with Arthur.

"One would do well to remember that gossip is not always entirely accurate," she said, trying to put a quelling note into her words.

"I did not mean to offend you," Juliana said. "But I wanted you to know that I understand that you have a very close relationship with St. Merryn. Why, they say he was seen kissing you quite passionately the other night in the gardens outside a certain ballroom." She paused. "He never kissed me like that."

"Yes, well—"

"In addition, there is a rumor going around that he actually promised to issue a challenge to a gentleman who spoke to you in the park."

"I assure you, that incident was inflated out of all proportion," Elenora said quickly.

"The thing is, St. Merryn actually issued the threat." Juliana sighed. "Several people overheard him. That is the whole point, you see. He did not even bother to give chase the night Roland and I ran away."

"Did you want him to go after you?" Elenora asked softly, suddenly very curious to know the truth.

"No, of course not." Juliana tapped the edge of her mask lightly against a wooden workbench. "Indeed, I was profoundly grateful that he did not come after us. I was terrified that he might hurt Roland or even kill him in a duel. Instead, I'm told that St. Merryn went to his club and played cards that evening." She made a rueful face. "Which merely confirmed what I had believed all along."

"What was that?"

"That while it was true that St. Merryn was betrothed to me, his passions were decidedly not engaged."

"I am glad that you were able to marry the man you love." Elenora said gently. "But I still do not know what you want from me."

"Do you not comprehend? My dear Roland took an enormous risk when he saved me from St. Merryn. And he has paid a terrible price."

"What price is that? You just told me that St. Merryn did not harm him in any way."

"I did not realize just how much Roland put at stake for me that night." Juliana sounded as if she was fighting tears. "My greatest fear was that St. Merryn would come after us, but the real danger lay elsewhere, in the very bosoms of our families."

"What do you mean?"

"We knew that my father would be furious and would likely cut me off without a penny, and that is precisely what happened. But what we did not anticipate was that Roland's father would be so enraged that he would stop Roland's quarterly allowance."

"Oh, dear."

"We are in desperate financial straits, Miss Lodge, and my Roland is too proud to go to his father and plead with him to restore his allowance."

"How are you surviving?"

"My mother, bless her, braved my father's wrath and secretly gave us some money from the allowance that Papa provides her for the household accounts. I sold some of the jewelry I took away with me the night that Roland and I eloped." Juliana bit her lip. "Unfortunately, I did not get much for it. It is quite astonishing how little good jewelry is worth when one is obliged to pawn it."

Elenora felt a twinge of genuine empathy. "I know. I, too, have had occasion to discover that sad fact."

Juliana did not seem interested in comparing notes on pawn dealers, however. She was focusing intently on her tale. "For his part, Roland has been trying his luck at the gaming tables. Recently he fell in with a companion who seemed to know his way around that world."

"What do you mean?"

"This man took Roland to a club where he promised the play was fair. At first Roland won quite often. For a while we believed that his luck would see us through. But lately his cards have been very poor. Last night he lost quite heavily, and as he had pledged my last necklace, we are now down to almost nothing."

Elenora sighed. "I understand that feeling very well indeed."

"We cannot afford to go about very much." Juliana shook her head. "I suppose it was very naïve of me, but I must tell you that I had no notion how much a simple ball gown and a pair of matching slippers cost until Roland and I found ourselves cut off." She touched the folds of the domino she wore. "The only reason I was able to come here tonight was because a friend allowed me to borrow this costume. Roland does not know I'm here. He is in the hells again."

"I am very sorry for your plight," Elenora said.

"I fear that Roland is fast becoming desperate," Juliana confided in hushed tones. "I do not know what he will do if his luck does not turn. That is why I have come to beg you for your assistance, Miss Lodge. Will you help us?"

Chapter Twenty

Twenty minutes later Elenora made her way back in the lantern-lit ballroom. The crowd of cloaked and masked dancers was thicker than ever. She found an empty palm-shrouded alcove and sat down on the small, gilded bench that had been provided.

Absently she watched the throng of dancers, trying to spot Margaret and Bennett while she pondered her conversation with Juliana.

Her musings slammed to a halt when she saw the man in the black mask and domino coming toward her. Not again, she thought with a shudder. She would not allow him to touch her a second time. She could not abide the feel of his hand on her waist or the smell of his unwholesome excitement.

But a few seconds later she knew, with a sweeping sense of relief, that this was most certainly not the same man. True, he sliced through the crowd with the same gliding, sure-footed movements of a predator, but this man's stride exuded power and control, not unnatural energy. The cowl of the domino was pushed back. Although his eyes were concealed behind a black silk mask, there was no disguising that proud nose or the manner in which his heavy, dark hair was combed straight back from his high forehead.

A fizzy anticipation that she could not suppress sparkled through her veins. She lowered her mask and smiled.

"Good evening, sir," she said. "You are early, are you not?"

Arthur halted in front of her and bowed. "So much for my clever disguise. I arrived a few minutes ago. Found Margaret and Bennett straightaway, but they said they had lost track of you in the crowd."

"I went into the conservatory to get some fresh air."

"Are you ready to leave?"

"Yes, as a matter of fact, I am." She rose from the bench. "But I'm not sure that Margaret will want to go home this early. I believe that she is enjoying herself with Mr. Fleming."

"That much is obvious." He took her arm and steered her toward the door. "She just informed me that she and Bennett were off to drop in on the Morgan soirée. Bennett will escort her home later."

She smiled. "I think they are falling in love."

"I did not bring Margaret to London to have a romantic fling," Arthur grumbled. "Her role was to act as your guide and to provide an acceptable female presence in my household so that your reputation would not suffer in the course of your employment."

She silently debated whether or not to tell him the gossip that Juliana had reported was circulating among the ton. In the end, she concluded that it would only complicate the situation if Arthur learned that the Polite World assumed that they were involved in an intimate relationship. Such information might cause him to worry excessively about his responsibilities toward her. That was the last thing she wanted.

"Come now, sir. It is a wonderful thing that Margaret seems to have found a very nice gentleman who makes her happy. Admit it."

"Huh."

"And the most charming aspect of the situation is that you deserve all the credit for allowing the romance to bloom," she could not resist adding. "After all, had you not invited Margaret to London, she would never have met Bennett."

"It was not part of my strategy," he muttered darkly. "I do not like it when things fail to go according to plan."

He did not sound truly annoyed, she concluded.

She laughed. "Sometimes it is good to have our most carefully laid plans overset."

"When in blazes have you ever known such an outcome to prove anything but disastrous?"

When I met you in the offices of Goodhew and Willis, she thought wistfully. She had been seeking a quiet post as a paid companion to someone like Mrs. Egan. Instead she had encountered Arthur, and now, no matter what transpired between them, she knew her life would never be quite the same again.

But she could not tell him that, so she merely smiled, hoping that she appeared mysterious.

When they reached the front steps of the Fambridge mansion, Arthur called for his carriage. A few minutes later Elenora spotted it as it swung out of the long line of vehicles waiting in the street. When it arrived at the bottom of the steps, Arthur handed her up into it.

He vaulted in lightly behind her, the black folds of

the domino whipping out behind him like the dark wings of a bird of prey that hunted by night.

He closed the door and settled on the seat across from her. This was the first time she had ever been alone with him in the vehicle, she realized.

"Enough of this masquerade nonsense." Arthur untied his mask and tossed it aside. "I fail to see the attraction of concealing one's identity unless one is intent on committing a crime."

"I have no doubt but that several crimes were committed in the Fambridge ballroom this evening."

"Ah, yes. Indeed." He lounged into the corner of the seat, mouth twisted slightly in amusement. "Most of them involved illicit liaisons of one sort of another, I suspect."

"Mmm."

He contemplated her with his dangerous eyes. "I trust you were not subjected to any indignities? It was Margaret's job to ensure that you were kept safe from the wrong sort of attentions, but it has become obvious that she is not concentrating on her role. If any man made improper advances—"

"No, my lord," she said hastily. "There was no trouble of that sort. But I did meet an old acquaintance of yours."

"Who?"

"Juliana. Mrs. Burnley now."

He grimaced. "She was present this evening?"

"Yes."

"She sought you out?"

"Yes."

He did not look pleased. "I trust the encounter was not unpleasant. She did not stage a scene, did she?"

"There was no scene, but the encounter, as you put it, was, shall we say, interesting."

He drummed his fingers on the edge of the door. "Why do I have the impression that I am not going to like whatever it is that you are about to tell me?"

"It is really not so very dreadful," she assured him. "Nevertheless, I suspect your initial reaction may be somewhat, ah, negative."

"I suspect you are damned right." He smiled in feral anticipation. "But you are going to try to make me change my mind, are you not?"

"In my opinion, it would be in everyone's best interests if you could manage to achieve a positive reaction."

"Out with it," he growled.

"I think it would be better if I explained the situation first."

"Now I am absolutely certain that I will have a negative response."

She pretended not to hear that. "Were you aware, sir, that both Juliana's and Roland's families have cut the couple's purse strings?"

He raised his brows. "I have heard rumors to that effect, yes. I am certain that it is merely a temporary situation. Sooner or later old Burnley or Graham will come around."

"Juliana believed that at first, too, but she no longer places any faith in that possibility, and evidently neither does Roland. They are convinced that both families have turned against them forever. Juliana is quite distraught."

"Is she?" He did not sound the least concerned about Juliana's feelings.

"Her mother gave her a little money, but that is not enough to sustain the couple. The threat of financial disaster has driven Roland into the gaming hells."

"Yes, I know. I daresay he'll soon learn that the hells

209

are a good way to lose whatever little money he has left."

"You knew that Roland is attempting to make his fortune at the tables?"

"It is hardly a secret."

Of course he had been aware of the situation, she thought wryly, just as he had known that Ibbitts was stealing from the household accounts. Making certain that he was well informed of all the events in his world was Arthur's way.

She decided to take a different approach. "Juliana is very frightened."

Turning his head, he gave her his fierce profile. He looked out the window as though he was bored with the conversation and had found something of extraordinary interest to observe in the street. The lamplight etched his cheekbone and the line of his jaw, but his expression was lost in dark shadow.

"That does not surprise me," he said.

She recalled once again the gossip she had heard concerning Juliana's feelings toward Arthur. *They say she was terrified of him.*

Watching his averted face, she suddenly knew with great certainty that he had been very well aware that his fiancée feared him.

The knowledge that he was aware of how Juliana had regarded him did not surprise her, but the realization that he might have taken a silly young woman's gothic imaginings personally, perhaps had even allowed them to depress his spirits, did astonish her.

"My understanding is that Juliana endured an extremely sheltered upbringing," Elenora said briskly. "Her youth and lack of experience of the world no doubt caused her to fall victim to specters produced by a young lady's naturally overheated imagination."

He turned back to her. "Unlike yourself, Miss Lodge?" he asked mockingly.

She waved that aside with the hand in which she held her mask. "A lady who intends to go into trade cannot afford the luxury of possessing overly refined sensibilities."

A flicker of a smile came and went at the corners of his mouth. He inclined his head in a gravely solemn manner.

"It is certainly true that delicate sensibilities can interfere with turning a profit." He regarded her very steadily. "I learned that fact myself several years ago. As a result, I never allow sentiment to influence my decisions in such matters."

That did not bode well, she thought. With his legendary, preternatural intuition concerning finances and investments, he had already guessed that she was about to ask him for a favor involving money. He was giving her fair warning that she might as well save her breath.

Nevertheless, she decided to press on, employing the tools that might sway him: logic and responsibility.

"Sir, I shall come straight to the point," she said. "Juliana approached me tonight to request a favor."

His eyes narrowed faintly. "Never say she had the nerve to ask you for money?"

"No," she said quickly, pleased to be able to put that issue to rest.

His expression lightened somewhat. "I am relieved to hear that. For a moment there I thought she might have tried to convince you to give her a loan, although why she would think that you might be willing to do such a thing is beyond me."

"She did not ask for a loan," Elenora said very carefully. "At least not directly. But you will recall that you have put it about that you are supposedly in town to form a consortium of investors."

"What of it?"

Elenora squared her shoulders. "Juliana pleaded with me to ask you to offer Roland a share in your new consoritum."

For a moment Arthur just looked at her as though she had spoken in some unknown tongue.

Then he leaned forward, elbows resting on his knees.

"I must conclude that this is your eccentric notion of a joke, Miss Lodge," he said.

She searched his eyes and knew that it was irritation, not rage, that she saw burning in his gaze. There was a difference between the two. When it came to Arthur, she was quite certain that only the second reaction was truly dangerous. The first could be dealt with if one applied reason.

"Kindly do not attempt to intimidate me, sir," she said calmly. "All I ask is that you hear me out."

"There's more to this nonsense?"

"I comprehend that it is a lot to ask of you under the circumstances, but I feel that you would be well-advised to grant Juliana this favor."

His smile was as cold as steel. "But I am not forming a consortium at the moment, if you recall."

"No, but you do form them frequently, and we both know that sooner or later you will find yourself brewing up another financial venture. You could offer Roland a share in your next project."

"I cannot envision a single logical reason why I should invite Roland Burnley into a consortium, even assuming that he possessed the funds required to purchase a share, which, as you just pointed out, he does not."

"The matter of the funds he would require to purchase a share is another issue. We will get to that shortly."

"Will we, indeed?"

"Are you attempting to intimidate me, sir? If so, it is not working."

"Perhaps I should try harder."

With an effort, she possessed herself in patience. "I am attempting to explain why you should consider allowing Roland to become a member of your next company of investors."

"I cannot wait to hear this."

"The thing is," she continued, determined to finish her argument, "When one views the situation from a particular perspective, one could conclude that *you* are the reason that Juliana and Roland find themselves in their present extremely unfortunate financial circumstances."

"Damnation, woman, are you saying I'm to blame for the fact that those two eloped?"

She squared her shoulders. "In a manner of speaking, yes."

He swore softly once again and sat back. "Tell me, Miss Lodge, do you feel that it was my fault that Juliana was so horrified by the prospect of experiencing a fate worse than death in my bed that she felt she had no choice but to flee into the night with another man?"

"Of course not." She was shocked to the core by his conclusion. "I am saying that you are, in part, responsible for the outcome because you could have gone after Juliana and Roland that night and stopped them. Moreover, if you had given chase, I suspect you would have caught up with them well before the damage was done to Juliana's reputation."

"In case you have not heard the tale in its entirety, there was a ferocious storm that night," he reminded her. "Only a madman would have braved it."

"Or a man madly in love," she amended, smiling slightly. "I have heard the story in several variations, my lord, and I must conclude that you did not fit that description. If you had been passionately in love with Juliana, you would have given chase."

He stretched his arms out full-length on either side along the back of the cushions. His smile was as thin and sharp as the edge of a blade. "Surely by now someone has explained to you that I am a man who is motivated solely by money. People credit me with many attributes, Miss Lodge, but I assure you, strong passions are not among them."

"Yes, well, I daresay that few people know you well enough to make such a judgment, and that, too, is no doubt your own fault."

"How the devil can you place the responsibility for that at my doorstep?"

"I do not mean to give offense, sir, but you do not encourage—" She broke off abruptly, aware that the word she had been about to use—*intimacy*—was not quite the *bon mot* she was searching for to describe his aloof, self-controlled nature. "Let us say that you do not encourage close personal relationships."

"And with good reason. Such associations frequently get in the way of sound business decisions."

"I do not, for one minute, believe that to be your motive for keeping most people at a distance. The truth, I suspect, is that it is your overriding sense of responsibility that makes it difficult for you to let down your guard. You do not feel that you can afford to take the risk of trusting someone else to take control for a while."

"You possess an unusual view of my temperament," he muttered.

"And in my *unusual view*, I am quite certain that you are a man of strong if tightly controlled passions."

He gave her an odd look, as though she had just provided him with cause to doubt her sanity. "Tell me, Miss Lodge, do you really believe that I would chase after a runaway fiancée under *any* circumstances?"

"Oh, yes, my lord. If your passionate nature was involved, you would pursue her into the gates of Hell itself."

He grimaced. "A very poetic image."

"However, sir, you did *not* pursue Juliana that night last year. Therefore, we are left with the results of your decision."

"Explain to me again why I should resolve the Burnleys' financial difficulties," he said grimly. "I do not seem to be able to grasp the crux of your argument."

"It is really very simple, sir. If you had pursued the lovers that night, the chances are excellent that Juliana would be your countess today and would, therefore, possess no financial worries of any sort. For his part, Roland would still be in his father's good graces and no doubt happily spending his plump quarterly allowance on tailors and boot makers."

He shook his head in wonder. "Your logic leaves me quite speechless, Miss Lodge."

"But you cannot fault it, can you?"

"Do you know what I think, Miss Lodge? I do not believe that you leaped to your conclusion through any process involving logic or sound reasoning."

"No?"

215

"I think you are pleading Juliana's case because of those damned delicate sensibilities you claim you do not possess."

"Rubbish."

"Admit it. Your soft heart was touched by Juliana's tears." He was amused. "As I recall, she has a talent for being able to cry on cue."

"She did not cry."

He raised his brows.

"Very well, mayhap there were a few tears," Elenora admitted. "But I assure you, she was quite sincere. I do not think that anything except the most extreme desperation could have induced her to approach me." She took a breath. "My lord, I realize that your private affairs are none of my business."

"A very insightful observation, Miss Lodge. I could not agree more."

"Nevertheless—"

"Nevertheless, you *are* interfering in my affairs," he finished for her. "No doubt because you simply cannot help yourself. Indeed, I believe that it is in your very nature to intrude into my private business, just as it is in the nature of a cat to bedevil a hapless mouse that it has cornered."

She flushed, shaken by his opinion of her.

"You are no mouse," she managed weakly. She did not add that if there was a hunting cat in this vehicle, he was seated directly across from her.

Arthur, however, did not appear convinced of her assertion. "You are certain that I am not playing mouse to your cat?"

"My lord." She swallowed, tightened her fingers together in her lap and glowered. "You are teasing me."

"Hmm."

He *was* teasing her, she assured herself. There was nothing for it but to ignore the deliberate provocation and conclude her plea on Juliana's behalf. She had promised the young woman that she would see this through.

"What I am attempting to convey here," she continued, "is that you are involved in this unfortunate muddle, whether you like it or not. Furthermore, it is within your power to set matters straight."

"Mmm." The prospect of setting matters straight did not appear to hold great appeal to him. He pinned her with a steely look. "Given your interest in the subject of finances, I'm sure you comprehend that if I were to offer young Roland a share in a consortium, I would also be obliged to loan him the money to make the purchase?"

"Well, yes, I do see that, but he could repay the loan with what he makes off the investment."

"And if it transpires that the investment founders? What then, my clever little cat? I must suffer Roland's loss as well as my own?"

"By all accounts, your investment schemes rarely, if ever, fail. Margaret and Mr. Fleming assured me that you are a genius when it comes to finances. Sir, I feel confident that, although you are not pleased with this turn of events, you will nevertheless give Juliana's appeal close consideration and decide to go to her rescue."

"You are confident of that, are you?" he asked politely.

"Yes."

He returned his attention to the scene outside the window for an uncomfortable length of time.

She was beginning to grow restless, wondering if she had pushed him too far.

217

"I suppose I should do something about the mess in which Roland and Juliana find themselves," he said after a while.

She exhaled a soft sigh of relief and gave him an approving smile. "I knew you were too kind to turn your back on Juliana and Roland, sir."

"It is not a question of compassion," he said, sounding resigned, "but rather of guilt."

"Guilt?" She considered that, lips pursed, and then shook her head. "That is putting too fine a point on it, sir. The entire affair was simply a very unfortunate mistake that you can correct, but I don't think you should feel guilt-ridden about events."

"Asking for Juliana's hand was, indeed, a disastrous miscalculation on my part, and it is true that I chose not to chase after her the night she eloped. But those two factors are not the source of my guilt."

She was not reassured by this twist in the conversation. Alarmed that he might be taking on more blame than was strictly necessary, she reached out unthinkingly and touched his knee.

"You must not be too hard on yourself, sir," she said very earnestly. "Juliana was very young, very sheltered and, I suspect, somewhat lacking in common sense. She did not realize that you would make an excellent husband."

There was a short silence.

He looked down at her gloved fingertips resting lightly on his leg.

She followed his gaze and froze at the realization of just how intimately she was touching him. She could feel the heat of his body penetrating the soft kid leather of her glove.

They both contemplated her hand on his leg for what seemed an eternity. Elenora could not move. It was as if she had been placed in a mesmeric trance. A strange panic sizzled through her.

She recovered an instant later. Mortified, she hastily removed her hand and folded it neatly in her lap. It seemed to her that the tips of her fingers continued to burn.

She cleared her throat. "As I was saying, there is no need to feel outright guilt in this affair. After all, you did nothing wrong."

He looked at her. She was startled to see that his eyes gleamed with wry humor.

"That is a matter of opinion," he said. "Who do you think was responsible for working out every damned detail of the plan for that elopement?"

"I beg your pardon?" And then comprehension struck. "You arranged for the pair to run off that night?"

"I took care of everything." He shook his head. "Right down to selecting the date, purchasing a ladder of the correct length to reach Juliana's bedroom window, and ordering the coach and team from the livery stable."

Chapter Twenty-One

She stared at him in astonishment. He allowed himself to savor the expression. It was not often that he was able to disconcert her like this.

But as amusing as it was to see her flustered and amazed, the sensation was nowhere near as satisfying as had been the touch of her fingers on his thigh a moment before. It seemed to him that he could still feel the warmth of her hand through the fabric of his trousers.

Elenora's shock turned to wonder. "Of course." Her lips twitched and then curved into a laughing smile. "You were the one who drew up that infamous escape plan, not Roland."

"Someone had to do it for him. It was obvious that young Burnley was quite passionate about rescuing his lady from the doom that awaited her. And an elopement was the only way I could escape the tangle without humiliating Juliana and her family."

"How on earth did you convince Roland to accept a

plot that you had crafted? He must have considered you his arch enemy."

"Quite true. I believe that I was very much the devil incarnate to him. I still am, for that matter. Bennett Fleming was my assistant in the matter."

"Of course." Her eyes sparkled with delight.

"He was the one who took Roland aside and convinced him that the only way to rescue Juliana was to run off with her. When Roland appeared enthusiastic but bewildered about how to go about it, Bennett gave him the strategy I had concocted." He thought about the entire day and a half he had been obliged to devote to creating the plan. "I wrote out every instruction. Do you have any notion of how complicated it is to stage a successful elopement?"

She laughed. The sound tugged at his insides. He had an almost irresistible urge to reach across the narrow space between them, pull her into his arms and kiss her until her amusement was transformed into desire.

The words she had spoken a short while before echoed again and again in his head. *Juliana was very young, very sheltered and, I suspect, somewhat lacking in common sense. She did not realize that you would make an excellent husband.*

"I must admit, I have never had occasion to consider what would be required in an elopement," she replied cheerfully. "But now that I stop and ponder the subject, I can see that it could get complicated."

"You may take it from me, it is not a simple task. Roland clearly had no notion of how to go about the business. I had a nasty feeling that if I left it in his hands, he would make such a complete hash of the business that Juliana's father would get wind of it in time to stop the pair before the, uh, damage was done, as it were."

"You mean before Juliana had been compromised to a degree that left no alternative but marriage."

"Yes. In the end it was a near thing, in spite of all my careful planning."

"The storm." She chuckled. "In spite of all your foresight, you could not anticipate such a dramatic change in the weather."

"I assumed that Roland would have the good sense to postpone the elopement until the roads were passable." He sighed. "But, no, the young hothead insisted upon sticking to every single detail of the scheme, including the time and date. You cannot imagine my dread when I got word that the pair had fled into the teeth of the gale. I was certain that Juliana's father would find them and drag his daughter home before she and Roland had thoroughly compromised themselves."

"That concern no doubt explains the reports that you played cards until dawn."

"It was one of the longest nights of my entire life," he assured her. "I had to do something to keep my mind off the possibility that my plan would fail."

He felt the carriage rumble to a halt. They could not possibly be home. It was much too soon. He wanted a little more time in the close confines of the carriage; a little more time to be alone with Elenora.

He glanced out the window and felt a whisper of unease when he realized that they had not halted in Rain Street. Rather, the carriage had stopped near a park. Another vehicle had drawn up alongside.

Arthur raised the cushion beside his leg and reached into the hidden compartment for the pistol he kept there. Across the way, Elenora's brows drew together in a concerned frown. He felt her tension, but she did not ask any bothersome questions.

The trap door in the roof opened. Jenks looked down from his perch on the box. "A hack just hailed me, sir. Says his passenger spotted this carriage and wishes a word with ye. What do ye want me to do?"

Arthur watched the door of the hackney fly open. Hitchins jumped down to the pavement and strode toward the carriage.

"It's all right, Jenks." Arthur put the pistol back into the compartment and lowered the cushioned lid. "That man works for me."

"Aye, sir." The trap closed.

Hitchins opened the door of the cab.

"M'lord," he said. Then he noticed Elenora. A broad grin crossed his rugged face. "A pleasure to see ye again, ma'am. And looking very fine, indeed."

She smiled. "Good evening, Mr. Hitchins."

"I told his lordship yesterday when he came to Bow Street to hire me that I remembered you well. I knew that day I escorted you out of your house that you would come about. You've got spirit, ma'am. And now look at ye, riding in a fine carriage and engaged to an earl."

Elenora laughed. "I can hardly believe it myself, Mr. Hitchins."

Arthur thought about the rest of what Hitchins had told him the day before, when they had talked about the time he had been hired to assist in the eviction. *"It was an amazing thing, sir. Amazing. There she was, sir, about to lose everything she possessed, but Miss Lodge's first concern was for the servants and the rest of 'em that worked on the farm. Not many people in her situation would have worried about anyone else at a time like that . . ."*

Arthur looked at Hitchins. "What have you come to tell me?"

The Runner swiveled his head back to Arthur, his manner very serious now. "I went to yer club, like you instructed, sir, but the porter told me you'd left. He said you were off to a fancy-dress ball and gave me the address. I was on my way there when we passed your carriage."

"Does this concern Ibbitts?"

"Aye, sir. You said I was to tell ye if anyone came to see him. Well, someone did. A gentleman went to his lodgings not two hours past. He waited there until Ibbitts returned from a tavern. They were private for a time. After a while, the visitor left. Had a hackney waiting in the street."

A cold mist sleeted through Arthur's veins. "Did you get a look at Ibbitts's visitor?" he asked in a voice that made Hitchins raise his brows.

"No, sir. I was not close enough to see his face. Nor did he notice me. You told me that I was not to let anyone know that I was watching Ibbitts."

"What can you tell me about his visitor?"

Hitchins's face scrunched in deep concentration. "As I said, he arrived in a hack. The light was bad, but I could see that he had on a cloak with the hood pulled up over his head. When he left he was in a great hurry."

Arthur realized that Elenora was following the conversation very intently.

"You're certain the visitor was a man, Mr. Hitchins?" she asked.

"Aye," Hitchins said. "I could tell that from the way he moved."

"What of Ibbitts?" Arthur asked. "Did he leave his lodgings again?"

"No, sir. As far as I know, he's still inside. I went around to the back of the building and checked the window. There's no light inside. Expect he went to bed."

Arthur glanced at Elenora. "I will see you home and then I will pay a call on Ibbitts. I intend to find out everything I can about his visitor this evening."

"What if he will not tell you the truth?" she asked.

"I do not think it will be difficult to get Ibbitts to talk," he said calmly. "I know his sort. All I need do is offer him money."

"It is quite unnecessary to escort me back to Rain Street before you talk to Ibbitts," Elenora said quickly. "Indeed, it would be a great waste of time. The streets are clogged with traffic and the journey will no doubt cause you a considerable delay."

"I do not think—" he began.

She did not allow him to finish. "It is the most reasonable course of action under the circumstances. I can see that you are eager to interview Ibbitts. There is no reason why I cannot accompany you."

"She's got a point, sir," Hitchins offered helpfully.

They were right, Arthur knew. Nevertheless, had Elenora been any other lady of his acquaintance, he would not have even considered taking her into that part of town. But she was not any other female. Elenora would not faint at the sight of a drunken tavern patron in the street or a prostitute plying her trade in an alley. Between Jenks, Hitchins and himself, she would be quite safe.

"Very well," he finally agreed, "provided you give me your word that you will remain in the carriage while I speak with Ibbitts."

"But I might be of some assistance in the interview."

"You will not enter Ibbitts's lodgings, and that is final."

She did not look pleased, but she did not argue. "We are wasting time, sir."

"Indeed we are." He shifted position on the seat. "Come with us, Hitchins."

226

"Aye, sir." Hitchins hauled himself up into the carriage and sat down.

Arthur gave the address to Jenks. He then turned down the interior carriage lamps and lowered the curtains so that no one in a passing carriage could see Elenora.

"It was a brilliant notion to set Mr. Hitchins to watch Ibbitts, sir," she said.

Arthur almost smiled. The glowing admiration in her voice was absurdly gratifying.

Chapter Twenty-Two

The carriage clattered to a halt in the darkened street outside Ibbitts's lodgings some thirty minutes later. Elenora had been correct about the traffic, Arthur thought, following Hitchins out of the vehicle. Escorting her back to the house in Rain Street would have cost him upward of an hour in lost time.

Before closing the door of the carriage, he looked back at her, intending to remind her of her vow to remain in the vehicle.

"Be careful, Arthur," she said before he could speak. Her face was pale in the deep shadows cast by the hood of her domino. "I do not like the feel of this situation."

The urgency in her voice took him by surprise. He studied her as she sat in the darkness. Until this moment she had seemed quite calm and utterly sure of herself. This attack of nerves surprised him.

"Do not be anxious," he said quietly. "Jenks and Hitchins will watch over you."

"It is not *my* safety that I am concerned about." She leaned toward him and lowered her voice. "It is just that for some reason I have developed a very nasty feeling about this business. Please do not go in there alone. I do not need the protection of both men. I beg you to take one of them with you."

"I have my pistol."

"Pistols are notorious for misfiring at inopportune moments."

This show of unease was uncharacteristic of her, he thought. He did not have time to talk her out of her agitation. It was easier to placate her.

"Very well, if it will soothe your nerves I will take Hitchins with me and leave Jenks to guard you and the carriage."

"Thank you," she said.

Her relief and gratitude worried him more than anything she had said.

He closed the door of the carriage and looked at Jenks. "Give us a lantern. Hitchins and I will go inside. You will stay here to watch Miss Lodge."

"Aye, m'lord." Jenks handed down one of the lanterns.

Hitchins lit the lamp and then took a wicked-looking knife out of a deep pocket.

Arthur glanced at the gleaming blade. "Kindly keep that concealed unless it becomes absolutely necessary to employ it."

"Whatever you say, sir." Hitchins obligingly slipped the knife into its hidden sheath. "Ibbitts's lodgings are upstairs at the back."

Arthur led the way into a dingy front hall. No crack of light showed under the door of the single ground-floor room.

"A couple of tavern girls live there," Hitchins

explained. "Saw them leave several hours ago. They won't be back until near dawn, like as not."

Arthur nodded and went swiftly up the steps. Hitchins followed close behind with the lantern.

The short upstairs hall lay shrouded in intense darkness. Hitchins raised the lantern. The weak yellow glare fell upon a closed door.

Arthur crossed the hall, made a fist and knocked sharply.

There was no response.

He tried the knob. It turned easily in his hand. Too easily.

He knew then that Elenora's apprehension had been well-warranted. There was something very wrong here.

He opened the door.

The stench of spilled blood, burnt powder and death wafted out of the darkness.

"Bloody hell," Hitchins whispered.

Arthur took the lantern from him and held it higher. The flaring light fell across the body on the floor. A portion of Ibbitts's face had been destroyed, but there was more than enough left to confirm his identity. The blood on the front of his shirt made it clear that he had been shot twice.

"Whoever the villain was, he wanted to make certain of his work," Arthur said quietly.

"Aye, that he did." Hitchins glanced around the small space. "Looks like there was a bit of a struggle."

Arthur studied the overturned chair. "Yes." He walked closer to the body. The light glared on the blade of a knife that lay near Ibbitts's outflung arm. "He tried to defend himself."

"No blood on his blade." Hitchins made a tut-tutting

sound. "He missed his target, poor bastard. Didn't even nick the villain."

Arthur crouched to take a closer look at the knife. As Hitchins had noted, there was no trace of blood. Several long, black threads were caught at the end where the blade was attached to the hilt.

"Looks like he snagged the killer's coat."

He straightened, an edgy dread tightening his innards. He thought of Elenora waiting downstairs in the carriage and turned immediately toward the door.

"Come, Hitchins, we must be off. We shall arrange for the authorities to be notified anonymously about this death. Whatever happens, I do not want Miss Lodge's name involved. Is that understood?"

"Aye, m'lord." Hitchins followed him out the door. "Set your mind at ease, sir. I've got too much respect for Miss Lodge to see her troubled in any way. She's been through enough."

The admiration in Hitchins's voice was genuine. Arthur was certain that the Runner could be trusted in this affair.

He went quickly down the stairs, cursing himself with each step. He had been a fool to let Elenora convince him to bring her along. It was one thing for her to risk being seen with him in a less-than-pristine part of town. The worst that could result was a bit of scandalized talk that would do no great harm.

It would be another matter altogether if someone noticed her sitting in a carriage in front of the scene of a murder.

When he and Hitchins reached the front hall, he turned down the lamp before moving outside.

"Do not run," he said to Hitchins. "But for God's sake, do not dawdle."

"Wasn't planning to take my time, sir."

They stepped outside and went quickly to the waiting carriage. Hitchins bounded up onto the box to join Jenks. Arthur heard him explaining the situation in low tones.

Jenks had the vehicle in motion before Arthur got the door closed.

"What's wrong?" Elenora demanded.

"Ibbitts is dead." He dropped down onto the seat across from her. "Murdered."

"Dear heaven." She hesitated a second. "The man Hitchins saw earlier? The one who waited for Ibbitts and then left in a great hurry?"

"Most likely."

"But who would kill Ibbitts, and why?"

"I suspect the villain got the information he wanted and then decided that death was the only way to keep Ibbitts quiet."

He kept the pistol in his hand and watched the street, searching each darkened doorway, trying to make out the shapes in the shadows. Was the killer still here, lurking in an alley, perhaps? Had he seen Elenora?

"Well, this certainly seems to prove that someone, is, indeed, aware that you are investigating your great-uncle's murder," she said quietly.

"Yes." He tightened his grip on the pistol. "This affair has become a game of hide-and-seek. If only Hitchins had gotten a closer look at the villain when he entered and left Ibbitts's lodgings."

"Was there no clue left at the scene of the murder?"

"I did not take time to conduct a thorough search. The only thing that was obvious was that Ibbitts tried to defend himself with his knife."

"Ah, did he cut the villain, do you think?" Enthusiasm laced her voice. "If he managed to wound his attacker, there may be some hope."

"Unfortunately, I fear that he only snagged the killer's cloak. There were a few black threads stuck to the knife, but no blood."

There was a strange silence from the opposite seat.

"Black threads?" Elenora repeated in an odd voice. "From a long cloak?"

"Yes. I suspect there was a struggle and Ibbitts's blade got tangled in the fabric. But I cannot see where that information will aid us. If only there were another witness."

Elenora took an audible breath. "I think there may well be another witness, sir."

"Who, pray tell?"

"Me," she whispered, sounding rather stunned. "I believe that I may have danced with the killer very soon after he committed the murder."

Chapter Twenty-Three

She sat in the chair nearest the fire, trying to warm her-self while Arthur paced the width of the library. She could feel the restless, prowling energy radiating from him.

"You are certain about the rip in his cloak?" he demanded.

"Yes. Quite certain." She held her hands out to the blaze, but for some reason the heat did not seem to penetrate very far into the room. "My fingers brushed against it."

The great house was hushed and dark, except for the fire that burned here in the library. Arthur had not awakened any of the servants. Margaret had not returned.

Arthur had said very little after she had delivered her startling news. The journey home had been con-ducted in near silence. She knew that he had spent the time pondering the information she had supplied, no doubt drawing up theories and arriving at possible conclusions. She had respected his deep concentration.

But as soon as they walked into the front hall, he had escorted her into the library and lit the fire.

"We must talk," he had said, tossing his black domino across the back of a chair.

"Yes."

Arthur unknotted his cravat with quick, impatient fingers and allowed the neckcloth to hang carelessly down the front of his jacket. He began to prowl the room.

"Did you comment upon his torn garment?" he asked.

"No. I said nothing about it. In truth, I did not wish to carry on a conversation with him." She shuddered. "At that point, it was my great desire to be finished with the dance as quickly as possible."

"He did not speak to you?"

"Not a single word." She caught her lip between her teeth, thinking back to the scene in the ballroom. "I suspect he did not want to provide me with such a significant clue to his identity."

Arthur shrugged out of both his coat and waistcoat and dropped the garments on top of a round pedestal table.

She took a deep breath and concentrated very intently on the flames. The man did not appear to realize that he was practically undressing in front of her.

Calm yourself, she thought. Arthur was merely making himself comfortable. A gentleman had a perfect right to do so in the privacy of his own home. His mind was clearly on murder, not passion. He did not realize the effect he was having on her nerves.

"That could mean that you have met him

somewhere else," Arthur continued. "He may have feared that you would recognize him if he spoke."

"Yes, it's quite possible. The only thing I can say with any certainty is that I'm quite sure that I have never before danced with him."

"How can you be so sure of that?"

She risked another glance at him. He was still moving about the room with the restless energy of a caged lion.

"It is difficult to explain," she said. "When he first came toward me through the crowd, I thought he was you."

That brought Arthur to a halt. "What the devil made you believe that?"

"He wore the same style of domino and a mask that was almost identical to yours."

"Damnation. He *intended* for you to be confused. The similarity in costumes cannot have been a coincidence."

She considered that briefly and shook her head. "I disagree. It could most certainly have been a coincidence. There were any number of gentlemen at the ball who wore very similar cloaks and masks."

"Did you mistake any other man for me this evening?"

She smiled ruefully at that insightful question. "No, as a matter of fact, I did not. Just the man in the ripped domino and only for a short time."

"How could you be certain that it was not me?"

She thought she heard an odd mix of curiosity and suspicion in his words, as if he was asking another question entirely. *Would you really know me in a dark and crowded room? No one knows me that well . . .*

I do, she thought. But she could hardly say that.

She pondered what she could tell him that would

237

sound logical. She certainly could not explain that the killer's scent had not been anything like his own. Such a remark would be far too personal, too intimate. It would reveal just how very aware of him she was.

"He was not the same height," she said instead. "I have danced with you, sir. Your shoulder is somewhat above his." She could rest her head on Arthur's shoulder, she thought wistfully. "And rather more broad." Arthur's shoulders were sleekly muscled and very inviting. "Also, his fingers were longer than yours."

Arthur's expression darkened. "You noticed his fingers?"

"Indeed, sir. A woman is generally very much aware of a gentleman's hands when he touches her. Is the reverse not true for a man?"

He made a noncommittal response that sounded like "Huh."

"Oh, and there were two other things I noticed," she continued. "He wore a ring on his left hand and a pair of Hessians."

"Like a thousand other men in town," he muttered. Then he glanced back at her, one black brow arched. "You noticed his boots, also?"

"As soon as I realized that he was not you, I became curious about his identity." She looked into the fire. "Whoever he was, he was definitely not an elderly man. He danced with a fashionable ease about his movements. There was no stiffness or hesitation in him. I can assure you he was not of your great-uncle's generation."

"That is a very useful piece of information," he said slowly. "I shall have to give it some close thought. Did you happen to note anything else?"

"It is difficult to explain, but at the time I sensed that there was something odd about his manner. He appeared to be in the grip of an unwholesome excitement."

"He had just come from killing a man." Arthur stopped in front of the window and looked out at the moonlit garden. "The horrid thrill of his deed was no doubt still upon him, riding him hard. So he sought you out and danced with you."

"It seems quite bizarre, does it not?" She shivered. "One would think that after committing murder, one would want to go directly home and take a hot bath, not go to a ball and dance."

"He did not go to the Fambridge ball to dance with just any woman," Arthur said evenly. "He went there to waltz with you."

She shivered. "I must admit it did appear that he deliberately sought me out. But I cannot understand why he would do such a thing."

"I can."

She turned her head very quickly, astonished by his bleak statement. "You comprehend his motive?"

"Tonight he no doubt learned from Ibbitts that I am hunting him. In his arrogance, he decided to celebrate what he perceived to be a triumph over me."

She pursed her lips. "Mayhap you are right, sir, but that does not explain why he danced with me."

Arthur turned to face her. She almost stopped breathing when she saw the savage anger that blazed in his eyes.

"Do you not understand?" he said. "There is a very ancient, very foul tradition among men who wage war against each other. More often than not, the winners seek to proclaim their victories by taking possession of their opponents' women."

"Possession? Sir, you speak of rape." She leaped to her feet. "I assure you, it was only a dance."

"And I assure you, Miss Lodge, that in the villain's mind that dance was symbolic of another act entirely."

"That is ridiculous," she began stoutly. Then she recalled how much she had disliked the feel of the stranger's hand on her waist. She took a deep breath. "Regardless of how he viewed the situation, from my perspective, it was nothing more than a short waltz with an unpleasant partner."

"I know. But your opinion is rather beside the point."

"I disagree," she said fiercely.

He acted as if he had not heard her. "I must concoct another plan."

She could tell that he was already formulating his new strategy. "Very well. What shall we do, sir?"

"You will do nothing, Elenora, except go up to your room to pack. Your employment in this household ends tonight. I will send your wages to you."

"What?" Outraged, she stared at him. "You are letting me go?"

"Yes. I intend to send you away to one of my estates until this affair is ended."

Raw panic jolted through her. She was not going back to the country. Her new life was here in London. Whatever happened, she would not allow herself to be packed off to some remote village estate where she would have to cool her heels for heaven knew how long.

But getting hysterical would only make matters worse, she told herself. This was Arthur. Logic worked best with him.

She fought to keep her voice even and controlled. "You intend to send me away merely because the villain danced with me?"

"I told you, to him it was more than a dance."

She flushed. "For heaven's sake, sir, it is not as though he forced himself upon me."

"What he did," Arthur said in a startlingly rough voice, "was demonstrate that he sees you as a pawn in this game that he is playing with me. I will not permit him to use you in any way."

She must make allowances for his rigid manner, she told herself. After all, he was attempting to protect her.

"I appreciate what you are trying to do," she said, striving to maintain her patience, "but it is much too late. I am involved in this affair, whether you like it or not. My lord, I fear that you are not thinking with your customary clarity."

He watched her very steadily. "Indeed?"

At least she had his attention, she thought. "Sir, you are obviously deeply concerned about my safety. That is very gallant of you. But what makes you think that the villain will forget about me if you send me away to rusticate in the country?"

"Once he understands that I have changed my strategy, he will lose interest in you."

"I do not think that you can depend upon that outcome. Have you considered the possibility that the killer may well decide that I possess even more valuable information about you and your schemes than Ibbitts did?"

There was a short, shattering silence. She saw the grim comprehension on Arthur's face and knew that he could not deny her logic.

"I will provide you with an armed guard," he said.

"You could do that, but it would not necessarily stop the villain. He moves freely in Society. What am I to do? Avoid all gentlemen? And for how long? Weeks? Months? You cannot keep me under guard indefinitely.

No, I am better off here with you, helping you find the killer."

"Damnation, Elenora—"

"And what of Margaret? If I am no longer conveniently at hand, the killer may well try to use her instead. After all, she is not only a member of this household but a member of your family. Removing me from the game may make her the villain's next target."

"Damnation," he said again, very softly this time. "You are correct. I have not been thinking clearly."

"Only because you have been under a great deal of stress this evening," she assured him. "You must not be too hard on yourself. Walking in on the scene of a murder would have a nasty effect on anyone's reasoning processes."

His mouth curved in a strange smile. "Yes, of course. I should have realized that was the source of my poor logic tonight."

"Do not concern yourself," she said, trying to sound bracing. "I'm certain that your customary powers of reason will return soon."

"I can only hope that is the case."

She did not trust that tone, she thought.

"Sir, let me remind you that I have been very helpful in this investigation," she continued, anxious to get back to the important matter. "If you continue to allow me to assist you, we will likely solve this puzzle far more quickly than if you work alone."

"I'm not at all sure of that," he muttered.

"Furthermore, if you keep me by your side in my role as your fiancée, not only will you be able to protect me, but the killer will assume that we know nothing more now than we did before Ibbitts was murdered."

His jaw tightened. "That is the truth, unfortunately."

"No, it is not the truth." It was her turn to pace the room. "I paid close attention when the villain danced with me. There is a very good chance that I might recognize him if I were to come into close contact with him again. At the very least, I can rule out any number of gentlemen based on their general age, height and physique and the way they move, not to mention the shape of their hands."

He narrowed his eyes, and she knew that she had made her point.

"Don't you see, sir?" She gave him an encouraging smile. "If we continue with your original plan, we will have an edge because the killer will never realize that we made a connection between my waltz partner and Ibbitts's killer. He won't know that we are aware of a few important physical details about him."

"You are right," he admitted. He flexed one hand in a small gesture of anger and frustration. "If I send you away immediately, he may suspect that we know he danced with you. If he thinks we know that much, he may wonder if we know more than we do."

"And that, in turn, would cause him to be more cautious. Surely it is in our best interests if he is emboldened instead, and becomes more reckless."

He considered her for a long, meditative moment. "Very well. You have convinced me that you would be no safer in the country than you are under this roof."

She stopped in front of the spiral staircase and smiled in relief. "Precisely."

"However, from this moment on, neither you nor Margaret will leave this house alone. Whenever either of you go out you will be accompanied by me or one of the male servants."

"What about Bennett Fleming? Surely he is an

acceptable companion? We know he is not the killer. Aside from all else, he is simply too short."

Arthur hesitated and then nodded once. "I think it is safe to say that Bennett is no mad alchemist bent on conducting a crazed experiment. I would trust him with my life. Very well, he qualifies as a suitable escort. I shall speak with him as soon as possible. He must understand that there is some danger afoot so that he will keep a close watch on you and Margaret whenever you are with him."

"Yes. We must also tell Margaret about this secret investigation."

A thick, heavy silence gripped the library. Elenora became acutely aware of the crackle and sputter of the flames. The discussion had ended. They had arrived at a compromise, one that would allow her to stay in this house and help Arthur find the killer.

The sensible thing to do now was go upstairs and seek her bed.

She glanced at the door but could not muster the will to walk toward it.

For his part, Arthur showed no interest in leaving, either. He continued to contemplate her with his fascinating eyes.

"Hitchins was right about you," he said after the silence had stretched to the breaking point. "You are a very strong-minded, very determined woman, Miss Elenora Lodge. You have spirit. I do not believe that, in the whole of my life, I have engaged in as many quarrels as I have with you in the past few days."

Her heart sank. He considered her a quarrelsome female. Everyone knew that men did not find difficult women attractive.

She cleared her throat. "I believe that we have had a

244

few heated discussions, sir, but I do not think it is fair to say that we have *quarreled*."

"Heated discussions. Is that what you call them? Well, I suspect that we are fated to have any number of them so long as you live in this household. A daunting thought, is it not?"

"You are teasing me, my lord. I doubt that such a prospect will cause either of us to tremble in fear."

His mouth lifted faintly at the corner. "Is there anything at all that would cause you to quake in fear, Miss Lodge?"

She gestured in what she hoped appeared to be blithe unconcern. The truth was, she was trembling a little at that very moment, but not in fear. She prayed that he would not notice.

"Any number of things," she assured him.

"Indeed." He started toward her with a deliberate tread, his voice darkening with sensuality. "What about the possibility that if we continue to work together in such an intimate fashion, we may do more than engage in a series of heated discussions? Is that one of the things that could cause you to quiver and shake, Miss Lodge?"

She met his gaze, saw the rising heat in them and nearly melted into the carpet.

"We are both exceptionally strong-minded individuals," she said, feeling oddly breathless. "I am certain that we are each quite capable of keeping our association entirely professional in nature."

He halted in front of her, the toes of his boots mere inches from the tips of her shoes. If she took a step back she would come up hard against the wrought-iron balusters of the spiral staircase.

"We may both be capable of maintaining a professional relationship," he said very softly. "But what if we choose not to do so? What happens then, Miss Lodge? Will you tremble?"

Her mouth went dry. Excitement snapped through her. She felt the knee-weakening warmth pooling in her lower body. She could not bring herself to look away from the smoldering fires in his eyes.

"I do not find myself trembling at that prospect either, sir," she whispered.

"No?" He raised his arms and reached around and behind her to grip the balusters on either side of her head. "I envy you, Miss Lodge. Because every time I contemplate the prospect of an intimate connection with you, I do tremble."

He was not touching her, but he had effectively imprisoned her. He was standing so close she could breathe in his unique, intriguing scent. Her head began to spin. She had to dampen her lips with the tip of her tongue before she could speak.

"Rubbish," she managed. That sounded rather weak, she decided. Unable to resist the very closeness of him, she touched his jaw with her fingertips. "You are not even quivering."

"That statement only proves how little you know about me."

He did not take his hands off the bars on either side of her head, but he leaned forward until his mouth hovered just above hers.

He intended to kiss her, she thought, but he was giving her time to protest or bolt for the door.

A wild, reckless rush of sensation swept through her. The last thing she wanted to do tonight was run from him. Quite the opposite. Everything in her yearned to plunge into his embrace and allow herself to experience the mysteries of the passion that she knew she would find in his arms.

She flattened her palms on the front of his white linen shirt. When she touched him she heard a low, hungry groan deep in his chest. The knowledge that she had such a powerful effect on him made her feel as though she were a sorceress.

She sensed rather than saw his hands tighten into fists around the iron bars, and then his mouth closed over hers.

Sensation whipped through her; a glorious, heady, dizzying whirlpool of passion. She knew that if she did not explore these thrilling emotions with him she would carry the regret with her for the rest of her life.

Her hands slipped upward to encircle his neck. He reacted immediately, crowding against her until she was pressed tightly between his aroused body and the staircase. He gripped the balusters as though they were the only things that kept them both fastened to the earth.

"Elenora." He drew a deep breath. "My brain tells me that this is not a good idea. But I do not seem to be able to listen to any more logic tonight."

"There are other things in the world besides logic, sir." She smiled up at him. "Things that are equally important."

"Until tonight, I did not believe that."

He kissed her again, deeply this time.

She responded eagerly, parting her lips for him and pushing her fingers through his dark hair.

He took his right hand off the baluster next to her left ear and began to unfasten the bodice of her gown. It fell away with shocking ease. When she felt his palm close over her left breast, surprise and pleasure rushed through her. A strange, delicious tension began to build deep inside. She heard herself utter a soft, husky cry.

He raised his head and looked down at her breast cradled in his palm.

"You are lovely." He used his thumb to circle her nipple.

She wanted to touch him just as intimately. She lowered her hands and went to work unfastening his shirt. He muttered something. She could not make out the words, but the exciting promise in them was crystal clear.

By the time she got the garment open, her pulse was racing, causing wave after wave of tiny shivers to pulse through her. She drew her fingertips down his bare chest, entranced by the sensual feel of his firm skin and the texture of the hair that covered it.

Unable to resist, she kissed his throat and then his shoulder.

He shuddered.

His response encouraged her to move her palm lower, gliding across the sleekly muscled expanse of bare flesh until she was stopped by the waistband of his trousers.

He made a sound that was half groan and half muffled laugh and captured her exploring hand.

"We are playing with fire," he said against the curve of her shoulder. "It is not a sport in which I often indulge. But tonight I am convinced that some flames are worth the risk."

She was not certain what he meant by that. But before she could query him on the subject, he released the other bar behind her head and picked her up, holding her snugly against his chest. The skirts of her partially unfastened gown spilled over his arms and brushed against the back of a chair.

He carried her swiftly across the room and put her down on the carpet in front of the fire. Before she could reorient herself to this new position, he lowered himself alongside her.

Cradling her in his left arm, he seized a fistful of her skirts in his other hand and crumpled the soft fabric all the way up past her thighs. She stopped breathing when she realized that she was exposed to him in the firelight.

A woman of the world would no doubt find this quite normal, she reminded herself. And it was certainly exciting to feel the heat of the flames on her bare skin.

She closed her eyes very tightly against the bright, shivery thrills that were tripping through her. His hand left her thigh. She realized that he was fumbling with the opening of his trousers.

A moment later she felt the firm thrust of his erection pushing against her bare hip. Curious, she opened her eyes just far enough to take a quick peek. She had seen aroused farm animals but she had never seen a man in such a condition.

The sight of his fully erect body rendered her nearly speechless.

"Good heavens," she gasped before she could stop herself. He was big, much bigger than she had expected. And so very *male.*

"What's wrong?" He asked, bending his head to kiss her throat. "Are you all right?"

"Yes, yes, of course."

She shut her eyes again very quickly. She wanted to ask him if such size was normal, but she feared that the question might disturb his current mood. She certainly did not want him to think that she was another Juliana, terrified of his lovemaking. She would have to be subtle about this, she thought.

Before she could summon the right words for such a

delicate inquiry, she got another jolt when he casually removed a linen handkerchief from a pocket and placed it to one side. Did he expect to sneeze in the middle of this business? she wondered.

But before she could ask about the handkerchief or the matter of size, his fingers threaded their way through the nest of hair that concealed her most private parts.

And then he was touching her in the most intimate fashion, setting off a delicious aching sensation. She twisted against him, seeking something more, something she could not describe.

"You are ready for me, are you not?" he said against her mouth. "So moist and plump and soft."

"Yes, *yes*." She had no notion of what he meant by those words, but she could give no other answer other than *yes* to him tonight.

He rolled on top of her, separating her thighs with a deliberate pressure of his own. She was aware of his erection probing the damp, throbbing entrance of her body and wondered if it was too late to discuss the question of size.

It was too late. Much too late. He was already easing himself into her body, pushing steadily, filling her until she thought she would burst.

A sharp, unexpected pain splashed through her. Startled, she cried out softly and dug her nails into his back.

"Hell's teeth."

Her eyes snapped open. She found herself looking up into his fierce gaze.

"Elenora." His face was taut with an emotion that might have been anger. "Why didn't you tell me?"

"Tell you what?" She wriggled a bit, aware that her body was already adjusting to his. It was a very tight fit, she concluded, but he did fit. Barely. That was the important thing.

"Why didn't you tell me that you were a virgin?" he said through his teeth.

"Because it wasn't important."

"I consider it important."

"I don't."

"Damnation, I took you to be a lady of some experience in this sort of thing."

She smiled up at him. "I have good news, sir. As of this instant, I am, indeed, a lady of some experience."

"Do not taunt me," he warned. "I am exceedingly annoyed with you."

"Does that mean that you are not going to finish what we have started?"

His face was fierce in the firelight. "I cannot seem to think clearly at the moment."

She speared her fingers through his hair. "Then you must allow me to make the decision for both of us. I would prefer to finish if you feel that you are capable of doing so."

"Capable? I am incapable of doing anything else."

He braced his elbows on the carpet, caught her head between his palms and kissed her ruthlessly. She felt him begin to move, slowly, cautiously within her. She sensed that he was at the limits of his usually exquisite control, and she delighted in the knowledge that she had been the one to push him to this dangerous edge.

He rocked against her, driving himself deeper, moving faster now. The muscles of his back were rigid bands beneath her palms. A sweet tension built inside her. She clutched him closer, eager to explore this new, uncharted territory.

"Elenora. Elenora, I cannot hold back. Forgive me."

Without warning he pulled himself free of her body,

251

reared back on his knees, and grabbed the handker-chief that he had placed conveniently at hand a few minutes before. He wrapped the square of linen around the head of his shaft. His mouth opened on a heavy groan and his eyes narrowed into intense slits as he spent himself.

When it was over, he collapsed, sprawling partway across her breasts, one leg flung over her thighs, his arm curved possessively around her.

She lay quietly for a time, taking in the sensations of the moment; the weight of Arthur's body, the warmth of the fire and the lingering tenderness between her thighs.

Arthur stirred eventually, raising himself on his elbows to look down at her.

"Not quite what you were expecting, was it?" he asked.

"It was . . . interesting," she said.

He winced. "Talk about damning with faint praise."

She had hurt his feelings, she thought. "Parts of the experience were quite . . . stimulating," she assured him.

He bent toward her, resting his forehead on top of hers, and kissed the tip of her nose. "I must apologize, my sweet."

Panic shot through her. She wriggled out from underneath him and sat up quickly, holding the bodice of her gown over her breasts.

She glared at him. "You must not blame yourself, Arthur."

He rolled onto his back, folded his arms behind his head and studied her with an unreadable expression. "No?"

"Of course not. I encouraged you, if you will recall.

My grandmother once told me about certain stimulating sensations that can only be experienced in the arms of a man. I have been curious about those feelings for some time now, and I assure you I was eager to discover the truth of her words."

"You used me to satisfy your curiosity?" He raised his brows. "And here I was under the illusion that you were simply attracted to me."

"I *was* attracted to you." She was horrified that he might think otherwise. "Very intensely attracted. Indeed, I have never been so attracted to a man."

"Kind of you to say so, but I cannot help but think that you are only trying to make me feel somewhat better about what just happened."

"There is no reason for you to feel badly about it, I assure you, sir. It was all my idea."

"You do realize, do you not, that if you had bothered to mention your own lack of experience at some point, things would have progressed in a somewhat different fashion?"

He was not going to let this go. He was still annoyed. She flushed, aware that she was starting to feel the pangs of an emotion that might well prove to be guilt.

She sighed. "Yes, I am well aware that if you had believed me to be inexperienced, your excessively strict sense of responsibility would no doubt have prevented you from making love to me."

A smile ghosted through his eyes. "I didn't say that."

"There is no need for you to speak the words," she muttered. "I am well aware that I had no right to put you into such a position." Anger jumped within her. "But I must tell you that it is extremely irritating to experience such an exciting sensation one moment and then be obliged to feel so much guilt and responsibility about it the next."

He startled her with a wholly unexpected, exceedingly wicked grin. "In that we are in complete agreement, Miss Lodge."

She glared. "Sir, I would remind you yet again that I am not in the same category as the young ladies on the marriage mart this Season. I am not another sweet, innocent, overly sheltered Juliana."

He sat up slowly. "Whatever else you are, Elenora, you are no Juliana."

"Yes, well, I just wanted to make certain that you understood quite clearly that what happened here tonight was in no way your fault. You bear no responsibility whatsoever for any of it."

He considered that for what seemed an eternity. Then he nodded once and rolled to his feet with a smooth, easy movement.

"Do you know, my dear, I believe I do, indeed, concur with you on that point." He went to stand in front of the fire and shoved his shirt back into his trousers. "Very well, you have convinced me. I shall be happy to place the whole weight of the blame on your charming head. I might even go so far as to say that I feel that I have been used."

"No." Shocked, she scrambled to her feet. "No, indeed, I never intended to use you, Arthur."

"Nevertheless, that is what it comes down to, does it not?" Finished with his trousers, he turned around to face her. "You took advantage of my great weakness where you are concerned to explore a stimulating new experience, did you not?"

She felt herself turn very warm. "You are most certainly not weak, sir."

"I appear to be when it comes to you."

"Nonsense."

He held up one palm. "Ah, but you knew full well that I could not resist kissing you. Admit it."

She thought she saw a suspicious gleam in his eyes. Was he laughing at her? No, that made no sense. This conversation was far too serious.

"That is absolutely untrue, sir," she said stiffly. "I had no notion that you could not resist me. Furthermore, I don't believe it for one moment."

"I assure you, it is the truth." He finished adjusting his trousers. "I fear I am merely a hapless victim of your charms."

He was teasing her, she thought. Or was he?

She searched his face, but she could not be certain. She was growing more confused by the moment.

"Hapless is the very last word I would ever employ to describe you, sir," she said.

"Now you are trying to evade the blame by implying that I should have been more resolute and strong-willed." He shook his head as he walked toward her. "You disappoint me, Miss Lodge. I believed you to be far too honorable to try that trick."

Damnation, she thought. She could not figure out what he was about.

"It is not a trick," she said. "Furthermore, I must tell you—"

The muffled sound of the front door opening interrupted her. Voices sounded in the hall. A fresh wave of panic roiled through her. Margaret and Bennett had arrived.

She looked around wildly, seeking escape. Perhaps she could slip out the window into the garden. But then how would she get back inside the house?

"What's the matter, Elenora?" Arthur asked very softly as he fastened his shirt. "Did you fail to plan for the possibility that your night of seduction might be interrupted at an inopportune moment?"

"Do not dare to taunt me, sir." She kept her voice to a hoarse whisper. "They might come in here at any moment. What are we to do?"

He swept her a gallant bow. "Do not fear. Although I am not at all sure that you deserve it, I will save you from the embarrassment of being caught in such an extremely compromising position."

"How?" she asked baldly.

"Leave the details to me."

He collected his domino and carried it to the far end of the room near the window that looked out onto the garden. He shoved the used handkerchief out of sight beneath the folds.

Then he scooped up her costume and draped it over her shoulders.

Taking a firm grasp on her arm, he urged her toward the spiral staircase. She frowned at the balcony that rimmed the library. "You expect me to hide up there?"

"One of the bookcases is actually a hidden door that opens into a linen closet." He hurried her up the narrow steps. "No one has used it in years. I had almost forgotten about it until I realized that it is where Ibbitts must have hidden when he eavesdropped on our conversations."

"A secret panel? Really?"

"Really."

"How thrilling," she breathed, going swiftly up the steps ahead of him. "Just like in a horrid novel."

"I see that you find the notion of a hidden door even more stimulating than my lovemaking."

"Oh, no, truly. It is just that, well, I have never had occasion to make use of a secret doorway."

"Do not try to make excuses. You have battered my delicate sensibilities quite enough for one night."

"If you expect me to take that remark as a jest," she said, "I must tell you that your sense of humor leaves much to be desired."

"What makes you think I am joking?"

On the balcony, he turned to the left, grasped the edge of a bookcase and tugged. Elenora watched, fascinated, as the entire section of shelving slid aside to reveal a darkened linen closet.

"In you go." He ushered her inside. "The door in the closet opens onto the hall very close to your bedchamber. I suggest you make haste before Margaret finishes saying good night to Bennett and makes her way upstairs."

She stepped quickly into the shadows and whirled to face him. "What about you?"

The suspicious gleam disappeared from Arthur's gaze. He turned coolly thoughtful. "I believe that this is an excellent opportunity for me to have a chat with Bennett. I shall ask him to help me keep an eye on you and Margaret."

"Oh, yes, of course."

"Good night, my sweet seductress. Next time I promise to do my utmost to provide you with a more stimulating experience."

He closed the bookcase door in her face before she could recover from the notion of a "next time."

Chapter Twenty-Four

Arthur went back down the spiral staircase, humming very softly to himself. The combination of guilt, panic and the afterglow of his lovemaking in Elenora's glorious golden eyes had been priceless.

High time she accepted the blame for toying with his emotions, he thought cheerfully.

The situation in which they were now embroiled had become stunningly more complex with tonight's events, but in spite of all that had transpired, he was feeling better than he had in a very long time.

Meanwhile, he now had not one but two murders to solve.

At the foot of the staircase he remembered to shove his fingers through his hair, raking it back from his forehead into some semblance of neatness. A quick check of his appearance in the octagonal mirror beside the door assured him that he looked like a man who had been relaxing in the privacy of his library after a busy night on the town.

He surveyed the room. As far as he could tell there was no evidence whatsoever that he had just finished engaging in a bout of wild, reckless passion with his fraudulent fiancée.

He opened the door and went down the corridor, taking his time and making enough noise to ensure that Margaret and Bennett had ample notice of his impending arrival.

The murmur of low voices stopped when he walked into the front hall. Margaret and Bennett were standing very close together. The air of intimacy that surrounded them was unmistakable.

They both looked at him. Margaret's face was flushed. Bennett wore a bedazzled expression.

"Good evening, Arthur," Margaret said brightly. "I didn't know you were still awake."

Arthur inclined his head. "I'm sure you're exhausted and anxious to go upstairs to bed."

"Well, not really—" Margaret began.

Arthur ignored her and looked at Bennett. "I'm having a brandy in the library, sir. Will you join me?"

Bennett tightened his grip on the handle of his walking stick. "Yes, of course."

Margaret frowned, looking distinctly uneasy. "Arthur, why do you want to be private with Bennett? You are not going to embarrass me by asking him to declare his intentions, are you? If so, I would remind you that I am a widow, not a green girl. My personal life is my own."

Arthur sighed. "Yet another female who thinks she should be allowed to make all her own decisions. What the devil is the world coming to, Fleming? At this rate the ladies will soon have no more need of us poor males."

"I am serious, Arthur," Margaret said forcefully.

"It's all right, my dear." Bennett kissed her hand. "St. Merryn and I are old friends, remember? I have no objection whatsoever to joining him for a brandy in his library."

Margaret did not look happy about the situation, but her eyes softened. "Very well. But promise me that you will not allow him to coerce you into making any statements or promises that you do not wish to make."

Bennett patted her hand reassuringly. "Do not worry about me, my dear. I am quite capable of dealing with this matter."

"Yes, of course." Margaret shot Arthur one last warning glance, picked up her skirts and went swiftly up the stairs.

Arthur motioned Bennett down the hall toward the library. "I think you will find that my new brandy is excellent."

Bennett chuckled. "I do not doubt that. You only purchase the best."

Arthur followed him into the library, closed the door and walked to the table that held the decanter and glasses. "Please be seated. I asked you in here this evening because I have something of great importance to discuss with you."

"I understand." Bennett sat down in one of the chairs that faced the hearth and stretched out his legs. "You wish to inquire into the nature of my intentions toward Margaret. I assure you, they are entirely honorable."

"Of course they are. Good lord, man, that is the least of my concerns. You are one of the most honorable men I have ever known in my entire life."

Bennett seemed oddly embarrassed but quite gratified by that remark. "Why, thank you. The sentiment is entirely reciprocated, as I'm sure you know."

Arthur nodded brusquely and picked up the two glasses he had just filled. He handed one to Bennett. "I am pleased to see Margaret looking so happy, and I comprehend that you are the reason."

Bennett relaxed and took a sip. "I consider myself a very fortunate man. I did not think that I would ever meet another woman I could love after I lost Elizabeth. It is not often that life gives us a second chance, is it?"

"No." Arthur reflected briefly. "You two make an excellent match, do you not? You read novels and Margaret writes them. What could be more ideal?"

Bennett choked and sputtered on his brandy. "You *know* about her career as an author?"

"Certainly." Arthur sat down across from him.

"She thinks that you are unaware that she writes for the Minerva Press under the name of Mrs. Margaret Mallory."

"Why is it that everyone assumes that I do not know what is going on in my own family?" Arthur began. He broke off at the sight of a narrow strip of pale blue ribbon lying on the carpet near the sofa.

It was one of the blue satin garters Elenora had used to secure her stockings.

He stood quickly

Bennett frowned. "Something wrong?"

"Not at all. Just thought I'd prod the fire a bit."

He grabbed the poker, made a couple of desultory stabs at the crumbling embers and then moved leisurely back to his chair, taking a path that brought the toe of his boot very near the garter.

"I did not ask you in here to discuss Margaret. What I wish to discuss with you is the status of my inquiries. There has been another murder."

"Never say so." Bennett paused in the acting of taking a swallow of brandy. His heavy brows came together in a bushy line above his nose. "What the devil are you talking about, sir?"

Arthur took advantage of the moment of acute distraction. Using the toe of his boot, he nudged the garter out of sight under the sofa. It was still visible if one knew where to look, but it was unlikely that Bennett would get down on his hands and knees to survey the carpet for signs of recent debauchery.

Satisfied that he had done all he could to conceal the evidence, Arthur continued back to his chair.

"I found Ibbitts shot to death this evening."

"Good God, man."

Arthur sat down. "The situation has grown considerably more dangerous. I am going to need your help, Fleming."

Elenora heard the knock on her bedchamber just as she got herself free of the domino and gown. Margaret.

"One moment," she called.

She stuffed the gown and costume out of sight in the wardrobe, seized her wrapper and pulled it snugly around herself. She yanked the pins from her hair, plopped a white cap on her head and removed her earrings.

A glance in the mirror assured her that she looked like a woman who had just been summoned from her bed.

She opened the door, hoping that Margaret would not notice that she was breathing rather quickly for someone who had been asleep.

But Margaret did not look as though she was in a mood to pay attention to extraneous details. She radiated anxiety.

"Are you all right?" Elenora asked, alarmed.

"Yes, yes, I am fine, but I must speak with you."

"Of course." Elenora stood back to allow her into the room. "What is wrong?"

"It is Arthur. He has taken Bennett into his library for a private conversation." Margaret paced nervously back and forth in front of the dresser. "I am terrified that he is going to force Bennett to declare his intentions."

"I see."

"I reminded Arthur that I am a widow and therefore have every right to a private life with a gentleman, regardless of his intentions."

"Indeed."

"But you've known Arthur long enough now to realize that he is inclined to take charge of one's life, whether or not one wishes him to do so."

"Yes, well, if it makes you feel any better, I think I can assure you that Bennett's intentions toward you are not the subject of the conversation that is taking place downstairs in the library."

Margaret stopped her pacing and turned to face her with a questioning expression. "Are you certain?"

"Quite certain. Perhaps you had better sit down. It is a long story that begins with George Lancaster's murder."

"Dear heaven." Margaret sat down quite abruptly on the dressing-table chair.

Bennett left, a man committed to a noble cause, some thirty minutes later. Arthur saw him out the door and locked it behind him. He turned down the lamps in the front hall and made his way back to the library.

Inside the long chamber, he went to the sofa, crouched on one knee and reached for the blue garter.

He picked up the damning bit of ribbon and got to his feet. For a moment he studied the garter coiled in the palm of his hand. It was delicate and enticingly feminine. He could feel himself getting aroused all over again, just looking at the thing. He recalled how he had coaxed it off Elenora's leg so that he could lower her stocking.

He would never walk into this room again without remembering what had happened here this evening, he reflected. Making love to Elenora had wrought some change in him that he could not yet describe, but he knew that it had affected him very deeply.

Whatever happened in the future, he would never be the same man that he had been before this night.

Chapter Twenty-Five

Elenora delayed going downstairs the next morning until she could no longer stand the pangs of hunger. Even then she hesitated and considered requesting that a tray be brought to her bedchamber.

But in the end, she opened the door and marched determinedly out into the hall. Eating in her room in order to avoid having to confront Arthur would have been cowardly in the extreme.

She was surprised to find herself feeling quite fit. She had expected to spend a restless night, but to her amazement she had slept soundly. That was fortunate, she told herself as she reached the bottom of the staircase. At least her eyes were not puffy and red and her skin was not dull from lack of proper sleep.

She had selected a green muslin gown and a white ruff to wear for this first encounter with Arthur. She felt that the vivid color made her appear somehow more confident and sure of herself.

She needed every ounce of self-possession she

could muster. What did one say to a gentleman the morning after making mad, passionate love to him in his library?

"Good morning, ma'am." Ned loomed in the hall, looking concerned. "I was just about to send the new maid upstairs to see if you wanted to take your meal in your bedchamber."

"Very thoughtful of you, Ned, but I only take breakfast in bed when I am feeling ill. And I am almost never ill."

"Yes, ma'am. Breakfast is in the breakfast room, just as ye directed, ma'am. Sally and her sister finished getting it ready yesterday afternoon."

"Excellent." She gave him a blazing smile, took a fortifying breath, and swept on down the hall and into the breakfast room.

In spite of her concerns about having to deal with Arthur, she took a few seconds to enjoy the changes that had taken place in this space.

The breakfast room had been cleaned and polished until it glowed. Enticing odors wafted from the silver serving trays on the sideboard. Warm spring sunlight poured in through the windows. The view of the gardens was somewhat marred by the fact that the foliage was still overgrown and unkempt, but that would soon change. The new gardeners were due to start work today.

She was startled to find that Arthur was not alone at the table. Margaret was with him.

"Oh, there you are," Margaret said. "I was worried about you. I was just about to send someone upstairs to see if you were feeling well this morning."

Conscious of Arthur watching her with what appeared to be amusement, Elenora tried not to blush.

"As I just told Ned, I enjoy excellent health," she said.

Arthur got politely to his feet and pulled out a chair. "We wondered if perhaps you had engaged in a bit too much exercise last night."

She shot him her most repressive glare.

"On the dance floor," he concluded with perfect innocence.

She searched his face very closely for a couple of heartbeats. Beneath the dry amusement she caught a glimpse of genuine concern. For heavens sake, had he really thought that she would find it necessary to take to her bed for a day in order to recover from the shock of his lovemaking? She was no frail flower.

"Don't be ridiculous, sir." Ignoring the chair he held for her, she picked up her plate and went to the side-board to examine the offerings.

"Arthur is teasing you," Margaret said quickly. "Of course I was not worried that you might have danced too much last night. I thought that perhaps the ghastly events of the evening had taken their toll, that's all. Arthur and I were just talking about them. A dreadful business."

"There is absolutely nothing wrong with me, I assure you." Elenora studied the contents of the steaming trays.

"I suggest the fish," Arthur said. "It is excellent."

"And do try the eggs," Margaret suggested. "I vow, Sally's sister is an excellent cook."

Elenora helped herself to a bit of everything and then turned to find that Arthur was still holding her chair.

She sat down. "Thank you, sir."

He looked at the food heaped on her plate. "Obviously your appetite has not been affected by recent events."

"Not in the least sir."

He sat down across from her. "I was rather hungry myself this morning."

She had had enough of innuendoes, she decided. She picked up her knife and buttered a slice of toast. "How do you plan to proceed in your inquiries today, sir?"

His expression turned serious. "What with all the excitement last night, I neglected to mention that I did obtain one interesting clue before we went to the scene of Ibbitts's murder."

Elenora lowered the toast. "What was it?"

"The name of the man who may have been Saturn. Evidently he died a few days ago. I intend to pay a call on his widow this morning."

"That is very exciting news," Elenora said, too elated by the clue to chastise him for having neglected to mention it earlier. "You must take me with you."

He cocked a brow. "Why is that?"

"A bereaved widow may be hesitant to talk about private matters with a gentleman she does not know. Having another woman present will make her feel more comfortable."

Arthur pondered that for a moment. "You may be right. Very well, we shall leave at eleven-thirty."

Elenora relaxed slightly. Whatever else had changed between them, one thing had not been altered. Arthur was still treating her as a partner in this affair, one whose advice he valued. She would cling to that knowledge.

Margaret beamed. "On another topic, Arthur just told me that he knows that I write novels. Is that not astonishing? And to think that I was afraid that he would send me back to the country if he discovered the truth."

Elenora met Arthur's eyes across the table. She

smiled. There was very little that would escape his notice when it came to those for whom he felt responsible.

"Somehow, I am not at all surprised to find out that he has been aware of your career all along, Margaret."

Forty minutes later, she opened the door of her bedchamber and surveyed the hall. It was empty. She had heard Arthur return to his room a few minutes before, to dress for the visit to Glentworth's widow. Margaret was hard at work on her manuscript, as usual at this hour.

That meant that there would be no one in the library.

She stepped out into the corridor and went quickly toward the linen closet. Her slippered feet made no sound on the carpet.

When she reached the closet, she glanced back along the hall one last time to make certain there was no one about to observe her actions. Then she let herself into the small, dark room and shut the door.

By touch she found the lever that opened the hidden panel and pulled it cautiously.

The bookcase slid back. She moved out onto the balcony and looked down to be sure that none of the servants had decided to dust the library at that moment. But as she had anticipated, she had the long chamber to herself.

Scooping up the skirts of her gown, she went swiftly down the spiral staircase and crossed the room to where she and Arthur had made love.

She searched the area anxiously, but there was no sign of her blue garter. It had to be here somewhere, she thought.

Last night she had not noticed it was missing until

271

after Margaret had left. When she had realized that her left stocking was rolled down to her ankle she had assumed that the garter had come undone in the rush of getting out of her gown and into her wrapper. She had made a note to look for the missing item this morning in the daylight.

But a thorough search of her room a few minutes ago had not produced the garter. That was when she had realized that it had likely been lost in the library. A vision of Bennett Fleming having seen it and come to the obvious conclusion had induced a fit of near hysteria.

It was one thing to be a woman of the world, a lady of mystery and experience. It was quite another to have a very nice, very proper gentleman like Bennett Fleming discover one's garter in a place where it had no business being found.

She allowed herself a sigh of relief when she saw that the blue garter was not anywhere in plain sight on the carpet. That meant that Bennet had probably not seen it the night before. Unfortunately, it did not rule out the possibility that one of the servants had come across it that morning.

She got down on her hands and knees to search under the sofa.

"Looking for this?" Arthur asked from somewhere above.

The sound of his voice gave her such a start that she rose too quickly. She narrowly avoided banging her head on the edge of a table.

She steadied herself and raised her eyes to the balcony where Arthur leaned casually on the railing. The blue garter dangled from the fingers of his right hand. He must have noticed her sneaking into the linen closet and followed her, she decided.

Irritated, she got to her feet.

"As a matter of fact," she said, careful to keep her voice very low, "I *was* looking for it. You must have known that I would be concerned about where it was lost. You could have said something earlier and saved me a good deal of anxiety."

"Don't worry, I recovered it last night before Fleming noticed it." Arthur tossed the garter negligently into the air and caught it just as easily. "He never guessed that you had had your wicked way with me only moments before he arrived."

She made a face, gathered her skirts in both hands and started up the stairs. "Allow me to tell you, sir, that, on occasion, your sense of humor is decidedly skewed."

"There are those who would tell you that I have no sense of humor at all, skewed or otherwise."

"One can certainly understand how those persons arrived at that conclusion." She came to a halt at the top of the staircase and held out her hand for the garter. "May I have that?"

"I think not." He dropped the garter into his pocket. "I've decided to start a collection."

She stared at him. "You cannot be serious."

"Buy another set of garters and have the bill sent to me," Arthur said.

He kissed her on the mouth before she could scold him. When he finally raised his head, she was breathless.

"On second thought, you had better buy several sets of garters." He smiled with deep satisfaction. "I intend to create an extensive collection."

Chapter Twenty-Six

"We buried my husband a few days ago." Mrs. Glentworth looked up at the portrait that hung over the fireplace. "It was quite sudden. There was an accident in his laboratory. The electricity machine, you know. There must have been a terrible shock. It stopped his heart."

"Please accept our condolences on your loss, Mrs. Glentworth," Elenora said gently.

Mrs. Glentworth gave a perfunctory nod. She was a frail, bony woman with sparse gray hair tucked up under an old cap. The cloak of genteel poverty and stoic resignation hung heavily around her thin shoulders.

"I warned him about that machine." Her fingers clenched around the handkerchief she held, and her jaw jerked as though she was grinding her back teeth. "But he would not listen. He was forever conducting experiments with it."

Elenora glanced at Arthur, who was standing near

the window, a full cup of tea in one hand. His face was a cool mask that did little to conceal his watchful expression. She was quite certain that he was thinking precisely the same thing that she was thinking. In light of recent events, the fatal accident in Glentworth's laboratory appeared to be more than a mere coincidence.

But if Mrs. Glentworth suspected that her husband had been murdered, she gave no sign of it. Perhaps she did not particularly care, Elenora thought. The shabby parlor was filled with the gloom appropriate to a mourning household, but the widow herself appeared tense and rather desperate, not sad. Elenora could have sworn that, beneath their hostess's proper words and civil manner, a simmering anger burned.

Mrs. Glentworth had received them willingly enough, suitably awed by Arthur's name and title. But she was obviously bewildered.

"Were you aware that my great-uncle, George Lancaster, was killed by a burglar in his laboratory a few weeks ago?" Arthur asked.

Mrs. Glentworth frowned. "No, I did not know that."

"Did you know that your husband and Lancaster were great friends in their younger days?" Elenora added quietly.

"Of course." Mrs. Glentworth squeezed the handkerchief. "I am very well aware of how close the three of them were."

Elenora sensed Arthur going very still. She did not dare to look at him.

"Did you say *three* of them, Mrs. Glentworth?" Elenora asked in what she hoped was a mildly curious fashion.

"They were thick as thieves for a time. Met at Cambridge, you know. But all they cared about was science, not money. Indeed, they devoted themselves to their laboratories and ridiculous experiments."

"Mrs. Glentworth," Elenora began cautiously. "I wonder if—"

"I vow, I sometimes wished that my husband had been a highwayman or a footpad." A tremor shook Mrs. Glentworth. Then, as though a dam had crumbled somewhere inside her, the pent-up anguish and anger poured forth. "Perhaps then there would have been some money left. But, no, he was obsessed with natural philosophy. He spent almost every last penny on his laboratory apparatus."

"What sort of experiments did your husband conduct?" Arthur asked.

But the woman did not appear to have heard the question. Her rage was in full flood. "Glentworth had a respectable income when we married. My parents would never have allowed me to wed him if that had not been the case. But the fool never invested the money. He spent it without thought for me or our daughters. He was worse than a confirmed gambler, always claiming that he needed the newest microscope or another burning lens."

Arthur tried to intervene to redirect the conversation. "Mrs. Glentworth, you mentioned that your husband had a third friend . . ."

"Look around you." Mrs. Glentworth waved the hand in which she held the handkerchief. "What do you see of value? Nothing. Nothing at all. Over the years he sold the silver and the paintings to raise money to purchase items for his laboratory. In the end, he even sold his precious snuffbox. I thought he'd never part with it. He told me he wanted to be buried with it."

Elenora took a closer look at the portrait above the

mantel. It showed a portly, balding gentleman dressed in old-fashioned breeches and coat. He held a snuffbox in one hand. The lid of the case was set with a large, red, faceted stone.

She glanced at Arthur and saw that he was studying the portrait too.

"He sold the snuffbox that he carries in that portrait?" Arthur asked.

Mrs. Glentworth sniffed into the handkerchief. "Yes."

"Do you know who bought it from him?"

"No. I expect my husband took it to one of the pawnshops. Probably got very little for it, too." Mrs. Glentworth's jaw trembled with outrage. "Not that I saw any of the money, mind you. He never even bothered to tell me that he had sold it."

Arthur looked at her. "Do you happen to know when he pawned it?"

"No. It must have been shortly before he managed to kill himself with that electricity machine." Mrs. Glentworth used the mangled handkerchief to blot up a stray tear or two. "Perhaps that very day. I seem to recall that he had it at breakfast that morning. He left the house to take his exercise and was gone for some time. That was no doubt when he went to find a dealer."

"When did you notice that the snuffbox was gone?" Elenora asked.

"Not until that evening when I found his body. That afternoon I had gone out to pay a call on a friend who was ill. When I returned, my husband had already come home and locked himself in his laboratory for the day, as was his custom. He did not even bother to emerge for dinner."

"That was not unusual?" Arthur asked.

278

"Not at all. When he got involved in one of his experiments he could spend hours in his laboratory. But at bedtime I knocked on the door to remind him to turn down the lamps when he came upstairs. When there was no answer I grew concerned. The door was locked, as I said. I had to get a key to open it. That was when I . . . when I . . ." She broke off and blew her nose.

"When you found his body," Elenora completed gently.

"Yes. It was some time before my nerves recovered to the point where I noticed that his snuffbox was gone. Then I realized that he must have sold it that very day. Heaven only knows what he did with the money. It was certainly not in his pockets. Perhaps he decided to pay off one of his more pressing creditors."

There was a short silence. Elenora exchanged another knowing glance with Arthur. Neither of them spoke.

"I never thought he'd part with that snuffbox, though," Mrs. Glentworth said after a while. "He was very attached to it."

"Was your husband alone in the house while you were out that afternoon?" Arthur asked.

"Yes. We have a maid, but she was not here that day. In fact, she is rarely here anymore. She has not been paid in some time, you see. I suspect that she is searching for another post."

"I see," Arthur said.

Mrs. Glentworth gazed around with a resigned air. "I shall have to sell this house, I suppose. It is my one asset. I can only pray that I will get enough for it to pay off my husband's creditors."

"What will you do after you sell the house?" Elenora inquired.

"I shall be obliged to move in with my sister and her husband. I detest them both and they feel the same way about me. They have very little money to spare. It will be a miserable life, but what else can I do?"

"I shall tell you what else you can do," Elenora said crisply. "You may sell this house to St. Merryn. He will give you more than you will obtain if you try to sell it to someone else. In addition, he will allow you the use of it for the remainder of your life."

Mrs. Glentworth gaped at her. "I beg your pardon?" She shot a quick, disbelieving glance at Arthur. "Why would his lordship want to purchase this house for more than it is worth?"

"Because you have been extremely helpful today, and he is happy to show his gratitude." Elenora looked at Arthur. "Is that not correct, sir?"

Arthur raised his brows, but all he said was, "Of course."

Mrs. Glentworth looked uncertainly at Arthur. "You will do such a thing merely because I answered your questions today?"

He smiled faintly. "I actually am quite grateful, madam. Which reminds me, I have one last question that I wish to ask."

"Yes, certainly." Hope and relief began to lighten Mrs. Glentworth's drawn expression."

"Do you recall the name of your husband's third friend?"

"Lord Treyford." Mrs. Glentworth frowned slightly. "I never met him, but my husband mentioned him frequently enough in the old days. Treyford is dead, though. He was killed many years ago while still a young man."

"Do you know anything else about him?" Arthur

pressed. "Was he married? Is there a widow I might consult? Any children?"

Mrs. Glentworth thought about that and then shook her head. "I do not believe so. In the early days my husband made several references to the fact that Treyford was too devoted to his researches to be bothered with the demands of a wife and family." She sighed. "Indeed, I believe he was quite envious of Treyford's freedom from such obligations."

"Did your husband make any other comments about Treyford?" Arthur asked.

"He used to say that Lord Treyford was far and away the most brilliant of their little group. He once told me that if Treyford had lived, England might have had its second Newton."

"I see," Arthur said.

"They thought themselves so clever, you know." Mrs. Glentworth clasped her hands very tightly in her lap. Some of her anger returned to her face. "They were sure that they would all change the world with their experiments and their elevated conversations about science. But what good did their study of natural philosophy do, I ask you? None at all. And now they're all gone, aren't they?"

"So it seems," Elenora said quietly.

Arthur put down his unfinished tea. "You have been very helpful, Mrs. Glentworth. If you will excuse us, we must be on our way. I will have my man-of-affairs call upon you at once to settle the business of the house and your creditors."

"Except for *her,* of course," Mrs. Glentworth concluded harshly. "*She's* still alive. Outlived them all, didn't she?"

Elenora was very careful not to look at Arthur. She was aware that he was standing just as still as she was.

"She?" Arthur repeated without inflection.

"I always thought of her as some sort of sorceress." Mrs. Glentworth's voice was low and grim. "Perhaps she really did place a curse on them. Wouldn't have put it past her."

"I don't understand," Elenora said. "Was there a lady among your husband's circle of close acquaintances all those years ago?"

Another wave of anger flashed across Mrs. Glentworth's face. "They called her their Goddess of Inspiration. My husband and his friends never missed her Wednesday afternoon salons in the old days. When she summoned them, they rushed to her townhouse. Sat about drinking port and brandy and talking of natural philosophy as though they were all great, learned men. Trying to impress her, I suspect."

"Who was she?" Arthur asked.

Mrs. Glentworth was so lost in her unpleasant memories that she seemed confused by the question. "Why, Lady Wilmington, of course. They were all her devoted slaves. Now they are all dead, and she is the only one left. A rather odd twist of fate, is it not?"

A short time later Arthur handed Elenora up into the carriage. His mind was occupied with the information that Mrs. Glentworth had just given them. That did not stop him from appreciating the elegant curve of Elenora's attractive backside when she leaned over slightly and tightened her skirts to step into the cab.

"You managed to make that visit cost me a pretty penny," he said mildly, closing the door and sitting down across from her.

"Come now, sir, you know very well that even had I not been present, you would have offered to assist Mrs. Glentworth. Admit it."

"I admit nothing." He settled back into the seat and turned his attention to the conversation that had just been concluded in the shabby little parlor. "The fact that Glentworth died in a laboratory accident only a few weeks after my great-uncle was murdered indicates that the killer may have struck not twice but three times."

"Glentworth, your great-uncle, and Ibbitts." She folded her arms beneath her breasts as though she had felt a sudden chill. "Perhaps this mysterious Lady Wilmington will be able to tell us something of value. Are you acquainted with her, sir?"

"No, but I intend to remedy that state of affairs this very afternoon, if possible."

"Ah, yes, just as you did with Mrs. Glentworth."

"Indeed."

"Your title and wealth certainly have one or two useful advantages."

"They open doors so that I may ask questions." He shrugged. "But unfortunately they do not guarantee that I will get honest answers."

Nor were they enough to win a lady who was determined to go into trade, maintain her independence and live her life on her own terms, he thought.

Chapter Twenty-Seven

"Oh, my, yes, I remember those Wednesday afternoon salons as though I had held the last one only this past week." A distant, almost melancholic expression veiled Lady Wilmington's blue eyes. "We were all so young, so very passionate in those days. Science was our new alchemy, and those of us who were engaged in exploring its secrets saw ourselves as the inventors of the modern age."

Elenora sipped tea from the paper-thin china cup and surreptitiously surveyed the elegant drawing room while she listened to Clare, Lady Wilmington talk about the past. The situation here was quite opposite the one that existed across town in Mrs. Glentworth's small, poorly furnished parlor, she thought. Lady Wilmington was clearly not suffering from any financial difficulties.

The drawing room was decorated in a version of the Chinoiserie style that had first come into fashion several years earlier. It had been well-maintained in all its original lush, sensual glory. The dark, exotic atmosphere produced by the midnight blue and gold flower-patterned wallpaper, the intricately designed carpet and the ornate, japanned furnishings was brightened here and there by beautifully framed mirrors. It was a room designed to appeal to the senses.

Elenora could well imagine their wealthy hostess holding court in such surroundings. Lady Wilmington had to be fast approaching seventy years of age, but she was expensively dressed in the current mode. Her dark gold, high-waisted gown looked as if it had been designed to be worn in this richly hued room. The fine bones of her face and shoulders testified to the fact that she had once been a great beauty. Her hair was silver now, and some of it was surely false, but it was styled in an extremely elaborate chignon.

In Elenora's experience, the older a woman got, the more jewelry she tended to wear. Lady Wilmington was no exception to that rule. Pearls dangled from her ears. Her wrists and fingers glittered with an assortment of diamonds, rubies and emeralds.

It was the gold locket around Lady Wilmington's throat that caught Elenora's eye, however. Unlike the rings it was surprisingly plain in style. It appeared to be a very personal keepsake. Perhaps it held a miniature of one of her children or her deceased husband.

Arthur wandered over to the nearest window and looked out into the perfectly manicured gardens as though whatever he saw out there fascinated him.

"Then you remember my great-uncle, Glentworth and Treyford?" he said.

"Very well, indeed." Lady Wilmington raised the fingers of one hand to the gold locket at her throat. "They were all dedicated to science. They lived for their experiments the way painters and sculptors live for their art." She lowered her hand, smiling sadly. "But they are all gone now. The last one to pass on was Glentworth. I understand your great-uncle was killed by a house burglar a few weeks ago, sir. My condolences."

"I do not believe that he was murdered by an ordinary thief he chanced to encounter in the course of a burglary," Arthur said evenly. "I am certain that he was killed by someone connected to the old days when the gentlemen of the Society of the Stones frequented your Wednesday salons."

He still appeared to be fixed on some sight outside in the gardens, but Elenora was watching their hostess closely. She noticed the tiny tremor that went through Lady Wilmington's shoulders as Arthur delivered his flat conclusion. Once again her fingers brushed against the locket.

"Impossible," Lady Wilmington said. "How can that be?"

"I do not have the answer to that question yet, but I intend to find it." Arthur turned slowly to face her. "My great-uncle is not the only victim of this villain. I believe that Glentworth's death was no accident, either. I am convinced that the same man killed both of them, and my former butler as well."

"Good heavens, sir." Lady Wilmington's voice quivered. Her teacup rattled when she put it down on the saucer. "I don't know what to say. That is . . . that is unbelievable. Your butler, too, you say? But why would anyone kill him?"

"To silence him after gaining information from him."

Lady Wilmington shook her head once as though to clear it. "About what, pray tell?"

"My inquiries into George Lancaster's murder, of

287

course. The killer is aware now that I am hunting him. He wished to discover what I had learned thus far." Arthur's jaw tightened. "Which is not much. Certainly not worth a man's death."

"Indeed not." Lady Wilmington shuddered.

"But this villain is not thinking in a wholly rational manner," Arthur told her. "I believe he killed my great-uncle and Glentworth to obtain the red stones set into their snuffboxes."

Lady Wilmington frowned. "I recall those extraordinary gems very well. Quite fascinating. Treyford felt that they were unusually dark rubies, but Glentworth and Lancaster believed that they had been crafted in ancient times from some sort of unique glass."

"Did you ever see my great-uncle's lapidary?" Arthur asked. "The one he brought back from Italy along with the stones?"

"Yes, indeed." She sighed wistfully. "What of it?"

"I believe the villain we are hunting is sufficiently mad as to believe that he can build the infernal device described in the *Book of Stones*," Arthur said.

Lady Wilmington stared at him, momentarily open-mouthed with astonishment.

"Surely not," she finally said with great conviction. "That is absolute nonsense. I cannot believe that even a madman would take the instructions in that old book seriously."

Arthur looked back at her over his shoulder. "Did the three men ever discuss the machine?"

"Yes, of course." Lady Wilmington collected herself. Her voice steadied. "The lapidary named it Jove's Thunderbolt. We discussed the device on several occasions. Treyford and the others actually tried to construct it. But in the end, they all concluded that it could never be made to function."

"What caused them to be so certain of that?" Elenora asked.

Lady Wilmington massaged her temples with the fingers of one hand. "I do not recall all of the details. Something to do with the difficulty of applying the energy of an intense fire into the heart of the stones in order to excite the latent energy of the gems. They all agreed in the end that there was no way to accomplish that task."

"I am aware that my great-uncle came to that conclusion," Arthur said. "But are you sure that Glentworth and Treyford did also?"

"Yes." A faraway expression flickered in Lady Wilmington's eyes. Once again she touched her locket in a fleeting gesture as though seeking comfort while she looked into the past. "Mind you, it was fashionable in those days for some who were consumed by the study of science and mathematics to flirt with the occult. In some circles the dark arts continue to fascinate even the most well-educated minds today. No doubt that will prove to be true in the future as well."

Elenora watched her closely. "It is said that the great Newton himself was fascinated with the occult and devoted many years to the serious study of alchemy."

"Indeed," Lady Wilmington stated firmly. "And if a mind that brilliant can be seduced by the dark arts, who can blame a lesser mortal for falling prey to such intriguing mysteries?"

"Do you think that Glentworth or Treyford might have continued to secretly pursue such researches after they had all agreed to abandon alchemy?" Arthur asked.

Lady Wilmington blinked and straightened her shoulders. When she turned to Arthur she was clearly back in the present.

"I cannot imagine that for a moment, sir. They were, after all, highly intelligent, educated men of the modern age. They were not real alchemists, for heaven's sake."

"I have one more question, if you will be kind enough to indulge me," Arthur said.

"What is it?"

"Are you certain that Lord Treyford died in that explosion in his laboratory all those years ago?"

Lady Wilmington closed her eyes. Her fingers went to the locket. "Yes," she whispered. "Treyford is most certainly dead. I saw the body myself. So did your great-uncle, for that matter. Surely you do not believe the killer you seek is an old man?"

"Not at all," Elenora said. "We are well aware that we are searching for a young man in his prime."

"Why do you say that?" Lady Wilmington asked.

"Because the villain had the nerve to dance with me after he murdered Ibbitts," Elenora said.

Lady Wilmington looked stunned. "You danced with the killer? How do you know it was him? Can you describe him?"

"No, unfortunately," Elenora admitted. "The occasion was a masked ball. I never saw his face. But there was a tear in his domino which we believe may have been created during a struggle with the butler."

"I see." Lady Wilmington's expression was troubled. "I must say, this is all quite odd."

"Yes," Arthur said, "it is." He glanced at the clock. "We must be off. Thank you for seeing us, madam."

"Certainly." She inclined her head in a regal nod. "You must keep me informed of your progress in this matter."

"Yes." Arthur took a card from his pocket and set it on a table. "If you think of anything that might assist me in this investigation, I would very much appreciate it if you would send word immediately, no matter what the time, day or night, madam."

Lady Wilmington picked up the card. "Of course."

Arthur said nothing to Elenora until they were both inside the carriage. He settled into the seat, resting one arm on the back of the cushions.

"Well?" he said. "What do you make of Lady Wilmington?"

She thought about the manner in which the woman had touched her gold locket time and again throughout the conversation.

"I think that she was very much in love with one of the members of Society of the Stones," she said.

Arthur's face tightened with surprise. "That is not quite what I had expected to hear, but it is certainly interesting. Which of the three, do you think, caught her fancy?"

"Lord Treyford. The one who died in the prime of life. The one she and the others considered the most brilliant of the three. I suspect it is his picture that she carries inside that gold locket."

Arthur rubbed his chin. "I had not noticed the locket, but I was certainly aware of the fact that her ladyship was concealing some information. I have done business with enough cunning people to know when someone is lying to me."

Elenora hesitated. "If she did lie to us, I suspect it was because she was convinced that it was necessary."

"Perhaps she is trying to protect someone," Arthur said. "Whatever the case, I am convinced now that we must learn more about Treyford."

The killer had dared to dance with Miss Lodge. He must have been mad to have taken such a daring liberty.

291

Mad.

Lady Wilmington shivered at the thought. She sat alone for a long time, staring at the earl's card and fingering the locket. Old memories rushed in upon her, clouding her vision. Dear heaven, this was so much worse than she had allowed herself to believe.

After an eternity, she straightened her shoulders and dried her eyes. Her heart was breaking but she no longer had any choice. Deep down inside she had known that eventually this time would come and that she would have to do what must be done.

Reluctantly she opened a drawer in the writing desk and took out a sheet of foolscap. She would send the message immediately. If she planned well, everything would soon be under control.

By the time she finished the brief note, some of the words had been smudged by her tears.

Chapter Twenty-Eight

St. Merryn had visited Lady Wilmington.

The killer could scarcely believe what he had seen. Shaken, he stood in the shadows of the doorway halfway down the street and watched the gleaming carriage disappear around the corner.

Impossible. How had the bastard made the connection? And so quickly?

He had not been surprised when the street urchin who was his paid spy had reported that St. Merryn and Miss Lodge had gone to Mrs. Glentworth's address. It was inevitable that sooner or later the earl would speak with Saturn's widow. But what had that silly old woman told him that had sent him straight to the Wilmington townhouse?

Frantically, the killer went back over his plans, trying to determine if he had made a mistake. But he could not find any errors in his elaborate scheme.

He could feel himself starting to perspire. The sight of the St. Merryn carriage parked in the street outside

Lady Wilmington's front door was the first indication that this amusing game of wits that he had begun playing with his opponent had taken a nasty, unplanned turn.

Enough. He did not want to risk any more surprises. He had everything he required now to complete the device. The time had come to end the affair.

He moved out of the doorway and set off down the tree-lined street, his clever mind already at work on his new strategy.

Chapter Twenty-Nine

Jeremy Clyde slouched out of the front door of the brothel. He ignored the handful of carriages and hacks waiting in the street hoping for fares. He needed some fresh air. His head was buzzing from the copious quantities of wine he had consumed.

He tried to think of where to go next. His club? One of the hells? The only other option was to go home to the shrew he had so foolishly wed. That was the very last thing he wished to do. She would be waiting for him with a long list of questions and demands.

He had thought that marrying a wealthy woman would solve all of his troubles. Instead it had increased his misery a thousand fold. Nothing had gone right since Elenora had lost her lands and her inheritance. If only her stepfather had not been so damnably stupid.

If only. It seemed to Jeremy that he repeated that phrase a hundred times each day.

It was not fair. Here he was, trapped in a dreadful

marriage, hostage to the whims of his wife's stingy parent, while Elenora had landed on her feet like the cat she was. She was going to marry one of the wealthiest and most powerful men in town. How could that be? It simply was not fair.

A man came toward him out of the darkness. Jeremy hesitated uncertainly. He relaxed when the light of the gas lamps revealed the fine, elegant coat and the gleaming boots that the stranger wore. Whoever he was, he was most certainly a gentleman, not a footpad.

"Good evening, Clyde," the man said with an easy air.

"Beg your pardon," Jeremy muttered. "Have we met?"

"Not yet." The stranger swept him a mocking bow. "Allow me to introduce myself. My name is Stone."

There was only one explanation for Stone's air of amused familiarity, Jeremy thought grimly. "I suppose you're going to tell me that the reason you know my name is because you witnessed my fall in the park the other afternoon or else heard the gossip concerning it. Save your breath."

Stone chuckled. He draped his arm around Jeremy's shoulder in a companionable way. "I admit that I was present on that unfortunate occasion, but I was not amused by your predicament. Indeed, I felt naught but a great sympathy. I also know that, had I been in your shoes, I would be eager for a bit of revenge against the gentleman who had caused me such humiliation."

"Bah. There's little chance of that."

"Do not be so certain, sir. I may be able to assist you. You see, I have made a study of St. Merryn. I have

296

set street boys to watch him from time to time, and I have interviewed his recently deceased butler who was, I assure you, a veritable fount of information. I know many things about the earl and his very unusual fiancée, things that I think you will find extremely interesting."

Chapter Thirty

Two days later, late in the evening, Elenora stood with Margaret at the back of yet another crammed, over-heated ballroom. It was nearly midnight and she had dutifully endured several endless dances. Her feet ached, and she was restless and anxious.

None of those things would have mattered a jot, of course, if the dances had been with Arthur, but that was not the case. He had been gone all evening, just as he had been the night before, pursuing his inquiries. She wished she had been able to talk him into taking her with him, but, as he had explained, he could not smuggle her into the various gentlemen's clubs where he went to interview the old men.

Her thoughts kept returning to the conversation with Lady Wilmington. It had occurred to her this afternoon that there was one very important question that she and Arthur had neglected to ask.

A pretty young woman, polite smile frozen in place, glided past in the arms of a middle-aged gentleman who could not seem to keep his attention away from the lady's fair bosom.

"I must say, the longer I play my part in this affair," Elenora murmured to Margaret, "the more my respect grows for the stamina and endurance of the young ladies who are being dangled on the marriage mart. I do not know how they manage."

"They have been in training for years," Margaret said dryly. "The stakes of this game are very high, after all. They are all well aware that their futures and in many cases the futures of their families are riding on the outcome of this one short Season."

Elenora felt a rush of sudden understanding and sympathy. "That was how it was for you, was it not?"

"My family was in desperate straits the year I turned eighteen. I had three sisters and two brothers as well as my mother and grandmother to consider. My father had died, leaving very little. Contracting a successful marriage was our only hope. My grandmother scraped together the money required to give me a single Season. I met Harold Lancaster at my very first ball. His offer was accepted immediately, of course."

"And you did what you had to do for the sake of your family."

"He was a good man," Margaret said quietly. "And I came to care for him in time. The greatest difficulty was the difference in our ages. Harold was twenty-five years my senior. We had very little in common, as you can imagine. I had hoped to take comfort in my children, but we were not blessed with any."

"What a sad tale."

"But a very familiar one." Margaret nodded toward the couples on the dance floor. "I expect there will be many similar stories repeated this Season."

"No doubt."

And the result would be any number of cold, love-less alliances, Elenora thought. She wondered if, in the end, Arthur would be obliged to make such a marriage. He had no choice but to wed, after all, whether or not he found a woman he could love with all the passion that was locked inside him. In the end, he would do his duty by the title and the family, regardless of his own feelings.

"I must say, you are right about this crowd," Margaret said, fanning herself briskly. "It really is quite a crush tonight. It will take ages for Bennett to get back to us with the lemonade. We shall likely per-ish of thirst before he returns."

The throng parted briefly. Elenora spotted the elab-orately curled, old-fashioned powdered wig that was part of the livery worn by their host's footmen.

"There is a servant over there by the door," she said, standing on tiptoe to get a better view. "Maybe we can catch his eye."

"For all the good it will do," Margaret muttered. "This lot will have emptied his tray before he gets any-where near us."

"Stay here so that Bennett will find you when he returns." Elenora turned to pursue the rapidly disap-pearing footman. "I'll see if I can catch up with that servant before he runs out of lemonade."

"Be careful you don't get trampled underfoot."

"Don't worry. I'll be right back."

With a few polite murmurs, Elenora slipped through a cluster of middle-aged ladies and made her way as quickly as possible toward the spot where she had last seen the footman.

She was only a few paces away when she felt the brush of gloved fingers on the skin of her bare back, just beneath the vulnerable nape of her neck.

An icy chill flashed down her spine. She suddenly could not breathe.

Just an accidental touch, she assured herself; the sort that could occur so easily when so many people were crowded together. Or perhaps one of the gentlemen had seized the opportunity presented by the tight quarters to take liberties.

Nothing personal.

But it was all she could do not to shriek out loud. Because her intuition told her that the touch of those gloved fingers drifting intimately across her naked skin had been very personal indeed.

It can't be, she thought. Not here. He would not dare. Cold terror prickled her skin in spite of the heat. Surely she was mistaken.

But the villain had come to her the last time in the middle of a crowded ballroom, she reminded herself.

Whatever she did, she must not give any sign that she was aware that he was near.

Forcing herself to stay calm, she turned slowly on her heel, trying to appear casual. She unfurled her fan with a flip of her wrist and used it to cool herself while she searched the crowd.

There were several gentlemen nearby, but none of them stood close enough to have touched her.

Then she saw the footman; not the one she had been pursuing, she realized, but a different man.

He had his back to her, striding swiftly away through the throng of chatting, laughing guests. All she could see was the collar of his green-and-silver jacket and the back of his powdered and curled wig beneath his hat. But there was something disturbingly familiar about the way he moved.

She plunged into the crowd, trying to keep the footman in sight.

"Excuse me," she mumbled to the people she forced out of her way. "Beg your pardon. So sorry about your lemonade, madam. Did not mean to tread on your toe, sir . . ."

Eventually she reached the fringes of the crowd and came to a halt. There was no sign of the footman, but she saw at once that the doors that stood open onto the gardens provided the only exit on this side of the ball-room.

She stepped out into the shadows. She was not alone on the terrace. There were a handful of couples engaged in soft conversations. No one paid any attention to her.

The footman was nowhere to be seen.

She crossed the stone terrace and went down the five broad steps that led to the night-shrouded gardens, trying to look like any other overheated guest who had decided to take the evening air.

A broad circle of large, marble statues loomed directly in front of her. Nothing moved in the deep shadows between the figures.

"Elenora."

She was so tense that she almost screamed aloud at the unexpected sound of her name.

Spinning around, she saw Jeremy Clyde standing a short distance away.

"Hello, Jeremy." She snapped her fan closed. "Did you happen to see one of the footmen go past a moment ago?"

"Why the devil would I take notice of a servant?" He scowled, moving quickly toward her. "I saw you come out here and I followed you. I've been looking for you. We must talk."

"I don't have time to chat." She picked up her skirts and walked toward the row of statues, searching for some sign of the vanished servant. "Are you certain you did not see the footman? He was in full livery. I'm sure he must have come this way."

"Devil take it, will you stop blathering on about a footman?" Jeremy hurried after her and seized her bare arm.

Impatiently she tried to get free of his grasp. He did not release her.

"Kindly remove your hand, sir." They were out of sight of the couples on the terrace, but she knew that voices carried on the night air. She spoke in a sharp whisper. "I do not want you to touch me."

"Elenora, you must listen to me."

"I just told you, I don't have time for this."

"I came here tonight to find you." He gave her a small shake. "My darling, I know *everything*."

Startled, she forgot about his hand and looked up at his face. "What on earth are you talking about?"

He glanced uneasily back toward the terrace and then lowered his voice to a hoarse whisper. "I know that St. Merryn has employed you to be his mistress."

Shocked, she stared at him. "I have no idea what you mean."

"He is using you, my darling. He has no intention of marrying you." Jeremy grunted in disgust. "Evidently you are the only one who does not know the truth."

"Rubbish. I have no idea what this is all about, nor do I wish to find out. Release me. I must return to the ballroom."

"Elenora, listen to me. Your name is in all the betting books in every club in St. James tonight."

She could feel a distinct fluttering in her stomach. "I beg your pardon?"

"Every gentleman in town is placing a wager on what will happen when St. Merryn tires of you."

304

"It is common knowledge that some gentlemen will place bets on anything that amuses them," she said tightly.

"We are talking about your *reputation*. It is going to be in tatters soon."

"When did you develop such a touching concern for my good name?"

"Damnation, Elenora, keep your voice down." Jeremy glanced around again with an agitated air, assuring himself that there was no one within earshot. He leaned closer. "I would remind you that I am a gentleman. Unlike St. Merryn, I had the decency to protect your reputation while we were engaged."

"Yes, your gallantry left me speechless, sir."

He did not appear to notice her sarcastic tone. "St. Merryn, on the other hand, is using you. He intends to toss you aside in the most humiliating manner after parading you around town as his fiancée for a few weeks or months. When he is finished with you, you will be ruined."

"From the sound of things, it is already too late for me, so I may as well enjoy the process."

"Oh, my dear Elenora, it is not like you to talk that way. I can help you."

"Indeed?" She was almost amused. "How do you intend to do that."

"I will take you under my protection. I have the money to do that now. Unlike St. Merryn, I will be discreet. You will not be obliged to face the sneers of Society. I will keep you safely tucked away out of sight. We can be happy at last together, my love, just as we were meant to be."

Outrage poured through her. Briefly she pondered sticking her fan in Jeremy's ear.

"Allow me to tell you, sir," she said through her

teeth, "that the prospect of being ruined by St. Merryn is considerably more thrilling than that of becoming your mistress."

"You are overset," he soothed. "I understand. Your poor nerves have obviously been under severe stress lately. But when you think about it, you will see that what I am offering is the best solution. It will save you from the great humiliation that awaits you at St. Merryn's hands."

"Let me go, Jeremy."

"I am only trying to protect you."

She smiled coldly. "The last thing I want is to be under your protection, sir."

"Do you prefer such an arrangement with St. Merryn because he is wealthier than I am? What good will his money do you when he is finished with you and you face the most complete and utter disaster? You will never again be able to show your face in Polite Society. Your future will be destroyed."

"You know nothing about my plans for the future."

"Elenora, you must hear me out. Then perhaps you will understand how dire your situation truly is. I just came from one of my clubs. I saw the entries in the book with my own eyes. This very evening young Geddings wagered two thousand pounds that St. Merryn will cast you off at the end of the Season. His bet was merely one of many. Some of the sums involved are quite enormous."

"It never fails to astonish me that so many well-educated men can be such fools."

"They are all wagering that the engagement is a sham. The only variation in the betting concerns the exact date when he will cast you aside. Most favor the end of the Season. A few believe he will keep you in his bed through the summer because the situation is so convenient for him."

In a sense, Arthur *was* going to let her go when this business was finished, she thought glumly. It was decidedly irritating to realize that so many of the gentlemen of the ton who were placing wagers on her future would make a handsome profit at her expense. It was not at all fair.

At that instant, a stunning thought struck her with more force than a bolt of lightning could have done.

I know precisely how this affair will end.

She could, in fact, see her own lonely future far more clearly than any of the gentlemen in the clubs. As soon as Arthur caught the killer, she would be able to fix an exact date for the end of their association.

It was a very depressing thought, but she could not ignore the financial implications. She was the one person in this situation, aside from Arthur, of course, who could place a wager on how it would end with absolute certainty.

It would not be a simple matter, she reminded herself. She tapped her folded fan against her palm, thinking quickly. There were one or two obstacles that would have to be dealt with. After all, no lady could walk into a gentlemen's club and ask to put down a bet. She required the assistance of someone who could be trusted to place the wager in his name on her behalf.

"Elenora?" Jeremy gave her a small shake. "Did you hear me? Wagers are going down all over town as we speak. Where is your pride? You cannot allow St. Merryn to treat you in this despicable manner."

Pull yourself together, Elenora thought. She was supposed to be playing a part here.

"Nonsense, Jeremy." She raised her chin. "I cannot believe that St. Merryn would be so callous as to toss me aside. Why does everyone believe that he would do such a thing?"

That, she thought, was actually a very good question. What *had* led to this sudden spurt of wagers this evening?

"They say he got you from an agency," Jeremy told her.

At that news she relaxed. "Oh, for heaven's sake, Jeremy. That nonsense about selecting me from an agency has been a joke from the start of this affair. Everyone knows that. Have you no sense of humor?"

He squinted slightly. "Until tonight I and everyone else believed that the tale was, indeed, St. Merryn's eccentric notion of an amusing jest. But now the gossip is going around that it is the truth, that he actually *did* obtain your services from an agency that supplies paid companions."

"Why would he do that? With his money and title, he could take his pick of fiancées from among the young ladies of the ton."

"Don't you see? The word is that he went to an agency to hire an impoverished paid companion precisely because he has no intention of marrying. He merely wished to amuse himself with a mistress he could keep conveniently at hand under his own roof and parade in front of the ton. It is just another one of his infamous stratagems. The man is notorious for his clever schemes."

"Well, this is certainly one of his more brilliant plans, if that is the case," she said lightly, "because I am quite convinced that he intends to marry me." It would not hurt to reinforce the notion that she believed St. Merryn's intentions were honorable, she thought. It might help to drive up the stakes in the betting books.

"My dearest, you do not need to pretend with me."

Jeremy gripped her more urgently. "I told you, I know everything now. It is true that St. Merryn did get you from an agency. Do not deny it."

"Rubbish."

"Goodhew and Willis, to be precise."

Dear heaven. *He knows the name of the agency.* To her knowledge this was the first time anyone had connected the supposed jest to Goodhew and Willis.

She swallowed hard, trying not to let him see that his knowledge had shaken her. She had to find out how he knew the name of the agency.

"I have no idea what you are talking about, Jeremy." Keeping her voice light and unconcerned took enormous effort but she managed it. "Where did you hear that odd name?"

"Oh, my poor, naïve darling. I can see that you really do believe that St. Merryn intends to marry you." He squeezed her arm. "Tell, me, what promises did he make? What lies has he told you?"

"Unlike you, Jeremy, St. Merryn has been entirely honest and forthright with me."

Jeremy's fingers became a vise on her arm. "You mean you actually agreed to his scheme? I cannot believe that you would sink to such depths of depravity. What has happened to my sweet, innocent Elenora?"

"Sweet, innocent Elenora is about to become my wife." Arthur glided out of the shadows of a hedge. "And if you don't take your hand off her immediately, I will lose what little patience I have left for you, Clyde."

"St. Merryn." Jeremy released Elenora's arm with blinding speed. He moved back warily as Arthur came to stand beside Elenora. "How dare you, sir?"

"How dare I ask Miss Lodge to become my wife?"

309

Arthur took possession of Elenora's arm. "Probably because the notion struck me as a very good one. Not that it is any of your business."

Jeremy flinched but he stood his ground. "Have you no shame, sir?"

"That is almost amusing, coming as it does from a man who cast Elenora aside to marry another."

"That is not what happened," Jeremy said tightly.

"Actually," Elenora said, "that is precisely what happened."

"My darling, you misunderstood."

"I don't think so."

"I certainly did not ask you to do anything so outrageous as pose to the world as my fiancée," Jeremy turned back to glare at Arthur. "How can you justify using Miss Lodge in such a manner, sir?"

"You know, Clyde," Arthur said, his voice going lethally soft, "I find you extremely irritating."

Alarmed by his tone, Elenora stepped nimbly between the two men. "Enough, Arthur, we have more important matters to attend to here tonight."

He glanced at her. "Are you certain? This was just starting to get interesting."

"Jeremy knows about Goodhew and Willis," she said very pointedly.

She felt his hand tighten on her arm, the same arm he had just retrieved from Jeremy. At the rate gentlemen were seizing hold of that portion of her anatomy tonight, she was going to be bruised in the morning, she reflected.

Arthur did not take his eyes off Jeremy. "Does he, indeed?"

"It is common knowledge that you hired her from that agency," Jeremy sputtered.

"There is, indeed, a tale going around that I made

good on my vow to select a wife from an agency that supplies paid companions," Arthur agreed. "But the name of that agency is most certainly not common knowledge. Where did you hear it?"

"See here, sir, there is no reason why I should explain myself to you—"

He broke off abruptly when Arthur, without any warning, released Elenora, grabbed the front of Jeremy's expensive coat and shoved him hard against the bare backside of a marble god.

"Who gave you the name of Goodhew and Willis, Clyde?" Arthur asked again in an even softer tone than he had used a moment before.

Jeremy gaped, but he managed to utter a wobbly protest. "Unhand me, sir."

"I'm more of a mind to call you out for spreading malicious gossip about my fiancée, just as I once promised to do."

Jeremy's expression in the moonlight was one of appalled horror. "You are bluffing, sir. The whole world knows that you could not even be bothered to call out the man who ran off with your real fiancée. You are hardly likely to risk your neck in a duel over a woman you consider to be merely a convenience."

"Clyde, you and the whole world know very little about me and what I might do. Tell me where you heard the name Goodhew and Willis now, or my seconds will call upon you within the hour."

Jeremy's defiance collapsed. "Very well," he said, striving to maintain some dignity. "I suppose there is no reason why I should not tell you where I heard about your true intentions toward Miss Lodge."

"Where was that?"

"At the Green Lyon."

Elenora frowned. "What is the Green Lyon?"

"It's a hell off St. James," Arthur said. He did not take his attention off Jeremy. "How did you happen to go there, Clyde? Or is it one of your frequent haunts?"

"Don't be insulting." Jeremy drew himself up to his full height. "I went there on a whim last night because I was rather bored and someone suggested that it might be amusing."

"You just happened to go there last night and you just happened to encounter someone who told you about Goodhew and Willis? I don't think so. Try again."

"It's the truth, damn your eyes. I was feeling out of sorts and someone suggested that we go to the Green Lyon. We went there together and played at hazard for an hour or so. Somewhere in the course of the evening, he mentioned the rumors about Goodhew and Willis."

"This person is a friend of yours?" Arthur asked evenly.

"Not a friend. An acquaintance. Never met him before last night."

"Where did you encounter him?"

Jeremy looked quickly at Elenora and then just as swiftly away again. "Outside an establishment in Orchid Street," he muttered.

"Orchid Street." Arthur's mouth curved humorlessly. "Yes, of course, that would be the address of the brothel operated by the old bawd who calls herself Mrs. Flowers."

Elenora made a tut-tutting sound. "You patronize brothels, Jeremy? That is very distressing news. Does your wife know?"

"I just happened to be in Orchid Street on business," Jeremy mumbled. "I know nothing about any brothel there."

"Never mind," Arthur said. "Tell me more about the

man who introduced himself to you last night and suggested that you go to the Green Lyon."

Jeremy tried to shrug. He was only partially successful due to the fact that Arthur still had hold of his coat. "There is not much to tell. I think he said his name was Stone or Stoner or something like that. Seemed familiar with the Green Lyon."

"What did he look like?" Elenora asked.

Jeremy's features contorted with puzzlement. "Why the devil does that matter?"

Arthur pushed Jeremy harder against the statue's rear. "Answer her question, Clyde."

"Damnation, I cannot recall any particulars about his appearance. I'd had several bottles of claret by the time I met him, if you must know."

"You were in your cups?" Elenora was surprised by that bit of news. During the time Jeremy had been courting her, she had never known him to be a heavy drinker. "There is nothing worse than a drunkard. Your poor wife has my deepest sympathies."

"I've got a bloody good reason to want to forget my troubles," Jeremy snarled. "My marriage is not what anyone would call a love match. It's a living hell. Before we were wed, my father-in-law implied that he would settle a considerable portion on my wife, but afterward he reneged. He controls our income and he insists that I dance to his tune. I am trapped, *trapped*, I tell you."

"Your marital woes are of no concern to us," Arthur said. "Describe the man you met in Orchid Street."

Jeremy grimaced. "I suppose he was about my height. Brown hair." He rubbed his forehead. "Leastways, I think it was brown."

"Was he fat?" Arthur prompted. "Thin?

"Not fat." Jeremy hesitated. "Seemed very fit."

"Were his features unusual in any way?" Elenora asked. "Did he have any scars?"

Jeremy glowered. "I don't recall any scars. As far as his looks go, he seemed to be the type that women find attractive."

"How was he dressed?"

"Expensively," Jeremy said without hesitation. "I remember asking him for the name of his tailor, but he made some joke and changed the subject."

"What of his hands?" Elenora said. "Can you describe them?"

"His hands?" Jeremy stared at her if she had asked him to an extremely complex question in mathematics. "I don't recall anything unusual about them."

"This is useless." Arthur let go of his coat. "If you think of anything else that might be helpful, be sure to send word to me immediately."

Jeremy adjusted his coat and cravat with angry movements. "Why in blazes would I bother to do that?"

Arthur's smile was as cold as the outer rings of Hades. "Because we have every reason to think that your new acquaintance has killed at least three men in recent weeks."

Jeremy made a gargling sound, but no actual words emerged. Under other circumstances, Elenora thought, she would have found the sight vastly amusing.

In any event, she did not have long to savor Jeremy's shocked expression because Arthur steered her away from the circle of statues and back toward the ballroom.

"What the devil were you doing out here with Clyde in the first place?" he growled.

"I thought I saw someone who might have been the killer."

314

"Damn it to the Pit. He was here?" Arthur halted so suddenly that Elenora tripped over his boot. She would have stumbled to her knees had he not held her upright. "Are you certain?"

"I believe so, but I must admit that I cannot be positive." She hesitated. "He touched my back, just below my neck. I could swear it was quite deliberate. The sensation made me go cold all the way to my bones."

"Bastard." Arthur pulled her close and wrapped a possessive arm around her.

It felt very pleasant to be pressed against his chest like this, Elenora thought. Warm and safe and comfortable.

"Arthur, it could very well have been my imagination," she said into his coat. "Heaven knows I have been somewhat tense of late. We must concentrate on what we learned from Jeremy."

"Yes."

She raised her head reluctantly. "There are very few people other than you and me who knew the name of the agency where you went to employ me. Of that number, Ibbitts is the only one who would have willingly related the information to anyone else."

"And the person he gave the name of the agency to was likely the man who killed him." Arthur loosened his grip on her and resumed making his way back toward the terrace steps. "Come. We must hurry."

"Where are we going?"

"You are going home. I am going to the Green Lyon to keep watch for a while. Clyde said his new acquaintance seemed familiar with the club. Perhaps he will be there tonight."

"No, Arthur, that won't work. I must go with you."

"Elenora, I do not have time to argue about this."

"I agree. But you are not thinking logically, sir. I must go with you tonight to keep watch. Poor witness that I am, I am still the only person who might be able to identify the killer."

Chapter Thirty-One

An hour later, Elenora wrapped her shawl more snugly around her shoulders and adjusted the blanket across her knees. The night was not especially cold, but one felt the chill when one sat in an unlit carriage for an extended period of time.

"I must say, this business of keeping watch is not nearly as exciting as I had expected it would be," she said.

Arthur, enveloped in deep shadow on the other side of the vehicle, did not take his eyes off the entrance of the Green Lyon. "I did warn you, if you will recall."

She decided to ignore that. Arthur was not in one of his more mellow moods this evening. She could hardly blame him, she thought.

They were seated in an aging carriage that he had instructed Jenks to hire for this venture. Elenora understood his reasoning in the matter. It was, after all, quite likely that his own carriage would have been rec- ognized if it sat parked for any length of time in the street outside the Green Lyon. But unfortunately the livery stable had had only one old vehicle left at that late hour.

It had quickly become obvious why none of the stable's other clients had selected it. When it was in motion, the heavy carriage jolted and lurched in an extremely uncomfortable manner. In addition, although the seats had appeared to be clean at first glance, it had quickly become apparent that the accumulated odors of years of ill use had saturated the cushions.

Elenora stifled a tiny sigh and finally admitted to herself that she had anticipated that the time spent with Arthur in the dark, intimate confines of the carriage would be pleasant. She had envisioned the two of them talking quietly for an hour or two while they watched gentlemen come and go from the club.

But immediately after they had taken a place in the long line in the street outside the hell, Arthur had sunk into one of his deep silences. All of his attention was fixed on the door of the Green Lyon. She knew that he was reworking his master plan yet again.

She studied the entrance to the hell, wondering what it was about the place that drew such a steady stream of men. It was certainly an unprepossessing establishment, in her opinion. The single gaslight in front cast a weak glare that illuminated the faces of the patrons who came and went from the premises.

Most of the men who tumbled out of the carriages and hackneys that halted at the front steps were clearly drunk. They laughed too loudly and told bawdy stories to their friends. There was a feverish look of expectation about some of them as they made their way into the hell.

Most of those who emerged from the club wore very

different expressions. One or two appeared positively jubilant. They boasted of their luck and instructed their coachmen to take them to another place of amusement. But a far greater number walked back down the steps with an air of dejection, anger or deep gloom. A few looked as though they had received word of a death in the family. Elenora knew that they were the ones who had just gambled away a house or an inheritance. She wondered if any of them would put a pistol to his head sometime before dawn.

She shivered again.

Arthur stirred. "Are you cold?"

"No, not really. What will you do if we do not spot him tonight?"

"Try again tomorrow night." Arthur rested one arm along the back of the seat. "Unless some new information falls at my feet in the meantime, this is the most significant clue that has come my way thus far."

"Does it disturb you that the killer chose to confide the information about my connection to Goodhew and Willis to Jeremy of all people? It cannot have been a coincidence."

"No. I am quite certain he intended to create some mischief by telling Clyde that you actually did come from the agency, and that the rumors were not a jest after all."

"What sort of mischief?"

"I do not know yet. Remember that he still believes that we have no way to identify him. He no doubt feels that the secret of his true identity is secure."

She tugged on her shawl. "I only hope that I will be able to make him out from this distance."

Another silence ensued.

"Arthur?"

"Yes?"

"There is something that I have been meaning to ask you."

He did not turn his head. "What is that?"

"How does it come about that you guessed the name of the brothel in Orchid Street when Jeremy mentioned it?"

For a second or two he gave no sign that he had even heard the question. Then she saw him smile in the darkness.

"Such establishments have a way of making themselves known," he said. "Men gossip, Elenora."

"I am not the least surprised to hear that."

He glanced at her, the amused smile still etching the corner of his mouth. "What you really want to know is if I am familiar with that brothel because I have had occasion to visit it."

She raised her chin and kept her gaze on the front door of the Green Lyon. "I have absolutely no interest in that aspect of your personal life, sir."

"Of course you have, and the answer is no."

"I see." She felt suddenly quite cheerful for a moment, and then she recalled the other, related question about his private life that had been bothering her from the start of this adventure. Her briefly elevated spirits immediately deflated somewhat. "Well, I suppose you did not require the services of such an institution."

"There is no other woman in my life at the moment, Elenora," he said quietly. "As a matter of fact, there has not been anyone else for some time. Is that what you want to know?"

"It's none of my affair."

"Ah, but it is, my sweet," he said in a low voice. "After all, we have formed an intimate connection. You have every right to know if I am romantically attached to someone else." He paused a beat. "Just as I would expect to be told immediately if you decided to form such an attachment to some other man."

Something in his tone raised the hairs on the nape of her neck. He was making it clear that he would not share her affections.

"You know better than anyone that there is no other man in my life," she said quietly.

"I will expect matters to remain that way as long as you and I are involved with each other."

She cleared her throat. "I will expect the same sort of loyalty from you."

"You shall have it," he said simply.

He turned his attention back to the door of the Green Lyon, leaving her to analyze in silence the combination of satisfaction and wistful longing that welled up inside her. She would have him to herself for the length of time that they were bound together in this odd affair, she thought. But that realization only heightened her awareness of how painful the eventual parting would be.

She was trying very hard to keep her thoughts focused on the future and all of her grand plans, but it was becoming more difficult by the hour to imagine life without Arthur.

Dear heaven, I've fallen in love with him.

The realization filled her with a bright euphoria that transformed almost instantly into dread. How had she allowed this to happen? This was a miscalculation of enormous proportions.

"Hell's teeth." Arthur straightened abruptly, leaning closer to the carriage window. "What is this about?"

His urgent tone yanked her out of her morose thoughts. She sat forward quickly.

321

"What is it?" she asked.

Arthur shook his head, his gaze never wavering from the scene outside on the front steps of the club. "Damned if I know. But this cannot be a matter of chance. Take a look. Might that be the man you danced with the night Ibbitts was murdered? The one who touched you this evening?"

She followed his gaze and watched a handsome man in his early twenties walk purposefully out the door of the Green Lyon. In the glare of the gas lamp his hair appeared to be a light brown in color. He was slender, and he moved easily.

Her pulse began to thud heavily in her wrists, and her mouth went dry. Was she looking at the killer? Was that the man who had touched her so intimately tonight and on the night of Ibbitts's death? From this distance there was no way to be certain.

"He is about the right height," she said, hesitating. "And he appears to have long-fingered hands. I cannot see from here if he has a ring."

"He is wearing Hessians."

"Yes, but as you once pointed out, a vast number of gentlemen favor that style of boot." She squeezed her fingers together tightly in her lap. "Arthur, I'm sorry, but I cannot be sure from this distance. I must get closer to him."

"He is not getting into any of the carriages."

She watched as the man in the Hessians turned at the bottom of the steps, lit a small lantern that he carried at his side, and walked off along the dark street. He was alone.

"Stay here with the carriage. Jenks will watch you." Arthur opened the door and jumped down onto the pavement. "I am going to follow that man."

Anxiously, she leaned forward. "No, you must not

322

go after him alone. Arthur, please, this may be exactly what the villain intends for you to do."

"I want to see where he is going. I will not let him see me."

"Arthur—"

"I am very curious to discover what business he has in this neighborhood so near the Green Lyon."

"I do not like this, sir. Please take Jenks with you."

Arthur turned his head toward the rapidly diminishing point of light that was the lantern his quarry carried. "It will be difficult enough as it is to keep my quarry unaware of my presence. He will surely spot two men following him."

He made to close the door.

"Wait. You recognize that man with the lantern, don't you?" she whispered.

"He is Roland Burnley. The man who eloped with Juliana."

Arthur closed the door before Elenora could recover from her astonishment.

Chapter Thirty-Two

The weak illumination supplied by the small lights of the carriages and the gas lamp at the door of the Green Lyon faded rapidly behind Arthur. He moved more quickly, trying to keep Roland's lantern in sight. He had to concentrate to keep his weight on the balls of his feet so that the heels of his boots would not sound a warning on the paving stones.

Roland, on the other hand, was making no particular attempt at stealth. His steps were swift and sure; a man who knew where he was going.

The cramped, twisted street was lined with small shops that were all closed and shuttered for the night. No lights shone in the rooms above the business establishments. It was not a particularly dangerous neighborhood in the light of day, but at this hour only a fool would come here alone.

What drew Roland here?

A few minutes later his quarry came to a halt in front of a darkened doorway. Arthur moved into a vestibule and watched as Roland let himself into a small, cramped hall. The lantern light flared briefly and then disappeared entirely when the door closed behind the young man.

It occurred to Arthur that Roland might be visiting a woman in this street. There would be nothing unusual about such a situation. It was common for gentlemen, even those who had been recently wed, to keep a mistress on the side. But that type of indulgence was expensive. By all accounts the Burnley finances were in exceedingly poor shape.

Arthur watched the windows on the floor above the door that Roland had just entered. There was no sign of lantern light. Roland must have gone to a room at the back of the building.

He would learn nothing standing about in this doorway, he concluded. He lit his own lantern, turned the light down very low, and moved out of the shadows. He crossed the tiny street and tried the door through which Roland had disappeared.

It opened easily.

The dim light of the lantern revealed the stairs that led to the floor above the shops. Arthur removed the pistol from the pocket of his coat.

He went up the stairs cautiously, watching for any unexpected shadows on the landing. Nothing moved in the darkness.

At the top of the steps he found himself in an unlit corridor. There were two doors. A slender edge of light showed beneath one of them.

He set the lantern down so that the weak glare lit the floor but did not throw him into strong silhouette. No sense making a perfect target of himself, he thought.

He went to the door and tried the knob with his left hand. It turned easily in his fingers. Whatever he was about here, Roland did not seem to be concerned that someone might walk in on him with a pistol. Then again, perhaps he simply did not intend to stay very long and wished to be able to leave quickly without having to fumble for a key.

Arthur listened intently for a moment. There was no conversation inside the room. He could hear only one person, presumably Roland, moving around inside.

A drawer opened and closed. A moment later there was a squeak. The rusty hinges of a wardrobe?

When he heard a lengthy scraping sound he used the noise as cover to open the door.

He found himself looking into a small chamber furnished with a bed, a wardrobe and an old washstand. Roland was crouched on the bare wooden floorboards, searching under the bed. He did not hear Arthur enter the room.

"Good evening, Burnley."

"What?" Roland jerked around, staggering to his feet. He stared. "*St. Merryn.* So it's true." Anguish leaped in his eyes. It was washed away an instant later by a searing anger. "You did force her into your bed. *Bastard.*"

He launched himself toward Arthur in a reckless fury, both hands outstretched. Either he had not noticed the pistol or he was too enraged to care about the threat it posed.

Arthur moved swiftly out of the doorway and into the hall. He sidestepped and stuck out one booted foot. Roland's momentum carried him forward with such energy and speed that he could not halt his rush.

He stumbled over Arthur's boot and flailed desperately in a vain attempt to catch his balance. He did not fall to the floor but he wheeled and collided with the wall on the opposite side of the hall.

Jolted, he steadied himself with both hands. "Damn you to Hell, St. Merryn."

"I suggest we discuss this like sane gentlemen, not a couple of wild hotheads," Arthur said quietly.

"How dare you call yourself a gentleman, sir, after the wicked thing you have done?"

Arthur slowly lowered the pistol. For the first time Roland appeared to notice the weapon. Frowning, he followed the motion with his eyes.

"What, precisely, am I supposed to have done that is so evil?" Arthur asked.

"You know the nature of your crime very well. It is monstrous."

"Describe it to me."

"You forced my sweet Juliana to give herself to you in exchange for your promise to pay off my gaming debts. Do not deny it."

"Actually, I am going to deny it." Arthur used the tip of the pistol to motion Roland back into the room. "Every damn word." He glanced toward the dark stairs. "Come inside. I do not want to conduct this conversation out in the corridor."

"Do you plan to murder me, then? Is that the final step in your scheme of revenge?"

"No, I am not going to kill you. Come back in here. Now."

Roland glanced warily at the pistol. Reluctantly he peeled himself away from the wall and edged into the room.

"You never loved her, St. Merryn, admit it. But you wanted her, did you not? You were furious when she ran off with me, so you concocted a cold-blooded vengeance. You bided your time. You waited until you saw that I was in dun territory and then you sent Juliana word that you would cover my debts if she would agree to surrender herself to you."

"Who told you this strange tale, Burnley?"

"A friend."

"You know what they say: with friends of that sort, you do not need any enemies." Arthur put the pistol back into his pocket and surveyed the chamber. "I presume you came here tonight because you expected to find Juliana with me in that bed?"

Roland flinched. His mouth thinned. "I received a message while I was playing hazard. It said that if I came to this address immediately, I would find proof of your crime here."

"How was the message delivered?"

"A street boy handed it to the porter at the club."

"Interesting." Arthur crossed the room to the wardrobe and examined the empty interior. "And did you find proof that I blackmailed your wife into bed?"

"I had not finished searching the room when you arrived." Roland clenched his hands into fists. "But the fact that you are here would certainly indicate that you are familiar with this room."

"I had just reached the same conclusion about you," Arthur said.

He turned away from the wardrobe and went to the washstand. Methodically he opened and closed the drawers.

"What are you doing?" Roland demanded.

"Looking for whatever it is you were supposed to discover in this room." He opened the last drawer and saw a black velvet sack closed with a leather cord inside. A chill of understanding crept through him. "Then again, maybe I was the one who was meant to make a discovery here tonight."

Arthur untied the thong and turned the black velvet bag upside down. Two objects bound in linen fell into his palm.

He set the items on the washstand and unwrapped both in turn.

He and Roland studied the two beautifully enameled snuffboxes. Each was decorated with a miniature scene of an alchemist at work. Each lid was set with a large, faceted red stone.

Roland moved closer, scowling. "Snuffboxes? What are they doing here?"

Arthur watched the lantern light dance on the gleaming boxes in his hand. "It appears that we were both meant to play the parts of fools tonight. We very nearly succeeded in our roles."

"What are you talking about?"

Arthur carefully replaced the snuffboxes inside the velvet bag. "I believe that someone intended for me to kill you tonight, Burnley. Or, at the very least, have you taken up on charges of murder."

The carriage rumbled into motion before Arthur had got the door closed. Elenora restrained herself until both men were settled on the seat across from her. She tried to read their faces in the shadows.

"What is going on here?" she asked, trying to ignore the anxiety coursing through her veins.

"Allow me to introduce you to Roland Burnley." Arthur shut the door and pulled down the shades to cover the windows. "Burnley, my fiancée, Miss Elenora Lodge."

Roland, slouched uneasily in the corner, slanted him an uncertain glance and then eyed Elenora. She saw both disapproval and curiosity in his gaze.

Roland had heard the rumors that were circulating

in the clubs about her, she thought, and did not know what to make of this business. Obviously he wondered if he was being introduced to a respectable lady or a courtesan. Such a situation was bound to plunge any properly bred gentleman into a quandary.

She gave him her warmest smile and extended her hand toward him with cool expectation. "A pleasure to meet you, sir."

Roland hesitated, but confronted with a lady's gloved fingers and a formal introduction, his early training in manners took over.

"Miss Lodge." He inclined his head over her hand in perfunctory acknowledgment.

He dropped her fingers almost immediately, but not before Elenora had taken the measure of his grip. She looked at Arthur.

"He is not the one you are searching for, sir," she said quietly.

"I came to the same conclusion myself, a short time ago." Arthur tossed a black velvet sack lightly into her lap and turned up one of the carriage lamps "But it would appear someone intended for me to believe otherwise. Take a look."

She felt the weight and shapes of the objects inside. "Never say you found the snuffboxes?"

"Yes."

"Good heavens." Quickly she loosened the cord and removed the small objects wrapped in cloth. She uncovered the first one and held the object up to the carriage lamp. The light gleamed on the enamel decorations and sparkled on the large red stone in the lid. "What can this mean?"

"I have been asking St. Merryn just that question for the past several minutes," Roland grumbled. "He has not yet seen fit to respond."

"It is a complicated tale, sir," Elenora assured him. "I'm certain St. Merryn will explain things to you now that you are both safe."

Arthur shifted slightly and stretched out one leg. "The long and the short of it, Burnley, is that I am hunting the villain who murdered my great-uncle and at least two other men."

Roland stared. "What the devil?"

"I was led to believe that the killer is a frequent patron of the Green Lyon, so Miss Lodge and I kept watch tonight. Imagine my astonishment when I noticed you leaving the club and walking off alone down a dark street."

"I told you, I had reason to think that—" Roland stopped in mid-sentence and glanced at Elenora. He flushed a dark red.

Arthur looked at Elenora. "Someone told him that his wife had betrayed him with me, and that if he went to a certain address, he would find proof."

Elenora was shocked. "What monstrous nonsense."

Arthur shrugged.

She rounded on Roland. "Allow me to tell you, sir, that St. Merryn is a gentleman possessed of the most elevated notions of honor and the most refined sense of integrity. If you knew anything about him at all, you would know that it is inconceivable that he would have seduced your wife."

Roland shot Arthur a ferocious glare. "I'm not so sure of that."

Amusement gleamed in Arthur's eyes, but he said nothing.

"Well, I *am* certain of it, sir," Elenora declared. "And if you continue to believe such rubbish, you are worse than a fool. Furthermore, I must tell you that you do your wife an equally great wrong by allowing

332

yourself to think for even one moment that she would betray you."

"You know nothing about this matter," Roland muttered. But he was starting to look somewhat hunted.

"You are mistaken in that regard as well," Elenora informed him. "I have had the privilege of making Mrs. Burnley's acquaintance. It was obvious to me that she loves you deeply and would never do anything to hurt you."

Uncertainty and confusion tightened Roland's features. "You've met Juliana? I do not understand. How did that come about?"

"That is neither here nor there at the moment. Suffice it to say that I have complete faith in the depth of her feelings toward you, even if you do not. I have even greater faith in St. Merryn's honor." She turned back to Arthur. "Pray continue with your tale, sir."

Arthur inclined his head. "It is clear that the villain arranged for me to see Burnley here this evening, assumed that I would follow him, discover him with the snuffboxes and leap to the conclusion that he is the man that I have been hunting. He no doubt intended the entire affair as a distraction to put me off the scent."

"Yes, of course," Elenora said slowly. "Whoever he is, he obviously knows that you and Mr. Burnley are not on the best of terms. He was certain that each of you would believe the worst of each other."

"Huh." Roland seemed to withdraw even farther into his corner.

Arthur exhaled heavily.

Elenora bestowed a bracing smile on both men. "The villain misread the pair of you rather badly, did he not? Then again, how could he be expected to comprehend that you were each far too insightful and intelligent to make such a dreadful mistake about each other's intentions? He no doubt judged you both by how he himself would have reacted in such a situation."

"Mmm." Arthur was evidently bored by the conversation.

Roland grunted and examined the tips of his boots.

Elenora looked into the faces of both men and felt a disturbing prickle in her palms. In that moment she knew that whatever had transpired between Arthur and Roland a short time before, it had been a very near thing.

"Well, then, that's over and done," she continued, determined to dispel the grim mood. "We have a good many questions to ask you, Mr. Burnley. I hope you don't mind?"

"What questions?" he asked, looking wary.

Arthur studied Roland. "Let us begin with you telling us everything you can about the man who suggested that you go to that room tonight."

Roland crossed his arms. "There is not much to tell. I made his acquaintance a few days ago over a hand of cards. I won several hundred pounds from him that first night. Unfortunately, I lost the whole of that amount and more in the following days."

"Was he the one who suggested that you visit the Green Lyon?" Elenora asked.

Roland's mouth tightened. "Yes."

"What was his name?" she pressed.

"Stone."

"Describe him," Arthur said.

Roland spread his hands. "Slender. Blue eyes. His hair is medium brown in color. He is about my height. Good features."

"What of his age?" Elenora asked.

"In the same vicinity as my own. That was one of the reasons we got on so well, I suppose. That and the fact that he seemed to comprehend the difficulties of my financial situation."

Elenora tightened her hold on the velvet bag in her lap. "Did he tell you anything about himself?"

"Very little." Roland paused as though trying to summon up the memories. "Mostly we talked about how my present financial problems had all been created by—" He stopped abruptly and shot Arthur a quick, annoyed look.

"He encouraged you to blame me for your difficulties?" Arthur asked dryly.

Roland went back to examining his boots.

Elenora nodded reassuringly. "Do not concern yourself, Mr. Burnley. Your financial problems will soon be behind you. St. Merryn plans to invite you to participate in one of his new investment ventures."

Roland jerked upright. "What's this? What are you talking about?"

Arthur gave Elenora an impatient look. She pretended not to notice.

"You and St. Merryn can discuss the matter of your finances later, Mr. Burnley. For the moment we must stick with the subject of this man who took you to the Green Lyon to gamble. Please try to recall anything that he might have said about himself that seemed unusual or interesting."

Roland was torn, clearly wanting to pursue the topic of investments. But he subsided.

"There really is not much else that I can tell you," he said. "We shared a few bottles of claret and played some cards." He paused. "Well, there was one thing. I got the impression that he was very interested in natural philosophy and matters of science."

Elenora caught her breath.

"What did he say about his interest in science?" Arthur asked.

"I cannot recall precisely." Roland frowned. "The subject arose after a game of hazard. I had lost a rather large sum. Stone bought a bottle of claret to console me. We drank for a while, talking of various matters. And then he asked me if I knew that England had lost its second Newton several years ago before the man could demonstrate his genius to the world."

Elenora's mouth went dry. She looked at Arthur and saw the dark glitter of comprehension in his eyes.

"That reminds me of the question that we neglected to ask Lady Wilmington," she said. "Not that it is at all likely that she would have told us the truth, of course."

Chapter Thirty-Three

I'm not at all certain that this is the right step to take, sir." Elenora adjusted her shawl and looked up at the darkened windows of the townhouse. "It is two o'clock in the morning. Perhaps we should have gone home and considered more carefully before coming here."

"I have no intention of waiting until a more polite hour to speak with Lady Wilmington," Arthur said.

He raised the heavy brass knocker for the third time and let it drop. Elenora winced as the clang reverberated loudly in the silence.

A short time before, they had dropped Roland off at his club, giving him instructions to keep silent about what had occurred that evening. Arthur had then ordered the carriage driven directly to Lady Wilmington's address.

Footsteps sounded at last in the hallway. A few seconds later the door opened warily. A sleepy-eyed maid dressed in a cap and a thin wrapper gazed out at them. She held a candle in one hand.

"What's this all about? Ye must have the wrong house, sir."

"This is the right house." Arthur shouldered his way through the opening. "Summon Lady Wilmington immediately. Tell her this is a matter of great urgency. Life or death."

"Life or death?" The maid stood back, her face scrunching in horror.

Elenora took advantage of the woman's startled nerves to nip through the doorway behind Arthur. She smiled calmly.

"Go and tell Lady Wilmington that St. Merryn and his fiancée are here," she said firmly. "I'm sure she will see us."

"Yes, ma'am." The clear instructions seemed to steady the maid's jangled nerves. She lit another candle on the hall table and then hastened up the stairs.

A short time later she hurried back down.

"Her ladyship says to tell ye that she'll join ye in the study in a moment."

I still say we should have given this matter more close thought before coming here tonight," Elenora declared.

She sat tensely in a dainty chair in the elegant little study. The candle that the maid had lit for them sat on the beautifully inlaid writing desk near the window.

"The reference to a second Newton cannot have been a coincidence. You know that as well as I do." Arthur prowled the small room, his hands clasped behind his back. "Lady Wilmington is the key to this puzzle. I can feel it in my bones."

She was in perfect agreement with his conclusions; it was the way he intended to confront Lady

338

Wilmington that worried her. This was a delicate matter. It should have been approached more subtly.

"Earlier this evening I could not help but recall our visit with her," she said. "I kept thinking about the way she touched her locket whenever she spoke of Treyford. It occurred to me that, if they were lovers, perhaps there had been a child—"

"Not a son." Arthur shook his head. "I investigated that possibility tonight. Lady Wilmington's only male heir is a staid, extremely stout, respectable gentleman who, by all accounts, takes after her husband in his looks and also in his intellectual interests. He is devoted to his estates and never cared for matters of science."

"St. Merryn." Lady Wilmington spoke from the doorway, her voice flat with resignation. "Miss Lodge. So you somehow discovered the truth. I feared that you would."

Arthur stopped his pacing and looked toward the doorway. "Good evening, madam. I can see that you know why we are here at this late hour."

"Yes." Lady Wilmington walked slowly into the study.

She looked much older tonight, Elenora thought, aware of a stark pity for the once beautiful and still proud woman. Lady Wilmington's gray hair was not in a fashionable chignon tonight. Instead, it was tucked up under a white cap. She had the haggard look of someone who has not slept well in recent days. Her hands were bare of rings, and no pearls gleamed at her ears.

But Elenora noticed that she wore the gold locket around her throat.

Lady Wilmington sat down in the chair that Arthur held for her. "You have come here to ask about my grandson, haven't you?"

Arthur was riveted. "Yes, of course," he said very softly.

"He is Treyford's grandson, isn't he?" Elenora asked gently.

"Yes." Lady Wilmington focused her attention on the flaring candle. "Treyford and I were passionately in love. But I was married with two children by my husband. There was nothing to be done when I discovered that I was to bear my lover's babe. I pretended that Wilmington was the father and, of course, under the law there was no question but that he was my daughter's sire. No one suspected the truth."

"Did Treyford know that you had borne his child?" Arthur asked.

"Yes. He was quite pleased. He talked at length of how he would supervise her education in the manner of a concerned friend of the family. He promised to draw up elaborate plans to see that she was instructed in natural philosophy and mathematics from the cradle."

"But then Treyford was killed in that explosion in his laboratory," Arthur said.

"I thought my heart would break that day when the news reached me that he was dead." Lady Wilmington touched her locket with her fingertips. "I consoled myself with the knowledge that I had his child. I vowed to educate Helen as Treyford had intended. But although she was extremely intelligent, she showed no interest in science or mathematics. The only subject that drew her was music. She played and composed brilliantly, but I knew that Treyford would have been so disappointed."

"However, when she married, your daughter bore a son who did possess both Treyford's great mind and his passion for science." Arthur gripped the back of a chair, watching Lady Wilmington very closely. "Is that correct, madam?"

Lady Wilmington toyed with the locket. "Parker is the very image of Treyford at that age. The likeness is astonishing. When my daughter and her husband were taken off by a fever, I vowed to raise my grandson as Treyford would have wished."

"You told him the truth about his grandfather's identity, didn't you?" Elenora said quietly.

"Yes. When he was old enough to understand, I told him about Treyford. He deserved to know that the blood of true genius ran in his veins."

"You told him that he was the direct descendant of the man who could have been England's second Newton," Arthur said. "And Parker set out to fulfill his grandfather's legacy."

"He studied all of the subjects that had so fascinated Treyford," she whispered.

Elenora looked at her. "Including alchemy?"

"Yes." Lady Wilmington shuddered. "You must believe me when I tell you that I tried to steer Parker away from that dark path. But as he grew older, he showed signs of taking after Treyford in ways other than his intellectual interests."

"What do you mean?" Arthur asked.

"Parker's temperament became increasingly unpredictable as the years passed. He would be joyous and cheerful for no obvious reason. And then, without warning, his spirits would sink to a level that made me fear that he might take his own life. Only his alchemical studies seemed to have the power to distract him when he was in such a mood. Two years ago he went to Italy to continue his investigations."

"When did he return?" Arthur asked.

"A few months ago." Lady Wilmington sighed in pain. "I was so happy to have him back, but I soon realized that whatever he had learned in Italy had only deepened his commitment to alchemy. He demanded to see Treyford's journals and papers. I had stored them in a trunk."

"You gave them to him?" Elenora asked.

"I hoped that would satisfy him. But I fear that I only made things worse. I knew he had embarked upon some secret project, but I did not know what it was that he hoped to create."

"What did you assume that he was trying to do?" Arthur asked coldly, "discover the Philosopher's Stone? Transmute lead into gold?"

"You mock me, sir, but I tell you in all truth, Parker is sunk so deep into his occult researches that he believes such things are possible."

"When did you first realize that he was determined to construct the device described in the *Book of Stones*?" Arthur asked.

Lady Wilmington looked at him with sad resignation. "Not until you came to see me the other day and told me that both Glentworth and your great-uncle had been murdered and that their snuffboxes had been stolen. I knew then what Parker intended."

"And you also knew that he had gone beyond being an eccentric genius," Arthur said. "You realized that he had become a murderer."

Lady Wilmington bowed her head and clasped the locket very tightly in her fingers. She did not speak.

"Where is Parker?" Arthur asked.

Lady Wilmington raised her head. A quiet resolve seemed to have settled upon her. "There is no longer any need for you to concern yourself with my grandson, sir. I have taken care of the situation."

Arthur's jaw tightened. "Surely you understand that he must be stopped, madam."

"Yes. And I have done just that."

"I beg your pardon?"

"There will be no more murders." Lady Wilmington's hand dropped away from the locket. "You have my word. Parker is in a place where he can do no one, including himself, any more harm."

Elenora searched her face. "What have you done, madam?"

"My grandson is insane." Tears glittered in Lady Wilmington's eyes. "I can no longer pretend otherwise. But please understand that I could not bear the thought of him being chained in Bedlam."

Elenora shuddered. "No one would wish such a fate on a beloved relative. But—"

"After you left me the other day, I summoned my personal doctor. I have known him for years, and I trust him completely. He made arrangements for Parker to be taken to a private asylum in the country."

"You have had him committed to an asylum?" Arthur repeated sharply.

"Yes. Dr. Mitchell and two attendants went to Parker's lodgings this afternoon. They surprised him as he was dressing to go out to his club, and they subdued him."

Arthur frowned. "Are you certain of that?"

"I went with them and watched those men overcome Parker and strap him into that dreadful strait-waistcoat. My grandson pleaded with me as they forced him into a barred wagon. And then they silenced him with a strip of cloth across his mouth. I could not stop crying for hours."

"Dear God," Elenora whispered.

Lady Wilmington stared dully at the candle. "I

assure you, tonight has been the most terrible night of my entire life. It was even worse than the day I learned that Treyford had been lost to me forever."

Elenora felt tears swim in her own eyes. She rose quickly and went to Lady Wilmington's chair. Sinking to her knees, she covered the woman's hands with her own.

"I am so sorry that you were forced to endure such a great tragedy," she told her.

Lady Wilmington did not seem to hear her. She continued to gaze at the candle.

"There is something I would like clarified, if you don't mind, Lady Wilmington," Arthur said quietly. "If Parker was taken away to a private asylum earlier today, who arranged for Roland Burnley to receive a note telling him to go to an address near the Green Lyon tonight? And who made certain that I would follow him and discover the snuffboxes?"

Lady Wilmington heaved a sigh. "Parker is extremely exacting when it comes to making plans. It is yet another trait that he inherited from Treyford. His scheme involving you and young Mr. Burnley this evening must have been in place before the attendants took him away this afternoon. I'm sorry, I knew nothing about it. If I had realized what was afoot, I would have sent a warning to you, sir. At least no one else has died since you came to me with your tale."

"True." Arthur flexed one hand into a fist and then released it. "Although the situation was somewhat uncertain there for a while tonight when I found Burnley with those damned snuffboxes."

Lady Wilmington used a handkerchief to wipe her tears. "I am so very sorry, sir. I do not know what else to say."

"Speaking of the snuffboxes," Arthur continued, "I

wonder why Parker arranged for me to discover them? You say he was obsessed with constructing Jove's Thunderbolt. If that was true, he needed the red stones. Why let two of them fall into my hands?"

Elenora got to her feet. "Perhaps we had better take a closer look at those snuffboxes. I can think of only one reason why Parker would let you find them."

Arthur caught her meaning at once. He opened the velvet sack and removed one of the snuffboxes. Then he lit the lamp on the small writing desk.

Elenora watched as he held the lid of the box in the light of the lamp and studied it closely.

"Yes, of course," he said, slowly lowering the snuffbox.

"What is it?" Lady Wilmington asked.

"I will take the boxes to a jeweler in the morning to make absolutely certain," Arthur said. "But I think it is safe to say that this stone is merely colored glass that has been cut to resemble the original gem."

"Now it all makes sense," Elenora said. "Parker removed all three of the red stones and had them replaced with glass replicas. I wonder where he hid the real gems?"

Lady Wilmington shook her head, perplexed. "I suppose it's possible he had them on his person when they took him away this afternoon. But perhaps they are hidden somewhere in his lodgings."

"If you will give me the address, I will search his rooms tomorrow morning," Arthur said.

Lady Wilmington looked at him with a despair that caught at Elenora's heart.

"I will give you the key to Parker's rooms," Lady Wilmington declared. "I can only pray that you will forgive me for not being more forthright with you from the start of this affair."

"We comprehend your feelings in this matter." Elenora soothed the woman's trembling hands. "He is your grandson, and he is all that you have left of your lost love."

A few minutes later Arthur got into the carriage after Elenora. Instead of sitting across from her as was his usual practice, he lowered himself down beside her. With a deeply felt sigh he stretched out his legs. His thigh brushed against hers.

His close physical proximity was somehow comforting rather than stimulating tonight, she noticed. It was a good feeling, and she knew that it was yet another aspect of their association that she would miss in the years ahead.

"It makes sense that he would have arranged his plans yesterday or even the day before," Arthur said after a while. "He used Jeremy Clyde, who unknowingly played his part and dropped the lure that took me to the Green Lyon this evening. In addition, Parker no doubt set some street boys to watch for me to arrive. One of them must have noticed me inside this hired carriage and delivered the message to Burnley."

"All in the hopes of distracting you by making you think that you had found your killer."

"Yes."

"He assumed that you would be all too eager to believe that Burnley was the villain. After all, Roland had run off with your fiancée." She smiled wryly. "How could the killer have possibly known that you bore no ill will toward Roland and had, in fact, orchestrated the elopement?"

"It was his only miscalculation."

"Yes. And speaking of mistakes, obviously it was, indeed, my overheated imagination that made me think that footman who touched me in the ballroom this evening was the murderer." She shivered. "I must admit I'm very glad I was wrong about his identity."

"So am I. The notion that he might have touched you again—"

"For what it is worth sir, I believe that Lady Wilmington took the right course of action," she said quickly, hoping to distract his thoughts. "Parker is mad. There were only two options, an asylum or the gallows."

"I agree."

"It is over," she said gently. "The affair is concluded. You have fulfilled your responsibility. Let your mind be at ease."

He did not speak. But after a while he reached out, clasped her hand and closed his fingers very tightly around hers.

They sat without speaking, holding hands, until the carriage arrived at the front door of the big house in Rain Street.

Chapter Thirty-Four

The clock on the table beside the bed read three-fifteen. Arthur looked at it from his post near the window. He had undressed but he had not yet bothered to climb beneath the quilts. There was no point. It was not sleep he needed.

He needed Elenora.

The house seemed to slumber around him. The servants had long since gone to bed. If past behavior was a reliable guide, Bennett would not bring Margaret home until dawn.

He wondered if Elenora was finding sleep as elusive as he was finding it.

He looked out the window into the night-drenched garden and thought about how Elenora would look curled up in bed. Then he reminded himself yet again that a gentleman must not knock on a lady's bedchamber door unless he had been invited to do so.

Elenora had not issued any invitations when he had said good night to her a short time ago. In point of fact, she had instructed him quite succinctly to get some sleep.

He was not in a mood to follow those orders.

He contemplated the darkness for a while longer. It would be irresponsible to go to Elenora's room. True, they had got away with that episode in the library, but he had no right to put her into such a potentially embarrassing situation again.

The risks were many and varied. Margaret and Bennett could easily come home early, and Margaret might discover that he was in the wrong bedchamber. Or one of the servants might hear the creak of the floorboards and, fearing burglars, come upstairs to investigate.

But he knew, deep down, it was not the risk of discovery that was holding him back. It was the possibility that all Elenora wanted or needed from him was a short-lived passion.

He thought about her dreams of financial and personal independence. For a brief, heady moment he pictured what it would be like to cast off the shackles of his responsibilities to the Lancaster family and run away with Elenora.

The fantasy of living a gloriously free life with her in some far-off clime, well beyond the reach of his relatives and the demands of those who depended upon him, shimmered in front of his eyes, an effervescent reflection on the window pane.

The image quickly vanished. He had commitments. He would keep them.

But tonight Elenora was only just down the hall.

He tightened the sash of his black silk dressing gown and turned away from the window. Picking up the candle, he crossed the room, opened the door and let himself out into the corridor.

He stood listening for a few seconds. There was no sound of a carriage out in the street, no noise from downstairs.

He went along the hall and stopped in front of Elenora's bedchamber. No light shone beneath the door. He told himself he should take that as a sign that, unlike him, she had been able to go to sleep.

But what if she was lying there in the darkness, wide awake? It would not hurt to tap lightly on the door. If she was sound asleep, she would not notice the small noise.

He rapped, not quite as softly as he had intended. But, then, what would have been the point of a sound-less little tap?

For a moment he heard nothing. Then he caught the unmistakable squeak of the bed frame followed by muffled footsteps.

The door opened. Elenora looked out at him with eyes that appeared fathomless in the glow of the can-dle. Her dark hair was pinned up under a lacy little cap. She wore a plain dressing gown patterned with small flowers.

"Is something wrong?" she whispered.

"Invite me inside."

Her brows knit together. "Why?"

"Because, as a gentleman, I cannot enter your bed-chamber without an invitation."

"Oh."

He held his breath, wondering what she would do.

Her mouth curved in a slow, sensual smile. She stood back and held the door wide. "Please, come in."

Desire so powerful that it threatened to consume every other sensation thundered through his veins. He was already hard, fiercely aroused. He was desperate for her.

It took all the control he possessed not to seize her and carry her straight to the bed. He forced himself to move silently into the room and set the candle down on the nearest table.

She closed the door noiselessly and turned to face him.

"Arthur, I—"

"Hush. No one must hear us talking together in here."

He took her into his arms and kissed her before she could speak another word.

Her arms went around him very tightly. He felt her nails sink into his back through the silk of his dressing gown. Her mouth opened slightly, allowing him inside.

He *would* control himself, he vowed. This time he would make the experience one that would ensure that she never forgot him.

He slid his palms down her spine, savoring the elegant curve. When his fingers closed over her hips, the feel of her firm, round buttocks under his hands almost sent him over the edge. He squeezed gently and urged her snugly against his rigid staff.

Another delicious little shiver went through her. She made a tiny, breathless sound and clung to him.

He moved his hands around her waist and undid the knot in the sash that held her wrapper together. The garment parted to reveal a simple white lawn nightgown trimmed at the throat with lace and blue ribbons. He could see the soft swell of her breasts and the peaks of her nipples pressing against the delicate fabric.

He kissed her throat and then caught her dainty, delicate earlobe between his teeth. She responded with more shivers and a choked gasp of pleasure. Her reac-

352

tion thrilled him and stirred him in a way that no drug could ever match.

One by one he removed the pins that secured her little cap. When the last one came free, her hair tumbled over his hands. He made a fist in the sweet, scented tresses and used it to anchor her head for more kisses.

She pushed her hand beneath the lapel of his dressing gown and flattened her palm across his bare chest. The heat of her fingers was so intense that it was all he could do to swallow his groan of raw need.

He looked down into her face. There was enough light from the candle to show him that her expression was drenched in wonder and passion. She parted her lips, and he knew that she had already sunk so far into the realm of sensation that she had forgotten the need for silence.

Hastily, he covered her open mouth with his hand and shook his head, smiling slightly. Rueful comprehension gleamed in her eyes. A teasing, provocative light quickly followed. Very gently, very deliberately, she bit the palm of his hand.

He almost laughed aloud. Half-drunk with the knowledge of what was yet to come, he picked her up in his arms and carried her to the bed.

He tumbled her down onto the rumpled sheets and stripped off his dressing gown and slippers. He was entirely naked now, as he had not put on a nightshirt earlier when he had prepared for bed. He suddenly realized that this was the first time Elenora had seen him in a state of complete undress.

He looked down at her, wondering if she would find him pleasant to look upon or if the sight of his uncovered, fully aroused body would make her uneasy.

But when he saw her expression, his tension disappeared. A radiant fascination gleamed in her eyes, making him smile. When she reached out to encircle him with her fingers, it was all he could do to contain himself.

Slowly, deliberately, he lowered himself onto the bed. For a few minutes, he relished the hot pleasure of being touched intimately by Elenora. But after a moment or two of exquisite torture, he was forced to catch and trap her exploring hands. If he did not stop her, he thought, he would not be able to finish this as he intended.

He pushed her gently onto her back, bent over her and slid his palm along her bare thigh. The bottom edge of her nightgown caught on his wrist and was carried upward with the movement of his hand.

He did not stop until he could see the triangle of dark hair that veiled her secrets.

He leaned down and kissed her soft, beautifully round knee. She brushed her fingers across the back of his neck. After a moment he gently separated her legs and touched his tongue to the inside of one silken thigh. This time her fingers tightened in his hair.

"Arthur?"

Reaching up with one hand, he covered her lips with his palm, reminding her of the need for silence.

When he felt her subside, he returned to his task.

He settled himself between her legs and inhaled the exquisitely feminine scent he discovered there. She smelled of the sea and spices too rare to be named. He could live the rest of his life on that drugging fragrance, he thought. Raising her knees on either side of his head, he found the small, sensitive bud and began to work it with his fingers.

She stiffened immediately, as though not quite certain how to respond. But her body knew precisely what to do. In a very short time she was so wet that his hands glistened in the candlelight.

She began to breathe more quickly. Her hips shifted, lifting against him. When he eased a finger into her she clenched around him and gasped.

He lowered his head and kissed the very heart of her desire, simultaneously sliding another finger into her and probing gently.

"Arthur," she gasped in a muffled whisper. She struggled to rise to a sitting position. "What are you doing?"

He did not raise his head, but he used one hand to push her gently but firmly back down onto the bed.

At first he thought she would resist. But gradually she moaned and fell back. He could hear her quick little breaths. He knew that she was in the grip of a force she did not fully comprehend.

"Oh, my, oh, my, ooooh, my goodness."

So much for her vow of silence, he thought, amused but also a little worried. He could not stop now, though. She was too close and he was determined to finish this properly.

He sensed her impending climax before she did. Her hands twisted in the sheets. Her entire body tensed.

She was lost, he thought. She no longer had any notion of what was going on around her.

In that moment he heard the unmistakable sound of the door in the front hall opening. He caught the distant, muffled murmur of voices downstairs.

Margaret and Bennett were home.

Elenora's release burst upon her like a storm. He raised his head quickly and saw her lips part. Her eyes were squeezed shut.

Disaster loomed.

He moved, propelling himself forward until he

covered her body with his own. He caught her head between his hands and clamped his mouth over hers, swallowing the high, desperate shriek of astonished pleasure.

A moment later she softened beneath him. Cautiously he raised his head, freeing her mouth. He put a fingertip to her lips and spoke directly into her ear. She looked up at him with dazed, uncomprehending eyes.

"Margaret and Bennett are here," he whispered.

Downstairs, the door closed. Margaret's footsteps sounded on the stairs.

Arthur did not move so much as a muscle. Beneath him, Elenora was just as perfectly still. They both listened intently.

Margaret's steps grew louder as she started down the hall toward her bedchamber. Arthur met Elenora's eyes. As one, they both looked at the candle that still burned on the table.

He knew that they were each wondering the same thing. Would Margaret notice the pale slant of light beneath the door?

Margaret's footsteps paused at her own bedchamber and then, just as Arthur had begun to believe he and Elenora had been spared, she continued on down the hall.

She was going to knock and she would expect Elenora to answer the door, he thought. He could only hope that Elenora would be able to come up with a convenient excuse for not inviting her into the bedchamber for a late-night chat.

He became aware of the fact that Elenora had both hands planted against his chest and was pushing upward with all her strength. Obediently, he rolled away and got silently to his feet beside the bed.

The inevitable knock sounded on the door of the bedchamber.

"Elenora? I noticed the candle. If you're not too exhausted, I have the most exciting news. Bennett has asked me to marry him."

"One moment, Margaret, while I put on my wrapper and slippers." Elenora bounded out of bed. "Your news is thrilling. I am so pleased for you."

She continued talking in bright, enthusiastic tones while she wrenched open the wardrobe door, yanked the billowing skirts of several gowns aside and gestured frantically at Arthur.

He realized that she intended for him to hide inside the damned wardrobe. He stifled a groan. She was right. It was the only place of concealment in the bedchamber.

He paused to pick up his dressing gown and slippers and then, with great reluctance, he got into the wardrobe. Elenora promptly closed the door. He was immediately enveloped in fine muslin, scented silks and darkness.

He heard Elenora open the bedchamber door.

"I think this calls for a celebration, don't you?" she said to Margaret. "Why don't we go downstairs to the library and sample some of Arthur's excellent brandy? I want to hear every detail of Bennett's proposal. Also, I have the most astonishing news to tell you, too."

Margaret laughed happily, sounding for all the world like a young lady in the throes of her first great love affair. Maybe that was precisely the case, Arthur thought.

"Do you think we dare help ourselves to the brandy, though?" Margaret asked with a hint of genuine concern. "You know how Arthur feels about it. He treats the stuff as though it were a rare golden elixir of the gods."

"Trust me," Elenora said with great depth of feeling. "In this instance Arthur will not have the slightest objection to us going downstairs to drink some of his precious brandy."

The door closed behind the two women.

Arthur brooded amid the shadows and the feminine skirts for a few minutes, wondering what had become of his orderly, well-planned life. He could not believe that he was hiding in a wardrobe inside a lady's bed-chamber.

Things like this had never happened to him before he had met Elenora.

Chapter Thirty-Five

The following afternoon was Wednesday, the day the servants had free. Elenora found herself alone in the house with Sally, who quickly disappeared to her room to read her new Margaret Mallory novel.

Margaret had gone out with Bennett a half hour before. Arthur had left soon thereafter, saying that he intended to search the rooms where Parker had lived. Elenora knew he had expected her to insist upon accompanying him, but when he had informed her of his plan, she had merely nodded absently and wished him luck finding the three red gems.

At two-thirty, she put on her bonnet and gloves and set out for a walk.

It was a warm, sunny day. When she arrived at her destination she found Lucinda Colyer and Charlotte Atwater waiting for her in the perpetual funereal gloom of Mrs. Blancheflower's parlor.

"There you are, Elenora." Lucinda reached for the teapot. "We are anxious to hear your news."

"I think you will find it very interesting." Elenora sat down on the sofa and surveyed her two friends. "I apologize for the short notice."

"Do not worry about that," Charlotte said. "In your note you claimed that there was a matter of great import that we had to discuss immediately."

"Good heavens, it happened, didn't it?" Lucinda's eyes lit with horrified expectation. "Just as I predicted. Your new employer took advantage of you. My poor, poor, Elenora. I did warn you."

Elenora thought about what Arthur had done to her last night and the incredible sensations she had endured as a result. She suddenly felt quite warm.

"Calm yourself, Lucinda," she said, and took a sip of tea. "I assure you St. Merryn has not perpetrated any grievous insult upon my person."

"Oh." Lucinda's face fell in acute disappointment, but she managed a weak smile. "I'm so relieved to hear that."

Elenora put the cup down on the saucer. "I'm afraid that I cannot regale either of you with thrilling tales of my employer's lechery, but I think that you will find what I have to say even more exciting. It should certainly prove to be a great deal more profitable."

Arthur stood in the center of the small room that Parker had used as a parlor. There was something very wrong about this place.

When Lady Wilmington had given him the key an hour before, she had assured him that he would find Parker's lodgings in the same condition that they had been in the day before, when he had been taken away to the asylum. She had made it clear that she had not yet had time to remove any of her grandson's possessions or furnishings.

Arthur had gone through each of the rooms with methodical precision. He had not found the red stones, but that was not what was making him uneasy. What bothered him was the appearance of these rooms.

On the surface, everything seemed entirely appropriate and unremarkable. The furnishings in the bedchamber, sitting room and kitchen were precisely what one would expect to see in lodgings that had been used by a fashionable young gentleman. The bookcase contained the works of the most popular poets and an assortment of the classics. The clothes in the wardrobe were in the latest style.

There was nothing unusual or out of the ordinary, Arthur noted. And that was what was wrong. Because Parker was a most unusual and extraordinary villain.

Elenora was amused by Lucinda's and Charlotte's reaction to what she had just said. They stared at her in appalled astonishment.

"In short," she concluded, "the gentlemen in the clubs have all concluded that St. Merryn has played a great joke upon Society. They believe that he hired me to serve as an extremely convenient mistress."

"They have concluded that you are his mistress posing as his fiancée. And that he has arranged to have you live right under his roof so as to have you conveniently at hand. How utterly outrageous," Lucinda exclaimed.

Charlotte gave her a quelling frown. "Do try to remember that Elenora is not actually St. Merryn's mistress, Lucinda. That is merely the rumor that is going around the clubs."

"Yes, of course," Lucinda said hastily. She gave Elenora an apologetic, if somewhat regretful grin. "Do go on."

"As I was saying," Elenora continued, "the wagers all involve the date that St. Merryn will end his little charade and dismiss me." She paused a beat to make certain she had their full attention. "I see no reason why we should not take advantage of this situation, to place our own bets."

Comprehension appeared first in their eyes. It was followed almost at once by the first glimmers of wonder and hope.

"It would be a certainty," Charlotte whispered, awed by the possibilities. "If Elenora could persuade St. Merryn to end their association on a specific day—"

"I do not think there will be any problem there," Elenora assured them. "I believe that St. Merryn will cooperate on the matter of the exact date."

"And we would be the only ones who knew that date," Lucinda breathed. "Why, we might each win a fortune."

"It would be tempting to wager several thousand pounds," Elenora said, "but I do not think that would be wise. A vast sum might make people suspicious. We do not want anyone questioning our bets."

"How much, then?" Lucinda demanded.

Elenora hesitated, thinking. "I expect that we could safely wager a total of seven or eight hundred pounds. I should think any amount under a thousand would be small enough to go unnoticed in the betting books. We will split the winnings three ways."

"Certainly sounds like a fortune to me," Lucinda declared, entranced. She glanced meaningfully up at the ceiling. "It is a good deal more than I expect to see from Mrs. Blancheflower in her will, and I probably stand a greater chance of collecting it. I am starting to think my employer may outlive me."

"But how would we arrange to place the bet?" Charlotte asked. "No lady can walk into one of those clubs in St. James and put a wager in the book."

"I have considered the problem closely," Elenora said, "and I believe that I have a plan that will work."

"This is so exciting," Charlotte said.

"I think the venture deserves to be celebrated with more than a cup of tea," Lucinda announced.

She rose from the sofa, opened a cupboard and took down a dusty decanter of sherry.

"One moment," Charlotte said, some of her enthusiasm evaporating. "What happens if we lose the wager? We could not possibly cover our bets."

"For heaven's sake, Charlotte, use your head." Lucinda removed the cut glass top of the sherry decanter. "The only way we could lose is if St. Merryn were to actually marry Elenora. Now, how likely do you think that is?"

Charlotte's face cleared instantly. "Likely? It is inconceivable that a gentleman of his wealth and position would marry a paid companion. I don't know what got into me to even suggest that we might lose."

"Quite right," Elenora said. With an effort of sheer will, she forced back the tears that threatened to fall. She managed a bright smile and raised her sherry glass. "To our wager, ladies."

Half an hour later she set off for the mansion on Rain Street with a feeling that she was walking toward her own doom. It was all very well to drink to a rosy future free of financial worries and filled with the challenge of running her little bookshop, she thought. And no doubt someday, when her tears had dried, she would be able to enjoy the life she planned to create for herself. But first she would have to deal with the pain of parting from Arthur.

She emerged from the park and walked slowly along the street that would take her home. *No, not home. This street leads back to your place of temporary employment. You do not have a home. But you will have one eventually. You are going to create it for yourself.*

At the front door of the big house she remembered that most of the staff was away for the day. She possessed a key and was perfectly capable of opening the door.

She let herself into the hall and removed her pelisse, gloves and bonnet.

What she needed was a cup of tea, she decided. She walked along the hall that led to the back of the house and went down the stone steps into the kitchens. She glanced at the door of the room through which she had overheard Ibbitts extorting money from poor Sally. Only two days later the butler was dead.

She shuddered at the memory and moved on down the hall. The door to Sally's bedchamber was open. She glanced inside, expecting to see the maid curled up with her novel.

The room was empty. Perhaps Sally had decided to go out for the day after all.

In the large kitchen, she prepared herself a tray and carried it upstairs into the library. There she poured herself some tea and went to stand at the window.

The house had been transformed in recent days. The task was not yet complete, but it was already a vastly different place than it had been on the day she had arrived. In spite of her sad mood, she took a quiet satisfaction in what had been accomplished thus far.

The floors and woodwork gleamed from recent

polishing. Rooms that had long been closed had been opened up and cleaned. Covers had been removed from the furnishings. The windows and once-dark mirrors now sparkled on the walls, drawing the sunlight into spaces that had long been filled with gloom. On her instructions, the heavy drapes throughout the mansion had been tied back. There was hardly a speck of dust to be found anywhere.

The gardens were starting to look much more inviting, too, she noticed. She was pleased with the progress that had been made. The gravel paths were all neatly raked. The overgrowth was being methodically trimmed. Fresh planting beds were being repaired. The work on the fountain had begun.

She thought of how beautiful the view from the library would be in another couple of months. The flowers would be in full bloom. The herbs would be ready for the kitchens. The waters of the fountain would sparkle in the sunshine.

She wondered if Arthur would think of her from time to time when he looked out this window.

She finished her tea and was about to turn away when she noticed the man in sturdy work clothes and a leather apron crouched over a flowerbed. She thought about the replacement tiles for the fountain. It would do no harm to have a word with the gardener to make certain that the order had been placed.

Hurrying from the library, she let herself out into the garden.

"A moment, please," she called as she walked swiftly toward the gardener. "I would like to have a word with you."

The gardener grunted, but he did not look up. He continued pulling weeds.

"Do you know whether or not the order for the

fountain tiles was placed?" she asked, coming to a halt beside him.

The man grunted again.

She bent down slightly, watching as he yanked out another straggly green weed. "Did you hear me?"

Her heart almost stopped. *His hands.* The gardener wore no gloves. She could see his long, graceful fingers. A gold signet ring glinted on his left hand. She remembered the feel of that ring beneath the thin glove the killer had worn the night he had invited her to waltz with him.

She caught a trace of his unpleasant scent and straightened quickly. Her pulse was beating so frantically now that she wondered if he might hear it. She stepped back and clasped her hands together to still the fine tremors. She glanced quickly at the door at the back of the house. It seemed a million miles away.

The gardener rose to his feet and turned toward her.

Her first crazed thought was that he seemed far too handsome to be a ruthless killer. And then she saw his eyes and knew there was no doubt about his identity.

"I personally selected a sample of the tiles that I wish installed on the fountain," she said crisply. She took another step back and gave him a thin, shiny smile. "We don't want any mistakes, do we?"

The gardener produced a pistol from behind the leather apron and aimed it at her heart.

"No, Miss Lodge," he said. "We most certainly do not want any mistakes. You have caused me quite enough trouble as it is."

Suddenly she remembered that Sally had not been in her room. Fear and a great fury raged through her.

"What have you done with the maid?" she asked tightly.

"She is quite safe." He motioned toward the shed with the pistol. "See for yourself."

Elenora crossed the short distance to the gardening shed, scarcely able to breathe through her terror, and opened the door.

Sally was inside on the floor, bound and gagged but evidently unharmed. Her eyes widened with desperation and panic when she saw Elenora. A sealed letter lay on the boards beside her.

"Your maid will stay alive so long as you cooperate with me," Miss Lodge," Parker said casually. "But if you give me any difficulty whatsoever, I shall cut her throat before your very eyes."

"Are you mad, sir?" Elenora asked without stopping to consider her words.

The question seemed to amuse him. "My grandmother seems to think so. She had me carried off to an asylum yesterday. And here I thought she doted on me. It is a sad day when one cannot even rely upon one's relatives, isn't it?"

"She was trying to save you."

He shrugged. "Whatever her intentions, I was able to escape within a matter of hours. Why, I was back here in London in time to proceed with my plans last night."

"That was you I saw at the ball."

He gave her a mocking bow. "It was indeed. You do have a very attractive neck, Miss Lodge."

She would not let him unnerve her with such intimate talk, she vowed. "Why did you want St. Merryn to believe that Roland Burnley was the killer?"

"So that the earl would relax his vigilance, of course. I felt it would be easier to snatch you and, later, him, if he let down his guard for a time." He chuckled. "Besides, I rather enjoyed playing games with his lordship. St. Merryn prides himself on his logical mind, but his powers of reason are nothing compared to my own."

"What is this all about?" Elenora asked in her most authoritative tone. Perhaps if she stalled for time someone would return to the house, see her out here in the garden, and come out to investigate.

"All your questions will be answered eventually, Miss Lodge. But first things first. Allow me to introduce myself." Parker inclined his head in a graceful little bow, but the pistol in his hand never wavered. "You have the great honor of meeting England's second Newton."

Chapter Thirty-Six

Arthur put one booted foot on the step and propped his forearm on his thigh. "What made you think that the gentleman who lived in Number Five was odd?"

The elderly housekeeper snorted. "No manservant. No chambermaid. No one to look after his clothes or cook his meals. Lived there all alone. Never knew a young man who could afford better to do for himself."

Arthur glanced back toward the door of Number Five. "Were you here when they took him away?"

"Aye." The woman followed his gaze and shook her head. "A terrible sight it was. They brought him out all bound in one of them strait-waistcoats like they use to bind the poor souls in Bedlam. The fine lady in the carriage was crying her heart out. Afterward everyone said they'd taken him off to a private asylum someplace in the country."

"Did the gentleman ever have any visitors while he lived in this street?"

"None that I saw," the housekeeper said. "But, then,

again, he was only there for a few hours in the afternoons and early evenings."

Arthur straightened and took his foot down off the stone step. "He didn't sleep there?"

"Never saw him come home until midday at the earliest. Figured he spent the nights at his club."

Arthur contemplated the door. "Or somewhere else."

Elenora smelled the damp, dank odor that told her she was underground before Parker removed the blindfold. When he untied the cloth, she opened her eyes and found herself looking at the interior of a windowless stone chamber lit with lamps mounted on the walls.

They had descended into this place in some sort of iron cage. Because her eyes had been covered, she had been unable to see the device, but she had felt the movement and heard the noise of the heavy chain that Parker had used to lower it. He had explained with great pride that only he knew the secret to operating the cage.

"There is a special lock that secures it, top and bottom," he had said. "One must know the combination in order to release it."

The low, vaulted ceiling told her that the room was very old. The gothic design was original, she concluded, not a modern decorator's notion of a fashionable interior. She could hear the faint sound of water dripping or lapping somewhere in the distance.

A number of workbenches were arranged around the chamber. Each was laden with an assortment of instruments and apparatus. Some, such as the balance, microscope and burning lens, she recognized. Others were unfamiliar.

"Welcome to my grandfather's laboratory, Miss

Lodge." Parker gestured widely with one hand. "His collection of equipment and apparatus was excellent. But, naturally, by the time I arrived, they were all several years old. Some were still usable, but I have taken the liberty of replacing many of the instruments with more modern and more advanced devices."

Her hands were still bound in front of her, but Parker had untied the bonds that he had used to secure her ankles during the carriage ride.

At one point during the nightmarish journey she had tried to throw herself out of the vehicle, only to discover that the door was locked and barred. When Parker had given his orders to the two ruffians on the box, she had quickly realized that there was no point appealing for help in that direction. The villains were clearly in Parker's employ.

"We did not travel far," she said, pointedly ignoring his verbal tour of the laboratory. "We must still be in London. Where is this place?"

She kept her voice very even, trying to sound as though she was in control of the situation. Whatever else happened, she would not let him see the terror that filled her heart. She would not give this madman that satisfaction.

"Very astute, Miss Lodge. Yes, indeed, we are still in London. This chamber is located in a rather remote section beneath the ruins of an ancient abbey. Very few people live in the vicinity, and those who do are convinced the place is haunted."

"I see." She glanced around, surveying the shadowy corners of the room. It was not difficult to believe that specters and phantoms lurked in this chamber.

Parker put his pistol down on a workbench and removed his coat. Beneath the well-cut coat he wore a snowy white linen shirt and an elegantly made blue and white patterned waistcoat.

"My grandfather encouraged the local legends surrounding the abbey, and I have continued the tradition," he said. "It is useful for keeping people away from the place."

"Why have you brought me here?"

"It is a somewhat complicated tale, Miss Lodge." He glanced at his watch. "But there is time to tell it." He walked to one of the workbenches and touched the large, malevolent-looking machine that sat there. He stroked the device the way a man might stroke a lover. A terrible reverence glittered in his eyes. "It is a tale of destiny."

"Rubbish. No serious student of science speaks of destiny."

"Ah, but I am more than a serious student of science, my dear. I was born to be its master."

"Your grandmother was right. You are mad."

He gave a short, derisive laugh. "She certainly believes that."

"You have committed murder."

"Murder was only the beginning, Miss Lodge." He moved his hand slowly, lovingly along a part of the machine that resembled the long barrel of a rifle. "Only the beginning. I still have a great deal more to do."

The manner in which he caressed the machine disturbed her. She looked away from his long, elegant fingers. "Tell me about your so-called destiny."

"There can be no doubt about it. Not any longer." He seemed to have become entranced by his machine. "St. Merryn and I share a bond. Neither of us can avoid our fates."

"What do you mean?"

Parker took a small red velvet sack from his pocket and untied the thong that secured it. "We have each inherited a legacy of murder and thwarted destiny. But this time around, matters will turn out much differently than they did last time."

Very carefully he removed a large red gem from the sack and slotted it into an opening on the side of the strange machine.

"What on earth are you talking about?" she asked, desperate to keep him talking.

"My grandfather and St. Merryn's great-uncle were friends until they became fierce rivals. Eventually the competition between them turned bitter. George Lancaster could not abide the fact that my grandfather was Newton's equal, you see. Called him mad. Mocked him."

"You have had your vengeance, haven't you? You murdered Arthur's great-uncle."

"Lancaster's death was an accident, you know. At least, I thought so at the time. I did not intend to kill him, not until after he had witnessed the success of my project. I wanted him to know that he was wrong when he jeered at my grandfather and called him a crazed alchemist. But the old man surprised me that night when he walked in on me while I was searching his laboratory."

"You were looking for the snuffbox."

"Yes. Jove's Thunderbolt requires all three of the stones, you see." He slipped the second dark gem into the device. "After George Lancaster was dead, I thought perhaps I had misinterpreted my destiny, but when I learned that St. Merryn was hunting me, it all became clear. I understood at once that he, not the old man, is the one who is meant to witness my great success. It is perfectly logical."

"How is that?"

373

"George Lancaster and my grandfather lived in a different time. They were men of an earlier generation. They belong to the past. But St. Merryn and I are men of the modern age. It is only fitting that the earl, not his ancestor, be the one to witness my triumph." Parker patted the machine "Just as it is right that I, not my ancestor, untangled the last mystery of Jove's Thunderbolt."

"Where did you discover this supposed destiny?"

"It was all there in my grandfather's journals." Parker eased the last stone into the machine, closed the opening and turned to look at her. "But like any good alchemist, Treyford often wrote in a coded language that is not easy to unravel. I made a few errors along the way."

"What makes you think that you have not made a huge mistake in bringing me here?"

"I admit that some parts of my grandfather's writings were quite murky. But they were all clarified when the Earl of St. Merryn ensured that our paths would cross."

"You mean when he set out to find the man who killed his great-uncle?"

"Precisely. When I realized that he was hunting me, I understood at last that we were, indeed, destined to be opponents in this generation, just as Lancaster and my grandfather were, all those years ago."

She understood now. "You have brought me here tonight because you knew that would be the simplest way to get St. Merryn here and take him prisoner."

"You are a very clever woman, Miss Lodge. St. Merryn chose well when he went to the offices of Goodhew and Willis. It is a great misfortune for you that he dragged you into this affair. But that is how destiny works sometimes. It is often the lot of the innocent to play crucial roles as pawns."

Chapter Thirty-Seven

Arthur jumped out of the carriage before it had come to a full stop in Rain Street and went up the steps.

"Do not put the horses away," he called to Jenks over his shoulder. "We have another call to make this afternoon."

"Aye, sir."

The door opened before Arthur reached it. Ned stood in the opening, his face stark with dread.

"Ye got my message, then, sir?"

"Yes." Arthur moved impatiently into the hall. "I was still at Parker's address when the boy found me and said that there was a matter of great urgency. What is it? I have another call I want to make today and I do not want to waste time."

He saw Sally standing in the hall behind Ned. The stricken look on her face made his stomach knot.

"Where is Miss Lodge?" he rasped.

Sally handed him a sealed letter and started to cry.

"He threatened to cut my throat if she tried to run away or call for help," Sally said through her tears. "And he would have done it. I saw his eyes, sir. They weren't human."

It is true that my grandfather failed in his attempt to complete Jove's Thunderbolt," Parker lounged against the workbench, arms folded. "But the fault lay in his instruments, not in the old alchemist's instructions."

"What do you mean?" Elenora asked, trying to sound genuinely curious. She edged closer to the workbench, as though intrigued by the strange machine. Parker was eager to talk about the device and his own genius. He had assumed the air of a lecturer.

"The directions in the old lapidary call for using a cold fire to excite the energy sealed in the heart of the three stones," Parker said. "That was the great stumbling block. My grandfather reported in his journal that he tried heating the gems in a number of different ways but nothing worked. Nor could he decide what was meant by a cold fire. He was conducting researches into the production of a suitably powerful heat source when he was killed in that explosion."

Elenora stopped on the other side of the table, pretending to study the device. "You believe that you have found the answer?"

"Yes." Parker's face lit as though with passion. "Once I had read my grandfather's journals and considered the instructions in the lapidary in the light of modern science, I understood at last what could be used to apply a cold fire to the gems."

"What is it?"

Parker caressed the device. "Why, an electricity machine, of course."

Arthur ignored the distraught butler who was attempting to announce him and walked swiftly into the study.

"Parker has kidnapped Elenora," he said.

"No." Lady Wilmington rose quickly from the chair behind the writing desk. "No, that cannot be possible."

"He escaped from that private asylum where you sent him."

"Dear heaven." Lady Wilmington sank back down onto her chair, stricken. "No one sent word that he was gone. I swear it."

"I believe you. No doubt they have not told you yet because they are hoping to find Parker before you learn that he escaped. After all, you are a very wealthy client. The proprietors of the asylum would not want you to take your business elsewhere."

"This is a disaster."

Arthur crossed the room in three strides and came to a halt on the other side of the little desk.

"Parker left a note instructing me to go alone to a certain address in the stews at midnight tonight. There I am to be met by two men who will convey me to some secret location. I can only assume that I will first be bound, blindfolded and disarmed before I am taken to see your grandson. I will not be of much assistance to Elenora in that condition."

"I am so sorry. So very sorry." Lady Wilmington seemed dazed with despair. "I do not know what to say or do. I never meant for this to happen. I thought I was doing what was for the best for everyone."

Arthur leaned forward and flattened his palms on the dainty desk. "Where is Parker's laboratory?"

Lady Wilmington was obviously confused by the question. "I beg your pardon?"

"I went to his house today and searched it thoroughly. The books and furnishings are nothing more than a stage set designed to imitate the lodgings of a fashionable gentleman."

"What do you mean?"

"I spent a great deal of my youth in my great-uncle's house," Arthur said. "I know what to expect in the way of furnishings in the home of a man who is consumed with a passion for science. I found none of those things in Parker's lodgings."

"I don't understand."

"There should have been a laboratory cluttered with instruments, apparatus, glassware. There should have been books on optics and mathematics, not poetry and fashion. Treyford's journals were not there either."

"Yes, of course, I see. I was too overset yesterday to even think about such things."

"Parker may be mad, but he is obsessed with his plans to build Jove's Thunderbolt. He must have a secret laboratory somewhere in London. It will be a place where he feels secure. A place where he is free to labor all night without drawing attention. That is where he will have taken Elenora."

"Treyford's old laboratory." Lady Wilmington rubbed her brow. "Parker no doubt discovered the location in the journals. He would have been fascinated with the notion of pursuing his research there where his grandfather had once conducted his experiments."

"What do you know of it?"

"Treyford constructed it after he broke with your great-uncle and Glentworth. They were never aware of the place and likely wouldn't have cared if they had

378

known. But Treyford took me there on many occasions," Lady Wilmington said wistfully. "He needed to share his research with someone who could appreciate his genius, you see, but by that time he was no longer speaking to Lancaster or Glentworth."

"So he took you to his laboratory to witness the results of his experiments?"

"Yes. The location was our secret. It was the one place where he and I could be alone together without fear of discovery."

The shorter of the two men waiting in the alley was the first to notice the flaring light of an approaching lantern.

"Well, now, what do you know? He came after all, just like Mr. Stone said he would." The footpad pushed himself away from the wall and raised his pistol. "You'd think he'd be too smart to risk his neck for a female."

A figure in a hat and greatcoat appeared at the entrance of the alley. He was starkly silhouetted against the light of the lantern.

"He's a fool, all right." The second man hefted the knife he held in one hand. With the other, he reached down to pick up the length of rope that he intended to use to bind their prisoner. "But that's his problem, not ours. All we have to do is take him to the old abbey and leave him in the cage that Mr. Stone described."

They went cautiously toward their prey, but the figure in the hat and greatcoat did not make any suspicious moves. He simply stood there, waiting.

"Stay right where ye are, yer lordship," the short man said, holding the pistol so that his intended victim could see it clearly. "Don't move so much as yer little finger. My companion here is going to play valet for ye and see that yer dressed right and proper for yer visit to Mr. Stone."

The figure in the greatcoat did not speak.

"Not feeling in the mood to chat, eh?" The taller man moved forward, rope in hand. "Can't say that I blame ye. I wouldn't be anxious to be in your shoes right now and that's a fact. Mr. Stone is a strange bird all right."

"But he's generous when it comes to our pay so we try not to notice his odd ways," the short man said. "Let's get on with it. Put your hands behind your back so my associate can truss ye up. We don't have all night, y'know."

"No," Jenks, said, removing his hat. "We do not have all night."

Ned and Hitchins stepped quickly out of the shadows of the doorway behind the two footpads.

At the sound of the footsteps behind them, the pair started to turn. But Ned and Hitchins were already upon them. They jammed the barrels of their pistols into the spines of the two footpads.

"Drop the weapons or you're both dead men," Hitchins said.

The villains froze. The pistol clattered on the stones. The knife followed.

"Now, hold on. My friend and I were hired to take his lordship to our employer," the short man said, unnerved. "We were told it was all arranged and that his lordship was agreeable to the plan. There's no crime here."

"That's a matter of opinion," Hitchins said.

The taller of the two villains squinted at him uneasily. "Are ye St. Merryn?"

"No. St. Merryn decided to take another route to meet up with your employer."

Chapter Thirty-Eight

Parker pulled his gold watch from his pocket and checked the time again. "Another half hour until my employees leave St. Merryn, neatly bound and secured, in the iron cage in the chapel above this room."

"You mean your men know about this laboratory?" Elenora asked, astonished.

"What do you take me for?" He gave her a disdainful look. "Do you think that I would risk telling a couple of footpads such a great secret? They were given instructions to secure St. Merryn, leave him locked in the cage in the back of the chapel and then depart. No one knows about this place except me."

"I now know about it," she pointed out.

He inclined his head, amused. "I stand corrected." He looked up at the vaulted ceiling. "And, in a short time, after the cage is lowered through the hidden trapdoor in the floor of the chapel, St. Merryn will learn of it also. I trust the two of you will both be suitably cognizant of the great honor that I have bestowed upon you."

"The honor of allowing us to view the secret laboratory of England's second Newton?"

"You sound so scathing, Miss Lodge. Really, you wound me." He chuckled and reached out to take hold of a handle on Jove's Thunderbolt. "But you will change your tune after you see what this device can do."

He began to turn the crank very quickly.

Elenora watched uneasily. "What are you doing?"

"Building up a strong store of electricity. When it is ready, I will use it to activate the machine."

She studied the device with mounting anxiety, paying close attention now. "How does it work?"

"Once the charge of electricity has been properly stored, I can release it by turning that knob on top of the machine." He pointed to it. "That is also how one turns off the thunderbolt. When the sparks of electricity come in contact with the three stones in the chamber it excites the energy stored in them, just as the old alchemist predicted. A very narrow beam of crimson light is released. I tested it once, just before my grandmother had me carried off. It worked perfectly."

"What does the beam do?"

"Why, the most amazing thing, Miss Lodge." Parker exclaimed. "It destroys whatever happens to be in its path."

She would not have thought it possible to be any more terrified than she had been already. But when she saw the madness burning in Parker's eyes, the icy sensation in the pit of her stomach became a thousand times more intense.

She knew then that whatever else he planned to do

with Jove's Thunderbolt, he intended to turn it on Arthur and herself first.

Arthur had thought that the darkness would be the worst part of the business, but in the end it was the odor that bothered him the most. The smell that emanated from the enclosed riverbed was so foul that he had been forced to wrap his neckcloth around his nose and mouth to block the stench.

But at least he hadn't had to walk along the narrow, rat-infested banks of the lost river, Arthur thought, dipping the pole back into the black water. He had found a small, shallow-bottomed boat and a pole at the secret dock beneath the old warehouse.

"Treyford kept extra boats and poles at both the entrance to the laboratory and here in the warehouse," Lady Wilmington had explained when she had led him down into the dark basement of the abandoned building and showed him the secret underground dock. "He told me that this way he could enter or leave the laboratory through the abbey or this place, according to his whim or if it became necessary to escape due to some disaster with an experiment. Parker appears to have followed the same practice."

The current of the murky river was sluggish, making it relatively easy to force the little boat upstream with the pole. The light from the lantern that he had positioned at the front of the craft splashed its glare across a bizarre scene.

More than once he had eased the boat around a twist in the river and had to crouch quickly to avoid an ancient footbridge.

There were other hazards in addition to the low bridges. Chunks of stone and ancient timbers had fallen into the river in places. Some projected above the waters, looming like the long-lost monuments of a dead civilization. Others were submerged and did not reveal themselves until the little boat bumped lightly against them.

He studied each fallen stone carefully as he poled past it, watching for the classical statues and the strange marble relief that Lady Wilmington had told him to use as landmarks.

"They had survived many centuries when I last saw them," she said. "I am certain they will still be there."

Parker checked his gold watch yet again and appeared satisfied, even eager. "Twelve-thirty. My employees will have locked St. Merryn in the cage and left by now."

Elenora looked up at the vaulted ceiling. "I heard no sound from the rooms above this chamber."

"The stone floors are very thick. They do not transmit any noise. That is one of this laboratory's most admirable features. I am able to conduct experiments that produce a great deal of noise and light and no one, even if he were standing directly above, would have so much as an inkling of what is happening down here."

"What makes you think your men will not wait and watch to see what happens?" she asked.

"Bah. They are as frightened of the old abbey as everyone else in the neighborhood. But even if their curiosity got the better of them, they would see nothing but the cage disappearing into the wall of stone behind the altar. Once the hidden panel closes, it is impossible to find the opening. They would not see the cage being lowered into this chamber."

He reached up and turned the great iron wheel that projected from the stone wall.

A section of the ceiling slid aside, revealing a

dark shaft overhead. Elenora heard the creak and rumble of heavy chain. She recognized it as the sound she had heard earlier when Parker had brought her here.

Her heart pounded. The only chance she would have to seize the rod on the workbench would be when Parker was occupied with the task of getting Arthur out of the cage.

The rattling of the chain grew louder. Elenora saw the bottom edge of the iron cage appear out of the shadows of the vault that housed the mechanism.

The tips of a pair of brilliantly polished boots came into view. Parker was riveted by the sight.

"Welcome to the laboratory of England's second Newton, St. Merryn," he said, never taking his eyes off the boots. The words rang with exultation and excitement.

Elenora took a step closer to the workbench. She reached out with her bound hands and picked up a heavy iron rod. There would be only one chance, she thought.

"Elenora, get down." Arthur's sharp command reverberated across the chamber.

She obeyed reflexively and dropped to the floor, still clutching the iron rod.

"*St. Merryn.*" Parker spun away from the sight of the empty boots in the cage, pistol lifting.

"No," Elenora screamed.

The twin explosions that ensued echoed through the laboratory. The acrid stench of burnt powder wafted through the air.

The two men were still standing, she saw. The pistols had both discharged, but the distance had been too great to allow any degree of accuracy.

Both weapons were now useless until they were

reloaded, but Arthur quickly drew a second pistol from his pocket. He came forward swiftly, never taking his attention off Parker.

"Elenora," Arthur's voice cracked across the space. "Are you all right?"

"Yes." She got to her feet. "What about you?"

"I am unharmed." He aimed the pistol at Parker.

"Bastard," Parker rasped. He looked at Arthur with eyes that glittered with fury, and moved a little closer to the workbench.

"He has another pistol," Elenora shouted. "It's on the table behind him."

"I see it." Arthur stepped forward and scooped up the unfired weapon.

"Fool." Parker stared at him from the opposite side of the workbench. "You do not know who you are dealing with."

Without warning, he flung himself toward the strange device and used both hands to turn the round knob on the top.

Arthur raised the pistol. "Do not move."

"Beware," Elenora warned. "He claims that the machine works."

"I doubt it. Nevertheless—" Arthur motioned with his pistol. "Get away from the device, Parker."

"Too late, St. Merryn." Parker's laughter echoed off the stone walls. "Too late. Now you will learn the truth of my genius."

A strange crackling came from the device. Elenora saw electricity snap and arc in the air around it.

A thin beam of ruby red fire blazed forth from the long barrel. Parker swung the mouth of the weapon slowly toward Arthur.

Arthur dropped to the floor. The ray of red light sliced through the air where he had been standing a second ago. It struck the stone wall behind him, hissing and sparking wildly.

Sprawled on the floor, Arthur raised his pistol and fired. But he had no time to aim properly. The shot thudded into the workbench.

Parker was already swinging the nose of the device downward in the direction of his target. The hellish beam sliced toward Arthur, charring everything in its narrow path.

Elenora tried to move soundlessly up behind Parker. She must not alert him until she was close enough to strike, she told herself.

"Did you really think that you could defeat me?" Parker shouted at Arthur.

He used both hands to make the barrel of Jove's Thunderbolt follow Arthur's rolling body. The action of the heavy machine was slow, and it was clear that Parker had to exert considerable force to continually readjust the aim.

Just a few more feet, Elenora, thought. She tightened her grip on the iron bar she had taken from the workbench and raised it.

"You are a madman, not a genius," Arthur yelled. "Just like your grandfather."

"You will acknowledge my genius with your dying breath, St. Merryn," Parker vowed.

Elenora took another step closer to Parker and swung the rod with all her strength, aiming for his head. But at the last instant, he sensed her presence.

He spun quickly to the side just as she brought the bar down in what should have been a deadly blow. The iron struck the heavy table and rebounded with such force that she lost her grip on it.

She had missed her target, but the distraction had

obliged Parker to release his hold on the killing machine. Enraged, he shoved Elenora to one side.

She tumbled to the floor, bruising herself on the hard stones. Her eyes closed against the pain.

It was the sound of a rush of motion that made her raise her lashes. She opened her eyes just in time to see Arthur slam headlong into Parker.

The two men went down together, hitting the floor with a sickening thud. They crashed violently from side to side, Arthur on top one second, Parker the next.

Abandoned by its operator, Jove's Thunderbolt was steady now, but the deadly ray continued to blaze from the mouth of the barrel.

The two men fought with a savagery that was unlike anything Elenora had ever witnessed. There was nothing she could do to intervene.

Without warning, Parker suddenly rolled free and surged to his feet. He scooped up the iron bar that Elenora had attempted to use against him and made to bring it down on Arthur's head.

Elenora screamed a warning.

Arthur hurled himself to the side as the rod descended toward him. The bar narrowly missed his skull. He reached out, seized one of Parker's ankles and jerked violently.

Parker shouted in rage and staggered in an attempt to free his leg and regain his balance. He raised the rod again, preparing to deliver another crushing blow.

Still half lying on the floor, Arthur suddenly released his captive.

Caught off balance, Parker swept out an arm and moved back hastily in an attempt to find his footing.

"No," Elenora shrieked.

But it was too late. She watched in horror, her hands to her mouth, as Parker's desperate attempt to catch his balance carried him straight into the path of the deadly beam of light.

He screamed once as the ray burned through his chest in the vicinity of his heart. The dreadful cry bounced off the walls.

It ended with horrifying suddenness. Parker collapsed like a broken clockwork toy. The searing ray continued to shoot into the stones directly behind where he had been standing a second before.

Elenora turned away, unable to look at the terrible scene. Her stomach lurched. She was afraid she was going to be violently ill.

"Elenora." Arthur was on his feet, moving swiftly toward her. "Are you hurt?"

"No." She swallowed heavily. "Is he—? He must be." She dared not turn around.

Arthur stepped past her, careful to avoid the light beam, and knelt to check the body. He rose quickly.

"Yes," he said. "He is most certainly dead. Now we must find a way to switch off that device."

"The knob on top, I think. "

A strange, low rumble interrupted her. At first she thought that the iron cage was once again in motion. Then she realized with horror that it was coming from Jove's Thunderbolt.

The rumble became a low roar.

"Something has gone wrong," Arthur said.

"Turn the knob."

Arthur ran to the workbench and started to wrench the knob. He drew his fingers back instantly.

"Damnation. It's as hot as live coals."

The muted roaring gradually changed into a high-pitched whine that was unlike anything Elenora had ever heard. The red beam projecting from the device grew less steady. It started to pulse in a strange pattern.

"Let's get out of here." Arthur came swiftly toward her.

"We can't use the cage," she warned. "Parker said it could not be made to operate unless one knew the secret for unlocking it."

"Not the cage. The lost river."

He reached her side, gripped her shoulder and propelled her toward the crypt at the back of the laboratory.

She did not understand what he was talking about, but she did not argue. On the workbench the machine was turning a dull red as though it was being heated in the intense flames of some monstrous forge. The strange, shrill sound emanating from it grew louder.

It certainly did not require a genius of Newton's caliber to conclude that the thing was about to explode, she thought.

She fled with Arthur into the crypt. The dank smell hit her with great force. Arthur lit a lantern. They got into a tiny, shallow-bottomed boat.

"I see now why you came alone," she said, balancing cautiously.

"This craft will only hold two people," Arthur said. He grabbed a pole and used it to propel the boat away from the stone dock. "I realized I might need to use it to bring you out."

"This is a river," she whispered, astonished. "Flowing beneath the heart of the city."

"Keep your head down," Arthur advised. "There are bridges and other obstacles."

The muffled noise of an explosion came a few minutes later, echoing down the ancient tunnel walls. Elenora felt a tremor go through the little boat, but it continued forward, riding the current.

There followed a horrific grinding, crashing,

shattering sound of stone on stone. It seemed to go on forever.

After a while an unnerving silence descended.

"Dear heaven," Elenora whispered. "It sounds as though the entire laboratory may have been destroyed."

"Yes."

She looked back into the darkness. "Do you think Parker really might have been England's second Newton?"

"As my great-uncle was fond of saying, there was only one Newton."

Chapter Thirty-Nine

Two days later, Elenora met with Margaret and Bennett in the library. She was feeling much more herself this afternoon, she thought. The shock of events was rapidly receding. She was pleased to note that her strong constitution had reasserted itself, and her nerves felt quite steady once again.

It was time to move forward into her new life.

She had seen very little of Arthur since they had made their way out of the lost river. The previous day had been spent dealing with the aftermath of the great explosion. Oddly enough, there was no visible evidence of the disaster aboveground. The abandoned abbey appeared entirely undisturbed.

Working under Arthur's direction, laborers had managed to locate the entrance to the secret chamber that housed the iron cage. But they had found the shaft sealed with rubble and broken stone.

Arthur and Bennett had taken small boats back along the hidden river to see if the crypt entrance was still passable. But there they had been met with another impenetrable wall of tumbled rock. The destruction of the hidden chamber had been complete.

The one thing she and Arthur had done together was call upon Lady Wilmington. Arthur had explained as gently as possible that it would be an extraordinarily expensive and quite possibly futile task to try to find Parker's body.

"Let the laboratory be his tomb," Lady Wilmington had decreed, tears in her eyes.

Today Arthur had left the house again very early, saying that he intended to talk to several people who were owed an explanation of events, including Mrs. Glentworth and Roland Burnley.

The moment he was gone, Elenora had sent a message to Bennett, asking him to call upon her at his earliest convenience. He had arrived within the hour, but he did not appear at all enthusiastic about the favor she was asking of him.

"Are you quite certain that you want me to do this, Miss Lodge?" he asked gravely.

"Yes," Elenora said. She had to go through with this, she thought. She must not turn aside. "My friends and I will be extremely grateful to you, sir, if you can arrange to place the wager for us."

Margaret's brow wrinkled slightly in disapproval. "I cannot say I like this scheme of yours, Elenora. I really think that you should discuss the situation with Arthur first."

"I cannot do that. I know him very well. He will be concerned for my reputation. If he learns of my plan, he will likely put his foot down and refuse to allow it."

Margaret stiffened. "Arthur may blame Bennett for placing the wager for you and your friends."

Elenora frowned. She had not thought about that

possibility. "I would not want to create a rift between you and St. Merryn, sir, since you are soon to marry into the family."

"Do not bother yourself on that account, Miss Lodge," Bennett said gallantly. "It is not St. Merryn's temper I fear. It is that you may have misjudged his feelings toward you."

"Bennett is right," Margaret said quickly. "Arthur is very fond of you, Elenora. I am certain of it. I realize that he may not have let you know his feelings, but that is because he is not accustomed to revealing his emotions."

"I do not doubt but that he feels some affection for me," Elenora said, choosing her words carefully. "But our relationship is, in truth, that of employer and employee, not that of an engaged couple."

"Your association may have started out that way, but I feel that it has changed," Margaret insisted.

It certainly had altered, Elenora thought, but she did not intend to confide all of the details to Margaret or anyone else.

"The nature of my personal connection to Arthur has not changed in any significant way," she said carefully.

"I'm not so sure about that." Margaret was starting to look stubborn. "I wouldn't be surprised if Arthur is considering an offer of marriage."

It required every ounce of self control Elenora possessed not to burst into tears. Somehow she managed to keep her voice steady. "I do not want Arthur to feel that he has an obligation to propose marriage to me merely because of recent events. Is that quite clear?"

Margaret and Bennett exchanged glances.

"I understand," Margaret said, "but—"

"It would be extremely unfair if he were made to

395

feel that he was honor-bound to offer marriage," Elenora said evenly. "You know how he is when it comes to his sense of responsibility."

Margaret exchanged another look with Bennett, who grimaced in response.

"Everyone knows that Arthur's sense of duty tends to be somewhat excessive on occasion," Margaret admitted.

"Precisely," Elenora said.

"You may be right about St. Merryn's attitude toward his responsibilities, Miss Lodge," Bennett said. "But in this case, I fear there is good reason why he will consider that an offer of marriage is the only honorable thing he can do."

Elenora lifted her chin. She tried not to clench her hands. "I will not have it."

Bennett sighed. "No offense, but after having posed as St. Merryn's fiancée and having been perceived to be on rather *intimate* terms with him, you will never be able to show your face in Polite Circles again unless you and he are wed."

"Bennett is correct," Margaret assured her.

"My future in Society is not a problem," Elenora said. "I have none. That was understood from the start of this affair. Indeed, Arthur and I discussed the matter thoroughly before we agreed to the arrangement."

"But Elenora, you were very nearly killed because of this post," Margaret said. "Arthur never intended that you be put into danger."

"Of course he didn't." Elenora straightened her shoulders. "And it is precisely because of the fact that I *was* placed in danger that I fear he may feel obliged to go beyond the original terms of our agreement and offer marriage. I refuse to allow him to be placed under such a ridiculous sense of obligation."

396

"I comprehend your meaning, Miss Lodge," Bennett said gently. "Nevertheless, don't you think it would be best if you talked to him about your scheme first?"

"No," Elenora said firmly. "Can I depend upon you to handle this matter for me, sir?"

Bennett heaved another sigh. "I will do my best to assist you, Miss Lodge."

At four o'clock that afternoon, Arthur came down the steps in front of his club, walked past the long line of waiting carriages, and stopped in front of the door of a handsome maroon equipage.

"I got your message, Fleming," he said through the open window. "What the devil is this all about?" Then he noticed Margaret sitting next to Bennett. "Are you two on your way to the park?"

"No," Margaret said. Her expression was one of grim resolve. "We came here to discuss a matter of the utmost importance with you."

"Quite right." Bennett thrust open the door. "Will you join us, sir?"

Something was certainly amiss, Arthur thought, resigned. He'd had plans for the afternoon; plans that included Elenora. But Bennett and Margaret were obviously extremely agitated. Best to find out what was wrong now rather than later. In his experience, problems were usually easiest to manage in the early stages.

Resigned to the delay, he vaulted up into the carriage and sat down on the empty seat. "Very well, what seems to be the trouble here?"

"It is Elenora," Margaret said bluntly. "She is packing as we speak. I fear she plans to be gone by the time you arrive home this afternoon."

Arthur felt his innards turn to ice. Elenora leaving? He had a sudden bleak vision of the big house in Rain Street devoid of her vital presence. All the gloomy shadows that had magically disappeared in the past few days would return the moment she walked out the door.

"Elenora and I have a business arrangement," he said in what he hoped was a calm and controlled tone. "She will not leave until certain matters are settled."

"She mentioned that the business of her wages and a certain bonus could be handled through your man-of-affairs," Margaret said.

Damnation, he thought, going colder. Elenora wasn't just terminating their business arrangement, she was running away from him.

Elenora put the last gown and a pair of slippers into the trunk and slowly lowered the top. She felt as though she was closing the lid of a coffin.

The wretched sense of loss that had been threatening to overwhelm her all afternoon grew stronger. She had to get out of here before she dissolved into a puddle of tears, she thought.

She heard the muffled clatter of a carriage stopping down in the street. The hackney that she had instructed Ned to summon had arrived. She heard the muted sound of the front hall door being opened. It closed again very quickly. Ned had no doubt gone outside to inform the driver that she would be down in a few minutes.

She turned slowly on her heel to take one last look around her bedchamber, telling herself that she did not want to forget any of her possessions. But her gaze went to the neatly made bed and lingered there.

All she could think about was the last night of passion with Arthur. She knew that she would carry those memories in her heart for the rest of her life.

She was vaguely aware of a man's footsteps in the corridor outside the bedchamber. That would be Ned coming to collect her trunk and take it downstairs to the waiting hackney, she surmised.

Moisture shimmered in her eyes. She seized a handkerchief. She must not cry. Not yet, at any rate. The sight of her leaving in tears would greatly alarm Ned and Sally and the rest of the staff.

There was a single knock on the door.

"Come in," she called, frantically dabbing at the incipient tears.

The door opened. She finished blotting her eyes and turned to face whoever stood there.

"Going somewhere?" Arthur asked quietly.

She could not seem to move. He loomed large in the opening, his hard face set in grim, unyielding lines, his eyes as dangerous as she had ever seen them. Her mouth went dry.

"What are you doing here?" she whispered.

"I live here, remember?"

She flushed. "You're home early."

"I was obliged to alter my schedule of appointments for today when I received word that you were planning to run away."

She sighed. "Margaret and Bennett told you?"

"They informed me that you were packing your bags and preparing to depart with no notice." He folded his arms. "And here I thought we had some matters to discuss."

"I felt it might be best if we concluded our business through your man-of-affairs," she said softly.

"My man-of-affairs is very competent in most

399

respects, but I doubt that he has had a great deal of experience conveying an offer of marriage."

Her mouth fell open. She got it closed again only with great effort. "Oh, dear." She could no longer hold back the tears. Frantically she blotted her eyes. "Oh, dear, I was afraid of this."

"It is clear that I am doing something very wrong when it comes to my personal affairs," Arthur said in a world-weary tone. "My fiancées all seem to want to run away from me."

"I beg your pardon?" She lowered her handkerchief and glared at him. "How dare you imply that I am running away from you? I am not a frightened rabbit like Juliana, and well you know it."

"I am very much aware that you are not Juliana." He walked deliberately into the bedchamber and closed the door behind him. He angled a glance at the closed trunk. "But you do appear to be about to run away from me."

She sniffed, wadded up the handkerchief in one hand, folded her arms beneath her breasts and hugged herself. "You know that this is an entirely different situation."

"Oddly enough, from my perspective it does not appear to be that much different."

"Oh, for heaven's sake, that is a perfectly ridiculous thing to say."

"Is it?" He came to a halt a short distance away. "You once told me that you thought I would make a very good husband. Did you mean it?"

"Of course I meant it." She unfolded her arm and waved the crumpled handkerchief about. "But for some other woman, one whom you truly loved."

"You are the woman I love. Will you marry me?"

All of the oxygen seemed to have evaporated from the room. The world and time itself stopped.

"You love me?" she repeated. "Arthur, do you mean it?"

"Have you ever known me to say anything I did not mean?"

"Well, no, it is just that . . . ." She narrowed her eyes. "Arthur, are you certain that you are not offering marriage because you feel you must?"

"If you will recall my history in such matters, my dear, you may remember that the last time I found myself trapped in an engagement that I wished to escape, I showed myself quite capable of getting out of the entanglement."

"Oh. Yes. Yes, you did." She frowned. "But this is not the same sort of thing at all. I do not want you to feel that you must marry me just because of what happened between us here." She paused. "And downstairs in the library."

"I shall let you in on a little secret." He closed the remaining distance between them. "I made love to you on both occasions because I had already decided that I wanted to marry you."

She was too stunned to summon up anything resembling a coherent response.

She swallowed. "Really?"

"I wanted you from that first moment when you came crashing through the doorway of the offices of Goodhew and Willis. I knew then that you were the woman I had been waiting for all of my life."

"You did?"

"My love, let me remind you that I am famous for my intuition when it comes to making investments. I took one look at you and I knew that you would be the best investment I could ever possibly make."

She smiled tremulously. "Oh, Arthur, that is the most romantic thing anyone has ever said to me."

401

"Thank you. I was rather pleased with it, myself. I practiced it during the carriage ride here today."

"But you know that a gentleman of your rank and wealth is expected to marry a young lady right out of the schoolroom. One with excellent social connections and a plump inheritance."

"Allow me to remind you that I am considered to be something of an eccentric. Society will be dreadfully disappointed unless I wed a lady who is equally unusual."

"I do not know what to say."

He tipped up her chin with one hand. "You could tell me whether or not you think it might be possible for you to love me enough to want to marry me."

The most delicious sense of joy unfurled within her. She moved her hands up around his neck. "I am so desperately in love with you that when I packed my trunk today in preparation for leaving, I thought my heart might break."

"You're certain?"

"Absolutely." She touched her fingertips to his jaw. "And, as you know, sir, I am a woman of very decisive temperament."

He laughed and scooped her up into his arms. "When it comes to that trait, we are well-matched indeed. No wonder you have swept me off my feet."

She realized that he was carrying her toward the bed. "Good heavens, the servants, sir. Ned will be coming up here to fetch my trunk, and the hackney is waiting."

"No one will disturb us." He dropped her lightly on the bed and peeled off his coat. "I sent the hackney and the entire household away when I got home a few minutes ago. I made it clear that no one was to return for at least two hours."

She smiled slowly. "Did you, indeed, sir? Were you that sure of yourself?"

"No, I was that desperate." He sat down on the side of the bed and pried off his boots. "I knew that if I could not convince you to marry me using logic, my only remaining hope was to make love to you until you could no longer think clearly."

"What a clever notion. That is one of the things that I love about you, Arthur. I have never met another man who manages to combine logic and passion with such amazing skill."

He laughed again, the sound low and husky and warmed by happiness.

When he came to her a short time later, she opened her arms to him. He undressed her almost as swiftly as he had undressed himself, tossing her gown into a careless heap beside the bed.

He rolled onto his back and pulled her down onto his chest. She framed his face with her hands and kissed him with an urgency that made him groan. She could feel him pressed against her thigh, heavy and rigid with desire.

He slid one hand down her waist to her hip and traced the cleft that separated the swells of her buttocks. His fingers dipped lower, finding the place where she was already damp and aching with need.

She kissed his throat and then his chest, tasting him. When she slipped lower and touched him experimentally with her tongue, wanting to give him the same pleasure he had once given her, he sucked in his breath. She felt his fingers clench in her hair.

"Enough," he rasped.

Then he tugged her upward and positioned her so that she straddled his thighs. He stroked her, watching her face.

She felt her lower body tightened at his touch. She moved against his hand, twisting and clenching.

And then, just when she thought she could not stand any more of the glorious stimulation, he clamped his hands around her hips and drove himself deep inside her.

She gasped and gave a choked cry as the waves of pleasure rippled through her.

Together they tumbled into the sparkling whirlpool.

Reality returned a long time later. It struck Elenora with such force that she sat bolt upright in bed.

The wager, she though, panic-stricken.

"I beg your pardon, I must get up. Right now." She tried to push herself free of Arthur's arm and leg. "Please, let me go. I've got to get dressed."

"No need." Arthur tightened his arm around her waist and lazily pulled her back down beside him. "No one will be home for another hour."

"You don't understand. I can't marry you unless I can find Mr. Fleming before . . . Never mind, it is very complicated and I don't have time to explain."

"Surely you would not be so cruel as to cast me aside now that you've had your wicked way with me yet again."

"It's not that. Arthur, listen, the most terrible thing is about to happen. I told Mr. Fleming to place a wager on behalf of some friends and myself."

"Yes." He gave her a stern look. "I heard about your scheme. You know how I feel about that sort of thing. Remind me to have a long talk with you about the perils of gambling."

She stopped struggling. "You know about the wager?"

"Yes. I cannot tell you how shocked I was when I

discovered that I was about to wed a confirmed gamester."

She ignored that. "You understand why I must stop Mr. Fleming from placing it in the betting books."

"Calm yourself, my dear." He used one hand to propel her firmly back down across his chest and chuckled. "It is too late to stop him from placing your bet."

"Oh, no." She dropped her forehead down onto his chest. "My friends and I cannot cover our losses."

"If it becomes necessary to make good on them, I will allow you to borrow the money from me. Think of it as a wedding gift."

"I shall have no choice but to take advantage of your generosity." She did not raise her head. "It was my fault. I convinced my friends that the outcome was a certainty. This is so humiliating. I am sorry to embarrass you like this, Arthur."

"Mmm. Well, as I said, Bennett placed your bet as you instructed. But upon my advice, he altered the terms ever so slightly."

Warily she raised her head. "What do you mean?"

"He also agreed to invite a few other people to join your little consortium of intrepid gamesters."

"Good heavens."

"The way things stand now," Arthur said, "You and your friends, together with Roland Burnley, Margaret and Bennett all stand to make a handsome fortune if you agree to marry me by special license before the week is out."

She was torn between laughter and the most profound astonishment. "*That* is the wager that Mr. Fleming placed in the betting books today?"

"Yes." He speared his hands through her hair. "What do you think the outcome will be?"

She felt her love for him well up inside until it filled

every part of her being. "I think that the outcome of that wager is a certainty."

"I am relieved to hear that." He gave her his rare, sensual smile. "Because I included myself in your little investment scheme."

"You took a share in my wager?" She laughed in delight. "I don't believe it. Were you that sure of yourself, sir?"

"No." His eyes grew intent and very serious. "But I reasoned that if I lost this wager, nothing else would matter, least of all the money."

"Oh, Arthur, I do love you so."

He kissed her, long and deep, setting the seal on the promise of a lifetime of love.

Epilogue

One year later. . . .

"What you must keep in mind when you contemplate a financial investment is that it is important to look beneath the surface." Arthur leaned back in his desk chair and studied his small audience. "Ask the questions that others neglect to ask. Make notes. Consider what can go wrong, as well as what you hope will turn out well. Is that clear?"

The twins gurgled at him from the depths of their cradles. Little David watched him closely, obviously fascinated with the lecture. His sister, Agatha, however, appeared more interested in her rattle, but Arthur knew that she was absorbing every detail. Like her mother, she was quite capable of doing two things at once.

He smiled at both of them. There was no doubt about it, he was the father of the most intelligent, most beautiful children in the entire world.

Outside the window, spring had arrived on the

estate. Warm sunlight poured into the room. The countryside was green and the gardens were in bloom.

He had brought Elenora here shortly after they were married. London was all very well for the occasional visit, he thought, but neither of them was suited to long periods of time spent in Society. In any event, the air here in the country was far more healthful for the children.

"Money is not the most important thing in the world," Arthur continued, "but it is an extremely useful commodity."

The door of the library opened. Elenora, fresh and vivid in a rose-colored gown, whisked into the room. She had a familiar-looking journal in her hand.

"Especially in this household," Arthur added dryly. "Because your mother appears to be able to spend an endless amount of it on her charities."

Elenora raised her brows as she walked toward him. "What nonsense are you telling the children?"

"I am giving them sound financial advice." He got to his feet and kissed her when she came to a halt in front of him. Then he looked warily at the journal. "Do not tell me, let me guess. You require more funds for your new orphanage, correct?"

She gave him her wonderfully brilliant smile, the one that never failed to warm all the places deep inside him, and leaned over the cradles to play with the infants.

"The construction is nearly complete," she said over her shoulder. "I just need a bit more to cover the cost of the changes to the design of the gardens."

"As I recall, the gardens were covered in the original budget."

"Yes, but I want them expanded. We did agree that the children will need a pleasant, attractive place to play. It is important that they get plenty of fresh air and exercise."

He had married a lady of many talents, he thought. Under her supervision, everything in his world, including the children and himself as well as her newly established charities and their various households, thrived.

"You are correct, my sweet," he said. "The children in the orphanage will need excellent gardens."

"I knew you would understand." She straightened, opened her journal and made a quick note. "I shall send word to the architect this very afternoon telling him to proceed."

He laughed. Very gently he removed the journal from her fingers and set it down on the desk.

"You once asked me what I did to make myself happy," he said. "I did not respond to your question that day in the park because I could not. I did not know the answer, you see. Now I do."

She smiled, her love as clear and bright as the morning sun. "And what is the answer, sir?"

He took her into his arms. "Loving you makes me the happiest man in the world."

"Oh, my dear Arthur," she whispered. Joy filled her heart. Her arms slid up around his neck. "I did tell you once that you would make a most excellent husband, did I not? You must admit that I was correct."

He would have laughed, but he much preferred to kiss her instead.